I0699879

Small Town Frenzy

FOLLOW ME

To keep up to date with her writing and more, visit S.L. Scott's website: **www.slscottauthor.com**

To receive the newsletter about all of her publishing adventures, free books, giveaways, steals and more:

https://geni.us/SLScottNL

Follow me on TikTok: https://geni.us/SLTikTok
Follow on IG: https://geni.us/IGSLS
Follow on Bookbub: https://geni.us/SLScottBB

ALSO BY S.L. SCOTT

Called "**The Most Romantic Book Ever**," We Were Once, is available and FREE in Kindle Unlimited.

We Were Once

The international sensation, **Best I Ever Had**, has won readers over and is available in ebook, audio, and paperback, and Free in Kindle Unlimited.

Best I Ever Had

Audiobooks on Audible - CLICK HERE

Peachtree Pass Series (Stand-alones)

Long Time Coming /Lead Me Knot /Small Town Frenzy

The Westcott Series (Stand-alones)

Swear on My Life / Never Saw You Coming

Forgot to Say Goodbye / When I Had You

Never Have I Ever / Speak of the Devil - Faris Family

Hard to Resist Series (Stand-Alones)

The Resistance / The Reckoning

The Redemption / The Revolution / The Rebellion

The Crow Brothers (Stand-Alones)

Spark / Tulsa / Rivers / Ridge

The Crow Brothers Box Set

DARE - A Rock Star Hero (Stand-Alone)

New York Love Stories (Stand-Alones)

Never Got Over You / The One I Want / Crazy in Love

Head Over Feels / It Started with a Kiss

The Everest Brothers (Stand-Alones)

Everest / Bad Reputation / Force of Nature

The Everest Brothers Box Set

The Kingwood Series

SAVAGE / SAVIOR / SACRED / FINDING SOLACE

The Kingwood Series Box Set

Playboy in Paradise Series

Falling for the Playboy / Redeeming the Playboy

Loving the Playboy

Playboy in Paradise Box Set

Stand-Alone Books

Best I Ever Had

We Were Once

Along Came Charlie

Missing Grace

Finding Solace

Until I Met You

Drunk on Love

Lost in Translation

Sleeping with Mr. Sexy

Morning Glory

SMALL TOWN FRENZY

S.L. SCOTT

PROLOGUE

Griffin Greene

A kiss?

Thanking her for the great sex?

Giving her my phone number?

One night was all this was supposed to be. At least that was the impression I got from her last night when she grabbed me coming out of a bar on Jaco Beach and kissed me.

Has she changed her mind?

I wouldn't be surprised. The sex was incredible. *Best I ever had.* It's safe to assume she feels the same, considering how many times I made her . . . I smirk, feeling cocky over the achievement.

I'm not opposed to the idea of sharing numbers if that's what she wants, but I'll let her take the lead. I turn back before opening the hotel door to see the beauty propped up on her elbows, my cowboy hat on her head, and a smile as wide as Big Bend National Park with her fantastic tits on display. I'm fully distracted, so it's hard to notice anything else. I force my gaze up to her eyes—because I'm a gentleman like that—and grin. "Oh yeah? What's that, babe?"

"Your hat." She taps under the brim of the hat that has traveled five continents with me over the past six years, raising it higher on her forehead. To say she looks incredible wouldn't do this vision justice.

With her arousal on full display, those perfect pink buds peaking for me, and a spark flashing in her green eyes, she sure tempts me to stay. "You keep it." The words are out before I can think them through, and the surprise on her features might mirror mine. That hat was one of the few things I took with me when I left Peachtree Pass. *How many years ago was that?* But it feels right to give it a new home.

If I've learned anything from my mom's passing or the ending to my baseball career, it's that nothing is meant to last forever. I say, "A little something to remember me by."

"A souvenir of our time together?" The smile doesn't falter even when she shifts on the mattress, eyeing me like she already knows exactly who I am without so much as exchanging a name. Granted, she didn't ask for or offer one. I didn't either, so it seemed like a settled subject. Wrapping her arms around her bent legs, she says, "I don't need a hat to remember you."

Although it was a bit of a hasty start to a one-night stand, I'd only had a few beers last night and got a good look at her. *She was fucking stunning.* The sky threatened a summer downpour, but she stood like an angel under a neon-pink bar sign. Brown hair wild from the wind, glistening tanned skin from too much sun and dancing in the heat of Costa Rica at night, and that fine body wrapped in not much more than two scarves—one tied around her back, and another at her hip that was seriously enticing to tug loose, only to discover a bikini bottom was hidden underneath and nothing else.

"Glad to know I'm unforgettable." I wink. I love the sound of her laughter as it fills the five-star room she's been calling a "crash pad." But it pales compared to her smile, which about knocks me over because it's so stunning. It's the kind of smile I'd like to spend more time appreciating, but I'm not sure staying is a good idea.

Names will get involved, potentially feelings or even hearts, and I'm in no position to be any good for someone like her. She was out of my league long before she kissed me, so she'll only be disappointed if I stay.

I unlock the bolt and take hold of the doorknob. "You don't have to rush out the door, you know?" Her guileless tone has me turning back again.

"I don't, but don't you think it's best?" I study her, the way her eyes are fixed on mine, but the corners remain soft as if she still believes in fairy tales and happy endings. *So beautiful.*

"No." She's simple and direct, a lot like last night. "I don't think it's best. I think it's easiest for you, though."

At one time in my life, those words would have stung. I know when it's time to make my exit, though. "Keep the hat. It looks better on you."

Sitting up, she grasps for words as her expression funnels through a few emotions before landing on annoyance. Her lips purse, the pink whitening when she bites the lower one. I'm not surprised. She seems like the kind of woman who's used to getting what she wants. "I don't want you to go. Not yet."

With the sheet puddled around her waist, I look her over again. She's not wearing anything under the covers, and there's just something about seeing this beauty in my hat that has me thinking about throwing caution to the wind with her. Again. "Why's that?"

"Because you remind me of home."

I don't expect my chest to tighten, but it causes me to lower my hand. "Aren't you in Costa Rica to get away from home?"

"I didn't know how much I missed it until spending the night with you, cowboy." She pulls the sheet up over her chest and wraps her arms around her legs again. "Where are you from?"

"I'm not sure we should travel down that road when we know it leads to a dead end."

She only responds with a barely discernible nod, her eyes watching me as if she already knows our ending.

Maybe it's that look, the one losing the hope that shone in her eyes only a minute prior, that gets me. Or how her shoulders are beginning to fold forward. As much as I've tried to close myself off to . . . *everything*, sometimes an emotion slips through. *Fuck.*

I rub the back of my neck, eyeing her. Those big green eyes are a trap I've fallen into. I lock the bolt and pull my shirt back off over my head. "Maybe just a little longer."

When I get my jeans off and dive back into bed with her, she says, "I'll make it worth your while."

CHAPTER 1

Cricket Dover

Four years later. . .

THE CRACK of the bat draws my eyes up from my phone to the ball flying over the far side of the baseball field. I visor my eyes to watch the ball breach the boundaries. *Home run.*

It's been a long time since I've seen a home run out here on Dover Creek field. Leaning forward on the metal bleacher, I watch the batter jog the bases. "Who's number twenty-two?" Without my glasses, there's no way I can see the name written in smaller letters on the back of his jersey from these nosebleed seats.

"Greene," Savvy replies, flipping the pages on her clipboard when I glance over at her.

"Greene with an E, as in Greene County?" The rivalry between our county and theirs runs back generations. I still don't know what caused the initial ruckus between the

Dover and Greene families, but it persists in the peripheries of the modern lineages for each, at least from my understanding. It always sounded like a bunch of old ranching tales from the wilder west days of the Texas Hill Country.

My cousin, and assistant, drags her finger down the roster, then taps it twice on a name. When she looks at me, she says, "Griffin Greene. Definitely a Greene with an E of Greene County."

"And of Rollingwood Ranch, Greene Farms, which is under the ranch umbrella, and the Greene family reviving their small town of Peachtree Pass." I sigh with a roll of my eyes. I've heard so many stories growing up about this so-called feud that I feel like I know the family myself. I don't, but I know enough to get by. "Ranching royalty in these parts."

Looking at me under the brim of a Dover Armadillos baseball cap, she adds, "And a former pro baseball player to boot."

Turning my attention back to him on the field as he rounds home base, I note, "Wonder why he's no longer in the Major Leagues when he still hits like that?"

"I don't know his story."

"Neither do I." *I'd like to, though.* "Just curious."

"He's cute," she tacks on casually as she stands, knowing her audience well.

I look up at her, my eyes still shielded from the sun with my hand. "How cute?"

"As a woman in a never-ending engagement, it wouldn't be proper for me to speak on such things." She laughs and plops down next to me again. Then, as if others in this empty stadium will hear us, she leans in, and whispers, "*Very* cute. Don't tell Blake I said anything. You know how jealous he gets, and they're teammates for this fundraising event. But he's just your type."

"First of all, I rarely talk to Blake. Our paths just don't cross that often, except at family events or the occasional dinner with you guys. I don't even think he likes me."

"He likes you, but we do tend to get in trouble together."

"Trouble as in have a good time? That's once in a blue moon at best. We rarely go out anymore. Anyway, second, your secrets are always safe with me. And third, I don't have a type."

"You have a type. You just don't want to admit it." She stands again and starts to shift down the row. "I need to get back to the office. Are you staying for the rest of practice?" She eyes the field and homes in on a certain baseball player. "I wouldn't blame you if you did." Her laughter trails her as she takes a few steps down.

"I'll be back in an hour or so," I reply. "I have emails to catch up on before the end of the day." And check this guy out a little longer . . . *maybe I do have a type?*

"I'll see you back at the office."

Savvy weaves her way to the exit and out of sight. My attention returns to the field as the players swap out. "Griffin Greene, huh?" I can tell he's a big guy, even from where I sit in the stands. Broad shoulders and muscular arms that tend to be exactly what I'm drawn to when I'm drinking, which isn't too often these days. But there was a time when life was less complicated, and from what I see, I'd certainly find him attractive if I were partying out on the town.

Let's just hope he's not as cute as Savvy says. Being a thirty-something single woman in Dover Creek is already a crime in some people's eyes. Falling for the enemy would not only be unforgivable in my family but it would also have me serving two life sentences.

"Oh Jesus." He covers third base, too? *I don't stand a chance.* I pray to the baseball diamond itself that he is hideous to look at up close and married. I'm doomed to make a big mistake with a ballplayer otherwise.

The sky rumbles through the few clouds above, but a storm is brewing not too far off, and dark clouds are moving in quickly. I stand and start down the steps, not wanting to get caught in a downpour.

The players jog to the dugout as I duck into the open-air stairwell. With the sky darkening, I make it to the main gate at the same time as some of the players heading for their cars.

"Did you catch that home run, Cricket?"

I stop to look back at the sound of a familiar voice. Seeing Coach Barth, I smile. "Impressive. It's all for a good cause, but I can't say I wouldn't mind kicking some ass out on the diamond. I'm glad you made the call."

"There's no calling Griff. The man's been out of pocket for so long that I was surprised to even find an active email for him." He crosses his arms over his chest. "He's our secret weapon, though we do have a few players coming in from the Round Rock Express. Grew up here. It's a solid team."

Lightning cracks almost as loud as that home run. I duck in reaction and turn toward the parking lot. "I should get going before the rain kicks in." I start walking backward, and add, "Maybe we can sign a few of these guys for the season."

"We can't afford 'em."

"You never know until we try, Coach." I turn around and slam into a hard chest. My body is sent backward, but hands the size of baseball mitts catch me by the back of the arms. My eyes meet his, and my breath stops hard in my chest. My heart clenches from the sight of him.

"You should be more careful," he says. The warning in his dulcet tone shoots through my body and straight to my toes. "Or you might get hurt." He looks away too quickly, releasing me when I'm steady on my feet again. "See you tomorrow, Coach," he calls over my head like I'm not even standing here, then turns to walk toward the lot.

The clip of Coach's steps echoes in the opposite direction as he returns down the hall toward the locker rooms.

"Hey," I say, not sure what the hell I'm doing or what should follow "hey" since he stopped. I just want to get a good look at him since the last one was too quick. I'm only granted his profile, which holds its own—killer cliff of a jawline dusted in scruff, eyes that have seen too much life to be concerned with what's behind him, and a nose that's near perfection. But it's a flaw I'm most drawn to, a bump on the bridge of his nose that makes me think it's been broken a time or two, and has me curious about whether it was earned in a baseball play, a bar fight, or an accident on his ranch. My mind goes wild with potential causes.

Not losing my initial train of thought, I ask, "Have we met before?"

Barely angled in my direction, he laughs under his breath without giving me more than an ounce of his attention. "You a fan?"

"I . . . um . . ." I'm so taken back by the question that I stumble further into this mess. "Uh . . ."

"It's okay. I'll give ya an autograph." He glances back at me but it's too quick to form an impression. His grumpy personality is doing a stellar job of making sure I want nothing to do with this guy. "If you have something for me to sign."

Mortified, I can feel my cheeks heating and hope to God

he doesn't see. With an ego like his, feeding it is the last thing I want to do. "I don't want an autograph," I snap.

"Suit yourself, sweetheart." No time is wasted. He turns away from me and starts walking again.

I'm left standing in the tunnel with my mouth gaping open. *What the hell was that?* Brushing his chin against his shoulder, he dares to look back at me before turning the corner. Who the hell does he think he is?

He clearly doesn't realize who I am . . .

My gast is too flabbered to bite back because I have never met a more arrogant man in my life. I've met a lot of jerks and dated plenty of assholes, and Griffin Greene is king of them all. If the rest of the Greenes act even an iota as jerky as he does, the ongoing feud between our families makes a whole lot more sense.

I stomp toward the lot again, but as soon as I reach the edge, the sky splits in half, rumbling above my head. The rain falls so hard that I teeter on the edge of the curb to keep from getting soaked. The roar of a Ford pickup races by, doing the job instead. I didn't even have time to react before I was splashed from the neck down. I throw my arms in front of me as if that will stop the water from soaking me. With my eyes clamped shut, I gasp.

The engine fades under the splattering of rain, leaving me pissed. I open my eyes, looking down at my drenched shirt and jeans. My flats are filled with water, and my leather purse has spots from the puddle.

Fisting my hands at my sides, I want to scream in anger. I don't because I can't lose my cool on the job, but I'm so close to doing it anyway. I peek out from under the concrete awning and spy my car—one of two vehicles remaining. I recognize the other as Coach's truck.

When I look up at the sky, there's no break in the dark clouds from what I can see. With no option but to run for it, and no reason not to since I'm already wet, I take off toward my vehicle. Popping the locks on approach, I duck inside and slide onto the leather of my dark blue SUV and look around for anything I can use to dry myself off with. Typically, I'd have a discarded shirt or even a towel available in the back seat. No luck today. That's what I get for having my car cleaned yesterday. It's also probably the reason it rained today. Mother Nature loves a good karma moment.

Checking my face in the rearview mirror, I find my mascara already running under my eyes. I grab a napkin from the console, which I got from the Sonic up the road, where I stopped on the way in for a soda. I pat my face and swipe the dark makeup away.

I start the car. And with irritation running through my veins as I drive home to change into dry clothes, I realize I made two errors in judgment today.

One—I allowed Coach Barth to send out the invites without checking the list for contemptibly rude and Dover family enemies first. *My dad will not be happy when he hears about this.* I'm not going to be the one to tell him.

Two—I let my guard down when talking to a man, a baseball player, and a Greene, of all things.

If I were being rational, I could blow this off under the guise that it's only a charitable game, a one-off event to raise money. *How bad could dealing with that man over the next week really be?*

I'm not in the mood to give him the benefit of the doubt, though. *Not yet.* Not when he just treated me like a fan and then wet me to my core. Oh no. I'm not in the forgiving mood at all.

Griffin Greene considers himself big stuff over where he lives, but in this stadium and in Dover County, my family reigns. So I'm not sure who he thinks he is to rudely assume I was a Dillo fangirl coming onto him, but I can guarantee that he just assured my generation of Dovers will uphold this feud with the Greenes if it's the last thing I do.

CHAPTER 2

Griffin

CROSSING into Greene County brings back many memories. The fields and large oak trees, the shops that make up the little downtown of Peachtree Pass— "What is going on here?"

I slow the truck and lean over the middle of the cab to get a better look at the construction, the progress this small town hasn't seen in decades, if not a century. I knew my brother was investing in the future growth of the area, but I had no idea he was building a metropolis in the middle of the hill country.

I'd recognize my dad's truck anywhere. No matter how much money the man makes, he'll never spend it on another vehicle. We used to joke that it'll be buried next to him, since he loves it so much. We no longer joke about death. Not since my mom died. Though he occasionally mentions being buried next to her up on the wildflower field.

I pull into a spot next to him and hop out. Is there a

protocol for walking back into their lives after so many years of being gone? If there is, it's lost on me, so I stroll into the construction of the new shopping space, only to hear my brother's voice carrying from somewhere else. I walk through and round the corner to find him pointing at a light fixture.

Hard hat on, tool belt wrapped around his waist, work boots, and paint-splattered clothes, he turns to see me when I enter the room. Baylor Greene is rarely at a loss for words, but I manage to stump him. "Brother," I say, holding my hand out.

He grabs hold and pulls me against him, accompanied by a strong back pat. "Holy shit. When did you get back into town?"

"Just now. Saw Dad's truck out front and stopped."

After directing the guy to finish up, he then turns back to me and crosses his arms over his chest. "Damn, dude, I did not have you showing up on my bingo card for today."

"Slipping back into town saved our sister from having to plan a big reunion."

"Christine won't let you off the hook that easily." He nods toward the back door. I follow him to where his truck is parked. He opens a cooler and tosses me a bottle of water, then grabs one for himself. After drinking, he shakes his head and stares at me. "It's good to see you, Griffin."

"It's good to be seen again. You look . . . not so much like a punk-ass kid anymore."

He chuckles. "Marriage will do that to you. You go from thinking this is as good as it gets to realizing how meaning-less it was without the love of your life in it."

"I'll have to take your word for it," I say, wanting to tease him since I'm no authority on either living life in a way that's considered "as good as it gets" or falling in love. "The closest

I've gotten to a relationship is a fan out at the ballpark earlier begging for an autograph. At least she was hot." And for some reason, she felt familiar. I didn't get as good a look at her as I wanted, even when I turned back. Fangirls are all the same, though. I'm sure I'll see her out there again.

I thumb over my shoulder at the shopping center in a not-so-subtle change of subject. "I thought you were remodeling the four shops? There are three more that didn't even exist the last time I was here."

"We're quick around here. A housing development is being built out off Ranch Road 36. Lauralee expanded the café of Peaches Sundries & More into two spaces, and the pizzeria is now open. We're adding a small Tex-Mex restaurant at the end with a patio for more seating and to host live music on the weekends. I fucking miss Mexican food, and the closest is forty miles over in Fredericksburg."

"So you're building an entire restaurant to suit your cravings? Sounds like a good idea if you've got money to burn."

He starts back toward the shops but stops to grab my shoulder and give it a squeeze as he passes. "It's not burning. It's reinvesting in the Pass. A couple from Pflugerville is moving here to rent the space. Now come on, before Dad hears you're in town and haven't gone to see him."

I follow him back inside, and we cut through the space to the front sidewalk on Main. He glances over at me. "Is there a reason you're walking around in an Armadillos baseball uniform with your name embroidered on the back?"

I'd forgotten I was wearing this. Funny how long it's been since I wore a uniform, yet the moment I put one back on, it feels like a second skin again. "Long story short, I'm playing in a fundraising game next weekend."

Baylor stops and looks at me with curiosity leveled in his eyes. "And what's the long version?"

"Neither Dover Creek nor Peachtree Pass High Schools has funds to support their baseball programs. The coach from Creek emailed me to ask if I'd come play in a fundraising game. The winery is matching dollar for dollar. The program at our high school paved the way for me to attend college and then pursue the majors. Other kids should have the same opportunity." I shift suddenly, feeling self-conscious about it, though I know I have no reason to be.

We didn't grow up like some of the other ranching families in the area. The money came later, after a lot of hard work and sacrifices on my parents' part. It was my sister who changed the game entirely. But we weren't spoiled rich kids by nature. We all worked hard—I hit home runs, Baylor threw touchdowns, and Christine topped the podium as a barrel racer. But we'd still return home to chores that had to be done before catching up on homework.

We all made our way, taking different paths to success, and now have more money than sense. My contract with the Cardinals set a record for the team. Six years after being released, I still have money to last generations long after me despite trying to blow through it while traveling the world and escaping reality, if I'm honest with myself.

"I did a sponsorship for the pizzeria. Thought it was a good way to get word out." We start walking again. "We were planning to go," he says, grinning. "I had no idea I'd be treated to watching my big brother play again." Tugging the door open to the pizzeria, he adds, "If you'd given me a heads-up, I could have picked you up from the airport."

"No need. I bought a truck on my flight in. It was ready for me when I arrived."

He looks past me toward the street. "Is that white Ford yours?"

"Fresh off the lot."

With a few customers at the tables, he keeps his voice low when he says, "It's a nice ride." Nodding toward the counter, he chuckles. "Peaches knows better than to leave Dad working the register, but he likes the power behind the counter." He tosses his hand in the air. "Hey, Dad, look who's here."

When he looks up, I see the way life has aged him beyond his years. He's not old, but he's led a hard life on the ranch as a child and then on his own property. When he sees me, he smiles. It's one I recognize as my own. "Griffin, what? When did you get here?"

"Earlier today, but not more than twenty minutes back in the Pass." I don't want him to feel like he wasn't a priority.

Coming around the counter, he embraces me. My father is not a hugging man, or he wasn't before today that I was aware of. But a lot has changed since my mother passed seven years ago. Notably, that my dad is hugging me and dating again.

Peaches comes in from the back. Her entire expression lights up when she sees me. "Griffin, you're back." I give her a quick hug because she's the lady who used to sneak a piece of candy across the counter at the Sundries store when I didn't have enough money in my pocket to pay for it. She's also now dating my dad, which in a strange way feels full circle somehow.

"Hey Peaches, how are you?"

She swats my arm. "Devilishly good these days." I catch how she glances at my dad when replying.

I thought I'd feel more hurt somehow by their relation-ship, but it's been the opposite reaction. I'm happy for them. Though I'm not sure how the newlyweds, Baylor and Lauralee, handle their parents hooking up. It's not something I care to think about at all. "The place is looking good. Dad said on our last call that he was enjoying the pace of the pizzeria."

She replies, "It's a lot different from working the ranch, that's for sure."

"And air-conditioned," my dad adds with a laugh.

"Don't blame you for that." When Baylor cuts out to return to the other space next door, I say, "So I know my showing up out of nowhere is a surprise. I can get a hotel room if I need—"

"I won't hear of it." My dad pats my arm. "Your room will always be your room, and you always have a place to stay."

"Even at thirty-five?" I can admit I'm old enough not to have a "room" at my dad's house any longer.

He chuckles. "Your age doesn't change that you're my son, kid. Why don't you head back to the ranch, get cleaned up, and rest before dinner? I'm sure you're tired after traveling and having practice today before that storm rolled in."

"How'd you know I had practice today?"

Gesturing to the uniform, he replies, "Besides you walking in wearing a Dover Creek Armadillos uniform, which is blasphemy in some circles, Coach Barth contacted me for your current email. I figured you wouldn't mind hearing about a chance to help the local high school teams."

"I'm glad you did. It feels good to be able to help." Taking a step back, I say, "I'm going to take you up on the offer and head back. I could really use a shower and a nap."

"You go do that. You know the way back."

We don't embrace again, but a shared look kind of says all either of us needs to. I walk toward the door but stop just shy of opening it. "Hey, Dad?"

"Yes?"

"It also feels good to be back with family again."

He's not a sentimental guy by any means, but even I can see the emotion swarming in his eyes. "I'm glad you're back, son."

I walk out into the shade of the covered sidewalk and stroll to the truck. The rain stopped before I crossed county lines, but the sun still struggles to come back out. I don't mind springtime storms. It's like the Earth's way of replenishing itself. I have so many memories of the rain in the Amazon while exploring, and the storm that rolled in too fast to escape when hiking in Nepal. The storms in Australia were wild one summer but a welcome reprieve from the heat. I remember recording the sound of raindrops hitting palm leaves as I stood underneath them during a quick shower in Hawaii.

After starting the truck, I pull out onto streets that haven't dried yet. These storms and the rain here are different. The dry ground begs for it to prevent cracking. The crops will only survive if we get what's needed to protect them. I will never complain about the rain after experiencing so many droughts growing up in Texas.

The drive isn't long—another fifteen, twenty minutes on a slow day. When I see the weathered metal Rollingwood Ranch sign arched high above the cattle guard embedded in the ground, I know I'm finally home.

CHAPTER 3

Cricket

"He wasn't cute," I say, unimpressed as I drop my purse on the top of my desk.

Savvy sits back in her chair, grinning like she already knew how this would play out, though I know she's still in the dark regarding splash-gate and the infamous Mr. Greene. "Do tell."

"He's an ass just like every other athlete I've met or made the poor decision to date."

"Do we have a number to assign to 'every other athlete' you've met, or are we just generalizing this morning?"

I flop down in my chair, already over this week, and it's only Tuesday. "Yeah," I say, laughing. "That number is none of your beeswax."

She laughs, sitting forward again and resting her arms on the wooden top. "You never share the good stuff."

"I've shared plenty of good stuff when there was good stuff to share." Popping my shoulders up playfully, I start shuffling papers around and organizing the top of my exceptionally messy desk. "There hasn't been any good stuff to share in so long that I'm not even sure what 'good stuff' entails anymore." I punctuate the statement by dropping two pens into a cup holder.

"But there could be." Savvy types on her laptop, her eyes locked on the screen. "When I look into those incredible eyes of his, ass is nowhere to be found." Her eyebrow quirks before she aims her gaze at me again. "Six-three. *Rawr.* Brown hair. Full. Thick with a perfect wave to entice fingers to run through it. Gorgeous blue eyes."

"Are we talking about twenty-two or some other rand—"

"Griffin Greene is smoking hot, if you ask me, which slightly offends me because you didn't." She cracks a smile.

I shake my head. The last thing I want to talk about is *that* guy. I can't help myself, though. It's like a carrot of tidbits being dangled in front of me. "The website actually says perfect wave to entice fingers and gorgeous blue eyes?" What site is she looking at exactly? I'm tempted to pull it up and do my own research.

"No. I added to it for flair, but I'm not wrong. Come see for yourself."

"No, thank you," I reply, trying to pretend I'm not utterly engrossed in this description as much as she is. I kind of hate myself for showing interest.

She double blinks as if she's returned to her original mission. "College degree in anthropology." *Guess she is.* "Single." She practically purrs the word.

Pretending to ignore this casual sales pitch, I tap papers on the top of my desk. "Did he recently hire you for his personal PR? Because you're doing a stellar job of selling him." Locking my gaze on hers, I add, "But I'm not buying. Men are nothing but trouble for me. Always have been. Always will be."

"No one said you had to marry the guy. And . . ." Raising her finger in the air like I imagine Einstein doing when he made a great discovery, she says, "Blake said he only flew in for the fundraiser. You can't have fundraising without a little fun. It's literally in the word itself."

I burst out laughing. It was a struggle to hold it in, but she wins. "You're an incurable romantic." I soften my smile to one less revealing. "But I'm not." I glance down at the papers still in my hands. The sweet blue-and-red squiggly drawings I got for my birthday maintain my smile, but the love for my guy still feels too big to carry inside, even after all this time. It only grows larger.

I tuck them in a file, then into the top drawer of my desk. "Are we getting any work done today?"

"Of course. I've already sent several invoices to wedding clients, and I talked to your mom for a bit."

"Oh yeah?" I haven't seen her in more than a month. "How's France?"

"Wonderful, and then she said c'est la vie." She laughs, but then loses all the humor. "And your brother got two accounts."

"It only took five months of traveling through France's wine country." I wanted that job so badly I could taste it. I have a few more things to work out since it wouldn't only be me, but I wasn't even under consideration. I'm bitter, but that's not my brother's fault. "That's good. Just one will open many other doors. Any word on their return?"

"Nope. She just left a message to check in with you."

"At least she hasn't forgotten me entirely," I tease, but I'm not sure how much of that is a joke.

Spinning in her chair, Savvy watches through the large glass panes behind her. Crowds of people cut across the grass with baskets hanging on their arms as they head toward the vines. "It's going to be a busy day if guests are showing up so early at the winery."

"It's smart to beat the heat when walking the vineyards with tour groups. By the time they return, it will be lunch and time to drink the day away under the oaks on the front forty." I try not to complain about the visitors to the winery since they've made the business what it is today, but I hate these large lookie-loo windows. "I'm glad we'll be moving into the new offices upstairs soon."

"I stopped in yesterday for a peek. I'd be surprised if it takes another week to finish."

"The pretty touches take time, my dear." Lowering my glasses from the top of my head to the bridge of my nose, I grin as I log onto my computer. "I'd rather have it done before furniture is moved in. I'll stop in later if I get a chance. Your Griffin Greene—"

"Mine? Now he's mine? Not sure Blake's going to like that." She giggles.

"He may not be yours, but you seem to really want to support this guy." I roll my eyes. "Anyway, Jerk-face hasn't signed the contract for the game. So—"

"Why, pray tell, is he a jerk-face?"

"I don't have the energy to go over that exhaustive list. Just trust me. Also, guess who needs to get the paperwork wrapped up?"

Her eyes widen. "You?"

"You guessed it. Can't wait," I reply sarcastically and throw in some jazz hands for good measure.

"Doesn't sound like a chore to me." She grins. "He graduated with a degree in anthropology. I find that so impressive and kind of dreamy. My heart be still."

"Why are we stilling hearts?" *Anthropology, huh?* The hard chest, the harder glare. The way he treated me like a fan of his . . . it's hard to imagine him studying anything other than how to be an asshole when he grew up.

"Because he cares about humanity."

I scoff, looking back at her again. "Studying humanity is not the same thing as caring about it."

Shaking her head, she laughs. "He really put a bee in your bonnet, didn't he?"

"No bees. No bonnet. But he did piss off his boss."

"Uncle Bryan?" she deadpans, dragging my dad into this.

Savvy's good. *Very good.* "It's amazing how you know just the right buttons to push with me."

"Aw, cousin," she replies with a laugh. "It's just because we know each other so well."

"Yeah. Yeah. Payback and all that."

With a heartier laugh, she stands just as the printer starts spitting out paper. "Can I quickly note that it's adorable you already have a nickname for him?"

"Please don't."

"Bah humbug, Grinch." After snatching several documents off the tray, she slaps them on my desk. "Good luck today. You're going to need it."

"I don't need luck, ye of little faith." Picking up the contract, I laugh. "But Griffin Greene does."

Settling back at her desk, she replies, "I have no doubt he'll need all the luck he can muster when he comes face-to-face with you. You're known as a hard-ass for a reason."

"No one says that." I start to laugh.

She huffs. "Fine, I just call you that behind your back to get the other employees to treat me like I'm part of the team instead of a Dover who got the job by association."

I can't even fault her for it. It's something we will always have to fight. We will always be proving ourselves even after succeeding. But I'm still not letting it go. "The reputation fits because I work my ass off to make it this hard, and I'm quite proud of it. Do you know how many squats I have—"

Her phone vibrating across the top of her desk silences me. It's fun to work with my built-in family best friend, but sometimes we forget we're supposed to be working, and as the events coordinator for Dover Creek Winery and operations manager of the team and stadium, our work never seems to end. We're busier than ever and growing like wildfire. We both take pride in our contributions to the Dover empire.

While she listens to a conversation on the phone, which is probably a vendor of ours, she covers the microphone with her hand, and whispers, "What time are you going to the stadium today?"

I hold up four fingers, then waggle them. "Are you still bringing Jacob with you?" I whisper back.

She nods. "We should be there by five." Returning to her call, she says, "But we ordered eight cases for the Mider reception. Five won't cover it, so what do you suggest?"

I return to the mass of emails that have accumulated in my inbox since I didn't bother returning to the office yesterday. After getting soaked, I went home to take a much-needed bath, then enjoyed dinner with my favorite little guy. That more than made up for the rotten ending to the workday.

Despite the emails demanding my attention, I'm still slightly distracted by this Greene guy. Sure, he's rude and utterly intolerable from our brief encounter, but I'm a little thrown by his biography. His hardened gaze pops into the forefront of my mind, and I have a difficult time reconciling the man I met with the one I just learned about. Everything happened so fast, though, so maybe I was blinded by rage and didn't give him a chance to right the situation.

Why do I always have to be the bigger person?

It's a weakness I really need to overcome.

Get the paperwork signed, check out these apparently notable eyes, and get out. No harm. No foul. No more encounters. I like having a plan, and this one is now in place.

Knowing I have a confrontation ahead of me, I click open the first email and get busy replying.

Despite the rain yesterday, no humidity clings to the air. *Thank goodness.*

It's a perfect spring day. My hair looks amazing to boot, putting me in a great mood. Bonus: I'm not sweating through the thin tee I put on before coming out to the field today.

April is such a perfect weather month in Texas. Though I know summer is just around the corner to torture me again, I'll enjoy seventy-degree temps while I can.

I wave to Coach Barth when I come out of the tunnel into the sunlight of the field and climb the stairs to a different section of the stands to mix it up today. As I settle onto the metal bench and set my bag beside me, the players switch positions. Just my luck, the third baseman is my direct line of sight, which means I'm in his as well.

Annoyance wriggles through my good mood, souring it. *No, don't let him win.* Maybe he was having a bad day. Or perhaps he gets hit up by fans all the time. I imagine that could be quite tiresome some days. *Or maybe, Cricket, he's just an asshole baseball player.* It's probably the latter despite wanting to try to justify his behavior yesterday.

I glance at the large manila envelope holding the

contract, unsure when to approach him to sign. I figure after practice would be best, judging by the nice day that remains, as it won't be called off like yesterday due to rain.

After watching a few plays, I grin. The team out of Rockwall isn't going to know what hit them. With current minor league players and a former major leaguer, the Armadillos are looking the best they ever have. My spy in Rockwall texted me that they also scored a Major League player, but that doesn't shake my confidence. I believe in our 'Dillos.

I wish my parents did. Why spend the money to own a team if you don't care about the game or the players? At least, Savvy and I enjoy it.

I grab my bottle of water and take a drink. The lack of breeze causes the sun to beat down stronger, but I start to wonder if it's the heat rolling off Greene. I'd put my glasses on to verify, but I don't need to. I can feel his eyes on me. It's equally unnerving and intriguing.

Footsteps running across the metal floors on my aisle pull my gaze to the source. I open my arms just as Jacob runs into them. I kiss his head, tucking mine against him and savoring his sweet little hugs. "Hi," I whisper, leaning back to see the blue eyes that matter most to me in this world. "How's my little guy?"

"We got to milk a goat, Mommy."

"You did?" Lowering my head so our eyes are level, I ask, "How was that?"

"Weird." I laugh, though he was being serious. I get it. I was always more of a winery girl than a farm gal. He hops onto the seat next to me. "Who's playing?"

"This is the all-star team and some of our Armadillo players. They're going to play a game to raise money for the two local high schools. Isn't that neat?"

He nods a few times, his attention glued ahead when

Savvy finally reaches us. "This kid can run. As soon as he reached the stadium, he took off as if he knew exactly where you were." She sits next to me and blows out a breath. "How are they looking today?"

"Incredible."

"And did you get the contract signed?"

"Not yet, but I'll get it done after practice." As if on cue, Coach Barth claps his hands to bring everyone in for the day.

"Looks like this is your chance." The players file off the field into the dugout, which will take them to the locker room. "Go get 'em, tiger!"

Dread suddenly fills my gut, which makes me more resolved than ever not to let that man win this round. "Thanks."

When I take Jacob's hand, he says, "Savvy said I could run the bases."

She adds, "I did promise him, and I don't mind waiting at the car afterward for you."

I kiss his head again. "Be good for Savvy, okay?"

"Okay."

This little boy is my world and all that really matters. So paperwork schmaperwork. I'm not afraid of confronting a Greene and feel more emboldened to do it. If I can raise Jacob on my own, run a winery, and manage operations of a regional baseball team, I can deal with a former pro ball player.

I march down the stairs and wait inside the tunnel for Mr. Greene with the allegedly gorgeous blue eyes. A few of the players walk by, saying hi as they pass.

It's been a while, so I check to make sure his truck is still parked out front. Is he the last to leave or what? Since I'll never forget the sight of it coming toward me yesterday, it's hard to miss. When I turn back, I run into that wall of muscle that's quickly becoming too familiar, considering we've never actually met.

"Are you stalking me?"

"You wish." I shove off him, backing up just enough to get caught in his gaze. *Oh* . . . My heart stops with a hard thud in my chest.

Jaco Beach.

Costa Rica.

Those unforgettable blue eyes.

There's no way . . . I even remember asking him where he was from that night.

"I'm not sure we should travel down that road when we know it leads to a dead end," he replied.

It was a dead end, but I'd know his face anywhere. I still see it in my dreams sometimes.

But being in his presence now, a man I never thought I would see again, words elude me as my mind scrambles through different scenarios of how this could play out. And knowing that I walked away with more than his cowboy hat as a souvenir that night.

Jacob.

My sweet boy.

I back up to a nearby railing, clinging to it as the foundation of the life I've built begins to crumble beneath me. A night I'll never forget is a nightmare four years later. There is no mistaking that face, or the man standing in front of me.

Griffin Greene wasn't just a good time in paradise. *He's the father of my son.*

CHAPTER 4

Griffin

"Do I need to call security?" I ask, looking her over again, since I had clearly underestimated what I was dealing with. She's got a tight little body wrapped in denim and a V-neck T-shirt. Her hair falls over her shoulders in waves of brown and deeper golds, but she's been staring at me with a slack jaw like she's meeting a celebrity for the first time. I'm sure she's starstruck.

Although her eyebrows squeezing together command their own attention, it's that damn V-neck that draws my gaze downward. Can't say I wouldn't have sex with her, even if she is currently a potential threat. It's not like I haven't hooked up with a fan before. Looking that good, she makes it hard . . . and has me forgetting the rest of what I intended to say. But even her curve appeal doesn't keep an all-star distracted for long, so I continue, "You show up two days in a row and just so happen to run into me like it's a coincidence when we both know it's not."

"First of all, my eyes are up here." I drag my gaze over

her collarbone and then higher to be greeted with a scowl. She crosses her arms over her chest, her knuckles whitening from holding on to herself so tight. "Second, you're insufferable, you know that?"

"That's rich, considering I'm the victim in this situation." Her scoff echoes through the tunnel. Grimacing, I say, "And if I'm so insufferable, why are you hiding around every corner of this stadium in hopes of seeing me again?"

Shifting her weight to the other hip, she snaps, "I wasn't hiding—"

"Look, I don't know what kind of game this is, but I'm not playing, lady."

"Lady?" Offense jerks her head back so fast that she might need to seek medical treatment. Hopefully somewhere away from me. She's quick to straighten her shoulders. Coming on strong with the defense, she balls her fists at her sides as if she's squaring up to me, which is kind of cute, coming from her. I mean, she can't be more than five-three, five-four tops. She's spunky for such a little thing. "I'll have you know—"

"This isn't fun—"

"No joke." Her eye roll is so big that her head accompanies it.

"I'll make you a deal so that we can get this encounter, or whatever we're calling it, wrapped up and go our separate ways."

A grin crosses her face, the kind a villain in a Disney movie would wear. All bark, no bite. "I cannot wait to hear this."

"If I give you an autograph, will you stop harassing me?"

Her balk could probably be heard in Austin, it's so loud. I rub my ear, worried about my drum bursting. But then she levels a glare on me, giving me the first full view of her entirety—orange fire flickering in green eyes contrasts with the delicate features of her face, her lips pursing but then pillowing again as if they're ripe for the kissing. But it's her eyes that transport me back to Costa Rica and the girl I left in a hotel room on Jaco Beach. Four long years couldn't erase the memory. *How could it?* It was one of the best nights of my life.

Frivolous fun and great sex. Kissing her was like kissing the sun. I knew I'd get burned if I stayed too long. But we were raw attraction, the night sultry with possibilities, and so fucking sexy while it lasted.

We shouldn't have been a one-off.

I should have stayed, and my gut twisted when I walked away.

I should have asked for her number.

Hell, or at least gotten her name.

But here she is in the flesh again, the woman I never imagined I'd see again. Of course, I didn't expect her to show up as a stalker either, so there is that aspect to deal with. Oh shit. *Did she track me down?*

Maybe she never asked me my name because she already knew it. The thought is a bit unsettling. I had built an entirely different story about what happened to her after I left, but this new information changes things.

She smirks, which puts me more on edge than I already was. "You got yourself a deal." Bending down, she pulls an envelope from the large bag she left on the ground at her feet and then digs through the mess until she retrieves something silver and shiny. Is she going to pull a knife on me, force me into her vehicle at gunpoint, and coerce me to perform lascivious acts on her? *If only . . .*

I take a step back before realizing it's a pen. Okay, maybe I need to slow my roll with the stalker thing. Although she's a bit mouthy and has a Mount Everest-sized attitude, which I fully respect as someone else who falls in that category, I'm starting to think she's harmless. I've slept with the woman, and she didn't kill me then, so I'm not sure why she'd want to after all these years.

I scratch the back of my neck, unsure what to make of her. I've had nothing but fond memories of our time together, but seeing her under these circumstances is confusing. More so, does she not even recognize me? What the fuck?

Did I just waste years thinking about her when I wasn't even worth a second thought in her mind?

When she stands back up without an ounce of the irritation that burned hot inside her previously, she hands me the silver pen, then pulls papers from a large envelope. Tapping two different spots on what oddly looks to be a contract, she directs, "Sign here. And then here."

Guess I wasn't worth it since she's moving on like that night never existed.

What-the fuck-ever.

My gaze bounces around the document to catch words like *donation* and *contribute* but also, *no legal standing*, and *not an offer of employment.* "What is this?" I ask as my eyes dart to the top to find the title.

"It's the contract saying that any monies earned, raised, or acquired by participating in the game on Thursday is one hundred percent donated to the cause." Tilting her head as if she's really done something there, she laughs. "It's to make sure you don't go back on your promise and undercut our support for the high school teams."

I look at her again. The girl I remember, who was sexy and sweet, flirtatious and self-assured in everything she wanted, isn't the one standing before me now. This woman is smug and has the patience of a ticking time bomb. Her hair is darker, which I'm not mad about. It makes those eyes of hers even more captivating than they already were. But I'm still confused about why she's here, having me sign a business contract instead of an autograph. When she clears her throat and checks her watch like I'm keeping her from somewhere more important, I realize maybe her self-confidence still tracks. I ask, "But why are *you* having me sign this?"

"Because it's my job as oper—"

"Cricket," Coach calls out, coming from the locker room. *Cricket?* The door slams closed behind him. "I'm glad I caught you." *Caught a bug?*

"What can I do for you, Coach?" she replies with such syrupy sweetness in her tone. It's the first time I'm hearing it. The change in her smile reaches her eyes, joy shining bright inside. I'm almost impressed with how fast she morphed from a fangirl demanding I sign something into the pleasantries exchanged with him. *Almost.* She's got me more curious than ever about who she is, if she's whipping out contracts and already in Coach's good graces.

"Your brother wanted to play in the game, but I haven't seen him this week for practice. Any word from him?" So she has a brother who plays baseball. *Interesting.*

"He won't be here. He's still in France negotiating deals."

"Okay." As if he just notices me, he tilts his chin up in acknowledgment and says, "Hey Griff, good hustle again today. That play in the second inning? Bring that same energy on Thursday."

"No worries there. I bring it every time I play." I look at her and then him again. He's looking at me like I interrupted them, giving me the opportunity to duck out of this awkward conversation. "I'll let you guys talk. I need to head out anyway."

I only take one step before she says, "Not so fast." She taps the papers again. "You need to sign this, or you can't play in the game."

Glancing at Coach, he's gone quiet on me, making me think this chick is legit. Am I missing the bigger picture of who she is? I turn to her again, taking a longer dive into her eyes this time. "You work here?"

Coach guffaws, then hides his eyes behind his hand. "Oh no."

She glances at him and back at me. "No *oh no* needed." She holds a hand up in surrender. "It's okay." Shooting me another look, she snipes, "Not everyone in the world knows who everybody else is. Sometimes you mistake them for someone they're not, and sometimes you hit the nail right on the head."

I have a strong suspicion that the brief monologue was for my benefit, but I'm not sure why. Until it hits me like the nail she just mentioned. "Okay, in my defense again, you knew who I was but skipped over your introduction each time we've met." *Notably, Costa Rica comes to mind.*

Coach leans in, and whispers, "Cricket is the Armadillos' operations manager."

I release a heavy breath, realizing how this has gone off the rails for both of us. Dragging a hand over my head, I ask, "So this contract is real?"

"It's real alright." There's a pause where I can practically see her mind spinning for a comeback, but then the tension in her shoulders eases, and she says, "We appreciate you coming out to help us raise money."

The line is so well-rehearsed that she almost has me

falling for it. "I should probably send the contract to my attorney or, at a minimum, read it myself."

"Probably," she adds matter-of-factly.

I look over again, my eyes latching onto hers. "That will take at least a week." I start to skim it. "I'll take the risk." It helps to know she's only here because she was doing her job and not to do any damage . . . *at least physically*. "Sign here?"

"Yes," she replies, her expression remaining indifferent. "And although you're trusting me, against any attorney worth his fee, I'll give you the quick notes." When I glance at her, her eyes are already fixed on mine. Before I have a chance to read anything more into it, she blinks and turns her gaze back to the paperwork. "This is the part that states your appearance fee is waived in lieu of a donation being made in your name." I sign while she keeps talking. "And this paragraph says that the company will match that donation to double it. Two schools. Two donations. We really want to see these teams thrive and create the next generation of players."

"I was raised on those fields and developed my skills on that diamond in Peachtree Pass." I sign the other line and hand the pen back to her. "I'm happy to support the teams in return. That I get to play baseball while doing it seems like a no-brainer to give back to the town that gave me the opportunity."

When she looks up at me, only embers remain of the fire that was burning angry hot inside her eyes a few minutes prior. Even the corners have softened as she turns away to study the paperwork. I'm only given a flash of a glance before she smiles, tearing her gaze away again. "Guess my job here is finished for the day."

I recognize that smile when it was sprinkled throughout our time together and sandwiched between some unforgiving hour of the night and before the sun rose in the morning. We didn't know each other at all, but peace was found in our physical connection, and the comfort I felt while holding her in my arms. We had sex, but afterward, she was mine for a brief time. *And I was so fucking hers.*

Now, I hardly recognize her. It's not her looks that have changed so much. It's her openness, the calm she shared through confidence, and our bond. I shake the memories away because it's best not to dwell on the past. I learned that after my mom passed away.

"Mission accomplished." Wanting to try her name on for size, I add, "Cricket." I'd never pinned one to her prior despite many crossing my mind over the years. Cricket isn't one I would have ever guessed, but seeing how she angles her chin to give me a full view of her face again, it somehow fits. "That's a memorable name."

"Too memorable on some occasions. That's why I don't always volunteer it."

I'm still shocked she's standing in front of me like it's the first time, like we didn't exist altogether in a different time and place before this. "I know."

Somehow, that's the thing that wins a genuine smile from her. "That's my bad, habits and all that."

"Cricket, huh? Like the bug."

She arches an eyebrow as sharp as her tongue can be when I'm not more careful. "I consider it more like the sport." She raises her chin even higher in defiance. "Since it's another bat and ball game, like baseball."

I laugh humorlessly. "It's nothing like baseball, though I can see how some might be easily confused when they're not as familiar with the ins and outs of the game."

An emotional cold front blows in, returning the tension to her body, her back straighter, stiffer, the windows to her soul closed shut, and her smile on lockdown. It happened so fast I didn't see it coming, much less have time to say anything to stop it. Though I'm fairly certain it's what I said that opened the door for it to blow in.

And now she's staring at me like I crossed a line. Again, though I wasn't the one stalking her for a signature—for an autograph or a contract. She kneels to tuck the paperwork into her bag like it personally offended her.

She effectively shuts down further discussion, turning her back to me to speak to Coach. "You needed something, Coach Barth?"

Opportunity lost.

"Yeah, the feedback over the speakers from the announcers' booth is still not fixed," he says. "I called in the guys to take another look. I'm hoping to get this sorted before the game this week."

"We need it working, but have them send me the invoice, and you keep me updated." She only glances at me briefly, her armor back in place, shielding her from the possibility of this turning too friendly for her liking. That's too bad because the past four years have only made her more gorgeous than she already was, referencing my memories. And although she wasn't as—should I say—temperamental back then, it's not something that would turn me away now. But what *will* do the trick is her forgetting we've ever met, much less had sex. *Fan-fucking-tastic sex at that.* It was unforgettable for me, but seeing how she hasn't acknowledged our past, I guess we don't feel the same.

That's too bad, but I'm not going out of my way to remind her. I'll be too busy nursing this blow to my ego for the rest of the night. "Anything else?" I'm ready to get on my way.

"Nope." She spins on her sneakers, causing her hair to

swing around her shoulders, and marches toward the parking lot, lugging that heavy-ass leather bag of hers. Waving over her shoulder, she calls back, "Good night, Coach Barth."

Wow. Guess I'm chopped liver over here . . .

Two can play that game, sweetheart.

"Night," he replies, looking at me like I fucked up. Shaking his head, he says, "It's probably best to know who your bosses are."

"First of all, I don't have a boss. It's a game I've volunteered for. Nothing else."

Grabbing my shoulder, he squeezes it. "Let me give you a little advice, son. Don't piss off a woman. She'll make your life hell. But especially never piss off a woman with the last name of Dover. You'll be paying that price for the rest of your days and nights."

Dover? "Wait. Back up." *No. Fucking. Way.* "As in Dover Creek Winery?"

"Yep." He nods with pride as if he had a hand in it. "Family owned and operated for more than forty years."

What are the odds I hooked up with a Dover in Costa Rica? Pretty slim, I'd imagine. If not nil. "Dover as in the town of Dover Creek?"

"One and the same," he replies, starting back toward the door to the locker room.

I'm having a hard time piecing this together in my brain. How is this even possible that two people who met in another country, and did a lot more than that, just so happen to also be a Dover and a Greene from the same tiny part of the world? "Let me guess . . . Dover as in Dover County?"

Using his foot as a doorstop, he nods again. "The very ones. Owners of the Armadillos and this here stadium."

Sympathy structures his face to fall as if I've already got one foot in the grave. He adds, "It was nice knowing ya, Greene."

"Come on," I waver, which is not something I often do. "How bad can it really be? It was a simple mistake. How was I supposed to know she was part of the family who owns the team?" Throwing my arms wide, I plead my case. "She never told me." He's not the judge and jury I'm worried about, though.

"If you say so."

"Way to have my back, Coach."

He chuckles. "I value my job more, kid." The guy is like twenty years older than me at most, and I'm still considered a kid? I laugh as he disappears. But when I turn back to face the parking lot, I realize what this new information really means. The issue at hand isn't that she's a boss over me, because she's not. It's that she's a Dover of the namesake county I've spent my formative years being told was the enemy by most folk in Peachtree Pass.

I head to the truck, wondering what mess I've gotten myself into by coming back here. Who would have ever guessed?

Of all the people in this vast world I could have hooked up with, it had to be Cricket Dover . . .

Fuck me.

CHAPTER 5

Griffin

"DID you know the Dover family owns the Armadillos?" I scratch my arm, still agitated from my earlier encounter with Cricket.

"Yes," my sister replies from the kitchen in front of me. "Everyone knows that."

"I didn't." Christine looks back at me over her shoulder, and her pointed glare and casual shrug kind of say what she's thinking without saying a word. Sitting on a barstool, I chuckle, shaking my head. "I'm a little out of the loop on the goings-on around small-town gossip in Texas."

"That's not even gossip. That's old news."

Old news . . . like how Cricket Dover is the operations manager of the entire outfit, and everyone in a hundred-mile vicinity apparently already knows? Or is it old news that I slept with the woman before being aware of who she was or her connection to the Greenes, which goes back generations? Both those stories have run their course. Let's hope that they stay in the past and don't make fresh news across the grapevines.

Her being a Dover bothers me. I didn't think it did other than regarding not knowing her role out at the stadium, accusing her of stalking me, and thinking she was trying to kill me at the first confrontation. Mistakes happen. Assumptions get made. If someone acts like a fan, they usually are.

I slept with her. None the wiser, but I didn't expect it to come back and haunt me. Would I not have gone back to the hotel with her if I had known? I smirk, knowing I would have. So this leaves us where we are—caught in an uncomfortable situation. Nothing more. Nothing less. Though I still dream about her perfect tits some nights.

My sister brings a glass of iced tea and sets it in front of me. "Just found out?"

"Found out today in not the best of ways either."

She's struggling to hide her smirk. "That sounds like a good story."

Twisting the glass on the counter, I reply, "I accidentally thought one of the Dovers was a fan."

"Oh." The cringe that drags the left side of her mouth down is how I feel on the inside, especially now thinking back on it. "And how did that work out for you?"

"Unsurprisingly, not well."

Her ponytail swings wildly as she starts laughing. The added clap wasn't necessary, in my opinion. "Glad I'm so entertaining to ya, sis."

"It's just funny." She still laughs under her breath. "The Dovers own pretty much everything in Dover County at this point, especially the fancy places. The winery. The stadium. The restaurant on Dover Creek near downtown. They're old Texas money. That wealth has traveled through generations and stayed in the family."

Thinking about the very ranch we're on right now, I ask, "Does that make us new money? Because we sure as shit weren't born with silver spoons in our mouths."

"Only to the Dovers, I suppose, and their fancy friends." Her laughter lightens as she busies herself in the kitchen again. I haven't fully cooled down from the walk down to their house on the lower part of the property, so I take the opportunity to drink some tea.

"Only the Dovers" echoes, the words rolling around until Cricket's face comes to mind again. I don't know why, but she's gotten under my skin. Was it because she was so smug with Coach around? I assume she really felt like she pulled one over on me by not introducing herself from the get-go. What was that about anyway? It's almost like she didn't want me to know who she was. Or should I say, who she *really* was, since we've done way more than just met yesterday.

I remember her looking so fucking sexy lying in that bed with my hat on . . .

"You forget something, cowboy?"

"What's that, babe?"

"Your hat."

"You keep it. A little something to remember me by."

"I don't need a hat to remember you."

She had no problem forgetting who I was when I left . . .

"I can't believe you're here," my sister says, dragging me from my thoughts. Christine looks at the clock hanging on the kitchen wall. "And you've stayed more than twenty-four hours, too. You've been here for twenty minutes. Breaking records." She hands me a fork with a teasing grin. "The jet not fueled?"

"The girl's got jokes." I grab my chest, feigning pain. "Aw, that hurts, sis." I start laughing, but I can't hold on to it because I do feel bad, which is interesting since I didn't feel much of anything while traveling. Just like when I was flying from one destination to another, being back comes with its own baggage. *Good and bad.* "Joking aside, sorry I've been gone so long—"

"The ranch. The family. Our lives." She lightens the guilt with a genuine smile. "It's been longer than it should have been, big brother." She leans on the light-colored stone counter of the island and slides a pie between us. "But you're here now."

So many memories come flooding back that I can't help but smile when I see it. "Blackberry pie. Damn, I've missed this." This is way better than the turmoil of earlier.

"Mom's recipe. Homemade like she used to make." She digs her fork right in without hesitation and scoops out a bite. My stomach growls just from seeing that filling. "Dig in."

I take my first bite, savoring the fruit and then the flaky crust. Memories of Mom and me sitting together at the table, eating and laughing while my brother and sister napped, come rushing back. I try to remember her smile and the sound of her laughter instead of her sudden death dragging me down, which is what usually happens. "She always made two pies. One for after dinner when Dad was there to enjoy it—"

"And one for her and us kids to devour as a treat before he even got home."

"We were really getting away with something back then." I take another bite. As soon as I swallow, I grin again. "It felt like robbing a bank." I chuckle.

My sister's smile reminds me so much of my mom's that it almost catches me off guard. The family sends me photos, but seeing it in person makes it hard to miss the resemblance. I'm not sure when my pipsqueak of a little sister grew up, but it's good to see that trait carried on even though the rest is uniquely her own.

"It kind of feels like we're breaking the law right now." Digging in again, she holds the bite in front of her, and adds, "I've carried on the tradition with the kids."

"I'm sure they love it as much as we did." I scoop another bite onto my fork. "You make a good pie, sis."

"It's even better because we're totally ruining our dinners." We both laugh again like we used to. Christine was never as annoying as Baylor. My brother is great, my best friend if I have one, but we've thrown down a time or two. Dad had to separate us more than a few times, and Mom would send us to our bedrooms to think about what we had done.

It was always the same result. We were both fine with what we'd done, even if it was sitting in front of our parents sporting a new shiner. We fought, but we made up fast like nothing had happened. He should be here delving into the pie with us.

"How's the ranch doing?"

She lowers her fork and grabs a napkin to wipe her mouth. Standing, she asks, "Is this an official meeting or are you asking your sister casually over blackberry pie?"

"I get the quarterly reports. I'm asking you off the record."

"Tagger has really come into his own, running a lot of it while I was pregnant. I was living in the lap of luxury in my air-conditioned office here in the house. And now that Julie Ann is here, I have her with me."

"You were doing the books anyway." I may have made millions in the majors, but my wealth has only grown because she single-handedly created an empire for our family. Even when Baylor and I gave her most of our shares a few years back because she had more than earned them, we still rake in the big bucks from the ten percent we each retained.

"He's a natural and has taken over most of the physical duties—"

"Well, he practically grew up at Rollingwood himself and knows it like the back of his hand."

The thought of him causes her to smile. She looks down as if she can hide it from me. *Is that what love looks like?* It's how Mom used to look at Dad. I shift, tempted to drop my feet to the ground to find a more solid surface to rest on than this thin metal bar.

I don't. I'm not giving Christine the satisfaction of proving she's right. Do I consider it running when I leave? *No.* I've always had a backup plan. Even when it came to settling down. I knew it was something I didn't want at her age. After all these years, though, and maybe being back in the Pass, my emotions are mixed up. I have no idea what I want anymore.

This is why I don't stay in one place. I start to face reality, and I'm more lost than ever. At least, the ranch is a nice detour to give me time to figure out where I go from here.

She says, "We have solid ranch hands in place as well. Now I don't have to do the outside chores, but I do miss riding my horse. I find her grazing out front most early mornings."

"When can you ride again?"

"The doctor said it was fine since having the baby four months ago, but I—" She sighs. "I just want to wait a bit longer. No need to rush it. I still spend time with Sunrise each day, though. And our little Julie Ann seems interested in horses already by how she wriggles when she sees them."

My niece was named after our mom, which I think is sweet. Though hearing her name is still not something I'm used to. I know I will in time. And she's so cute that it fits her. My mom would have loved having grandkids.

"Maybe she'll barrel race like you did."

"I'd love it, but only if it's something she loves. I'm not forcing it, but I'll support her own goals. You had baseball. Baylor was all about football. I had the rodeo. The ranch is the perfect place to dream as wide as the sky."

I'm not sure I've seen this side of my sister. Maybe it's because I've been out of the house since before she turned fifteen because of our age difference, or perhaps it's because she's a mom with a family of her own. Either way, I'm glad to see it now.

I steal one more bite of pie and then stand. Three kids and a husband keep her busy enough. She doesn't need me to add myself into the mix. "I'm heading back to Dad's house. I need to ice my shoulder."

"I'm still not sure how you got roped into this game, but I'm glad you said yes. I love having the family together again. Greene Farms is a sponsor—"

"Oh yeah? Guess I can't let the family down, then."

That makes her laugh again. "No pressure from us, old man."

Chuckling, I reply, "Let's hope the ice helps, or you'll be sneaking out of that stadium not wanting to be seen."

"We're stepping over enemy lines to watch you play again, so there's a little pressure." She holds her fingers almost pinched together. "Just a wee bit."

Since she brought it up again . . . "Speaking of enemy lines, what is the history with Dover County? What caused the ruckus between our families?"

She shrugs. "I don't know how that legend began. I've

just always known there was a rivalry. Not sure I ever heard the cause."

"Yeah, me neither, but I'm curious."

"Oh great. Now I'm curious, too. I'm sure I'll be thinking about this at three a.m." She rolls her eyes. "If you find out, let me know."

"I will." I walk around the island and playfully lock her into a hug, kissing her head. "I'm glad to be back."

My nieces waking from their nap gives me time for a quick hello before I start back across the field and up the hill to the other house. While working out my arm, I start to wonder if I'm getting too old for this.

It's not something that's crossed my mind even as the years ticked by. I've played here and there, picking up a few games in Mexico and Japan as a fill-in when their third basemen got injured, but it's been a while since then. I'm feeling it, and don't know if ibuprofen can put me back together like it used to. Here's to hoping.

One thing I know is it sure does feel different walking on this hard earth at thirty-five than it did at fifteen or even twenty-five, when I'd come back to visit. I can kid myself that some things change and others stay the same, but it's not the things or the land. *It's me.* And that's never been more apparent since returning.

Life has moved on without me.

I rub my shoulder, feeling the tightness of the muscles while wondering where I fit into this world, or even how I fit anymore. Maybe I don't. But I'm still hoping to figure out why I jumped on a plane the first opportunity I was given instead of booking that ticket to Fiji like I'd planned.

I'm pretty sure I'm not getting the answers on a ten-minute walk. I'll set that aside in my mind to enjoy being here again.

A few animals are sheltering in the nearby barn when I pass it to head up the front porch. As I tug the screen door open, it squeals like no one found the time to oil it in the past ten years. Probably didn't.

My dad tended to overlook those kinds of tasks, which annoyed my mom. He could work and run an entire farm and cattle ranch, even manage the small crew working the orchard, but taking two minutes to oil a squeaky screen door always remained on the list at the end of the day.

I'll take care of it like I did back then. I just won't have my mom standing nearby praising me like I was Superman who just saved the world. She always valued the little things the most, preferring a horrible finger painting from school to a piece of jewelry. Being home again pulls random memories closer more often. I can still see her holding the necklace I bought when I signed my Major League contract, and the way she admired it around her neck. *"This is too much, Griffin. Where would I wear something so fancy?"* The words are still so clear. It's her voice that's fading.

When I open the freezer, packs of ice line the door compartment like my dad still has athletes at home to nurse back to health. I have a feeling it's another thing left on a list somewhere. He's also recovering from knee surgery, so I leave some in there for him. I grab a couple of packs and head to the hall closet. If I'm home, I want to soak in the time I'm here. I drag my finger down the boxes, landing on a puzzle, then tug it free from the others.

Moving into the living room, I pull the coffee table closer to the couch and dump the pieces out. I don't remember a time when my mom didn't have a work-in-progress puzzle set out on this table. But when the others went to bed, she would sometimes let me stay up later and scavenge for pieces with her.

The house was quiet, except for the low hum of a late-night TV show in the background. That time meant more to me than she knew because she always made me feel special.

I open the side table drawer and pull out a roll of athlete's tape. She always made me sit in this very spot on the couch and get taped up when I was injured and heading into a game. If she could see me now . . . Trying to pretend I'm still twenty-five. I wrap the tape around the packs and over my shoulder to secure them in place. The ice doesn't bother me. I'm used to the numbing sensation.

The first few puzzle pieces come together easily, but the green pasture will be a challenge. I have the time, it seems—a few days at least to knock this out.

But busying my hands doesn't busy my mind, which is already wandering back to Cricket Dover of all things. Talk about a wrench being thrown into a plan. She may have popped up at the stadium and back into my life, but I know one thing for certain. I don't believe in coincidences.

Damn. *I did not see her coming . . .*

CHAPTER 6

Cricket

THE SOFT SLUMBERING sounds on my chest have me tightening my hold around Jacob. Should I have kept him up an extra hour just to spend more time together? Probably not, but I don't regret it. My father would say I'm spoiling him. If loving him and giving him my undivided attention is spoiling him, he'll be rotten to the core. Seeing his pure joy from eating french fries and chicken nuggets while watching cartoons together is worth it.

It was important to me to give Jacob what I always wanted as a child, especially since he only has me. Rushed routines or the staleness of eating dinner at a banquet table in the formal dining room weren't things I valued. And my mom remained oblivious to our misery as we sat ten feet from each other while we were served dinner. Why pretend we're living like it was the Gilded Age when we could have been a real family? My brother and I just wanted parents we could talk to and hang out with.

I want fun and laughter with Jacob, heartfelt conversations, and to create memories worth retelling one day. I want to see the light in his eyes as he grows instead of him witnessing the stress in mine. I want him to get nights at home with his mom rather than wondering where I am.

After trying to use my core to get up, I relax back when I realize that's not going to work. He's grown so much that I just might be trapped on the couch for the night. I grin, trying not to laugh. But then one thought wipes it free from my face.

Griffin Greene.

Damn him.

I kiss my son on the head, aware that Jacob inherited many of his traits from his dad. I mean, I already knew, since I spent a night with the man with nothing hidden between us . . . except our names and where we came from.

His tall frame and broad shoulders were the first things that drew me to him. After clubbing the night away with my friends, we danced onto the streets, and there he was. He had me in a chokehold the moment I laid eyes on him, those blue eyes piercing right through my walls that night. *So annoying.*

That's what I get for trying to pretend I was someone else.

Unlike *his* eyes, Jacob's are so full of love when he looks into mine. I kiss his head again and linger there. I can still smell the soft scent of bubble bath from earlier on his hair. Closing my eyes, I relish the feeling of just the two of us. Tomorrow is another day, and in light of it, I'll have to start considering the steps I take, or am willing to take, in this situation with Griffin.

The worst plays out in my mind like a stab to the heart. I'm not about to give up my son to some random guy to take away from me, not even fifty-fifty. I'll fight for him. Whatever it takes. However much it costs. No matter how long it takes, I'll fight for full custody. I just hope it doesn't come to that.

I'm jumping to conclusions. From what I've seen of Greene, he won't care to step into Jacob's life or want to deal with me. I can only hope. I'm not going to solve anything tonight, though, so I leverage the back of my legs against the front of the couch and put my core back to work, lifting to my feet. Carrying this sleepy toddler down the hall, I stay steady like I have his whole life. I whisper, "I'll always be here for you."

I enter his bedroom and kiss him once more before settling him into his small bed in the corner. The threat of his father's sudden presence in our lives causes my throat to tighten and my heart to hurt. It shouldn't be like this, but I don't know this man from a serial killer, so I have no idea what battle is ahead. Maybe he'll just fall off the map like he's done for years, from what Savvy says, and disappear again. That's a whole other set of worries. I can't let Jacob get attached to someone who won't stay for him. Ugh. My brain hurts from running through the scenarios.

I'm getting worked up for nothing. I have no idea how he'll react or what he'll do, so I just need to hope for the best. But do it tomorrow, Cricket.

Stay calm. Act cool. Always appear collected. It's the only way to show strength in the face of potential danger.

Closing the door behind me, I smile once more, seeing him sleeping so peacefully. I take pride in the fact that he has a few traits of mine as well, mainly his tenacity. So whether *they* share traits or not, he's my son, and I'll do what I need to protect him.

"I NEED to know how to address your absence, Dad. Mom and Will have their trip as an excuse, but what's yours? The *Gazette* will be there for photo ops and to write up a story for the weekend edition. So help me out. You don't know if you're going or don't want to go?" I stand at the corner edge of a large, intricately carved wooden desk that's too elaborate for my taste, but to him, it reeks of money. He loves that. I'm not that showy. Or try not to be anymore. We all have our journeys.

"You're asking me to drop everything I'm doing to go to a high school fundraiser, Buggy."

I hate that nickname. Cute at five. Not so cute at thirty-one. "I'm not asking you to do anything. If you don't want to be there, that's fine. I'll tell everyone that you had prior commitments. I can hand out the checks. I was only wondering if you wanted to come out to support the teams and event."

Glaring at me with his hand over a landline phone, he seems to catch his irritation and releases a heavy breath. "This is something you can handle," he says in a lowered voice.

"I know I can handle it." I don't bother saying anything more because he's already putting the phone to his ear and a fake smile on his face as if the caller can see him.

"Richard, it's been too long, old buddy."

I walk out of his office, still respectful enough to shut the door quietly after exiting despite the anger building inside me. I'm not sure why I can't learn the lesson and stop the expectations. He's never going to change.

"Have a great day, Cricket," his assistant, Sarah, says from behind a large filing cabinet. Just like my dad, this office is run like we're still in the past. I had to beg for more duties after I shamed him by getting pregnant out of wedlock. So old-fashioned. I'm the family disappointment. It took me a long time, but I finally realized it didn't matter what I did or do now. He needs to place his own discontent in life somewhere, and it's never been on my brother, so it falls on me instead.

"Have a good day."

Pushing through the door, I enter the main corridor that leads to the winery's great room. The soft carpet deadens my heels as I make my way toward the exit to the executive suites on this side of the building. My heels clack against the Spanish tile of the great hall that greets the winery guests when they arrive on the property for tours, tastings, and events. It's a beautiful room overlooking the magnificent view of the rolling hills lined with endless rows of grapevines. Framed by my hands, it looks like Italy when I squint and not the harsher landscape of Texas.

I cross through the room and tug open the far door to enter the other corridor of offices, including mine and Savvy's. My back hits the door as soon as I enter, releasing an exhaustive sigh from the gut as if the room itself gives relief. My shoulders slump the moment I know I can relax.

"You okay?" Savvy asks, spinning in her chair to face me.

"I'm good." I push off the door and head for my desk inside this little pocket of safety from the world. "Tired."

"Didn't sleep well?"

"Tired of—" I cut myself off because someone in my position doesn't have a right to complain. No one cares if a rich girl's dad doesn't give her the time of day. "Yeah," I reply, hoping that slips by her as I busy myself by logging into my computer.

I scroll through emails, noting that the presentation check needs to be picked up by the end of the day, and add it to my never-ending to-do list for this event.

Although I appreciate the lack of questions and the quiet to allow myself to decompress, it's rare for silence to last long. There's not a click of the mouse or a tap on her keyboard, and her phone doesn't buzz on her desktop. Just . . . *silence.*

Maybe I'm the one who can't deal with it because I glance over at my cousin, bordering on gobsmacked by the quiet. "Okay, Sav, what's going on?"

"Huh?" She looks up from her computer screen. My reply is a few very pointed slow blinks. Laughing, she punctuates the sound with a perfected eye roll. "I figured I should let you get the upset out of your system before piling on even more. Seems now is as good a time as ever."

"With an intro like that, I'm worried." I angle to face her. "We've worked so hard on this event. Please don't tell me we're getting rained out or a player has dropped from the roster." I'm startled by an image of Griffin Greene popping into my head. And then irritation courses through me. He had to ruin the past two days with his presence, and now he's invading my thoughts. Typical arrogant athlete. They're all the same.

"I—"

"It was Greene, wasn't it?" I'm already shaking my head, knowing deep down that whatever the issue is, he's the cause of it. I stand and start pacing across the small room. I need to shake this off, but my mood only sours more. "I knew he'd do this even after signing that contract." Crossing my arms over my chest, I stop in front of her desk, and although she's just the unlucky messenger, I narrow my eyes as if she's to blame.

Anchoring my fists on my hips, I say, "He's not getting his fee back. That document is legal, so that money is mine." I waffle my head on my neck. "Not mine personally, but you know what I mean." Throwing my arms out, I'm still bracing for the bad news. "Well, are you going to tell me?"

"Haven't had much of a chance, considering that display." She rocks back in her chair, then kicks her feet up on the desk. She taps the end of a pen on her chin. "That's quite impressive—"

"What is?" My mind bounces through every hoop she throws out, but I still manage to trip over myself and come up empty-handed. *Until*— "No." I shake my head in denial because there is no way . . . "Absolutely no way. You cannot possibly mean you're impressed by that intolerable . . ." My hands punch down at my sides. "Disrespectful, annoyance of a man. I don't care if he does have a stupidly perfect face or that one could easily grapple off the sharp-edged cliff of his jawline. You are not allowed to date him."

"Moi? I am not allowed to date him?" She lowers her chin, keeping her grin at bay. "I love you dearly, but you do not have a say in whom or with whom I date."

My shoulders slouch from that earlier sinking returning. "Don't tell me you and Blake broke it off again?"

Standing, she snaps her fingers in front of my face. "Snap out of it, cuz. No one is talking about me and Blake. Blake is Blake and will always be Blake. That's . . ." She playfully shrugs. "It's one of the things I love about him. I'm not talking about him, or me, or Griffin Greene for that matter, though I think you have a few things that you need to get off your chest to cause such a reaction at the thought of that man."

Raising my chin ever so slightly, I reply, "I'm good. Thanks. Now spill the bad news."

I'm answered with an arched eyebrow. "The umpire threw his back out and can't officiate the game tomorrow."

The exhale I release causes her eyes to widen before I

understand what I did. "No. No. I'm not glad he threw his back out. That's awful. I'll send flowers—"

"You mean I'll be sending the flowers from you?"

"Fair point," I reply. "Thank you for doing that."

"You're welcome. I did it an hour ago."

"See?" I signal toward her as I return to my chair. "You're the most amazing assistant. Always two steps ahead of me. Since that's settled, I'll try to find a replacement umpire."

"Done. I found a guy out of San Antonio through Coach Barth. So no need to worry. It's been taken care of as well." Her eyes return to the monitor, but then she drops, "Now you have time on your hands to figure out why you got so worked up over a man who is apparently intolerable." She peeks around to make eye contact with me. "It was intolerable, right?"

I nod just a little, embarrassment slipping in. "And disrespectful," I whisper. Trying not to think about Griffin at all, I don't bother whispering this time. "Can we pretend I didn't go off on that tangent?"

"Of course. I mean, why would we want to talk about that perfect face?"

I don't bother looking up from my computer screen. "Stupidly—"

"Oh yes, we don't want to forget that it was a stupidly perfect face of his." She stands, picking her phone up off the desk. "Or even have that jaw cross our filthy minds again. Nope. We wouldn't want that."

With tightly closed lips and another shake of my head, I reply, "I definitely don't want that. I'm trying to forget him altogether."

"I think you're going to need to try harder next time. Soda? Coffee? Water? Food? I'm heading to the restaurant to get lunch before it sells out. I heard they're serving nachos today."

"No. Thanks, though. I'm heading back out to the stadium to make sure all the sponsorship signs are displayed properly."

She turns back in the doorway, grinning like she's in on some big secret. "I'd just like to note at this day and time that I just watched the most put-together woman I know unravel before my very eyes. And I suspect that a certain insufferable—"

"Intolerable." Rolling my hand on my wrist, I bow down my head. "But I'll allow insufferable since it works as well." I might as well embrace the shame and play along. Fighting it will mean discussing it another time, and I'd rather just forget this conversation ever happened.

A lack of good sleep.

Pent-up frustration from our encounters.

Dealing with his arrogance.

All lead to these buildups and breakdowns. Top it off with dealing with my father this morning, and I was bound to explode at some point. I'm just glad it was with Savvy instead of at the jerk himself. *Never show weakness.*

"Ballplayer is pulling the thread."

"He's not pulling anything. Not the wool over my eyes or over my head. Not a bone in my body finds that man attractive despite the slip of my tongue." Exasperated by getting myself into this mess, I sigh again. "Rant over."

"As long as you're good."

"I'm good." I throw my hands up as if that proves some point. "Go get your nachos. If I don't see you before I leave, I'll pick Jacob up today."

"Okay." Pointing at the console, she says, "Don't forget to grab your jersey for tomorrow. It's right there."

"Thanks."

As soon as she leaves, I return to my emails to ensure I don't have any emergencies waiting for me. Looks to be clear since she's already gone through them. I grab my bag, the list of sponsors off the printer, and the jersey before heading out.

I take a deep breath, inhaling calm, already feeling more myself than I was earlier. Nothing about that Griffin Greene is worth getting worked up over. I must only tolerate him for one more day, and then he'll be back to flying wherever he's headed, and I'll have my good little life back again.

It sounds so easy when I know this is the most difficult challenge I've ever faced. I know what the right thing to do is, but as Jacob's mother, I will always prioritize his needs and safety. *What a nightmare.*

CHAPTER 7

Griffin

WHILE TRACKING the ball across the sky, I start for first base. When it lands on the other side of the fence, I take a home run victory lap around the bases, high-fiving the guys as I pass them by.

I spot a certain little ball of fire as I round third, heading down the home base line. Standing ahead, past the home plate, she leans against the fence in front of the stands. The heat of her glare extends across the field, stabbing me like a sword to the heart.

For a Dover, she's a hot-tempered little thing. I always heard they were too good for everyone, so to see her emotions worn so openly is surprising. She looks away when my eyes catch hold of hers, though she pretends she doesn't notice me, or maybe it's a bad acting job of not caring. Whichever it is, there is no way she doesn't remember being together. *None.* It's not possible when my memories hold every minute of that night.

That night has been playing on repeat since I got a good

look at her yesterday. Now I'm left wondering what to think. It's confusing. Should I remind her who I am? Do I wait for her to remember? What if she never does? *Fucking humiliating.*

That's probably more her style, based on seeing her in action here.

I'm still not sure how I'm supposed to feel about her. I shouldn't feel anything, but it's hard to resist pushing those buttons of hers, so I pass the dugout and head toward her instead. "Can't get enough of me, huh?"

She rolls her eyes before righting her expression to indifference, and replying, "You don't need to waste all your energy at practice. It's only a fundraiser game."

I look over my shoulder at the teams changing out, then turn back to her. "I have plenty more where that came from."

"I rem—" She looks away with clamped lips, then glances back at me with a chill rolling off her entire being. "You should really see a doctor about that swollen head of yours. It can be dangerous if left unchecked for long."

"So I'm sensing." I smirk. "What brings you by today, *Ms.* Dover? Got more paperwork for me to sign?"

Her body loosens under the release of a hard breath. So she *can* relax around me. *Good to know.*

"No paperwork. And I'm not actually here to see you at all."

Resting my hand on the fence above my head, I keep my eyes steady on her while she tries so hard to keep her gaze from returning to me. Only judging by how she's looking anywhere and everywhere else except at me. "That's too bad. I love meeting fans."

She grumbles under her breath and shoots me a look before lowering her glasses from her head to her nose. "Listen, Greene, I don't know what you think this is, but it's nothing. Not a friendship. Not a working relationship. Nothing but a short blip on our life's radar, so if you'll excuse me—"

"Excuse you from what?" She's adorable in that sexy librarian way when she's wearing those black-rimmed glasses.

"From this little tête-à-tête, so I can do my job." With a clipboard and papers held to her chest, she points across the field. "I'm verifying the sponsorships are hung and their placements are correct."

She doesn't owe me anything, but I'm keenly aware she felt the need to share with me. "I appreciate the update."

Annoyance glazes over her green eyes like I just lit the match. *Fiery little thing.* I turn away and look out at the signs.

The first to catch my eye is the Greene Farms logo hanging from the scoreboard. If I didn't know better, I might suspect my sister of trying to make a point in what she considers "enemy territory." I grin.

Cricket says, "Your family bought the largest sponsorship . . . behind mine. Please tell them thank you."

"You can thank me instead."

Her gaze slides down to me. "I'd rather not." Her honesty makes me chuckle. "Also, I don't remember you being our contact and booking it." She sways to the side and dips at the hips to rest her arms on the railing again, basically getting as close as she can to me. "Tell me something, Twenty-two."

"Anything." Angling my shoulder against the wood, I reply, "I'm an open book."

That seems to cause her to pause as she stares at me, but then she exhales, and asks, "Did you get a ticker-tape parade when you got back to Peachtree Pass? It's not every day the prodigal son returns home."

I fucking knew it. I grin while pushing off the wall to get some distance so I can see her face in the sunshine again. "So you *have* heard of me and knew who I was even after so boldly denying it to my face the other day. *Tsk tsk* for lying, *Ms.* Dover."

A smile tries to creep onto her face, but she shuts that shit down real fast. "In my defense"—she places her hand over her heart—"I hadn't heard of you when you played in the majors."

"Ugh. That hurt." I'd act like it injured me, but it was my soul that took that blow. "You really have a knack for stabbing me right in the heart."

She laughs. "Will it make you happy if I tell you that's an impressive accomplishment?"

"I'm quite proud of it, so yes, it will, but be sure to say it nice and slow. I want to savor every syllable."

Trying so hard not to give in, she can't stop from laughing even louder this time. "Why are you like this?" Waving me off, she says, "Never mind. From my experience, most pro athletes are like this."

That "from my experience" pangs in my chest. "Is that something you have a lot of experience with? Pro athletes?" Why do I sound like a jealous fool? "Not that I care."

Her right shoulder rises and drops suddenly. "Why would you? You wouldn't."

"Nope." I swear she's fucking with me again. Am I going to have to spell out our past for her to remember it? That doesn't just sting. It burns. *Forget that.* I won't give her the satisfaction like I did in Costa Rica. "No reason whatsoever."

Straightening her back, she says, "Coach is calling you."

I turn to look back toward the dugout and see Coach waving me back in. "Come on, Greene. Mind on the game."

Her steps reverberate over the metal base of the stands, reaching my ears as if intended. She's got my full attention, alright. When she glances over her shoulder, I catch a smile that I know she'd deny sharing, and say, "Yeah, Greene. Mind on the game."

If I had a sec, I'd come up with some snappy comeback. But she's got my mind twisted instead of on baseball or anything else but her. I look back once more as she crosses the far side of the field when I return to the dugout. Situating myself at the back of the other end of the bench, I cross my arms over my chest and sit back to watch as she circles around, taking photos of the signs.

As Coach talks about tomorrow's game, I can appreciate how seriously everyone is taking this. A few of the guys from the Round Rock Express remind me a lot of myself back when I could run bases a little faster and throw a ball to take out a player sliding into home without having to ice my shoulder.

I don't feel old, but I feel my body wants to wind down a bit more than I'm ready for. My identity has been wrapped up in the former Major Leaguer package for years, but who am I if I officially retire? Just another has-been.

Fuck. That's depressing.

We're dismissed, and everybody files into the locker room to find tomorrow's game jersey hanging in each player's locker. The practice jerseys only sported the Armadillos logo. I turn this one around on the hanger. It's good to see my name matter again, even if it's just for one more game.

I change out my shoes and untuck my T-shirt, but there's no use showering when I'm heading back to the ranch. I'll just get dirty all over again. I plan on getting some of those tasks that never get done taken care of. It beats sitting around the house puzzling my day away.

Surely, my skills on the diamond aren't the only thing I'm good for. If so, I need to figure out what I'm going to do with the rest of my life.

Any other man my age knows where the rest of their life is heading. Hell, it's probably been mapped out for more than a decade. So it's strange how money and even a taste of fame can derail one's plans when their career abruptly ends.

I need to feel useful again.

After saying bye to the guys, I make my way out of the locker room and into the main tunnel to the parking lot. Just as I'm about to step into the sunlight, a blue BMW slams to a stop. The window rolls down, and there's who's becoming my favorite feisty friend. Would she call me a friend? Shit no. But that's just because she can't admit that she's drawn to me in some way, or she wouldn't keep ending up in my orbit.

Resting her elbow through the open window, she has sunglasses covering her eyes, and she smirks. "You're lucky it's not raining. But when it is, revenge is going to taste so sweet."

"What are we talking about?" She rolls the window back up and drives away, leaving me wondering what she means. Should I be concerned? It wouldn't be a first with her, considering I barely scraped by with my life when she stalked me the past few days. I need to stay on my toes with that one. She sounded way too smug about that sweet revenge she mentioned.

Revenge for what exactly?

She's a complete mystery, which is a first for me. I know what women want. I'm not here to make their dreams come true, so if they want the white picket fence, a husband, or to settle down and start a family, I say more power to you.

That's not what I'm interested in. I'm here for the entertainment, the good time, and I always leave them satisfied. But I don't think Cricket wants anything from me other than this so-called revenge.

Is this about me leaving after our night of fun? It was morning. I was starving and wanted to get back to my rental to shower and get some sleep. Now I'm the bad guy when she didn't think it was necessary to share so much as her first name?

She wants control back. She wants to be the one who leaves me this time. I laugh. *Good fucking luck with that, sweetheart.* I walk to my truck, too tired to be riffling through the riddle that's Ms. Dover.

I TRACK down a rusted can of metal lubricant in the barn and return to the front porch. Spraying the hinges, I test until all three no longer squeak when opened.

It's the simplest job, but it feels good to get it done. When I return the can to the barn, gravel crunches outside. The roar of a diesel engine pulls in behind me. I step through the large open doors as Tagger climbs out of his truck. "Hey, Griff, how's it going?" he asks, shutting the door.

"Good." I wipe my hands on a rag I found tossed on a shelf. "What's going on?"

"Keeping busy." He joins my side, and we walk back into the barn. "How's practice?"

"It's fine. I'm already having to ice my shoulder in the evenings." I chuckle.

He chuckles as well and stops just inside the doors. Looking over at me, he crosses his arms over his chest. The brim of his hat shadows his eyes, his boots are scuffed, and his jeans are worn in. Farm life isn't pristine, and I'm not sure when I convinced myself that this life wasn't worth my time. I almost miss the gritty feeling of dirt and sweat from a hard day's work. He asks, "What happens after the game tomorrow?"

"What do you mean?"

"You coming back or taking off? Just think your sister should be prepared if she's not going to see you on Friday."

I shift, looking at this guy who was always my brother's best friend, but now stands strong at my sister's side as her husband. "I can appreciate that you're protecting Chris, but I haven't packed my bag yet."

He stares at me a good long while. "A heads-up is all we're asking for this time."

"I can do that."

His guard seems to lower when his arms return to his side. "It's only been a few days, but it's good to have you around."

"You'll get sick of me soon enough." I laugh, but it's lost its humor. "I can't sit around this place. You got any odd jobs that need to get done come Friday?"

Nodding, he grabs an old wrench from the tool table. "I can find something for you, but until then, get to icing." Reaching out, he offers his hand. "Tomorrow, we need you to show your nieces and nephew how great a player their uncle is."

When my hand clasps his, I reply, "I can do that."

He gets what he needs from this barn, then drives toward the equipment barn. Not a lot was said, but what was said feels bigger than the moment we gave it. Don't go running off too fast and show everyone how it's done in the majors even though it's only a fundraising game.

I go inside, ready to clean up and prepare some dinner.

The smell of the old house still hits me each time I walk in through the door. It's not musty, but a house with a history. It was once bustling with a busy family and all the things that remind me of home—my leather mitt, stinky cleats left by the door, a roast cooking on Sundays, and peaches picked fresh from our very own orchard. So many memories come back at once that I close my eyes and take a deep breath. I can almost hear my sister banging on the bathroom door for Baylor to get out so she could wash her hair, the boiling pot of potatoes on the stovetop, a game on the TV in the living room, and my dad going on about the cattle not wanting to leave the wildflower field again.

Smiling, I welcome the flood of memories instead of pushing them away like I usually do. Exhaling an easy breath, I rush upstairs with renewed energy to take a shower. It's not the memories, although they're good to have, but come Friday, I have a purpose. I don't have plans to leave or know how long I'll stay. That's the freedom of no obligations. But I can't wait to be back in the saddle again.

CHAPTER 8

Cricket

THE JERSEY FEELS a little snug when I pull the two sides together to button over my chest. This polyester might be breathable, but I'll need a little spandex to make this work. As I'm buttoning it up, the top one refuses to stay through the hole, so I undo it, which exposes my bra and a whole lot of cleavage. Probably not the look my father would approve of when representing the family.

My boobs aren't going to shrink, and there's no way I can fit a tank under this shirt. I change out my bra to one with more coverage and smooth cotton. Buttoning up the shirt, I leave the top undone since it won't behave anyway. I check my appearance in the mirror. If I'm looking to meet a guy, this would be a great outfit to wear. Maybe not as great at a professional event that carries the weight of my name as the organizer on it.

But I'm not terribly upset. It feels good to finally like what I see in the reflection.

All those early morning Peloton and yoga sessions are

paying off. *Finally.* It took three years to lose most of the baby weight, and I'm happy with where my body is in its journey. Glancing once more in the mirror, I grin because these jeans and this top are showing off all my better assets, and my name embroidered on the back is a nice touch.

I walk into the living room to find Jacob stacking building blocks on the coffee table. His nanny looks up, her long brown ponytail swinging to the side. Hairs have escaped the band like it's been quite the rambunctious day, but she smiles when she sees me. "It's beautiful outside with a nice breeze."

"I was hoping for good weather," I say, smiling as if I accomplished controlling Dover Creek's temperatures today. "And it was far exceeded."

With a block in each hand, she says, "I'm taking Jacob to the park in a little while. I think it will be good to get some of his energy out so he's not running wild at the stadium."

"That's a good idea. He loves hearing his stomps echo off the metal flooring." I laugh to myself. "People there to watch the game may not appreciate it as much as he does."

I move to my purse on the kitchen counter and then hesitate. For the past five days, I had no qualms about Jacob being at the game, but with Griffin Greene wandering around the stadium, I'm not sure it's a good idea. "Judy?" She looks up from gathering blocks that have scattered across the floor.

She's been a great nanny over the years. Jacob adores her, and being in her early twenties, she has the stamina to keep up with my busy boy. He doesn't stay still unless he's sleeping. I wouldn't get any work done if I didn't have her help. She's also someone I've come to rely on heavily with my busier schedule more recently since organizing this event has taken more time than anticipated. "Yes?"

"I'm thinking tonight might be too long a night for him to stay up. And there's the possibility of overtime, plus awarding the checks and acknowledging our sponsors. It could be a very late night."

"I can bring him for a while, but also stick to his regular bedtime schedule. I don't mind staying until you get home."

"Are you sure? It may be late."

Her smile never fails. "I don't mind, Cricket. You rarely take an evening. You've put a lot of time and effort into raising money for these kids. I want you to be able to enjoy the event from start to finish. I really don't mind." She glances at Jacob, ready to catch anything that falls as he stacks the blocks ten tall this time with a steadier hand.

"I appreciate that." Slinging the purse strap over my shoulder, I ask, "I'll see you both around six thirty?"

"We'll be there."

I kneel beside Jacob. "Hey, buddy, I'll see you later, gator."

With a silly grin on his face, his small hand rests on my cheek. "After while, cocky-dile."

I giggle. He's just so darn cute. "Good job." I kiss his head. "I'll see you at the baseball game. Love you."

"Love you, Mama." As soon as the words are spoken, his attention returns to the blocks. Ha. It's hard to compete with toys.

I move to the door, and say, "Bye," before slipping out and going to my car parked out in front of the cottage. My mom spent years renovating and building structures all over the thousands of acres of Dover Creek Estates, which houses the winery, horse stables, a barn that is fit for a king to live in, the lodge where my parents reside on top of the highest hill, a country house my brother inherited, the quaintest holiday home for our guests to the property, and the cottage that I received for my college graduation. I've lived here ever since because it's a cottage only in name. With four bedrooms, each with its own bathroom, an office, a living room, and a stunning kitchen, I don't think I'll ever outgrow this home. How could I when it's only me and Jacob?

Running the day's itinerary through my head, everything seems to be in place. I'll verify once at the stadium, but I'm feeling good about this event. Once ticket and concession sales are added to the fund, I'll write out the checks, and it will be easy sailing afterward.

Easy sailing is the last thing my relationship with Griffin Greene has been. Torrential rains and rough seas might describe it more accurately. "Relationship." I scoff, and then exhale, the harsh breath reaching my hands on the steering wheel. "Proceeding with caution is the only thing on our horizon." It's good advice, even if I don't always follow it.

I can't deny it wasn't the worst conversation I've had in my life. But it's not like him being courteous for once makes him a knight in shining armor. So let's not get ahead of ourselves here. I pull into my parking spot at the stadium and get out, making sure I have everything I need. My purse should be it, but I check the trunk just in case anything got left behind from the past few days.

Coming in from the bright sunshine into the dark tunnel takes my eyes a few seconds to adjust to the change in light. But I know this place inside and out, so I keep walking. The door to the locker room flies open, bouncing against the heavy-duty door stop. Two players deep in conversation cut me off, oblivious to my presence, and then jog toward the field ahead.

I'm just about to start for the offices when the closing door is pushed open again. Our eyes connect first, his skies to my pastures, and we share a moment of peace. No verbal weapons locked and loaded. No provocation on the tip of his tongue. Just two people who shared something amazing and then lost it. Maybe it's not peace, but acceptance that I see in his eyes.

Though I know it's for the best, I'm not comforted by how fast he surrendered. Did our night mean nothing?

"Couldn't stay away, huh?" And then he had to open his mouth again and ruin everything.

I start walking toward the first door down on the right, and reply, "Being here is part of my job."

"Ah, operations manager, right?" I like how he makes himself sound *soooo* innocent. Ridiculous. He knows exactly who I am.

I stop just past him, giving him a full view of my back, and point at it over my shoulder. "That's the rumor." I keep walking, then tap my card against the security pad. Grabbing hold of the handle, I yank the door open like I'm really showing him up. I should just go before I keep embarrassing myself. I'm not sure why he brings out this side of me, but it's not cute, and more so, it's unprofessional.

"Hey, Dover?"

I stop and glance back. A smile lifts the corners of his lips. It almost appears genuine, like the one I remember from so long ago. "What is it?"

With his eyes locked on mine, he says, "I'm gonna hit a homer for you." It's the cluck of his tongue that breaks the spell he almost put me under. I'm surprised he didn't wink.

"I bet that line works well for you." I try not to scowl, but I fear I'm failing. "Give me a ballpark figure. Each game, how many women did you promise to hit a homer for when you were in the majors?"

He chuckles, glancing down and rubbing his thumb

over his bottom lip. Looking back up, I'm hit with those eyes that I couldn't get enough of once upon a time. But I've grown up and know a line when I hear one. "A few." He doesn't even have the gall to feel shame over that confession.

"Did it work?"

"Like a charm every time." *And there's the wink.*

"I had no doubt. Go win today." I walk inside the small hall of offices here at the stadium, letting the door close behind me, then drop my back against it. From the way he looks into my eyes like I'm the only other person who exists, that wry grin that supports the arrogance he can back up in bed and on the field, to the way he carries himself like shame is the last thing he's ever felt, I'm still, apparently, a sucker for a hot guy. And to give credit where it's due, he's one of the most attractive men I've ever seen. Damn him.

I take a deep breath and force myself forward. I can't stop thinking about him and how easy it would be to fall again. I won't, not even for one more night. I'm just lonely in that department, so even scraps have me salivating.

After tucking my purse into my desk, I pocket my lip gloss and slip my glasses onto my head, so I'll actually be able to watch the game instead of just making out figures on the field. I lock the door behind me and start for the stands, where I need to find Savvy. With my eyes shadowed by my hand from the bright sunshine, I do a quick scan.

The owner's box is nice, but we prefer to be closer to the action and love the energy of the crowd. That's not something the folks being served fancy hors d'oeuvres with flights of wine from our private label seem to have.

A beer, a hot dog, and the occasional crowd wave are much more entertaining. And because I have the best friend in the world, Savvy has already set me up by the time I find her. "For moi?"

"Oui." She grins, but as soon as her eyes land on me, her jaw drops. "Va. Va. Voom," she replies, looking me over.

I don't know if I should take the compliment or be self-conscious. Looking down at my cleavage, I find it's debatable. "Yeah. I wanted to ask you about this jersey—"

"I ordered a size down . . ." Looking around to see if anyone is eavesdropping, she cups her hand on the side of her mouth and whispers, "Or two, so it would show off what the good lord gave ya. But holy sexiness, Crick." She laughs under her breath. "I'm glad your dad isn't here to see this. He'd be fuming."

"He would, but how did you think I'd react?" I sit beside her. "So you plot a plan out to purposely sabotage the fit of my shirt for this family-friendly fundraiser for high school sports for some reason, but then when said plan *works*, I'm lucky my dad didn't show up? Got it." I shake my head. "You're lucky I'm such a forgiving boss, or you'd be fired."

"Fired for creating a smoke show in the stands?" Her casual shrug and half smirk aren't doing her any favors. "And let's state the facts, ma'am. You didn't have to wear it, but here you and the girls are in all your glory. So how upset can you really be?"

I face forward, my hackles up from being called out like that. "Oh my God. I can't with you." She's not wrong, though. I had choices, but I still wore it like I didn't.

She bursts out laughing. "You do look incredible, if that makes a difference."

"It does, and," I start, readjusting on the seat cushion. "I needed the boost today."

"You're welcome."

"I didn't say thank you."

Her shoulders pop up, then fall again. "I knew what you

meant, though." Pointing at the field, she locks her eyes onto her man in uniform. "Now shhhh. The show's starting."

"What show? The game doesn't start for another fifteen minutes."

"The real show. Warm-up." Glancing at me, she adds, "It's my favorite part of the game."

"It's not part of the game. It's the preshow."

"Exactly. Just take a look for yourself."

I follow her gaze to her fiancée on the field, but he doesn't hold my attention for long when the guy near him steals it instead. All six-three of that man is on the ground stretching his legs. With his weight on his hands, he's leaning forward with his pelvis aimed down. A slow, calculated gyration forward has my throat going dry. When he shifts back and does it again, sweat beads at my hairline. Up. Down. Back and forth. "Oh." Words elude me. I lick my lips and narrow my eyes for a better look.

Savvy slides my glasses from the top of my head to rest on the bridge of my nose. With a clearer picture, I chuckle when she asks, "See?"

"I most definitely see." *Boy, do I ever.* I adjust my glasses to sit properly on my face. When I look back at the field, I swear he's staring right at me. It's not his eyes that get me. It's the heat emanating from him across the field to me. I glance down at the cup of beer next to me, then pick it up to chug some down. Alcohol probably isn't the best way to cool down, but it's worth trying. *And the distraction I need.*

I don't know why or how he affects me so much, but I'm beginning to think that Costa Rica isn't so far behind us that it isn't worth a revisit. *Good lord, Cricket!*

Absolutely not. "Jesus." I use the back of my hand to wipe my forehead. "I might need to—"

"Walk it off?" Fake sympathy shapes her expression, but a grin wins out. "I get it."

I level a glare at her. "Funny."

"I thought so."

She's always good for some laughs, but her jokes are on point today. Or maybe it's me being sloppy with my slips when it comes to him. He's thrown me off-kilter, messed with my focus, and it shows.

Returning my gaze to the field, I dart my eyes from one place to the next with no luck finding him. I could be disappointed, but as air returns to my lungs, I'm grateful for the reprieve. He may not play pro ball anymore, but he's every bit of a professional at getting a reaction out of me. Good or bad.

Savvy nudges me with her elbow and then whispers, "He's in the dugout."

Not ready to admit that I'm starting to see the man a little differently since he ironed a few things out between us. Namely, I'm not the enemy, stalker, or fan he made me out to be in the beginning. Since my righteous indignation has started to subside, I realize I might have been a bit hard on him. Maybe, just maybe, he's not as bad as I first thought he was.

It's too soon to decide.

There's always a chance he'll open his mouth again . . .

CHAPTER 9

Cricket

Seven innings in . . .

MY ENTHUSIASM HAS WANED as the other team scores again. "What the hell?" I grumble. Standing up, I cup my mouth and shout, "Come on, Armadillos." My shouting may not change the trajectory of the game, but it feels good to release some of my pent-up frustration.

Maybe I should be yelling at the man on third base since he hasn't hit that much-needed homer he promised me, and it would be really nice about now. Or he could catch a ball and take a few players out for me instead. *If only one would fly his way.*

"The money raised still gets divided between the two schools," Savvy says like watching these pro and former pro ballplayers doesn't mean as much.

"We worked hard bringing these players together. Is it wrong to want our team to win?"

"No. Just making sure you knew."

She knows I know. I glance at her. Her cheeks are pinker as the heat kicks in during the hottest hours of the day. A hat shields her eyes from the sun as she stares at the field in the distance, but it's her bouncing knee that makes me wonder why she's acting out of character, even for her. "Everything alright, Sav?"

Peeking at me briefly, she stops bouncing her knee. "Blake is going to be in a pissy mood if they lose." She leans forward on a heavy breath, resting her arms on her legs as if that will keep the nerves abated. Looking over at me again, she says, "That means no going to that new pizza place in Peachtree Pass." Her tone has changed, resolve taking over, and a string of disappointment runs through her words. It's in direct opposition to her usually chipper tone.

Wrapping my arm around her back, I lean in. "Talk to me."

"It's just that . . ." She exhales, shaking her head. "It's hard to date a pro athlete. I know you have in the past."

"Years ago and it wasn't serious, so my situation is different. You're engaged to Blake."

"He's playing out of Austin right now, but it's looking like he might be called up for the majors."

"Ah." I sit up, grabbing my bottle of water to pick at the label. "You might leave." Not a question but I know she hears it in my voice.

"I don't know what I'll do. It's not a conversation he wants to have at this time."

I don't like that, which is not something I should admit to her. It would make her feel defensive, and that's the last thing I want my cousin to be with me. "What are your thoughts?"

That prompts half a grin out of her. "Is it wrong to want to know which city first?"

I laugh. Lightly, but it is funny. "I'd feel the same."

She nods with a smile growing on her face. "I knew you'd understand."

"I'm always here for you and forever team Savvy."

Bumping into my arm, she laughs this time. "We're Team Dover forever."

"Team Dover forever." The teams on the field swap, sending the Armadillos into the dugout and up to bat. "I knew this couldn't be about pizza."

"Oh, it's about pizza, alright. If Blake loses, he'll get home and zone out playing video games for the rest of the night. No talking. No dinner together. It's just his method, his way to grieve, relieve the stress, and then he's ready to play again the next day."

I'm hearing a lot about him and nothing about my strong and beautiful cousin. It bugs me. "If they lose, how about you and me go to the pizzeria?" I eye an Armadillo taking first base in my periphery.

Her grin spreads on solid ground, more like herself. "That'd be fun."

"It's a plan, then." We watch another batter hit a single, sending the other to second in a close call of being taken out by the ball. We both clap. "This is our comeback," I say. "I can feel it."

"If they win, though, we can all go. You can ride with us. Sound good?"

Do I want to be a third wheel to their twosome? It would be fun to get out, even with Blake there, taking up all my cousin's time. "Sure." It's been too long since my social life involved anything outside of work obligations and family events. "Judy said she'll stay late if I need her to, so that sounds good."

The whack on the bat sends everyone to their feet to get a better view of the action. I clasp my hands together in front of my chest. My excitement grows as I watch the ball flying through the air. My breath halts in my throat in anticipation of turning this game around.

As soon as the ball crosses over the fence on the far side of the stadium, cheering erupts into a thunderous roar of celebration. "*Homerunnnnnnnnnn,*" the announcer's voice echoes through the speakers of the stadium. "Griffin Greene is rounding the bases along with two other players to put the team in the lead by one. Get on your feet, Armadillo fans, and let's cheer to bring 'em home."

My clapping slows, and I'm just about to sit down when I see him point at me. "Jesus. That man has the arrogance of the Trojan army." I sit, too embarrassed to remain standing any longer.

"It didn't work out well for them." She side-eyes me. "But history doesn't always have to repeat itself."

"You're about to be kicked off Team Dover. Maybe Team Greene takes traitors."

She bursts out laughing. "I'm starting to think all this talk about number twenty-two is not just talk."

I remain silent, choosing not to indict myself.

With a nudge of her elbow, she says, "It's okay. Anyone with eyes can see the guy is more than hot. He's gorgeous. And I'm not upset about that for you. It's been a long time, cuz. If memory serves, the last time you hooked up was in Costa Rica."

My heart starts thumping in my chest, the beats filling my ears. I take a breath to calm it down, hoping everyone in the stadium can't hear it. "And I ended up pregnant, so I've been a little busy since that trip."

"Too busy to live a life outside of being a mom? Come on, Crick, it's okay to want more for yourself. It's not selfish to have needs or want to fulfill them."

I turn to look at her. "Are we really talking about sex in the middle of this baseball game?"

"Seems like a good time to me."

"I'm sure it does. I'm just glad my kid left three innings ago. Wouldn't want him to overhear his auntie exposing his origin story."

"All great superheroes have a backstory they must overcome to reach the highest level of their superpowers. Jakey's getting it easy if his mom hooking up a random hottie in Costa Rica is the worst of it."

Other than mortification starting to make me sweat, I can just feel Greene's eyes on me again as if he has nothing better to do than stare at me. It's not like he's in the middle of a baseball game or anything . . . "Can we please not revisit this again?"

"Jake reminds me of him."

I still, bracing myself from her words. Gripping the edge of the metal bench, I steady my voice, and whisper, "Not me." Guilt coats my throat, the lie burning as I swallow the words back down.

She looks at me but doesn't stare. Returning her gaze to the field, she nods, not saying anything else, which I'm grateful for.

By the ninth inning, we leave the stands with the Armadillos still in the lead, praying the other team doesn't score on us again. With the large checks in hand, we rush back to the tunnel at the edge of the field and watch the final batter step up to the plate. I'm holding my breath when he hits the ball, sending it into the outfield where it's promptly caught. "Yes!" Savvy and I hip bump in celebration of winning the game. We're also thrilled by the amount of money raised.

The teams are shaking hands and chatting as they line up in a designated area. The two high school teams run out to join them when Savvy and I walk out with the checks. Coach Barth speaks on sportsmanship, camaraderie, and our community. The Dover Creek Bank president shares words of gratitude, then introduces me. After a quick wave to the cheering in the stands, I make my speech. I didn't write it down, wanting it to be genuine and from the heart. That's easy to do when we raised so much money.

"I'd like to thank the volunteers who made this possible, our sponsors who supported this event and the continued growth of these high school programs, the players," I say, looking off to the side where they're standing. Those eyes aren't hard to find in a crowd, especially when I'm so drawn to them. Even standing in the back row doesn't hide him from me. "You made this day possible, you brought in the crowds, and the opportunities you have given these future pro ballplayers are because you gave up your time and paychecks to be here. Thank you."

Savvy steps up to the microphone. "We are thrilled to present checks to the baseball teams at Dover Creek High School and Peachtree Pass High School. Enough was raised to support their programs for the next two seasons, including travel fees and new uniforms. We're also hoping to make this a yearly ev—"

A round of applause drowns out the rest of her words, so we take the opportunity to hand the checks to the teams.

When everyone disperses, Savvy runs and jumps into Blake's arms. Since we won, I guess it's going to be a good night after all. After thanking Coach Barth and the players again, I head back toward the tunnel.

He doesn't say anything yet and isn't next to me to see, but I can feel his presence behind me. So I say, "Thanks for the homer."

"My pleasure." His voice is deep, cockiness ever-present in his tone. His words shouldn't, but for some odd reason, having confirmation that he's near makes me smile.

I keep walking, but then stop just on the edge of the grass. I don't turn back but stand there, allowing everyone else to pass. He doesn't—I knew he wouldn't. I don't have to be a player to be cocky like he is. A thrill flows through my veins like butter on hot pancakes. Satisfyingly predictable. He's exactly who I thought he was.

When the scuffle of cleats and the chatter of the others leaves me in silence, I turn around. My eyes connect with his, and that smile he retrieved from me grows. Like my joy is contagious, Greene's grin looks suspiciously like I planted it on his face myself. "If you're not careful, I might get the wrong idea."

"Wrong ideas are sometimes the most fun."

"Hmm." *He's not wrong . . .* Tossing my arms loosely from my sides, I ask, "What do you want, Twenty-two?"

That smile turns on a dime, a smirk replacing it in point two seconds. With his baseball glove wrapped around his other hand, he takes a step closer. My breathing shallows as he keeps his eyes locked on mine like the prey he's ready to devour. "So many things come to mind, Little Chirp. None of them are appropriate for my boss."

My lips part, my lungs desperate for air. I picked this man out of a crowd four years ago. I'm feeling that same draw to him now. But I exhale and take a step back, needing the space and clarity without him causing my hormones to go haywire. "Probably best to keep them to yourself then." I turn to walk away because it's what *I* need right now. Otherwise, I'm going to end up in bed with this guy. *Again.*

"Hey, Cricket?"

I stop at the sound of my name, having never felt a pull to the very sound of it before. I hate that I like the way it rolls off his tongue with such ownership. Looking back at him, I ask, "What?"

"The fun's all over." A smile has lifted his cheeks but not enough. If he's not careful, I might think he's being genuine. "You going to miss seeing me come tomorrow?"

I grin because, annoyingly, the guy can be kind of charming when he wants to be. Also, that he'd think I'd miss him is just funny. "In your dreams, Greene." I start walking away again.

"If that ain't the truth."

This time, I don't turn back, and I don't slow down, my pace picking up before I feel the need to counter again by flirting with the enemy.

When I enter the parking lot, Blake's pulled up in his truck. With the window down, Savvy leans over from the passenger's side, and says, "Let's go. I'm starving."

I get in the back seat of the King Cab and shut the door. Sitting back, I see Griffin's build shadowed in the tunnel as he walks toward us. I slide down but spy on him. "Me too," I reply, but I'm not talking about pizza.

CHAPTER 10

Cricket

THE PIZZERIA IS BUZZING. Players, family, friends, and even the stodgy ole operations manager have shown up in support of all who participated. And since I'm the OM, I'm picking up the tab for the pizzas. I'll decline any anointing of sainthood since the restaurant gave us a hell of a deal tonight. They mentioned our dedication to helping both high schools with the fundraiser, which was nice.

Chatter and laughter ring through the air, and indecipherable music we can barely hear plays in the background. After letting the last of my second beer slide down my throat, I lower the empty pint glass to the table and giggle. It's been too good a day. My mood can't be ruined. "Do you have money for the jukebox?" I ask my cousin.

She sets a large custom coin down on the table. "It takes tokens. Play something good."

I push up from the table. "I'm going to walk off the pizza and beer I devoured," I say, rubbing my stomach. Although I know it won't do much to make me feel less stuffed, I take the long way, lapping the place. The red-and-white checkered tabletops are reminiscent of New York pizza joints. The red glass candle holders add a romantic glow, although daylight still sneaks in the large front window. A few velvet paintings hanging on the wall are just a classic touch to complete the vibe they seem to be going for. It's nothing like anything Texas and right out of the movies or an old Italian restaurant where I once dined when visiting Rome years ago. I move to the outside of the center tables and follow a path along a row of booths to the jukebox. They're a charming touch, giving the place a vintage flair as if this joint has been around forever instead of officially opening its doors in the past few weeks.

Savvy said this is the second time she's come out to Peachtree Pass in the past week to eat here. I can see the appeal—low-key, casual dining, good food, and comfortable atmosphere. I should bring Jacob. We don't get out of Dover County as much as I like. This would be a fun little dinner adventure for us.

I don't recognize most of the songs on the playlist, so I drop my token into the slot and punch in a random code, taking a chance. The Flamingos scroll across the small screen on the inside just as a song begins to play. I lean my hands against the glass and smile when I hear the harmonizing of what sounds like a song from the 1950s, conjuring images of couples slow dancing.

What happened to romance? It seems to have disappeared from my life entirely unless it's in a book I'm reading, or I catch a movie on TV. I grin, remembering how much I used to eat up romance, even if it was only a crumb tossed my way. If some guy I found attractive gave me attention, I was a goner. Getting hurt too many times taught me a hard lesson. Now, I can handle my own life and thrive in my independence. I don't need a man, but it would be nice to have a partner. Savvy has a point. Being a single mom doesn't mean I can't be an individual with my own needs as well. Or does it? I have no role model to know the difference.

"I'm starting to think you really are stalking me." The deep, dulcet tone wraps around my shoulders like his strong arms once did. The heat between us electrifies when his arm brushes against mine. Even his words aren't so irritating after a few beers. *Damn him.* When did I turn into a fan of his? No way can I let him win. But is it so bad to find him attractive despite his usual demeanor? Sue me for noticing.

I couldn't have timed his entrance better to snap me back to reality despite the creature comforts I briefly felt. Keeping my eyes on the pastel lights flashing across the top of the jukebox, I reply, "Or maybe it's *you* stalking *me* since I was here first."

"True." He comes around, leaning against the side of the machine, acting way too comfortable, like we're old friends. I'm not even allowing myself to look into those eyes of his. I know I'll crumble under the intensity. "But it's not so far-fetched to find me in my own family's restaurant."

I look around as if I missed the clues, but I don't see the name Greene anywhere. Finally, I glance up at him. "It is?"

"It is, but they don't feel the need to name everything after themselves. And you have nothing to worry about. They allow all sorts in here, even Dovers on occasion." He only gives me a flash of that smirk I know gets him his way too often.

"Funny," I remark, but fail to restrain a laugh. I blame the beer and my lack of defenses in this condition. Making sure my cousin does not bust me, I slide my gaze to Savvy, who's oblivious to my current predicament as she yucks it up with her fiancé and some of the other players. When I look back at Griffin, I show him the indifference he deserves despite that being a difficult emotion to hold on to when he's standing so close that I can smell his aftershave.

My knees weaken, but I grip onto the jukebox to keep myself from falling for his lines any more than I already have. Don't get me started on his stupidly handsome face. Why does he have to smell so good and then back it up with that incredible gift of attractiveness? I huff, and then add, "So you're here for the celebration?"

"Is that what you want me to say?"

Shifting, I anchor my hand on my hip and tilt my head. "I can't figure you out. It shouldn't have to be this hard, Greene."

There's a pause as if he's thinking about it. Then he replies, "You're right. Weapons down, Dover?"

"At least for tonight, okay?" Dropping my hand to my side, I even manage a smile . . . a small one, but it's better than the other extreme reactions he usually elicits from me.

He holds his hand out. "I'll take that deal."

I hesitate, knowing I'm going to feel some way about that kind of contact with him—hate or the opposite. I won't know until I-I stop overthinking, take a deep breath, and slip my hand into his.

My first thought, *it's not hate . . .*

My second, *I'm in trouble.*

I pull my hand back like the connection was flaming hot. Not a lie. I hate that I'm so conflicted when it comes to him. Does he not remember our time in Costa Rica? The pregnancy may have been a surprise parting gift, but I don't regret any part of that night, especially not Jacob.

The more I get to know Griffin, the more I start to loosen the tight constraints on my inhibitions around him. That got me in trouble once before. It's probably best if I don't repeat that mistake. I'm so conflicted when it comes to Griffin Greene. Why does he have to be such an anomaly?

Hot. Cold.

Friendly. Annoying.

Attracted to him physically. Turned off by his arrogance . . . *kind of.*

Safe to tell him about Jacob or a danger that he might take him away?

He pulls out so many emotions that I'm not sure what to think. I want to slap him one minute and kiss him the next. Surely, that can't be normal. How does he affect me like this? I just know I felt something with him during that one night we shared. I should have acted on it instead of pretending it meant nothing and let him walk out the door.

"Can I buy you a beer?" he asks, his eyes staring into mine as if he doesn't hear the ruckus over on the shuffleboard table as some players wager over the next shot. He blinks, not rushed, but like we have all the time in the world on our side.

But it's the subtlety of him leaning closer, just barely noticed but fully caught by me, that sends a zip of electricity through me, reaching my toes, and has me replying, "Yes."

"Come on." He nods toward the bar at the back. With a little pat to my hip, he passes, gliding between tables like he's familiar with the place, a confidence that makes me tingly. In turn, I dodge customers and revelry, ducking to avoid a serving tray full of drinks as a server passes between Griffin and me. He's in his element, and I have no clue what I just agreed to.

Reaching the bar, I slip onto a vacant stool and tap my

fingers on the wooden bar top edged with a fresh brass trimming. He nods to the older gentleman behind the bar who smiles when he sees him. "Son, how's it going?"

My chest tightens. Oh great. I wasn't expecting to meet the family tonight . . . me, the mother of this man's grandson. "I'm in Greene County, alright," I whisper under my breath.

He chuckles, glancing over at me. The heat from his hand brushes across my lower back in comfort, sending every bump straight up on my body in a thrill zipping up my spine. He whispers, "You're safe with me."

God, I want to believe that, but am I? *Is Jacob?* My heart is softening but my brain won't let me enjoy any of this. He asks, "What are you drinking, Little Chirp?"

"Is that what we're going with? Little Chirp? That's it?" My shoulders fall. "That's my nickname?"

Spinning on the stool to face me, he rests an arm on the bar. "You don't like it? I was growing partial to it."

"You've used it once. Now twice. I didn't even know if I'd see you again after today, and you're already growing partial to a nickname for me?"

He glances at his dad. "Two lagers please."

"Coming right up," his dad replies before walking toward the taps.

"I didn't want to keep him waiting. Lager work for you?"

"That works."

He eyes me. "I'm starting to think you might just argue about everything. Do you ever take off your boss hat and relax?"

I'm ready to defend myself, but then why would I? He's not wrong. I laugh humorlessly to myself, and confess, "No."

That makes him laugh, his shoulders ease under the

rattle of his chest, the sound deep but light with what sounds like genuine happiness. The beers are set in front of us, and his dad disappears too quick for me to offer to pay. Picking up one glass, Griffin taps his against mine. "Here's to honesty."

With my knee grazing against one of his, I drink, peeking up at him over the glass as I take the first cold sip. "I probably shouldn't have said that. It's not very . . . um. I don't even know cool terms to use anymore. I'm not that exciting, and my life is less so."

"I can't imagine anything about you being boring."

"You're not so bad sometimes, Twenty-two."

"Is that what you're going with for me?" He laughs again. "I thought you were preferring Greene. You know, a Dover bossing around a Greene must give quite the high." He takes another long pull of beer, but his gaze returns to me faster than it left.

"I can't say it's not been fun watching you discover who I am, but don't you think we're more than the roles we've been playing this week?"

"I'm hoping so." There's no waffle in his tone. Nope. He's as steady and confident as can be. It's as if he actually did set his weapons down, and I finally get to see the real him. Maybe I should do the same and stick to the agreement we made.

Whether I should or not, I toss caution to the wind, pick up my glass, and hold it between us. "Let's toast."

When he picks up his glass, he holds it close to mine. "What are we toasting to?"

I take a breath and leap of faith, trusting this is the real him, the man behind the player, and beneath the annoying layer of cockiness that gets under my skin. At least for tonight. "To new beginnings."

He grins, and there's no arrogance to be found, only knock-my-socks-off sincerity. "To a fresh start."

When his glass clinks against mine, I don't worry I've made a mistake. I drink in the moment I'm sharing with him, reminded of how good we once were together. "Cheers."

CHAPTER 11

Griffin

I KEEP THINKING that at some point Cricket will bring up Costa Rica, even in a casual mention or slipup. *But she doesn't.*

It's becoming a fixation I don't need, a little like her. I have no idea why it's so fun to banter with her, but the slight twitch of her lips is another of my new addictions. The way her eyes seem to glow with joy when she's pretending to be annoyed makes me want to prod a little more to expose the recognition I know must rest somewhere in her mind.

It isn't possible that she doesn't remember me. Our time together was unforgettable. So why won't she end this charade? She laughs with the group sitting at the nearest table, then returns her attention to the game when it's her turn. There must be some way to get this out of her.

Since everything is a game to her, a challenge of wills, I'll just have to charm it out of her instead. There is no way I'm going to lose this battle, especially not to a Dover. Whatever history lies between our families, I might have resurrected it to win.

Lifting my ball cap, I scrape my fingers through my hair before setting it on my head backward so I don't have any distractions while planning my strategy.

She slides the puck down the shuffleboard table, knocking my puck right off the side. With a grin that reeks of victory before the game is even done, she struts toward me at the other end of the table and pokes my arm. "Take your best shot, Greene."

With a mouth that can hold its own in any shit-talking arena, why does she have to be so fucking beautiful when she does it? *Fucking hell.*

I give her a little wink as I pass. "One shot is all I need, Dover."

"You sure about that?"

Glancing back at her, I grin. "Abso-fucking-lutely, sweetheart."

She rolls her eyes, but I see the smile that's tugging her lips up at the sides. Maybe I've been coming at this from the wrong angle. Is banter her foreplay? I laugh as I grab the puck, bend down, and narrow my eyes on the target at the other end of the board. But my gaze lands on her when she leans over the edge of the table in that damn sexy jersey that no button could hold closed. Two fingers tap the lane in front of her and then lift. When I follow them higher, she points at her eyes with a formidable look shaping her face under raised eyebrows, a discerning glare in her eyes.

"Up here," she mouths.

I grimace, knowing I fell right into that trap of hers. Shifting my eyes back to the target, her puck, I slide mine down, knocking hers out of contention. I stand, and my arms go wide. "Looks like I won."

She laughs and doesn't let me appreciate my win long before she sidles up to me and says, "It's a beer, not the World Cup." Before I can snap back with something I know would have her reeling in the cutest way, she's back at the bar.

When I rest my forearms down next to her, she adds, "I'm closing the tab, so if you want something else, better order it now."

"A beer is reward enough."

My dad sets the pints in front of us, eyeing me with disapproval. "Don't ya know to let a lady win, son?"

"Trust me, Dad, Cricket here wouldn't accept anything less than an honest and fully earned victory."

"No one has to let me win, Mr. Greene. I can hold my own."

Giving her a smile, he says, "I have no doubt you can. You're gonna need to with my son." He shoots me another look before he starts for the kitchen.

"Oh, nothing is needed with your son because I don't . . ." She gives up when he's out of earshot. Turning to me, she says, "I don't need anything with you."

After taking a sip, I smirk. "It wasn't a dare." Bumping my foot against hers, I add, "Weapons down, remember? I know you can hold your own. You don't have anything to prove."

She takes a drink, her eyes staring ahead at the mirrored wall full of glasses. As if a thought occurs out of nowhere, she looks up at me. "Why do I feel like I do?"

"Generational belief system?"

"Huh?" It's cute the way her nose scrunches and her eyes blink quickly before her expression settles back to a natural, sweet little shape again. "I don't understand."

Angling to face her, I reply, "Dover versus Greene. It's something I've been thinking about lately."

"I'm still lost." She takes another drink and slips onto the stool like she just might stay a while.

"Did you ever hear any stories about the Dovers not liking the Greenes?"

She pauses, and then under a soft laugh, says, "A little. Who hasn't? But I never heard anything that could be substantiated. What about you?"

"No specifics from anyone, which makes it more confusing. Why is there a preexisting competition of sorts, like one is better than the other and they don't like each other?"

Her eyebrows shoot straight up as she asks, "The Greenes don't like my family?" Offense coats her tone as much as shock widens her eyes.

"As the official spokesperson for my family, they have no issues with your family. I'm assuming by your reaction that your family has no issues with mine." Leaning closer, I lower my voice. "That's the thing, though. Is this just folklore passed through generations of our families with no actual evidence to back it?"

She blinks again, several times, before her lips twist to the side. "I'm going with folklore." Her tone is curt as she's over this topic of conversation. "What is there to say anyway? Of course everyone talks about the Greenes because of the ranch, the farm, and even the orchard. Then there's the county. I've heard a few jokes over the years about crossing enemy lines, but nothing that would give it legitimacy." She looks out at the restaurant behind us. Some tables have emptied, but a healthy crowd remains. When she turns back to me, she whispers, "Why do rumors run rampant like we're the Hatfields and you're the McCoys?"

"I've been trying to figure that out myself."

There's no guard in her eyes and no walls keeping her shoulders from relaxing. She pulls her long hair over one shoulder, but when she looks up at me again, there's a sparkle, a light I haven't seen in her pretty green eyes before. And for the briefest moment, I wonder if I put it there.

She tilts her head to the side. "Sure makes you wonder what happened back then to keep this rivalry alive."

"Sure does." I take another long drink of my beer before setting it down and turning the glass around on the circle of condensation puddled under it, suddenly worried this is going to end too soon. She could leave any minute because I haven't given her a reason to stay. *Fuck.* Just talk to her, Greene. "So what's next for—?"

"What are your plans—?" She laughs, making me smile as well that we're both nervous like two teens talking at the same time. Looking down between us, she says, "You go."

"I'd rather hear you speak."

The sun set a bit ago, only leaving the dimly lit room to help me see her as well as I want. It's not enough, but I'm not going to demand the brightest lights be turned on for my benefit. I swear I detect the faintest deepening color of her cheeks that even this light can't hide from me.

She replies, "I was just going to ask if you had plans now that the game is over? I hear you like to travel."

"I do. Did . . ." Not sure why the words stumble on my tongue. "I've been traveling a long time. I might stick around for a bit."

"Yeah?"

The right side of my grin rises higher just from looking at her. "Yeah. It's good to spend time with my family and help where I can. It's nice to be a part of things again."

"What do you think you'll do while visiting?" There's a

shyness to her question that has her glancing away before standing behind it and staring up at me for a response.

This moment between us is different. The energy has shifted into something more mellow, as if the deal turned into a truce without requesting it. "Visiting?" I shake my head. "It's weird to be a visitor in your own hometown, but I suppose I am these days." Turning my back to the bar, I rest my elbows on the wood top and stare out over the thinning crowd. "Help my brother with some of his projects and," I say, glancing at her, "my sister and brother-in-law out on the ranch. I'm not really sure other than to go where I'm needed."

"I know a fabulous winery you can visit if you're into that kind of thing." Her smile is so genuine that she makes me wish I were into wine.

Swinging the bill of my hat back to the front, I say, "I heard it's real nice out there." Nudging her with my elbow, I laugh. "In Dover County."

"It is. It's a beautiful property. The views," she says, raising her hands in the air in front of her as if she can picture it now, "are stunning." Her breath catches, and she slowly exhales with her smile softening. "I'm sure you have similar views on the ranch. You own most of the county and some of the next from what I hear."

"I only own a small share these days, but I still get to claim that it's the most beautiful place on earth."

Her elbow taps against mine this time. "Maybe that's how the feud started. Dueling properties."

"I have no doubt it involved property somehow."

"Hey, Cricket?" Blake's fiancée stands up next to him and waves her over. "You ready to go?"

My gaze slides to the woman next to me, kind of hoping she'll stay . . . fine, there's no *kind of* about it. I want her to.

Cricket whispers, "They're my ride."

"I can give you a ride," I say before having time to think twice. Shit. The heat of rejection strikes fast, making me want to take it back. "No press—"

"That's quite a detour out of your way."

"I don't mind." I face her, watching her eyes for any reaction she'll give me. But I see something steady that I can only identify as certainty.

"If you really don't mind?"

I'm not sure what we've just gotten ourselves into, but I don't want to untangle myself. "I promise I don't mind."

Her smile just about knocks me out. "Okay. I'll go tell my cousin." She walks off with a bounce to her steps, the ends of her hair swinging back and forth while cutting through the tables to reach her.

While they talk, I turn around. "Hey, Dad?"

My dad comes over with a rag in his hand, wiping the bar on approach. "Cricket Dover, huh?"

I chuckle. "Let's not make something out of nothing." I tap the top. "I'll cover the tab."

"She was charging everything to her card."

"I know. I'll cover it. They spent a lot to make this event happen, so I don't mind."

Taking the black card I pulled from my wallet, he heads for the computer, and says, "You'll get the family discount."

"As long as it's a discount and not cutting into profits. You need to get this place on its feet."

I sign the tab just as Cricket returns. "*Soooo*." She rocks back on her heels. "What do you want to do?"

Too many ideas come to mind, none of them appropriate for the current situation between us. Unlike the last time we were alone together, this time is about getting to know one another outside the bedroom. "Do you know how to swim?"

CHAPTER 12

Cricket

"Did you have to secure the life vest so tight?" I ask, tugging on the straps to loosen the top one so I can breathe normally. "This isn't even necessary. I know how to swim."

Standing toward the back of the rowboat, Griffin pulls the paddle through the water. He glances down at me, a grin set on his face, seemingly enjoying my struggle. "Better safe than sorry. It's dark. You can't see to the bottom of the water, especially when we're stirring up the mud."

I pop the latch, freeing my chest from the confines, and take a deep breath. "Good lord, is this a kid's vest or what?"

"It's small. You're small. Figured it'd work."

"If you're so worried about falling in the water, why didn't you have to put on a life vest?"

"Because I know my strengths. I'm not going down in five feet of water. I can literally walk to the shore. But you . . ." Sitting down on the back bench of the boat, he sizes me up, then says, "You'd be underwater, hence the life vest."

"For your information, I'm five-four. I could walk out of this river as well."

"Not without your mouth underwater." He rests the paddle on the side of the boat, and asks, "Is this what you want to argue about? Your safety?"

"I'm not arguing. I'm simply—okay, fine." Yeah, okay, I was arguing, but this isn't a battle I need to fight, not with him anyway. "I'll zip my lips."

"No need to go to extremes there, Little Chirp."

I drop my head to the right, having a strong suspicion this is the name I'm going to be stuck with from him. "Little Chirp doesn't even make sense." Annoyance coats my tone, and I cross my arms over my stomach since this vest keeps me from holding them higher.

"Sure it does. Crickets chirp, and you definitely do," he deadpans with half a smirk on his face. "You're not so tough or big, so little fits."

"I'm not so unique. Everyone is little compared to you."

He chuckles. "True." Digging into the brown paper bag he had packed at the pizzeria, he pulls out a can of beer and pops the top before handing it to me.

Four beers are more than I usually drink, but considering it's been over a five-hour period, and I didn't finish the last two, I'm not worried about the aftereffects. I take a sip and set it in a cup holder so I can rest my hands on the small board at the bow of the boat.

He cracks open a bottle of water. "You're not drinking?" I ask, suddenly feeling like a lush for accepting the beer.

"Since I'm driving you all the way back to your place, I'm good with water."

The beer isn't as appealing when I'm drinking alone. "Got another water in there?"

He nods and digs a bottle out of the bag. Twisting the top to loosen it, he hands it to me. I take a sip. It's cool but not too cold. Just how I like it.

Soon, the sound of cicadas will overwhelm the summer nights, so I appreciate the gentle breeze rattling the leaves, the water soft around the paddle as it wades through, and frogs croaking from the shoreline of springtime.

The moon lights the way as we glide through the still waters. I look out into the night between trees that grow tall from the water. Moss hangs down, but Griffin steers us clear of the patches of grass and the lower branches. I keep my voice down so as not to disturb the peace of our surroundings. "This reminds me of Louisiana more than Texas."

"An alligator wouldn't be so shocking in this part of the marshy Colorado River. They've found practically everything else floating in these waters."

I sit up, a bit alarmed by the implications. "How do you know about this place?"

"Been coming out here since before I could ride a horse—"

"Which was?"

"Almost four." His downplaying that he could ride a horse as a toddler is interesting, and so unlike the side of him I've known prior to tonight. Seems like a child who's Jacob's age riding a horse on his own is something worth bragging about. "My dad and Mr. Riggins were old friends. We'd come out to help him now and again with plowing his field so he could plant a garden each year. We'd return to help harvest."

I look back toward the shore, though we're a long way from where we pushed off. I didn't see a house or area marked off for a garden. There was a rusted tractor with flat tires and the boat that Griffin dusted the cobwebs before grabbing a vest from it and squeezing me into it. We didn't spend any time exploring the property for me to get a look at anything much prior to boarding the boat. "So what you're saying is we're trespassing?" I quirk a grin at him, not wanting to hold any competitive nature for the time being despite him typically bringing it out in me.

His chuckle sends birds' wings flapping nearby, the frogs to quieten, and the boat to gently rock. "I'm allowed out here anytime I like. One of the perks of helping Riggins back in the day."

"What's another?" I ask, staring off into the darker parts of the river.

"Owning it."

My gaze darts back to him. "What does that mean?"

When his eyes slide to mine, he stops paddling, and replies, "He left it to me in his will."

"The house?"

"All of it. The house, the acreage, even this shoreline is still a part of it." He starts paddling again as if this wouldn't be news to anyone else. I find it incredible.

"He left you his property because you used to help him with his garden? That's quite a gift."

His smile is small, but I can still spy the upturned corners. "Twice a week every week, sometimes more, I helped him until I left for college. He had no kids. No wife." He shrugs. "Guess he felt like leaving it to someone who had tended the land."

"Weren't you busy at your family's ranch? You also had baseball. I know that keeps kids busy."

"Sure, but neighbors help neighbors when they need it. He needed someone steady he could rely on, especially in his later years."

He makes it sound so easy to fit in all those obligations and even has it sounding like it's common every day to give that much of himself. I'm left wondering how he fit it in, and he's sitting there as if it was nothing. He adds, "He came to every one of my home games. I'd see him sitting in the stands, proud as if he were part of the family. He was in a lot of aspects. My mom would invite him over on holidays, or I'd bring him a plate she'd made if he wanted to stay home."

Hearing about his life growing up, even just this small glimpse of what it was like, has my chest aching. I swallow, not wanting to project my emotions onto him. It doesn't sound easy, but I hear no complaints either. The anomaly of him returns, leaving me conflicted. Is he a good man in disguise?

"At what point did the cockiness take over? And why did you decide to bury this side of yourself? Which, by the way, is much more attractive."

"Attractive, huh?" A glimmer of arrogance dances in his eyes, but maybe it's just the moonlight playing tricks on me.

"I misspoke. It's the alcohol."

"You sure about that?"

Sighing, I knew I had messed up as soon as the word left my mouth. This is him. Griffin Greene, not Savvy. The slip might have been of the Freudian kind, but he's the last person who needs to be told he's good looking. He's already well aware of that fact. "What do you want me to say? You're unattractive?" I laugh, glancing away briefly before returning to see him still staring at me. "What? Just say whatever it is you want to say and let's get it over with."

"I think you're beautiful."

You would have thought the compliment came on the point of a sword by how it hit. I'm left searching for a reply that's not coming and throw in the towel. "What am I supposed to do with that?"

Laughing, he rows a little faster. I'm sure he's ready to escape this awkward moment that I'm certain neither of us intended to be a part of. "You don't have to do anything with it, Cricket. Just enjoy."

My head juts back on my neck. *Enjoy?* The man just told me I'm beautiful, and I'm supposed to sit here and just take it like he really might have meant it.

"Hey," he says, nabbing my attention. "You don't have to overthink it. It's not that deep."

"I don't know, Greene. Sounded kind of deep to me." I rest my hands back again, feeling like myself when bantering with him. "Next thing you know, you'll be proposing marriage or something ludicrous like that."

"Don't worry. I'm not the marrying kind."

I eye him while his gaze dips away and returns quickly like a yo-yo back to me. "Not surprised."

"Why is that?"

"Because you're not even a relationship guy, much less the marrying kind." I shake my head, remembering how it felt to be left in that bed the following morning. Doubt ran deep as if I should have gotten something from him—a name, number, social media handle, or anything that would allow me to find him again in the future. It would have come in handy when I was giving birth to his child. "Because I had to talk you into staying the night—" I gasp, covering my mouth.

The paddling stops. His eyes latch onto mine like he might lose sight if he looks away. His mouth just barely opens, his tongue dipping out and sliding back and forth along the center of his lower lip.

Dropping my head, I close my eyes in disbelief that I

screwed up like this. Screwed up big time. At this point, remaining silent might be my best alibi.

When I look up, a slow smile glides onto his face. It's not anger or confusion, indifference, or shame that shapes his expression. It's arrogance that blazes like a wildfire in his eyes. *Figures.*

I look away, needing the few seconds without him distracting me to get my story straight. But lying is not my friend, so I go with the truth. Carelessly throwing my arm out to my side, I snap, "Like you didn't remember." I want to roll my eyes, but I won't give him the satisfaction of knowing he's gotten to me.

He doesn't bother saving me as I dig myself deeper into this hole I'm trapped in. My heart starts thumping hard in my chest, my breath growing shallower as panic starts to set in. It's not just the night. It's Jacob who stays at the forefront of my mind every time I think of our night in Costa Rica. What if Griffin connects the dots before I'm ready to expl—

"I remembered." His confession is loud and boastful. It's not soft either. It's steady and sure, his tone a force of honesty. "I never forgot."

"You didn't?" I hate how weak I sound, as if he's made everything better by his admission.

"No," he replies, grinning. No cockiness is found despite the earlier spark of it. "I just didn't know if you did. I felt foolish."

I whisper, "Why would you feel foolish?"

"Because that night meant a lot to me. You did." It's the first time I've seen him with any doubt caving his shoulders. "I should have gotten your information."

I breathe easier knowing we were on the same page. "You don't know how many times I wished I had done the same." I take a deep breath and slowly release it, and then ask, "Why didn't you say something sooner?"

Tilting his head to the left, he glances just to my side and then back again. "Probably the same reason you didn't."

"Spite?"

He balks, his laughter echoing through the marsh. "Ego, but spite works as well."

I hadn't noticed we'd turned around until we bumped up against the shoreline where we originally found the boat docked. Seeing the old tractor up on the level ground ahead makes me wonder if we just walk away now like nothing happened, when it feels a lot like something shifted in my universe. Good or bad, I feel different.

What happens once we get off this boat?

He stands and hops to solid land, and then tugs a rope attached to the boat, pulling it up on the shore. After tying the rope around the base of a tree, he comes back and offers me a hand. Before I can take it, he grips me under the bottom of the vest and lifts me to the shore next to him. Being this close has me thinking about things I shouldn't. Kissing him probably wouldn't be a great idea. Not when so much has been revealed, and there's so much more to share in time.

Time. I don't know how long he plans to be here. He doesn't even know.

He pops the latches on the vest and then drags it from my shoulders and tosses it in the boat. Neither of us rushes to walk away or say anything. Just a shared look that says more than we should exchange.

The back of his hand brushes against my chest, causing my breath to momentarily catch. I part my lips, needing air in my lungs, but when he leans down, I stop breathing altogether. He whispers, "What happens if I kiss you?"

The whole world can hear me gulp when I swallow, but then I say, "We blame it on the moonlight?"

His lips meet mine in a rush like time is running out. The pressure firm and his hand strong as he cups my cheek, tilting me up for better access. When his other arm comes around my lower back, my lips part. Our tongues meet as I melt into him, the kiss, and the reunion I never in my wildest dreams imagined would happen.

CHAPTER 13

Griffin

BEER AND SWEETNESS mingle on Cricket's lips. The swipe of her tongue around mine is possessive, wrapped in assurance. Her hands slide over my shoulders, and her arms come around my neck to press her body against mine.

When the softest of moans lodges in her throat, she holds me tighter. Sliding my hands over the curve of her waist and then lower under her ass, I lift her to bridge the height difference. She wraps her legs around my waist and rubs the apex between them against me. My thoughts spin from the past and present, and what this looks like come tomorrow. I never fucking worry about the future since it tends to work in my favor, but this is Cricket and me, four years after Costa Rica. This is being with someone in my hometown, which complicates not just when I leave, but when I come back to visit. She'll have expectations. What woman hasn't after being together like this? And it wouldn't be unreasonable, which means this needs to stop.

I pull back, not because I want to, but if I don't, this is

going to get out of hand and fast like my spinning thoughts. "Damn," I whisper, and then lick my lips.

Her eyes are lit with desire, and the push of her hips tells me all I need to know about where she wants this to go. But I peel her off the front of my body and set her on her feet again. "What's wrong?"

"Nothing." I brush some wild strands of hair stuck to her cheeks and tuck them behind her ears. Seeing her now reminds me so much of how she looked back then. She's more woman than girl, a greater curve from her waist to her hips than I remember, and her tits are fuller, which she made the stars of that tight-fitting jersey. I have a deep-seated craving that she wore it for me. I noticed, alright. Somehow, she's more stunning than ever if that's even possible. She was a fucking wet dream back then. Now she's a goddess before me, so fucking beautiful it hurts. "I was just thinking we might not want to take this much further."

"Speak for yourself, Twenty-two." Her hands slide down my chest and then grip onto the hem of my jersey. Not even trying to act shy, she smirks up at me. "I'm perfectly good with moving forward."

Chuckling, I take hold of her hands before they go lower, where I actually want them. If she goes there, I'm done for. "I think I should take you home."

"But—"

I touch her lips with my finger, which she promptly kisses, and then her grin returns, blooming even wider for me this time. She's a little vixen who knows how to get a reaction out of me. This is probably a losing battle, and by losing, I win if we sleep together again. And here I am, trying to be so good . . . "Not because I don't want you."

Glad I left my hat in the truck, I run my fingers through my hair without the hassle, and say, "I've thought about you more times than would be considered healthy over the years. So *when* we do this again, it's not going to be in a tin can of a boat, or against a tree." Glancing at the truck parked up the hill, I add, "Not even in a truck. It will be where I can appreciate every inch of you all night long without interruption."

Her eyes search mine as she fists my shirt, but words seem to fail her. Taking a deep breath, she looks down. When she slowly glides her gaze back up, she whispers, "Nights without interruption aren't something I really have these days." She takes a quick breath and then opens her mouth as if she wants to say more, but then doesn't. She licks her lips instead and releases my jersey.

She takes a step back, but I catch her wrist and bring her back. "Hey, I just don't want you waking up the next day regretting it."

"Why would I regret it? We'll use more protection this time." *Ummm, okay . . .*

Not sure where that came from, I narrow my eyes, and ask, "What do you mean by more? I wore a condom last time."

"Did you?" Her brows squeeze together as she stares up at me in question. She seems to have a point to make, but I'm lost on what that might be.

"Of course, I did. I always do." Bringing her wrist to my mouth, I place a kiss and then another across the soft skin before slipping my hand around hers.

Her head tilts. "All three times?"

"Are we having two different conversations because I can't make sense of it? What are you getting at?"

She releases a breath and my hand jointly, and then says, "I was on the pill, but that's not one hundred percent."

I take a step back, needing space to follow the bricks she's laying. "Are you saying we didn't use a condom?"

"One of the times. We ran out because we only had two."

That's not a detail I've held on to, much less recall at all. "It's not something I do."

"Well, you did. The one time," she emphasizes. "We were drinking, and it was years ago, so I understand why it would slip your mind."

"But you remember it like it was yesterday. Why is that? Why does it matter now? It's ancient history."

She moves out from under the overhang of the large Cypress trees lining the banks of the river. Looking up at the stars, she smiles and then returns her gaze to me. "I just want to make sure there are no accidents, if you know what I mean."

I nod and move out to see a sky full of stars above us. Texas sure knows how to flaunt her beauty sometimes. "Sure. I know what you mean. That's another reason not to continue tonight. I don't have a condom tucked into this baseball uniform." I crack a smile and give her a wink.

"I'm surprised knowing you." She laughs. I'm thankful for the sound as it cuts through the silence of the night. There's my fiery little chirp. I'm not sure she knows me as well as she thinks, but she's definitely onto me and might have me figured out more than most.

I like the easiness we've fallen back into together and run my thumb over my bottom lip while studying her. "I have to admit this isn't my kind of foreplay if this is the angle you're going with to seduce me, Dover."

Walking to me, she touches under my chin with her finger. "If I were seducing you, you'd know it." She flicks her finger off my chin like a match against the striker. Turning on her heels, she leaves flames in her wake. *So fucking sexy.*

That tight jersey of hers made it hard to look away, but her backside is giving a damn good show of its own. As if she knows she's left like a dog with his tongue hanging out and tail wagging, she stops and looks back over her shoulder. I'm given a glimpse of a playful smile toying with her lips. "You going to hang around here all night, Greene, or are you going to drive me home?"

"I'm coming." I catch up, taking her hand like it's mine to hold. "But you're making me think twice."

She doesn't pull her hand away. Her fingers wrap around mine as she walks next to me, our arms brushing against each other. "Too late. You had your chance. Now I'm ready to pull on some pajamas and call it a night. No offense."

"None taken. I only have myself to blame." I peer over at her to catch her nodding. Her eyes connect with mine just as we approach the truck. Instead of separating and returning to opposite sides of the truck, our arms stretch between us with our hands still clasped.

Standing there, neither of us in any hurry, she asks, "Would it be so wrong to make a night of it another time?"

"I like the way you think, Ms. Dover."

"I'm matching your energy."

"No doubt about that." I've never met a woman like her. It's damn attractive. I pull her close, wrapping my arms around her once more, knowing it's the last time I'll get to do it tonight. "Listen, I can respect that you have a comeback quip on the tip of your lips ready to fire at the first opportunity." The way the moon shines in her eyes and her smile is carefree when I'm holding her like this, it tempts me to kiss her again. I've been dying to, actually. I don't because I'm not going to escalate things between us again when we just wound them down. "But instead of teasing, I'd rather kiss and make up."

She bursts out laughing. Covering her mouth, she mutters, "Sorry. I'm not laughing at you."

"Considering I'm not laughing, I'm figuring it's not *with* me either." *She's downright irresistible.*

"No. No." She pats my chest. "No, for real. You do make me laugh, but in a good way." Reaching up, she runs the tip of my fingers over my bottom lip, then replaces them by lifting onto her toes and kissing me. It's gentle and probably placating a bit, but I'll take anything she's willing to give me.

This time when she pulls back, I say, "I'm really trying to be good here, but you make it really fucking hard." I regret the reference as soon as I say it.

Her eyes go lower, and with a smug little grin on her mouth, she leaves me standing there, growing erection and all, and tugs the door open. She takes a step up and then drapes her arm over the top of it. "Disappointingly, you're being a perfect gentleman, Griffin." Only a short distance separates us, but I can see the genuineness. It's also the first time I think she's said my name. I liked hearing it from her. "I'm the one stirring things up. Since we've slept together before, it seemed like an easy habit to form."

"Hooking up every four years?" I ask, walking to the driver's side. I duck inside just as she drops into the seat next to me.

"Giving myself permission every four years." She reaches away to grab the seat belt, but I'm still stuck on what she just said. Is she saying . . .? Surely not. *Maybe?* Oh shit . . . Before I can say anything, she adds, "It's definitely time for me to go home. I don't make the best decisions when I drink." She waves me off. "Just ignore me. I'm talking nonsense."

Cricket Dover is impossible to ignore. Not just because of her beauty, but I'm attracted to how clever she is. Quick-witted and snarky. A slightly dry sense of humor layered under a landing pun. I haven't smiled this much in a long time.

She looks good in my truck. Her dark hair has been pulled over one shoulder, and she leans back, rolling her head to face me. By that grin, I'm thinking she's not too upset with me sitting next to her. A lot has changed between us in the past few days. It's been nice to see her this way, relaxed with the stresses of the event behind her, but the silence brings her to say, "I'm sorry. I've not acted myself. I'm sure you're used to women wanting to maul you, but it's not something I do." She laughs under her breath. "Costa Rica and tonight aside, of course."

"You don't need to apologize." I start the truck and shift into Drive. With the distraction of being behind the wheel, I confess, "I find you quite beautiful, and have tried to manufacture excuses just so I could look at you a little longer instead of leaving."

Holding her hands on her lap, she looks forward as I pull up to the main road from the property. "We're even then."

A lot of life has been lived since we were last together, but it's like no time has passed between us. The chemistry is there, and the attraction stronger than ever. I may not have definitive plans in the future, but she's making me want to hang around a bit longer. "Where to?"

"Dover Creek Winery."

CHAPTER 14

Cricket

"You live at the winery?" After looking both ways and glancing at me, Griffin pulls onto the main road. His eyes now stay ahead on the dark two-lane road, but his interest shines a light on me.

This isn't the first time I've answered this question. I'm sure it won't be the last, but with him, I worry my response might make him see me differently. Spoiled rich kid. Born with a silver spoon in my mouth. Entitled brat. I've heard it all. I was once even called a nepo-baby from inheriting a name that is known well beyond the boundaries of the county.

I never much cared since the people who knew me never held my last name against me, but I suddenly feel my heart racing, wondering if Griffin will. I don't want that. Not after that boat ride and kiss. He was nothing but an annoying gnat in my busy life, but all it took was time for us to talk to change that. "It's on my family's property. They built the winery some twenty or so years ago."

"Sounds like the kind of expansion we've been seeing out at Rollingwood Ranch."

"That's your family's ranch?" He nods, taking a turn on the road that crossed from Greene to Dover County. We've not passed another car. For it only being midnight, I would think there'd be more action around these parts.

"Rollingwood is the ranch. Greene Farms is the commercial farming side, and we have the peach orchards, which were established many years ago. I think it all kind of grew from there." Two lights in the distance look to be heading this way.

"I heard your sister's been running it."

"She has. Christine took over when my mom died. I . . ." I hear the long exhale and slow draw of his inhale as he steadies his breath, pulling my gaze over to him.

I still my fidgeting hands when a memory of that news returns and how it rocked the hill country. *Julie Ann Greene Killed in a Car Crash.* The news spread fast. It always does when something happens to one of our own in this part of central Texas. His mom was special from the stories I heard. *Beloved.* Generous of time and spirit to the community.

. . . I remember overhearing my mom yelling from inside my dad's home office. I ran to find out what was happening, but stopped when my mom's voice carried into the hallway. *"You will not attend that woman's funeral. I won't allow it."*

"I must." Two words. His tone was unwavering, though I sensed something broken in him.

"Then I'll do what I must." The spite was dripping with anger that was foreign to what I knew of my mom. Stern was more typical, but she was very good at leveling her emotions and getting her way.

"Are you threatening me, Delancy?"

"Not a threat. But I won't let your careless whims from high school bring down what we've built."

"There was nothing careless about how I felt—"

"End this nonsense once and for all, Bryan. I won't come in second to a ranch hand's daughter in the next county over. We're Dovers, dammit. This discussion is over." Hearing her heels clack against the wood floor sent me running. I hid in the large niche beside the fireplace in the living room and waited for her to pass. Threats, whims, nonsense?

I'd heard my parents argue over the years. It didn't happen all the time, but it wasn't something new. The context of the argument was, though. That was the first time I realized there was a feud with the Greenes . . .

NOT SURE WHAT I can do to comfort Griffin, but I reach over and touch his arm in an effort. My heart squeezes when I catch the oncoming headlights reflect off the glassy surface of his eyes. "You don't have to talk about it."

He glances at me in silent understanding before turning on the radio. It's not so loud to drown the option for conversation, but the song seems to shift his mood. He reaches over and rubs my thigh. The gesture makes my heart race for a different reason this time. "I want to take you out," he says with a small smile returning to his handsome face.

"That could cause a small-town frenzy if anyone finds out a Greene and Dover went out on a date."

"It doesn't have to be anybody's business but ours." He keeps glancing between me and the road ahead. "We can go to Austin or even down to San Antonio. I can have you out at the ranch, or we can go back on the boat. There's a million ways to hide what you don't want seen."

"Sounds like you know a little something about that."

"Don't act like you don't. You grew up around here as well. If you didn't want the church choir teacher or the cashier at the market reporting your wrongdoings to your parents, or worse, your pastor, then your dirty deeds were kept out of sight."

I laugh as I look out the window at the vast fields, the twinkling of lights on a house speckling the distance. Coming up to a four-way stop, he stops the truck and looks over at me. "What do you say? Will you go out with me?"

"Yes," I reply as if the answer was already there just waiting to be asked. "Take a left. It's quicker by a few miles."

He makes the turn. We're not far behind another car, but it doesn't change the feeling of emptiness these roads hold. With room and time to think, my mind always returns to Jacob. Why am I pretending to be something I'm not with Griffin? I'm hiding parts of myself like I can somehow capture that girl I was in Costa Rica again.

I'm a mom. There's no shame in that, only bliss with that little boy. My most important role isn't something I need to hide, especially from Griffin. I swallow hard, gripping the side of the leather seat. That it's his son is beside the point in this moment, but it still weighs heavily on my heart.

Chewing the inside of my cheek, I debate like I've been doing a lot of lately. It doesn't feel like the time to spring this on him. Definitely too soon for me even though it's locked and loaded and ready to share at the drop of a dime. His hand squeezes my leg before he grips the steering wheel again. "Hey, what's on your mind?"

"I was thinking about this feud between our families," I lie, kind of. Is this rivalry a real thing or something that's become a legend with no substance behind it?

"Let's just settle this right here." He adjusts in his seat, stealing a glance before looking ahead through the windshield again. "I know for a fact that the Greenes don't have beef with the Dovers or anyone else in this area." His throaty chuckle fills the truck's cab. "It's probably just gossip, like we said, to give everyone something to talk about." His smile is so endearing that it would be easy to fall for this man.

I may have let my guard down a little too much around him. I need to get my head on straight and my thoughts together. A lot is on the line. I know I'm just lonely. It could be anyone sitting there giving me attention, and I'd probably feel the same. God, I'm getting good at lying to myself. I know nothing about that is true. As scary as it is to admit, Griffin Greene has me feeling this kind of way. I say, "Maybe we'll be the ones to break from tradition."

He gives a little wink. "Maybe."

With my mind spiraling, I realize a change of subject is needed. "Do you live in the house back there?"

"No." He shakes his head with his eyes fixed forward. "I live on the ranch with my family. Well, I'm staying there. As for live, Rollingwood is the closest thing I have to a home base."

"Sounds . . . I'm not sure what that sounds like." It sounds a lot like he might be lonely as well, but I won't put him on the spot to have to defend himself. And there's no other way that will come off if I say it. So I'll skirt around the issue, gobbling up the breadcrumbs he gives me. "Do you prefer roaming more than committing to someon—some *place*?" I can tell he caught the slip at the same time I did. I want to roll my eyes, but I also don't want to make a big deal out of it.

"Are you asking if I have commitment issues, Ms. Dover?"

I try to restrain my grin but fail. "Not in so many words, but I am curious." He appears to stall on the rebound, which is so unlike him. Letting him off the hook, I say, "Maybe some things are best left a mystery."

"I'm not trying to be evasive. I just don't have an answer." He takes a breath that fills his chest, and when he slowly releases it, he says, "I hope to figure some stuff out while I'm back in the Pass."

I don't know whether to joke or not since I'm not used to this side of him. "Sounds serious."

With a chuckle, he replies, "Not so serious, but time to face the next stage of life." He peers over out of the corners of his eyes. "Or at least consider it."

I'm glad he understood what I meant, but now he has me even more curious about this next stage. Looking ahead, I spy the turnoff. "Take a right up ahead." I cross my legs, leaning my elbow on the door. "Can I ask you something personal?"

"I feel like personal is all we've been doing tonight, but sure, hit me with some more."

I could play off his vibe, but I need to know who he is beyond what I've seen tonight. My heart thumps in my chest as I circle in on what I really want to know. "Do you run when you get scared?"

"Doesn't everyone? I've been in enough fights in my life. Flight keeps me out of jail." He chuckles and makes the turn. "The winery is located up ahead?"

I can sense his discomfort behind his jokes. "I don't mean scared for your life. I meant—"

"I know what you meant, Cricket." His tone doesn't hold an ounce of anger. No indignation or impatience is heard. But the door certainly looks to be closed if I want him to open up tonight. He slows the truck when he sees the entrance to Dover Creek Winery ahead. "Where am I taking you?"

"Stop at the gate. The guard will let us in." He could say so much about that, but there's no judgment on his face. He stops under the bright overhead lamp just shy of the guard hut. When he looks at me, I say, "He'll come out."

On cue, the door opens and Joe steps out, shining a flashlight on Griffin's face. As soon as Griffin rolls the window down, I lean over the console. "Hi Joe. Mr. Greene is dropping me off."

His eyes pivot back to Griffin, and he asks, "Dropping off Ms. Dover and then exiting the property?"

"Just as the lady said." His charm is laid out, though I know Joe well enough that it won't go far. I've known him for about ten years now. He can be protective, if not overly sometimes, and judges any guy I bring home. Sounds ridiculous even to me since I'm a grown woman, but I know it's from the good of his heart, so it's okay.

I catch the way Griffin is studying Joe. For someone so cocky, I didn't take him for the jealous type.

Joe leans down and nods at me. "Have a good night, Cricket."

"You too, Joe. Good night."

Griffin says, "Good night, Joe."

With one foot in the hut, he shoots Griffin a hard glare. "Drop-off only, Mr. Greene."

He salutes Joe, and as soon as the crossing gate rises, the truck is already moving forward. Griffin says, "I have a feeling Joe isn't looking out for you from the good of his heart but from a part that's lower."

"Why do you say that?"

"Um." His eyes dart between the road and me twice before he looks at me like the answer is obvious. Opening his mouth, he closes it again, but then says, "Good to know you're safe here."

"Aw." His caring about me makes my heart clench. "That's sweet."

Leaning over, he rests his elbow on the console and raises an eyebrow. "Must make it hard to date or have someone stay over." *If he only knew . . .*

"It's not something I've dealt with in a long time, so it's not a concern."

"How long?"

I point off to the side in the distance. "Take the first right and follow the curve of the road left just after the bend." He's looking around as he slowly cruises the property. When he looks at me in anticipation, I reply, "Maybe college since I brought someone home."

"And since someone stayed over?"

No need to lie. The truth comes easily on this one. "Not ever in this home. A boyfriend back in college once or twice. That relationship didn't stick for long. It's up on the right."

His eyes widen as he looks through the windshield. "Nice house."

"Thanks. It's . . ." I look out the window at it when he pulls up to the front. "I've enjoyed having the space."

"Looks big." He glances at me. "Do you get lonely being out here all alone?"

Guilt sets in, as I'm holding on to a lie about my son instead of being honest. I pop the door open. "Thank you for tonight and for driving me home. It was completely out of your way."

"And I wouldn't have it any other way." Reaching over, he asks, "When can I see you again?"

"I have a busy few days ahead. My cousin and I are

moving our office to a new space on the second floor. I imagine I won't be good company when I'm tired."

"How about I give you my number. When you're ready, just give me a text and I'll take you out."

When I hand him my phone, I take the time he's busy to admire him. There's no denying the man is gorgeous, but seeing who he is tonight makes him even more attractive to me. He's not a monster or an asshole. Griffin seems like a good guy. He makes it so much harder to keep this secret. I say, "Hey, I—"

"I'll see you soon, okay?" He leans over and kisses me. It's too quick and way too sweet, but I like the way his lips feel against mine, and I hope we can find the time to connect again.

"Okay." I hop down to the ground and shut the door. Backing onto the curb, I stand tall and raise my hand. "See you around, Greene."

He about levels me with a hit of his smile, weakening my knees. "See you around, Dover."

I turn to walk inside, though the pull to him is stronger than my will. I can only hope he drives away before I give in entirely. I reach the front door and watch his taillights disappear around the bend. As soon as the truck is out of sight, I go inside.

I almost slept with him. I would have if he hadn't put the brakes on. "God, Cricket, what are you doing?" I should feel shame for how I behaved, but I can't muster the energy. I head upstairs and pass the guest room where Judy is sleeping. Since she left the door cracked open, I shut it and go to the next room in the hall. Jacob's.

Seeing him tucked in and hearing his soft slumber makes me smile. "Love you, buddy," I whisper and then walk down the hall toward my room.

As soon as I shut my door, I go to my bed and flop face-first. But being squashed in the blanket can't stop my smile from beaming. I roll over, throwing my arms out wide, and stare up at the ceiling. Griffin Greene, who would have thought he'd come into our lives like he did—unexpected but potentially just what we need.

I kick my legs and silently squeal, letting giddiness take over. This was the best night I've had since the last time we were together. I'm starting to see a pattern with this man. And he sure is making it hard not to fall head over heels for him. I sit up and pull my phone from my back pocket. Pulling up his number, I text: *Thank you. I had an amazing time with you.*

I set it on my nightstand and get ready for bed. When I return, I see his response on the screen: *Tonight was worth the wait.*

And just like that, I swoon to death.

CHAPTER 15

Griffin

Didn't matter where I lay my head in the world, I used to sleep like a baby. Here in the Pass, I'm wide awake at five in the morning, cursing at the dark sky beyond the curtains. It's too early for this. Groaning, I put my feet on the floor and hunch over, rubbing my eyes. Seems I have no choice but to get up since I've lain here for the past hour staring at the ceiling. My body has fallen back into the rhythm of ranch life without my permission.

My mind is groggy despite my muscles itching to start moving, stretching with the day as night becomes morning. I stand, grabbing my phone from the nightstand to check for messages that came in overnight. It's clear, and I'm surprised by the disappointment that floods my system as the little chirp races to the forefront of my groggy mind.

A quick pit stop to the bathroom doesn't help with the exhaustion. Splashing cold water on my face revives me somewhat, but it will take some caffeine in coffee form to really get me moving. I bypass the closet, knowing nothing from high school or even college will fit me anymore. I'm a few inches taller, and my shoulders aren't shrinking despite playing ball a lot less over the years.

Sliding on a pair of jeans, I kneel to dig through a box of clothes I shipped from St. Louis when I was sent packing. I pull a solid light blue cotton shirt with pearl snaps along the front from the box and slip it on. It slides easily over my bicep, and I know I'm good to go. It slips on, so I snap the front closed and tuck it in, remembering one of the golden rules when working around farm equipment: loose shirttails lead to losing limbs.

After digging out an old pair of socks from the dresser, I reach over the sneakers to grab my old boots that are as well-traveled as I am. The leather has softened, but the form still holds strong.

Standing in front of the wall with hats that range from Little League to pro ball caps, I shift to the cowboy hats. Black felt is too hot, and my beige one is too formal. I pull the lighter summer straw cowboy hat from the wall and set it on my head. It's snug but fits the way it should. It's identical to the one I gave Cricket four years back. Wonder what ever happened to that hat. Broken in just right, soft around the band, but the brim still stiff and holding its shape. I don't regret giving it to her because damn, she looked so fucking incredible in it, but I do miss it.

I leave my room but stop when a flashback of the sun flooding this landing, the curtains my mom made hanging wide open, comes back. She always put special touches around. I wish I had paid more attention when she was around. I can still feel her in the details—floral curtains at the top of the stairs, a teacup on the side table my dad never put away, the blanket she handmade using all my jerseys from my childhood draped over my desk chair.

Dropping my head back, I close my eyes and soak in the memory, letting the comfort of being near her again wash through me. Mom may not be here, but I know she's watching over us. And sometimes I can even still hear her voice calling me downstairs for breakfast, in the creak of the steps when she used to come wake us up in the morning, and through the calm breeze after a passing storm.

I open my eyes and take a deep breath. It's good to be back as I breathe a little easier, feeling more attached to this life with each passing day. My mom's death was a catalyst. Maybe being home can tether me again.

Heading downstairs, I pause when I hear the TV. The volume is the lowest, just above silent. I continue down, quieter this time, and see the top of my dad's head over his recliner. "Can't sleep?" I ask, entering the living room.

I hadn't realized he was actually asleep. His lap is covered in a blanket, and an empty cup sits next to him. I walk more carefully into the kitchen, but I know I can't make coffee without waking Dad. So I slip out of the house and make my way through the first spot of light to the barn.

The large spotlight hanging over the entrance shines bright, so when I open one of the doors, the horses start to softly neigh as if I caught them off guard. I walk to Sunrise, my sister's horse, and open the stall. Letting her mosey out, I know she'll stay close. She's always been a good horse, not one for trouble like Nightfall has found himself in a few times.

I take a brush to her coat, allowing her to get used to my presence. My sister is a lot lighter than I am, so I'm not sure how she's going to appreciate the extra weight, though she's more than built for it. And since Nightfall is the bigger horse of the two, my brother-in-law rides him most of the time.

Sunrise rubs her head against me, causing me to smile. I

rub her nose and then fit her with a bridle collar and head-gear. There are options of saddles, but I go for the one my dad used to ride when he was running the place.

It doesn't take long before I'm riding again. Learning to harness the power beneath me, the ways in which the horse listens to commands or reacts, and speed will come when I'm ready to let her loose to run. She gallops down the grassy knoll and heads straight for my sister's house. It's a good reminder of who's really in charge around here.

When she stops about twenty feet from the front porch, she starts to graze, and nothing I do—from asking politely to trying to lead her in the other direction—deters her from her current mission. So I sit and wait.

The front door opens. My sister pushes open the screen door with my new niece in her arms. She doesn't say anything at first, the grin getting her amusement across loud and clear. But then she says, "Looks like you'll be here a while. You're welcome to join us for breakfast."

Leaning forward, I ask, "She's not going anywhere, is she?"

"She's loyal through and through." Christine steps to the railing of the porch and holds her hand out. Sunrise comes without a command to get nose rubs. My sister leans forward and kisses the bridge of her nose and then holds her baby up and whispers, "Look at the pretty horse, Julie Ann." Looking off to the trees in the east, she smiles. "Sun's coming up. Come on in."

I hop off, not bothering to tie Sunrise to the railing. She's got a mind of her own and seems to do as she pleases. I follow them inside the house and get a cup of coffee before taking over scrambled egg duty while Christine changes the baby. I pull the bacon from the oven and plate up the eggs, lining the sides with toast. I cut them on the diagonal, like my mom used to do. By the time I get some company, break-fast is served.

My sister says, "You didn't have to finish—"

"It's okay. I don't mind earning my keep." I pull out the chair for her and tuck in under the table.

Tagger walks into the living room to find us sitting down. "Morning. You're here early?" Though I suppose it's not a question, it still rings as one.

"I'm ready to be put to work."

He kisses the top of my sister's head as he walks to the other side of the table to sit. "I have plenty of that this morning."

We eat but don't take long. With the sun rising, it will only get hotter. Fortunately, Sunrise is more compromising now that she's had her visit with Christine and takes direc-tions as I follow Tagger around to the far field where the cattle have been. We round them up and drive them to undeveloped back acreage. The wildflowers are in full bloom out here. Bluebonnets and prairie fire splash the green landscape with swaths of color.

Cricket Dover shouldn't come to mind, but there she is, making an appearance with a smile so bright that I can't stop thinking about her.

Tagger and I stop the horses shy of the fence line near the cliffs and look out across the land. "You played like a pro yesterday," he says.

I glance over at him. Unlike my brother, who always seems to have something up his sleeve, or an idea that he's testing for reception, Tagger is straightforward. "I miss it."

He nods. "Sometimes I miss hearing sirens." Chuckling, he says, "Who would think I'd be missing New York and the constant noise of the streets?" Sitting back in his saddle, he looks over at me. "I go back occasionally for a meeting or to visit, and that's all it takes to cure me. It's heaven out here in comparison."

Picking up what he's dropping down, I get the unsubtle hint. "My body couldn't handle playing pro ball anymore." I look out ahead at the view, adjusting the brim of my hat higher on my forehead. "So I don't have a choice in the matter."

"You always have a choice. You're just choosing not to go out in flames."

I chuckle. "I did that the first time."

"You ever going to talk about what happened?"

"Talking about it never did me any good, Tagger."

Nightfall sidesteps, anxious to get going again. Animals are in tune with humans, so he's probably feeding off my energy. Even with a trusted friend by my side, someone who only wants the best for me, I don't sit in my discomfort for long. I usually book a plane ticket and get out before the feeling has time to settle.

"Did it do you any harm?"

"Drudging up problems from the past and opening old wounds doesn't sound like a good time to me." I back my horse away from the view, turning to face the cattle in the distance, chewing on wildflowers and tall grass.

He turns his horse around, sidling closer. With his gaze locked ahead, he says, "One day, you'll find out that running away from your problems only landed you right back in the middle of them. You can face up to them now or later, but the toll will eventually have to be paid." He and Nightfall take off running, leaving me stuck with his advice. He's probably not wrong . . . I know he's not. But why'd he have to be so right?

We finish up and return the horses to the barn for water and hay, but once that's done, Tagger says the ranch hands have the rest covered for the day. If I thought baseball was hard, this is about to break me. I forgot how hard this work really is, so I take the opportunity to shower and clean up. I pull on a clean tee, slip my dusty boots back on, and grab my hat before heading out.

I've been running away for years, but for the first time, I feel the need to run toward something instead. I get in my truck to see a girl about a date, and if I'm lucky, another kiss in Dover County.

CHAPTER 16

Cricket

"I can't hang on much longer, Savvy." My fingers begin to slip, so I slide my back down the wall to get a better grip under the loveseat.

"We shouldn't have done this," she says, worry smothering her tone.

"Too late." I take a breath to help heave it up just a bit more, but I'm failing. "Now we're wedged here on the stairs. I just know this is how we're going to die."

"I love you, cuz, but this isn't how I'm going down. Death by loveseat isn't my destiny. I haven't had the chance to have sex at the stadium—"

"Ew." But I see what she means. "Or in a rowboat in the moonlight."

"Oddly specific, but I'll allow." I can see her thinking when she looks up at the ceiling. When her expression reflects her excitement, she says, "I haven't kissed my soul mate at the top of the Eiffel Tower."

"Or at midnight at the top of the Empire State Building."

I grin despite my fingers and muscles in my arms aching. "I haven't . . ." I close my mouth as the weight of guilt sets in.

I can see the strain of concern weaving across her sweat-glistening forehead. "You haven't what?"

"I haven't given my son a father."

She anchors her leg under her end of the small couch with a heavy sigh escaping her. "You can't beat yourself up over that. Accidents happen, Crick."

"But what if . . ." My arms begin to shake. "What if I could right the situation?"

"You already know the answer to that." A small smile spreads across her face. "If you can right it, then you should."

I have no idea why I thought we could carry this beautiful, leather loveseat up a flight of stairs. I'm for sure going to be bruised from this dumb idea. "I'm about to drop it."

A bead of sweat runs down her forehead as fear widens her pupils. "Don't. You can't. It will fall back on me, and I can't hold it by myself."

"We must let it go. It's us or the loveseat." My voice cracks, the last of my strength snapping with it. Just as my fingers slip off the side, the thunder of footsteps pulls my gaze past Savvy. "Griffin?"

I didn't expect him to dive to catch the loveseat from falling and save the day, but it's a nice touch. Lifting the center of the furniture to balance my end on a step, he asks, "No movers available?"

"It wasn't in the budget," I reply, still pinned to the wall by the cushioned corner of the couch.

Savvy stretches her fingers as Griffin holds the bulk of the weight in his arms. He eyes her and then me. "What's the plan here?"

My cousin readjusts, appearing to be ready to take this

battle on again. "Getting this piece of furniture up the stairs into the new office was the goal. Now I'm leaning toward the trash," she deadpans. "It's not worth the effort anymore."

When Griffin is amused, he struggles to hide it. His grin is quick and reaches his eyes, crinkling them at the sides. This lightheartedness on display last night and today is the opposite of how I initially judged him. "We can do this as a team." Looking straight at me, he says, "I can lift, but I want you to guide it up."

Savvy snorts. "Why do I feel like I'm interrupting something here?" I practically lose my footing on the staircase as mortification strikes like lightning. I want to cover my face, hide in shame, but my hands are still stuck holding this damn thing. "You know, that's what he—"

"We get it, Sav." I don't dare look anywhere in the vicinity of Griffin. *No way. No how.* I can only imagine what he's thinking. We're grown adults and still cracking jokes like we're teenagers. I mean, we do, but that's between us, not for others to hear.

While I shoot my cousin with a thousand dagger glare, Griffin is kind enough not to add any commentary fuel to the proverbial fire. "We should get moving," he says. Spinning the couch a few degrees away from me, he frees me. I take two steps up to get a hold of it to guide it from hitting the walls or railing. With a devious grin still on her face, Savvy takes the other end.

Ready to get this over with, I take the glasses that were slipping down my nose from sweat and tuck time onto my head. "I'm good to go."

Without much effort on either of our parts, the weight falls on Griffin, and he replies, "Two steps at a time." Fortunately, there are only about twelve steps left since we made it around the split in the staircase. I help guide it up and around the corner, but each time I look back, he doesn't seem bothered and makes it look as light as a feather. When we get into the office, his patience is one of a saint as Savvy and I discuss where we want it, though I can't say his expression doesn't slip a few times as the couch bears down on him.

As soon as it's set down, he flops on the center of it. "How'd you get the other furniture up here? Don't tell me you two did it all?"

"Ding. Ding. Ding." Savvy taps her nose, then points at him. Sitting down on her chair, she rolls to the window and looks out.

Looking at me, he asks, "What gives? Is the winery having money issues?"

My father would blow a fuse if that was ever even hinted at in his presence, especially by Griffin, a Greene of all people. "No money issues," I say, acting nonchalant. "Long story. Not worth wasting time on when we could be talking about what you're doing here, which is much more interesting to me."

I sit in my chair and glide a little closer since there's no desk to separate us.

He grins. That's all the sign I need to make me want to roll right up on him and kiss that mouth of his. I don't. Well, I roll over to close the gap, but the kiss is going to have to wait. "Hope you like surprises."

"Sometimes." His eyes are bluer in the defused sunlight drifting through the large windows, especially against the white of his T-shirt. That tee is doing me all the favors. too. Tight around the biceps, fitted across the shoulders enough to see the dips and hills of his muscles even when he's sitting still. I don't think I realized men could be built like Aphrodite had a say in the matter. Good lord almighty.

Griffin Greene is quite the man indeed. "This time it's more than welcome. In the area?" I ask as if I wasn't just drooling when I checked him out. *I need professional help with my totally shameless behavior.*

"Nowhere near it. I just wanted to see you again."

Just as my usually dormant heart roars to life again, like it did when I was with him last night, a clearing of the throat drags our attention toward the door. My cousin stands in the doorway with her arms crossed over her chest and one quirked eyebrow. "Don't mind me. I'm going to pop out to . . ." She investigates the hallway and then doesn't bother finishing the sentence. She just walks out, shutting the door behind her. She was always good with the subtleties. In this case, we're practically skywriting that we'd like to be alone, so not-so-subtle messaging that was hard to miss.

Being alone with Griffin plants a smile I don't want to hide right on my face. Giddiness zips through my veins. It's been years since I've felt like this, and all because this guy came to see me. I glide my chair the rest of the way, closing the gap between us until my knees bump against his. "You came all this way to see me?"

"It's not that far, LIttle Chirp. Like twenty minutes."

"If you're speeding."

The rogue grin splitting his cheeks tells me he might have been. "A few speed limits were broken, but all for a good cause." He shrugs so casually that I honestly don't think he'd care if he had been ticketed. "What can I say? I was looking forward to seeing you."

I can feel the heat flooding my cheeks as he stares at me. It's so tempting to look away, to hide my face like I should be ashamed by the pinkening. I don't. I force my chin up and soak in his gaze because I've never had a man look at me as he is now, like I'm endgame material.

Overanalyzing would typically be my go-to in these types of situations, but is it so wrong just to enjoy the moment we're sharing? I deserve nice things, and he's proving to be a really nice thing in my life.

He spreads his legs farther apart as his boots loop with the metal base of the chair to slide me even closer. Leaning forward, he whispers, "I haven't stopped thinking about you."

I gulp. *So embarrassing.* I blush for different reasons now but he's quick to caress my cheek and soothe it away, replacing it with comfort from the warmth of his hand. I take a quick breath, and whisper, "Same. I've been thinking about you since you dropped me off last night."

"What do you say we do something about it? I know a little swimming hole not too far from here—"

"I can't," I say, starting to think whatever this is between us is more real than I first imagined. Last night I was saying yes to anything he asked because I was right there with him. But it's not smart for me to act like I don't have responsibilities when I do. Jacob being the main one. As much as I want to toss my work aside and run off with him for a few hours, I know I can't. It's not my job either. It's the secret I'm keeping from him. It's time for me to face my fears and make a decision. I'm either going to tell him or not, and I know the answer, even if I'm not ready to fully admit it yet. "I'm sorry." I look around as if that's enough for him to know what I'm thinking. "We have more to move, and it must be done today. And then later—"

"Later? I could stay and help you and make later come a lot sooner." The gleam in his eyes makes me want to say yes to him so badly.

I don't want to disappoint him or myself. This is fun, carefree, and lacks the heaviness that so much of my life contains. But I look away, knowing there's a secret that could make it, if looking on the bright side, or ruin everything, if it heads downhill after being revealed.

I've made no plans with Judy to work late either, so she and Jacob will be expecting me at the house just after five. I check the time on my watch, and it's just gone one. Lowering my gaze to the floor between us, I shake my head. "I can't. Not today."

He lifts my chin with the tip of two of his fingers. When our eyes meet, he says, "It's okay. Don't feel bad. I know you're busy, so we can see each other another time." He waggles his eyebrows. "Hopefully soon, though."

Dread drops like a rock into the pit of my stomach. What are we doing? I'm on top of the world with him, and then reality sets in again to remind me that he doesn't even live here. "Promise before you leave?"

His head juts back, but he chuckles, and the lines crease between his brows. "Who said anything about leaving?"

My head's a mess with the right path to take. What's best for Jacob is not the same as what's best for me in this situation. And what's best for me is nowhere close to what's best for Griffin. God, what a tangled web we weave. "I'm sorry." I start to backtrack, not wanting to mess this up any more than I already have. "Truth?"

His hand finds my knee and rubs gently. "Always."

"This is happening fast." I should be allowed to be deliriously happy for more than one night. The man just showed up because he missed me, and I'm saddled with a secret that feels like I'm turning it into a lie by omission. I'm not sure what I did wrong in a past life, but it's quite a punishment I've been dealt in this one. "It was unexpected. Getting real honest here, but I didn't even like you a few days ago. It's a fast transition on the emotions."

A smirk pops onto his face like I summoned it with a spell. "Look how far we've come in such a short time."

"From you drenching me with a puddle to saving me from certain death by loveseat."

"Not all heroes wear capes."

"Nope." I eye him . . . fine, I ogle him. Again. "Sometimes they wear white tees."

He's still smiling, but it fades when he tilts his head in curiosity, and asks, "What do you mean?"

"What?"

With his brows tugged together even tighter, he narrows his eyes at me. "What do you mean I drenched you with a puddle? I didn't do that."

"Yes, you did. You and that big truck of yours soaked me to the bone." Since he's still staring at me like I've presented a riddle he can't figure out, I add, "I didn't take photos or anything as evidence. But there's no mistaking that you hit that dip in the concrete just right to make sure you covered me." His silence is unnerving, so I start to overcompensate. "You know that giant puddle when you exit the tunnel at the stadium? You made sure to hit it, but my point is, I forgave you for that even without an apology."

With his mouth now draped open, I start to wonder if I've grown a third eye by how he's staring at me. "I would have never done that on purpose, Cricket." He sits a little straighter. "If I did that, I'm sorry. I didn't know."

"Not if you did it. It did happen, but I thought—"

"You thought I was such an asshole that I would splash you on purpose?" Shock infiltrates his expression from the wide eyes to the mouth still hanging wide open. "No wonder you hated me." He takes hold of my hands, turning them over so my palm is up and cradled by his. "I'm sorry. I didn't do it intentionally. I hope you can forgive me."

He pulls me gently, encouraging me forward. As soon as I stand, he guides me to his lap. I shouldn't like this as much as I do, but why are these simple gestures so sweet and attractive? The apology doesn't hurt either. "You didn't know? I could have sworn you saw me standing there and aimed."

"What kind of person would do that?" Running his fingers through his hair, he says, "I feel like a piece of shit not only for drenching you but that you thought I'm the kind of man who would knowingly do that to you. I've left quite the impression."

"Griffin?"

When he looks at me, genuine anguish is written in his eyes, darkened pupils with deep-set emotion weighing on his brow. I run the tips of my fingers over the edge of his jaw and lean down to kiss him. I don't want him feeling less or horrible for an accident that I mistook as a cruel act. He's right. Now that I'm getting to know him better, he wouldn't have done that. That alone shows how far we've come and so quickly.

The pressure is light at first, but I deepen it. His hands slide around my waist, and then his arms wrap around my body, holding me close. Just like last night, I could get lost in him if I let myself, but this isn't the time or place, so I reluctantly pull back. When our lips part, I slowly open my eyes again. "I'm free tonight."

"I thought—"

I'm not a romantic, but he makes me want to believe in the notion again. "Doesn't matter what I said earlier. I want to see you again, as much as I can."

When he cups my cheek, I lean into it, briefly closing my eyes and just feeling the joy he brings me. Is it so wrong to want one night without complications? One night when he sees me for who I am just like he did four years ago. My own person again. Not as my father's daughter or someone's mother, though the latter is a role I'll never take for granted. But as a woman with her own needs and wants, goals, and ambitions.

He's wearing his heart on his sleeve for me, so I can do the same for him. For one night, we can just be together. But I also know that I can't control this situation forever. I need to tell him before he finds out. Because if that happens, I could lose my son.

CHAPTER 17

Cricket

"RIGHT THERE," I say, holding my palms up. "Perfect." The desks are angled toward the window to maximize the view. I slide my chair under but stand to admire the new office. With Griffin coming around to stand next to me, I slip my arm around him. I do it partly because I can. And the rest because I want to. I'm already struggling to keep my hands off him. Maybe I'm more of a romantic than I could admit before.

He doesn't flinch or step out of my reach, doesn't seem to mind at all, as if this is normal, everyday behavior for us, rather than something new and shiny. He slips his arm around me and leans against the desk, getting us closer to eye level, though I'd still need to gain another few inches for that to happen.

Holding me by the hips, he pulls me between his legs, then cups my face. "Your cousin," he whispers with his eyes fixated on my lips, "went to get drinks for us."

"That gives us a good ten minutes alone," I say, insinuating so much as I drag my hand up his neck and dive my fingers into the hair on the back of his head.

"Best make the most of it." He lifts my glasses to the top of my head and kisses me, caressing my face and holding me to him. Our lips part, and his tongue finds mine in a swift and sweeping motion before they tangle together. His breathing picks up, and when I lean against him, my stomach to his middle, I can feel how quickly things have escalated.

My body becomes a traitor to the impulses of being with him again, the memory long faded and needing a new one to replace it. Lifting myself on my tiptoes, I brazenly rub my body against him and kiss him deeper while holding him tighter. I moan into his mouth. He swallows it down, as his hands lay claim to the small of my back.

I want to lose track of time, but it's hard to forget where I am. I pull back. Through heavy breaths, I ask, "Will I get to see you tonight?"

"I like this side of you."

"What side is that?"

"Your spontaneous side." His grin gives me the answer I want, but then he asks, "What time should I pick you up?" I feel more beautiful under his gaze as his eyes graze over my features like he's going to be quizzed on them later. He even lingers over each part of me like he's right-clicking and saving them to memory. Licking his lips, he leans back just enough to get a better view of me. "Or we could take off when we're done here?"

Running my hand over his cheek, I stop to admire his tanned face. As a baseball player, he practically lived outdoors. That's been a while, though this week was mostly sunny. I met him in Costa Rica, but I wonder if he was always traveling to warm-weather destinations. Tapping the tips of my fingers across his chin, I move to just barely touch his bottom lip before kissing him again.

"I can meet you out tonight and save you the trouble."

"You're no trouble."

"It's okay." I calculated the math to see how much time I'll need before leaving again. I need a shower, though I won't have to wash my hair. I want to spend time with Jacob, catching up on his day and making his dinner. It might be best to go later once he's in bed. He won't be upset, and I won't need to worry about the two of them crossing paths just yet.

He says, "How about you text me later. Tell me when and where, and I'll be there."

"That sounds like a good plan."

Stroking my hair back on one side, he's still smiling like it's become a permanent installation. "How did I never hear about you before? No way news of someone this pretty wouldn't have crossed county lines." Still standing taller in front of him, he kisses me.

I rub my hand around the back of his neck to bring him closer and go deeper, my body urging me to rock against him again. I resist, needing to control myself just a little since I'm still at work.

"Honey, you didn't greet us like you—"

I push off Griffin; my glasses fall to the bridge of my nose, and my eyes dart toward the door to see my mother and brother standing there staring. I push the frames in place and swipe the back of my hand over my lips. The shock of seeing them, of them catching us, makes my heart thunder in my chest. I'm lost for words, and don't dare look at the man I step in front of as if my body can hide the evidence, mainly him.

Their gazes establish the disapproval I knew they'd feel

when they glare at him over the top of my head. Yeah, pretty sure they see him. Throwing my arms wide, I cross the room. "I wasn't expecting you today." I hug my mom tight, but her arms are too languid to make me feel any love in return.

"You were on the itinerary," she says. I step back, looking her in the eyes with a nervous smile on my face. "I expected you to be waiting out front."

"Why?"

"Because I'm your mother. Or have you already forgotten . . ." The way her words trail off gives me no reprieve. I know she's distracted by the man behind me who I'm still pretending is invisible, while my mind rolls through fifty scenarios of how to explain what they just walked in on.

I go to my brother and hug him, only to get a strong pat on the back from him with a loud chuckle. "It's been so long, Will. How was the flight?" When I shift to the side, he flips his finger out, pointing in Griffin's direction. "You do know we can see him, right, Buggy?"

My lips tighten when I hear that nickname again. It's something I did not miss with him being gone. But he's right when it comes to Griffin. I need to own the situation. Never let them see you sweat.

Glancing back, I can't stop the smile when I see him standing there, looking rugged in his jeans and tee, sweaty from moving our furniture for the past hour, and so handsome as his confidence remains intact after getting busted kissing me. *Or was it me kissing him?* Either way, this will make news among the Dover family if I don't take control of the situation and fast.

"Yes." I return to his side this time and say, "Griffin Gr—" *Oh crap.* What mess have I gotten myself into?

"Griffin Gr?" my mom asks, genuinely curious as her

expression tightens. "That's unique. What's the origin of such a unique last name?"

My brother doesn't fall for it. I don't know if he knows where I was going with it, but he's shrewdly aware of my detour by how he shoves his hands in his pockets, rocking back on his heels, and trying to keep himself from laughing.

Griffin replies, "Can't tell you. I think it got lost in translation many generations back."

"Delancy," I say, holding my hand in the direction of my mom. "This is my mother, Delancy Dover."

Griffin cuts across the room to shake her hand. "It's nice to meet you, Mrs. Dover. I've only heard wonderful things about you."

"That's such a lovely thing for you to say." I didn't take my mom for the blushing kind, but guess she'd never met Griffin Greene before either. "Cricket hasn't told me anything about you, but I look forward to hearing more. Hopefully soon, considering what we walked in on—"

"During business hours as well," my brother adds. "Tsk. Tsk." *Jerk.*

Aggravated by him, I mumble, "This is my brother, William Dover."

"Will," my brother says, reaching out to shake his hand. "Good to meet you."

I should be nervous, even on edge with the two of them walking in on us like they did, but I'm not. What started as anxiety at first has turned quite calm since the introductions.

"Your mom and Will are," Savvy shouts, running down the hall. Her feet stop so fast at the sight of us that she almost tips forward.

My mom asks, "Are what, dear?"

She grins, and I've never seen someone swallow a

canary, but she seems to have the whole damn bird stuck in her throat. She coughs, glancing at me before replying, "Are here, Aunt Delancy." Leaning forward, she gives her an air kiss. "How was your flight?"

Savvy is somehow the best and absolute worst actress ever. It's either over-the-top dramatic or not bothering to even try. Although it's usually entertaining and I love her dearly, she can't seem to decide which she wants to be.

"Long. I'm going to take a short shower, have something small for dinner, and go to bed early tonight." My mom likes to do things in littles—short, small, early. She claims it's how she stays slim, ageless, and sharp. Despite her best efforts to convince me and Savvy to follow her path to success, we like to mix in some fun, drink on occasion, and stay up way past our bedtimes. Basically, the opposite of her advice. But it works well for her.

My mom looks around, then sets her eyes on me. "Before I retire for the evening, I was hoping to see my grandson." Her eyes are set on mine, but all signs of life have left my body. From my lungs functioning to my heart beating, I'm frozen to the spot.

Will grins, entertained by my downfall. Savvy's expression wreaks of the horror I feel inside. I don't turn to look at Griffin. I can't. What will he say? Seems like having a kid should have been a high priority to tell someone you're sneaking off property to sleep with later. Yet it didn't seem so obvious just a few minutes prior to this intrusion. Like Griffin said, we happened so fast. There was no time for logic or reason. Prudence was tossed out the window. I was running off lust and instincts for this man. Ugh. *Look where that got me.*

Will says, "Jacob, your son. My nephew. Where is he, Cricket?"

My gaze pivots to him and the asshole grin on his face. We'd been getting along so well, too, lately. Of course, he's been in Europe for months. Distance always helps our relationship, but still . . .

When Savvy covers her face and turns away from witnessing this trainwreck, I face the collision head-on. Glancing up at Griffin, I say, "My son should be back soon from preschool." I turn back to my mom. "Judy can bring him by to see you if you'd like."

"No, it's fine. I'm tired, so I'm going to stop in to see your father and then go home to rest." She comes to me and gives me a hug. "Next time I return from a long trip, I'd like to see you and Jacob waiting to greet us." She likes us all in a row —her staff, her kids, and now her grandchild.

My gut twists, not from her request, which is a little annoying, but from the music I'm about to have to face with Griffin. "Sure. Next time."

William escorts my mom into the hallway, but calls back over his shoulder, pleased as punch, "See you around, sister dear."

I stand where I was left, unable to bring myself to make any moves and steer well clear of any fast reactions. I let this new information simmer between us for a few seconds, thinking he might need the time to process the news.

So many questions populate my brain that I don't know where to lend my focus. What does he think about me having a child? Does he want to date someone with a kid? He doesn't come off like the type who wants a family, but would he want to be in his own child's life?

I feel sick. Wrapping my arms over my stomach, I watch Savvy slip farther into the hallway. She says, "I'll give you two some time to talk."

Talking feels like the last thing I want to do, yet I know

this is going to be the beginning of one of the most important conversations I'll have in my life. As soon as she shuts the door, I say, "I'm sorry for not telling you sooner."

"I'm sorry you felt you couldn't."

My heart sinks a bit. "Please don't say that. You don't owe me an apology, Griffin."

"You don't owe me one either." He leans against the desk again, stretching his long legs in front of him. Taking me by the hand, he slowly brings me into the fold of his side. Kissing the side of my head, he asks, "So you're a mom?"

I purse my lips, hoping to keep this damn smile from appearing, but I lose. "Why do you make it sound like that?"

"Like what? Sexy? Because you are."

Rolling my eyes, I'm tempted to poke him until he sees the situation for what it is. I don't, though, because I realize he's seeing it how he always would have. Having a child doesn't make me a detriment to him.

Unlike to my father . . .

Unlike to my family . . .

Unlike to our business . . .

As I stand in front of him, he reaches up and rubs my shoulders. His smile is sweet and his eyes full of understanding, and then he says, "Tell me about your son."

CHAPTER 18

Griffin

"HE's the best thing in my life." Cricket covers her chest with her hands clasped, and joyful tears fill the corners of her eyes, and says, "The best thing I ever did." Leaning against my leg, she looks at me with a glow that shines from the inside. I thought she couldn't be any more beautiful than she already is, but here she is, proving me wrong. *Again*. "He's silly, so funny, and the cutest kid I've ever seen, if I do say so myself." *I like her sass.*

"That's fair." Her smile is contagious and causes me to react. Her smile falters as she hesitates. Angling away, she slips from the confines of the arm I had resting on her hip and busies herself by shifting a table that didn't need shifting. Swiping the dust from the top with her hand, she says, "I think it looks better here, don't you?"

I'm not sure how to read her reaction. It's just his name that her family called him. Shouldn't inspire any reaction, much less her discomfort. And she was talking so openly about him before that I'm confused by the shift. "Looks great." I stand, wondering if I've overstayed my welcome. "I didn't mean to pry. I figured since your—"

"It's okay. This is new with you, but you didn't say anything wrong." She's still gripping the side of the table when she replies, "His name is Jacob." Even looking down, she can't hide the love that shines through the smile that follows as if just saying the name evoked it. "Jacob Justin."

"It's a good name. Strong."

"Thanks," she replies quietly. I hadn't given any thought to the possibility of Cricket being a mom, though I shouldn't be shocked. We're in our thirties. It's not like it would be uncommon. I've gone out with a few women who had kids, so it's not new to me. But it does have me wondering why she kept that part of her life a secret.

Thinking back over the interactions we've had, did she have an opportunity to tell me, or a reason that slipping that information in wouldn't have come off as out of the blue? Or maybe she just wanted us to get to know each other better before parading the kids out and an ex that's tangled in her life. Is that what it is? The dad is still hanging around, and he's the jealous type of any man stepping into his son's life or even Cricket's? Will I be dealing with a difficult ex? Is that why she's not comfortable talking about her son or his dad?

She didn't have a chance to tell me at the stadium. I still need to redeem myself from those encounters, especially for splashing her with a puddle. I cringe inside just thinking about it. That she thought it was on purpose . . . I need to make better first impressions and make it up to her.

Last night, she could have told me at the pizzeria or later in the boat, or even in the truck, if it was something on her mind she was ready to share. That's the most logical explanation. She wasn't ready to share. Her family forced the issue. Is it wrong for me to do the same? I need to know what I'm dealing with. "Is his father still in the picture?"

With her eyes cast down, she squeezes them shut. She grounds her jaw before looking up and replying, "Kind of." Her voice isn't any louder, but it's more determined in tone.

"Kind of?" I ask, grimacing. How do I navigate a situation with the response being "*kind of*"?

"It's complicated and something we should talk about soon." She's not shut it down entirely. That's good, so I can respect her not wanting to delve into it right now.

Since I have every intention of spending more time with her, and that includes the son I just found out about, I ask, "What is he into? Cars? Horses? Dinosaurs?"

She nibbles on her bottom lip, but a giggle bursts free. "Don't laugh, okay?"

"You think so highly of me," I reply, sarcastically. "I'm not going to laugh at a kid."

She takes a deep breath as if she's bracing herself for an onslaught. Damn, what is this kid into? She says, "Baseball."

"Baseball?" My eyebrows hit the ceiling, and my mouth drops open like an idiot to the floor. "That's what he likes to do?" I ask while a smirk takes hold of my face. "I did not expect to hear you say baseball. You had me worried by your behavior. All that buildup over baseball." I nod, feeling pride for something I had no part in making happen. "Sounds like my kind of kid."

"Something like that," she mumbles.

"Huh?"

Batting her eyelids a couple of times, she smiles so sweetly. "I was saying he got a glove and bat for Christmas and hasn't stopped playing with it since."

"You have any scouts calling to recruit him into the majors?"

She laughs. "Not yet, but there's still time."

"There sure is." Moving closer to the windows to see how the building is situated on the property, I cross my arms over my chest. "I had early encounters with scouts coming out to Peachtree Pass to watch me play."

She comes to lean on the other side of the large window and appears to relax under the change in topic. "I bet you were quite the player then as well."

"I was young and dumb and played like I was running after the last train leaving town. Fast and aggressive. Just what colleges are looking to tame—the next hotshot they can add to their claim-to-fame wall." I look through the glass at a group of women walking across the lawn with wineglasses in hand. "My brother is rebuilding Peachtree Pass to bring more people to town." Looking across at her, I add, "Seems the Dovers figured it out a long time ago."

"Alcohol is always a draw." Her eyes slide back from the people below to me, and she says, "Why did you leave?"

"I left for college."

Her head tilts, and she rests it against the wall. With a half smile relaxing on her face, she asks, "Why did you never return? Even when your career in the majors ended, you didn't come back. Why?"

"What was here that I couldn't get anywhere else in the world?"

"Your family."

"Ah." I roll my shoulders to the flat of the wall and chuckle as I stare across the office. "You got me there." I go with my old standby and pretend we weren't going where I didn't want to travel. Pushing off the wall, I weave through the pieces of furniture, thinking it's probably about time to go. "I know you're busy, so I should—"

"Please talk to me, Griffin."

I stop with my back to her, the pleas in the sound of her voice pulling me to respond. I turn my head, keeping her in my periphery. "Opening wounds doesn't heal them. It only exposes them to new pain."

She slowly starts toward me as if I'm skittish around confrontation. I'm not. I just avoid it when it's unnecessary. "I told you about Jacob. That wasn't easy for me."

I drop my head, my chin hitting my chest, and close my eyes. "My family became the last people I could face because I failed them."

Her hands run over the tops of my shoulders from behind, and she rests her cheek against my back. "I saw how close you and your dad were at the pizzeria. You talk about your brother and the respect you have for your sister. I can't imagine a world where your family would rather have you gone than see the amazing man you are on a daily basis."

Turning around slowly, I take her in my arms. With her tucked against me, I rest my head on the top of hers before tilting to kiss it. "You barely know me, and you already have me all figured out." Leaning back, I catch her eyes that are filled with sympathy for me instead of the love for her son that put the sparkle into them. It looks all wrong on her. "I'm back now."

"You said it was time to face the next stage of life. What does that mean to you?"

"I'm not sure I have a better answer today than I did yesterday, but I'm starting to see things in a new light. That's progress."

"Do you want a family?"

I chuckle, totally unprepared for the gunfire of questions aimed at me. "Um." I scratch the back of my neck, and reply, "A life I rejected before, maybe isn't so awful to me now?"

She laughs lightly, looking as confused as I feel. "Are you asking me if that's how you feel?"

"Do you have the answer? Because I sure don't."

She steps back and sits on the couch. Shaking her head, she says, "Nope. That's for you to figure out, but it does sound like you're open to the idea of change. Like you said, that's progress."

I should still go. Cricket hasn't made me feel like I've overstayed, but I think we both need a break before this gets any heavier. "I'm going to take off and let Savvy, who I have a strong suspicion is waiting in the hallway for me to leave, back in." I start for the door but turn back to kiss her. It's not slow or romantic, but for purely selfish reasons. It fills a need I have inside me to taste and feel her once more until I see her again.

Backing toward the door again, I grin. "You're going to text me later, right?"

"Yep. I'll text you as soon as I can." She stands in the middle of the room where I left her, her gaze fixed on mine, and a smile that I left on her face. "Thank you for helping move the furniture."

"Anytime." I open the door to see Savvy stand straighter like she was caught slacking on the job. To Cricket, I say, "Bye, Little Chirp." I knew I could get an eye roll from her. I chuckle as I pass her cousin. "Thanks for letting us talk."

I gallop down the stairs to her, saying, "I'm going to be highly disappointed if talk is all you did in there."

Looking back before I round the split in the staircase, I reply, "I never disappoint."

Her laughter echoes above as I work my way out.

I'm still smiling like a loon by the time I reach the guard gate. Joe wasn't on duty earlier, but he makes a show of it now. "Another drop-off, Mr. Greene?"

"Helping Ms. Dover and Ms. Dover move some furniture."

"Brawn wins again. I'm more of a brains guy myself." The punch would be swift and right to the mouth. Joe wouldn't know what hit him before dropping to the ground. Such a fucking tough guy when he's wearing a Winery Security badge like he's FBI.

He can think I'm as dumb as rocks all he wants, but I'm the one Cricket will be texting later. *So who's the real fool?* Anyway, I know better than to get in fights with people who think they're real police. I will be the one paying the price, but it doesn't stop me from wanting to knock him out. "You have a good day now, Joe."

He pushes the button like he has the power to access nuclear weapons. I'm not bashing the job because it's solid work, but what exactly is he securing at a winery? *Such a punk ass.* The gate rises, and I nod before driving away from him.

Rolling down the windows, I let the April breeze blow through the cab. I can't stop thinking about Cricket. She's beautiful and seems into me, but she's also a mother. I don't know the age of her kid, or if the father is still in her life. Those tidbits feel important for me to know how to navigate the situation. But we can talk tonight. She seemed to have more she wanted to ask anyway, so we should get it all out on the table before we're in too deep to turn back.

When I park the truck in front of the house, I see Beckett playing hoops. Tagger's son has gotten tall. Not surprising since he's a big guy, but his kid is only ten or so with a lot of growing ahead of him.

I shut the door to the truck and walk over to the makeshift half-court in front of the barn. "Hey?" I hold my hands out.

He tosses the ball to me. "Can you make that free throw?"

Jumping, I shoot for the basket. Circling the net, I can taste victory, but then it rolls off the side in defeat. "Can't win 'em all."

Beck starts to laugh as he retrieves it. "I thought it was gonna go in, too." He tosses it from the side and makes it.

"Good job, man." While he dribbles the ball, I walk closer. "You going to play for the middle school team?"

"Can't until seventh grade, but I'll try out next year."

"You got good aim, which is half the game." I hear a high-pitched chirp and look down to find a bug covered in dust on the dirt court. Kneeling, I smile when I see what it is. *My little chirp.* I bend to pick it up so I can relocate it to the safer plains of the field behind me, but pause when Beckett's shoe speeds past my reach, landing on top of it with a loud stomp. My eyes shoot up to see Beckett standing with a grin like he's destroyed the enemy. "Damn, dude, it was a cricket, not a cockroach."

"Same thing."

I stand back up. "No, they're not. Crickets are a good insect to have around."

"Sorry." He doesn't sound sorry, but I also shouldn't be as affected as I am by what he did. I've done the same. It was just a bug. So why'd it feel personal?

Don't overthink it, Greene. She's a woman who has a kid. Does that make me feel differently about where we were headed? Of course. That changes things. More important things will need to be considered. It's not frivolous fun anymore. I need to be careful with her as much as she needs to feel I'm someone worthy of introducing to him. That's not something that can be rushed.

Her questions are valid.

I'm not in a hurry, but am I willing to stay to see where things go with her?

I catch the ball again and shoot. This time, I make it. Reputation saved. "You have fun, dude." I hold my hand out for a low five, which he smacks. "I'm going inside."

I'm ready for a tall glass of tea and to kick back on the couch for a bit. See if any games are on and return to the puzzle I left on the coffee table. Otherwise, I'll be sitting around staring at my phone the rest of the day, waiting for a certain pretty woman to text me where and when. And feel like a fool if she doesn't.

Not that I don't think she'll text. She will. But it won't serve me well if I'm only hanging around this town hoping for her to give me the time of day. I need to get my shit together and really think about the next steps in my life.

The Riggins house comes to mind. An opportunity in disguise? Is it a chance to have a piece of the peach pie for myself? I have no idea, but it's not a bad situation to be in.

It's not as nice as her so-called cottage, but the old farmhouse isn't so bad, especially if I fix it up. But I'm no fool. Thoughts like I'm having about Cricket Dover only lead to one thing—me breaking her heart. She's a mom. I can't do that to her. Getting ahead of myself won't do me any good, though. But I'm also not ready to walk away from her. I adore everything about her, especially that mouth.

We're adults who know what we're getting into.

No one is getting hurt.

Even if a little damaged, hearts will remain intact.

I sit down with a cold glass of iced tea and flick on the TV. After I find a preseason game out of Houston, I discover a puzzle piece to complete the corner I've been working on. This life isn't so bad.

I glance over at my phone. No message. *Yet.*

This is different. I can't say I'm comfortable waiting to hear from someone I like. It's a bit eye-opening to feel anxious, wondering if she'll contact me. With my knee bouncing, I place a puzzle piece to connect a whole corner and am immediately reminded of the table Cricket moved in her office when she didn't need to. Her nerves were getting the better of her.

I don't know what she's doing to me, but I shake my head, guessing this is karma paying me back. But I smile right after because I can't wait to see her again.

CHAPTER 19

Cricket

"So you know . . ." Savvy starts, handing me her phone. "I approve of him."

I work through a few word search options with no luck, but ask, "Who?"

"Nice try," she says with a laugh. "He's cute. Just like I said the first time you saw him."

No point playing dumb when she saw more than she probably wanted of me and Griffin this afternoon. "I'm glad you approve, but don't get too ahead of yourself. No matchmaking." I glance at her next to me. "No leaving me to hitch a ride from him tonight. No setups at all." As I try a few new words and am victorious with the word crawl, I add, "Please let things happen organically. If it happens, it happens. If it doesn't, it doesn't." I hand the phone back to her.

She looks at the progress of the game we're playing, then back at me. "And if it doesn't, are you still going to tell him about Jacob?"

My breath stops hard in my throat before I can exhale.

In the dark of the back seat of the car we hired to drive us to Whiskey's Bar tonight, I can barely make out her features, other than the little light drifting in through the windows. The gas station lights are blinding for two seconds as we pass. When my eyes adjust to the dimness of the vehicle, I whisper, "I told him about Jacob, Sav. This afternoon."

"You know what I mean."

I lick my lips as my heart starts thumping. "I'm not following." Fine, I wasn't going to play dumb, but I feel forced into a corner, and it's all I can think to do to protect the secret I've been keeping from her about Griffin.

She angles her back against the car door, knocking her knees into mine. "I'm not trying to put you on the spot or upset you. But we both know he's Jacob's father. You basically copied and pasted that kid straight from his dad."

I catch the driver's eyes on us in the rearview mirror. Readjusting for more privacy, I face my cousin and lower my voice even more. "What makes you so sure?"

"First, you're not denying it. Second, I wasn't that drunk in Costa Rica. You were."

I try for indifference when I reply, "I knew what I was doing."

"I'm the last one to judge. We've both had plenty of good times in our lives. Some of those times, we made a pact to go to the grave with those stories. But this isn't the same as going topless our senior year of college at the Paldino's private pool in Vegas."

The way she can recall events in an instant is impressive, but also a tactic to take me down. *The traitor.* "Do you remember everything?"

Shaking her head, she says, "No, but I remember him. Hard to forget. I'd imagine it's tougher for you since you got a parting gift before he left." Leaning forward, she glances through the windshield. "I also saw him leaving your room the next day. The man is a giant, and if I must admit, which I feel strongly that I do, he's gorgeous. He's hard to miss all around, which is probably what drew you to him in the first place."

"It did," I confess too quickly, but I don't need to lie to her. "The moment I saw him, I was tripping over myself to meet him. And maybe a few too strong margaritas played a part as well." Pointing my finger at her, I add, "But I didn't really drink after that, so I was sobering up all night with him."

She throws her hand up with her clutch in it. "Again, I'm not judging. But even I saw him enough back then to recognize him on the team now. So I know you did."

The red sign in the middle of nowhere shines like a beacon around these parts.

Want a good time? *Go to Whiskey's.*

Rough day? *Go to Whiskey's.*

What's not to love about strong drinks, fried food, bar games, and live music to dance to? *Nothing.* That was how I knew it would be the perfect place to meet up. "If you knew all along, why didn't you say something sooner?"

"Because this was the one time," she says, reaching over to rub my arm, "I knew you needed to figure it out on your own. I can't tell you what to do or force you to do anything. Trust me, I've tried over the years." She gives a glimmer of a smile, which I find reassuring. I know my cousin only wants the best for me, as I do for her. Despite all of our family issues, we can always rely on each other.

"Admittedly, I've been stubborn in the past." Holding my hands up in surrender, I say, "Guilty as charged."

"The past is the past, but you usually do play it safe."

"I have to because of Jacob."

"I know. I just wanted to note the only time you seem to cut loose is with Griffin. Tonight, you're going out on a whim like you did in Costa Rica. Something about him has you tossing caution to the wind."

"I'm being careless, which isn't good, and I know it's fast, but Griffin isn't like anyone else I've ever met. I like him. *A lot.* And you know what? He likes me a lot, too, and isn't afraid to show it." I lean my head back, smiling at the image of him that pops into my head. Rolling my head to the side, I say, "I thought he was arrogant. Well, he is, but I find his confidence so attractive. It's not just in baseball or whatever. He's confident in me. He sees me for the woman I've wanted my family to see for years and haven't. He makes me feel . . ." I almost feel dumb for saying it, but I do anyway. "Invincible." I take a breath, and say, "Sexy. Smart. Beautiful. Responsible. And lovable. Not in the teddy bear kind of way, but that he could love me for who I am. It's an aphrodisiac, Savvy."

"I need to break up with Blake."

"What?" I sit up and stare at her. "What are you talking about?"

She sighs, glancing out the window as the car pulls into the gravel parking lot. I hear the pop of rocks under the tires as the driver drives us to the front. "He doesn't see me as any of those things. Most of the time, I don't think he sees me at all."

I'm left stunned. I lift my jaw back up and say, "I'm sorry. I . . ." It's ridiculous that I've had all this attention when she's been going through so much. "You deserve better."

"I'm starting to realize that." Her gaze returns to mine, and she says, "He's supposed to be here tonight. I asked him to come."

"You should talk to him and tell him your real feelings."

"Probably. Either way it goes down, I'll get an answer." The car stops.

The driver says, "We're here, ladies. Make sure to call me if you need a ride home."

"Thank you." I open the door and slip out, reaching in to grab my hat from where it was set between us. I put on the dark brown felted cowboy hat as the pièce de résistance to my outfit. My brown leather boots reach just under my knee and have seen everything from countless rodeos to twirling around the dance floor more than a few times. The white skirt with eyelet trim is Savvy's, but she insisted, and since I fell in love with it, it was an easy decision. The denim vest exposes my midriff but hugs my chest just right.

I hope Griffin likes my outfit.

Savvy tips him on the app, then slides across the seat to get out next to me. When she shuts the door, she pulls on her own hat and catches my arm before we go in. "Just remember that falling fast doesn't mean it's not real. You both know what you're doing and are both on board, so if he makes you happy, I'm happy for you." Her head bobbles as laughter trickles from her. "It's like watching destiny play out in a fairy tale right before my eyes. It's romantic that you're meeting for real this time around instead of only for a roll in the hay."

"Trust me, no hay was involved." I laugh too as we walk to the front entrance of Whiskey's. I may have gotten her approval, but it's her support that means the most to me. Heaven knows my parents aren't going to be happy. "Thousand thread count sheets were, though."

"Okay, that's too much." After grabbing the handle, she tugs the door open while laughing. Holding it open for me, she says, "You don't have to listen to a word I say. But you do need to consider all angles of this situation, including

Jacob's." She's not wrong, but would I be if I just had fun tonight? There's always tomorrow to face reality. The music filters out through the open door, the lights shining into the darkness around us. "Ready?"

"As I'll ever be." I walk into a busy Friday night. The volume of conversations being had from as far back in the corner where some guys play darts to the closer end of the bar to us almost drowns out the music. The band plays on the backstage as couples two-step their way around the dance floor.

If we wanted a drink, it would be hard to figure out where to even squeeze in to place an order. But a drink is a priority to calm the nervous energy overtaking me. I'm both excited and anxious about seeing Griffin again. I do like him, but so much still lies unsaid between us. What happens when it all comes to light? Will he still like me, then?

I sidle up between two guys talking to other people and wait for the bartender's attention. Savvy stands close. But then I hear, "What are you drinking?"

I turn to see it's not my cousin at all. A black cowboy hat shadows Griffin's face, but those blue eyes pierce, setting my heart on fire and my pulse to quicken beyond my control. The smile he seems to save only for me touches his lips, and he stands so close there's no mistaking we're together. Even if we're not, technically, we *are* tonight.

"I'm thinking about tequila."

When his hand slides across the bare skin of my back, he dips his fingertips under the hem of the denim vest. Shaking his head, he chuckles. "Nothing good happens when tequila is involved."

"I drank a lot of it the night I met you in Costa Rica."

"Okay, so some good things happen." He tips the brim of

my hat up before he leans down to kiss me. Licking his lips once he pulls back, he whispers, "You've never looked sexier, Little Chirp." He wavers his head but then smiles again. "Except when you were wearing my hat in that bed. I can't choose which I like better."

I slide my hand down the front of the pearl snaps on his western shirt, stopping just before I hit his hard as Rocky Mountains abs. "Good thing you don't have to. You can have both tonight." Am I jumping five steps ahead? *Yep.* Do I care when I'm close to him like this? *Absolutely not.*

"Don't write checks you can't cash, sweetheart."

"I can cash it, alright." God, I feel inspired and beautiful when he looks at me like he is now, like I'm the golden ticket he found in a Willy Wonka candy bar. "But I'm starting to wonder if you can handle a windfall." I drag a finger up his chest, neck, and flick the tip off that sexy, scruffy chin of his. "It's like winning the lottery."

The heat from his hands sears my hips as he pulls me close, my middle tight against his. Breath rushes from my lungs when he tilts my head up with his fingers. "You're telling me." His eyes spark with desire, causing butterflies to flutter to life in my stomach. Leaning down, he kisses me. This time just as quick, but only so he can hold his hand up for the bartender. "Two tequila shots, please."

CHAPTER 20

Griffin

Cricket Dover is unequivocally the most captivating woman I've ever met.

Her laughter is music, her body a map I want to travel every inch. Those green eyes are electric when she's happy and softer when she's deep in thought. That smile, though . . . it had my attention the first time I ever saw it. It made my heart ache to leave her behind when I walked out of that hotel room, and seeing it now shining for me, *because of me*, I'm already too deeply invested in this woman.

I don't have the strength or desire to take my eyes off her. Me and half of Whiskey's. She's owned this bar since the moment she walked in. She didn't notice how everyone stopped to look at her, how conversations altered to the topic of her entrance, or the way men were about to line up to talk to her. Did I stake a claim? *Fuck yeah, I did.*

The way she can't keep her hands off me, she's done some staking herself tonight. I even caught her giving a nasty glare to Maple Thornton, who works down at the feed store. *The crime?* Maple had the nerve to look at me. Granted, it was a certain way that gave her intentions a specific direction, but no one stands a chance with me when I'm standing next to the prettiest woman in two counties. I can easily say two countries. And since I've traveled so much of the world, I can confidently back that claim as well.

With her arms around my neck, she sways to the right and then the left with her eyes closing as she takes in the music. It doesn't matter that it's a line dance. Cricket is happy just slow dancing with me without a care for what's happening around us. She's not alone. I don't even like dancing, but I like doing it with her. She spins away, raising her arms in the air. I swear the world just shifted beneath my feet as I watch her skirt twirl away from her legs. The long strands of her hair are sent flying around her shoulders, but it's the lights reflecting in her eyes that have me wanting to make sure that light never leaves them, not when she's this carefree and happy.

Fuck, I'm sunk.

Not sure when it happened because I was blindsided, but I'm in way deeper with her than I realized.

She does a quick toe-tap dance step and rushes back to me. Falling against my chest, she grabs my shirt, laughing like nothing can dampen her mood. "Let's get a beer," she says, looking up at me like this just might be the best idea she's ever had. Just as she pulls away, I capture her around the waist, bringing her against me, her back to my front, my lips to her neck as a slew of giggles escapes her. "Why do I get the feeling you're craving something else, Greene?"

My hat falls off, but I don't care, I'm exactly where I want to be—with my lips pressed to her skin. I move higher just behind her ear to steal one last kiss before whispering, "I've been thinking about you more than would be considered healthy . . . or legal."

Her laughter quiets, and she leans into me. Taking a breath, she bends to pick up my hat and turns around. Setting it on my head, she gives it a little tug into place, then admires her work, or maybe it's me that puts those stars in her eyes. A guy can hope. Arching into me, she says, "I don't know what you did with that guy I met earlier in the week, but I really like this one."

Wrapping my arms tight around her waist, I lean over her, ready to kiss those tempting lips once again, but tease by replying, "Same guy. You just get the real version now."

Her hands brush against my cheeks, and her smile ascends into place. "The real version is dangerous to my heart, Griffin Greene."

"Don't worry, Cricket Dover. I won't hurt you." I kiss her as a promise to both of us.

This time, she leans back, and says, "I think I need water."

"Come on." I take her hand and lead her to the bar to order two cups of water. Cricket promptly takes one and starts sipping. Guess she's feeling the heat as much as I am. I'm left wondering if it's this overcrowded bar or the chemistry between us. Though I already know the answer, it's fun to pretend that she isn't the best thing to happen to me since the last time I spent with her.

This vibe in Whiskey's is going strong. The music is getting louder, and the hustle over on the pool tables involves throwing in more money in the late hours if you want to play. But I'm only into the woman at my side and wouldn't mind being alone with her again. Lifting my hat to cool off, I wipe my forehead with the back of my hand, and ask, "Do you want to get out of here?"

She stands straighter as if an opportunity has just presented itself. "Where do you want to go?" Knowing she's up for anything with me feeds a part of me that has been starving for so long. I just didn't know how much I was missing until she brought it to light.

"Anywhere with you." Setting my hat on my head, I take another drink of water.

A smile tickles her lips as she glances down at my chest. Fidgeting with a snap on my shirt, she peers back up at me, and says, "Anywhere, cowboy? You sure about taking that risk? I'm a Dover, after all. The D stands for dangerous."

She holds a straight face long enough for me to second-guess that she might not be joking. When a laugh bursts free, she pokes my chest. "You looked worried."

"Not worried. I was thinking it was dessert."

"Oh," she starts, her brows wriggling into concern. "Are you hungry?"

Should I tell her? *Nah.* Showing her is best.

Taking hold of her hand, I bring it to my mouth and kiss her fingers. Turning it over, I place another kiss on her palm and then lower on her wrist, letting my lips linger in hopes of feeling her heartbeat. "Risk doesn't scare me, especially not if you're involved." I chuckle, though. "The legendary feud between our families will either end or continue with us. Which will it be?"

"There's only one way to find out." She lifts on her toes and kisses me as if she's stealing from a candy shop, and when she lowers, the grin on her face shows me she got away with it. She takes a drink of her water and then another. When she drags the tip of her tongue over her lip, she's got my full attention, as if she didn't have it already. She did. *Wholly.* Appallingly consuming every minute she gives me. Why the fixation? The fascination? Why her?

She's unfinished business from years prior, the one time I made a mistake in my personal life, and the second chance I've been given. I'm not fucking it up this time. She was worth the wait, better than I imagined. Vibrant and drop-dead gorgeous. Funny with her quirks and full of secrets I want to uncover. Got a hot little temper and a side of vinegar to her snapbacks. I like that she holds her own and find her whip-smart wit so fucking sexy.

Cricket Dover is the full package.

Not that I could have known what I do now, but I was stupid for letting her slip away in the first place. I knew it then, and now I regret leaving her behind.

She grins with a tilt of her head and bats her eyelashes. "Should we get out of here?" Gotta love how she takes ownership of the idea. I don't mind letting her take credit. *She's hot as fuck.* That also gives her a lot of leeway in my book. "I need to let Savvy know. Be right back."

She starts to saunter across the bar like she owns the place, her confidence on full display. Such a turn-on.

She only gets a few feet away before she stops. The way she angles gives me a stunning view of her profile. The straight of her nose, and the long lashes that curl skyward, her chin the southernmost point of her sweet face, and the gentle slope of her neck when her hair is pulled to one side as she studies the view ahead. I sure like looking at her, but it only gets better when we're talking.

I hadn't felt my heart in years until I laid eyes on her again. The beats were subtle, barely detectable thumps that confused me at first. But every time I'm near her, they grow louder, harder until I feel every beat deep through my bones. I feel it growing stronger. I *feel*, which is something I wasn't doing at all before returning, before seeing her again.

I'm not sure what to think anymore. Women have never

been a priority, but that was before I met her, and before I was set up like it was kismet to fall into the same place at the same time again. The signs are getting really hard to ignore, so I'd best start accepting that some things might be meant to be.

She comes back to me, stopping at my side while facing the exit. "I'll text her. She'll be going home with Blake anyway. I'll save them the trouble if you can take me home?" Looking back in her cousin's direction, I see she's propped on Blake's lap. Judging by their engaging conversation, I understand why Cricket came back. "Or I can call a—"

"You're not calling anyone." That I selfishly get more time with her isn't worth mentioning, or that I like the way she looks sitting next to me in my truck. I'll happily take the wins when they come. "I'm happy to do it."

"Be careful, cowboy. I may not be a romantic, but you've managed to charm me before."

We start walking toward the front of the bar. Her words are playing on my mind, and a smirk wants to reveal itself, so I ask, "What happens if I don't heed your warning?"

Pushing through the door, I follow her and the sound of her laughter outside. "You just might be stuck with me."

"Torture," I tease, covering my heart with my hand.

She spins around and tucks her fingers into the top of my Wranglers to pull herself closer to me. I can't lie and say I don't like how handsy she is. But just when I think I can read her mind, she surprises me all over again. Holding her hand on top of her hat, she looks up at the night sky. I thought her profile was quite the sight, but damn, I could stare at her all night and see something new and untamed, a side of her that wants to break loose while she walks such a steady line on the daily. She's both otherworldly yet standing before me like I'm worth her time.

She turns to look at me. "I thought about you more times than I didn't."

I want to kiss her so badly that I cup her face and lean down. With our eyes closed and only a breath between us, I whisper, "I never forgot you, babe."

Her eyes flutter open, her gaze connecting with mine in a moment of silence shared between us. I breathe her in, running the tip of my nose along the bridge of hers. She sucks in a breath, then on the exhale, she asks, "Are you going to kiss me, Twenty-two?"

Smiling against her cheek, I lower my mouth to reach her lips. "I want nothing more, Little Chirp."

A smile touches her lips before I can. Her eyes close softly, waiting so patiently that it's hard to resist giving her what she wants. But the way her body leans into mine lets me know that what she wants and what she needs are two very different things.

I eye the pink of her plush lips, the round of her breasts in that vest as they start to heave from heavy breaths, and the trust she's giving me to do as I please. I should reward her for being such a good girl, though I'm the one making out like a bandit in this situation. I brush my mouth over hers, then come back to steal her breath away entirely. Covering her mouth with mine, I start gentle, but like so much else with her, it escalates quickly. Our lips part, allowing our tongues to find sanctuary inside each other's mouths.

Running my hand down the side of her neck, I lean in, going deeper. I want her so badly that my discomfort starts to be apparent. I shift to create some space but am given a harsh reminder that Wranglers aren't the most forgiving denim. Needing relief, I point to the left in the parking lot. "I'm parked over here."

I barely beat her to the door. Opening it, I help her step up and settle in before shutting the door, then walk around to the other side. Passing in front, I slow down just to give myself a moment to appreciate Cricket tucked snugly in my truck. I'm insanely attracted to this woman, but I like the way my chest warms when I see her sitting there. It's like that's where she belongs. *With me.*

Climbing in, I buckle up and start the engine. I reverse out of the space but stop when I pull up to the main two-lane highway out here. Right leads us to Austin. Left leads us back home. We live miles and a county apart, but somehow, the two of us met in another part of the world, and we live in the same direction.

She turns on the radio and rolls down her window. When I roll down my window, the wind whips through the ends of her hair while the hat holds the top in place. "Tonight has been perfect. Look at that full moon, Griffin."

I lean forward to look through the top of the windshield. Big and bold, the moon rides high in the sky and lights our way between fields and farms. "Pretty amazing."

Sitting back, she pulls her knees up to her chest. Her skirt slips down her legs but stops mid-thigh. With her arms around her boots, she says, "This is the most fun I've had in a long time. Thank you."

I reach over and rub her bare knee, then slide just a little lower. "I can say the same. Feels like we're getting away with something every time we're together."

"You think the feud is buried in our bones." She laughs, looking out the windshield again. "A Greene and Dover getting together . . ." She stops too soon as if she shouldn't have said it.

Giving her leg a squeeze, I shake my head. "There's nothing wrong with what we're doing."

"It doesn't feel wrong. My brain just makes me wonder sometimes."

"Give me the night and I'll convince you." The slight part of her legs to allow me more access has me sliding my hand lower. I reach the bend to her bliss and slip a finger between the fabric and her soft lower lip. With her mouth open and eyes set on mine, she closes it and bites her lip.

I could make her come before we reach Dover Creek Winery. Gliding through her slickness, she makes it hard to concentrate on the road ahead. Add in the strangulation of these jeans, and I should probably wait. "I want to touch you, but we only have a few miles left, and I don't want to rush this."

She nods as the words won't come. When I slide my hand from the embrace of her legs, I bring the tip of my finger to my bottom lip and slide it across a few times, then follow with my tongue to taste her.

Volleying my gaze between the highway and her, I hit the gas pedal. "I can't wait to take my time with you."

Her breathing picks up. "I can't either," she whispers breathily and reaches over to rub the back of my neck.

I spy the winery sign lit up in the distance. When she sees it, she puts her feet back on the floorboard and sits upright with her hands tucked in her lap. I turn in and drive the other fifty yards to the guard shack.

Oh joy, I get to deal with *Joe* again. He steps out, adjusting his belt that's hanging down from the giant ring of keys hooked to a loop of his pants. It jingles with each step. For a security guard, he doesn't seem to have a sense of sneaking up on the enemy. "What do we have here?"

I don't worry about safety out on the ranch, and it's accessible in any direction if someone wants to hop a fence. But Cricket is different, and she has a son to worry about. I have the need to know they're actually safe out here, especially with this heehaw "guarding" the property.

Cricket leans over like she did the last time. "Hey Joe, it's us again."

Shining his flashlight in my face, he's fucking lucky he turns it to the dashboard just as fast. With his gaze locked on Cricket, he asks, "Same as last night? Just a drop-off again?"

It's funny how I suddenly don't exist as he peers over me like the driver's seat is vacant. Her eyes find mine in the darkened cab, excitement making the little light from the shack shine brighter while a wild streak runs through them. With the smallest of nods like we're in this together, she replies, "He's staying."

That's an invitation I won't turn down.

Joe sighs a little too heavily for my liking. He's getting on my last nerve. "How long?" he asks, just to shred that nerve into smithereens.

"As long as he wants, Joe. Have a good night." She's not curt, but her tone is firm. It's the nicest way I've ever heard someone say it's none of your fucking business. She's better than me.

The arm of the gate lifts, and I drive on, not wanting to make a spectacle of what she said, but I'm riding that wave all the way down the property and up again to reach the "cottage" as she likes to call this big house. I shift into Park, cut the lights so they don't shine on the house, and let it idle. Angling to face her, I chuckle. "I'm staying the night, huh?"

With a shrug, she replies, "Assumed you wouldn't mind." But her cute face cringes. "I hoped you wouldn't."

"You assumed correctly." I cut the engine, and we both get out. While we walk quietly to the front door, she steals a glance at me that I catch. With her eyes forward, though, I watch the smile I caused bloom like a night flower across

her cheeks. As if she couldn't be more breathtaking . . .
She is.

Under a full moon, our mouths crash together as her back lands against the side of the porch. I shove a knee between her legs and plant my hands above her head. Kissing her becomes erratic and carnal. I lean down to scoop her up and take her inside, but she tugs me by my belt loops toward the door first. With her hand behind her back on the knob, and her mouth still attached to mine, she pulls back. Her head hits the wood, but it doesn't deter her from opening the door.

This is it.

I finally get to be with her again.

Before I step inside, I say, "I've waited four years to be with you again."

Her grin is naughty and equally sweet. Pulling me inside the house, she whispers, "Let's not waste any time, then."

CHAPTER 21

Griffin

Cricket hasn't wasted a minute. As soon as she hangs her hat on the hook by the front door, we tiptoe like we're sneaking out of our parents' house and not sneaking into her own.

She slows and walks even more carefully when we pass the second door on the left. Glancing back at me, she smiles and picks up her pace again before pulling me into the last room on the right.

My eyes aren't quite adjusted to the darkness, but when they do, I look around at her bedroom. Bed against the far wall and two nightstands with a couch at the end of the bed anchoring it. I approve of the large screen TV hanging on the opposite wall from the bed.

The curtains are open, and although the moon isn't hanging over this side of the house, some of its light still manages to filter inside. "It's very . . . neat."

She laughs after shutting the door. It's not as boisterous as it was at Whiskey's, but it holds the same joy in it. "I don't think you'd be surprised that I have someone who helps me out."

"It's not a crime, Little Chirp. I paid someone to clean my apartment in St. Louis—not because my mom didn't teach me to clean up after myself, but because I was exhausted and busy icing my body when I dragged my ass in after practice or being on the road."

After locking the door, she comes closer, taking smooth but calculated steps as she approaches. "My mom didn't teach me how to clean because she's never cleaned a day in her life." I'm still not judging, though I think she set me up for a reaction. But cleaning isn't why we snuck into her house and tiptoed to her bedroom. And I have no intention of letting that steam slip away.

I meet her halfway, cupping her cheeks and angling her face up for our lips to meet in the middle. We start slower than we did outside the front door, sweeter, and when her hands tug to untuck my shirt, I deepen it.

Suddenly putting air between us, she rips the snaps apart and smiles like she got herself a treat when she sees me.

Tucking a finger under her chin, I lift it. "Eyes up here, sweetheart."

She giggles. "How long did you have that ready to use?"

"Since you said it at the stadium."

"All's fair in love and war." Between the smile gracing her face and the magnificent sound of her laughter, I feel like I just won the World Series. "But for the record, you're very distracting." She moves ahead with what seems like her plan all along and strips the cotton from my shoulders. When it falls to the floor behind me, she adds, "There. That's better."

Before I have a chance to say anything, she attaches her

lips to my chest and kisses upward until she's lifting on her toes to reach my shoulder. I rub around the soft skin exposed at her waist and then move higher to run my fingertips under her denim vest. "I want this off." The words come in the form of a rumble in my chest. The buildup of this moment with her, after the years of imagining it would never happen, I can't be patient. Fortunately, she's grappling with my belt, appearing to be in a bigger hurry than I am.

She pauses, then abandons my belt for her vest. "You want this off?" The glint in her eyes says she already knows the answer. Starting on the lowest button, she frees it from the buttonhole.

"That's what I want." I run my hand to mess up my hair, wishing I'd done it earlier to remove the dents I know I'm sporting from my hat.

She undoes the middle button and says, "Those jeans look really uncomfortable."

"They are. I should take them off."

Her smile grows. "Great idea." The last button is released, revealing a white lacy bra bright against her tanned skin. She slips the denim down her arms and tosses it to the couch at the end of the bed. She slides her skirt down, giving me a full view of the lace thong that matches the bra. My smile fades when I glance down as she steps out of the skirt. Seeing her standing before me in nothing but lace and leather boots, I watch as shyness washes through her, brightening her cheeks.

Doesn't matter that spice and moxie got us here. I won't allow her to have any doubts about us being together. "Look at me, babe." When she does, I brush her hair back to admire her face. "We're just having fun. No pressure or strings. Whatever you want, I'll do for you."

"It's just been . . ." Taking a harsh inhale, she holds it

before exhaling. I hope it's not nerves, but I feel some in my belly, too, and that's never happened before. "It's been since you."

The message is heard loud and clear and causes my chest to ache. Bringing her against me, I wrap her in my arms and kiss the top of her head. I can feel her heart beating and her breath breeze across the plains of my chest. I kiss her once more and then whisper, "Understandable once you've tasted greatness."

She cracks up, her entire body rattling in my arms from laughter. Shoving her way out of my arms, she says, "I knew I'd regret telling you."

I reach for her again, sliding my hands under her fine ass and lifting her. Her legs wrap around me, her boots crossing behind my back. With her looking in my eyes, humor still dancing in hers, I whisper, "Thank you for trusting me."

Her breathing picks up, and with her arms around me, she pulls me down for a kiss. I grip her tighter. When she grinds against me and moans, I turn around and move to the side of the bed. After laying her down, I take hold of one boot of hers and then the other. She strips her socks off while I start tugging off my boots, hopping on the opposite foot like it somehow helps.

They're both dropped at the foot of the bed, and time seems to slow a bit. I take my socks off and then my boxer briefs. Moving to the bed where I left her, I study the beauty as if she's my next art piece, noting the small patch of freckles just off her belly button, and how her hair falls to the side of her delicate neck.

Her gaze travels over me and down, her mouth opening for more air to enter her lungs, judging by the rate of her chest rising and falling. "Like what you see?"

"I always did and still do."

I run my palms slowly across the top of her thighs and down again, detouring to the underside of her knee. In one quick motion, I pull her back to me. Legs spread. Her tempting mouth rounded from surprise. The sight of her makes me as hard as steel. "You deserve to feel good." Selfishly, I take my time taking her in, drinking in the beauty of seeing every inch of her body again. Almost every inch since bits of lace cover the sexiest parts.

The curve of her waist has me wanting to slide my hands along the flow and into the swell of her hips. The soft slope of her stomach is such a turn-on. Womanly and makes me want to spend time kissing right there.

Moving back up, I lean over, anchoring my hands on either side of her head to kiss her. No way am I going to miss out on tasting her mouth before I get to taste her pussy. Pushing up, I say, "I want to make you feel amazing." I take a harsh breath, my erection pulsing for attention. "I'm the luckiest fucking guy in the world that I'm the one you chose to pleasure you."

She brushes the tips of her nails around my ears and down my neck to cover the top of my shoulders and then my back. It both tickles and arouses me, though it might be the way she's looking at me like I just gifted her the moon that has me aching to be inside her. "God, I want you."

"I want you, too. So much," she replies through bated breath as she watches me pull away to kneel beside the bed, dragging the lacy thong until it's on the floor behind me. When I look up at her, she's freeing her amazing tits from the other confines of lace. The bra is dropped over the edge of the bed just as I lift her legs over my shoulders.

Kissing the inside of one knee and then the other, I go

higher to trail kisses up her thighs and follow with a swipe of my tongue to tease before I reach my destination.

Her head falls back, but I can still see her hands grabbing the blanket in my peripheral vision. "It's going to feel so good, babe. I promise."

The first touch from the tip of my tongue causes her to buck, so I maneuver my hand higher to her hip to hold her in place while sliding through the softness of her lower lips. The first taste is sweeter than the ripest peach in high season, delicate on my tongue as I explore the forbidden enclaves of her body. Each time she pushes against me, my tongue holds position, letting her help herself. I rise to reach her clit, encircling it to tease a moan out of her and a gentler buck from her hips.

When I dive into her entrance, the bed dips as she pushes into it and arches her back. I look up to see her reaction just as I start fucking her with my tongue. Her face is hidden, but I can hear her breath on the other side of her breasts that are peaked at the tips. I never forgot those beauties and can't wait to have my lips wrapped around her nipples again.

Her fingers find my hair and pull hard as moans escape her on every delve and dip, pull back and thrust again. I reach up to toy with her needy bud when she whispers, "Oh my God." Her thighs shiver as her body stiffens. "Please, please, please," she chants between breaths as she sinks against my mouth, her fingers ready to pull my hair out. Her breath catches before her release hits.

I taste every tremor, feeling the squeeze around my tongue. It's when her body melts to the mattress, replete with her arms falling wide, that I place a kiss, then dig a condom from my pocket. She warned me, so I don't show up anywhere with her without protection.

Rolling it down my length, I catch her propping up on her elbows to watch as if this is the entertainment when we both know damn well this is only a preview of what's to come. She says, "Thank you."

"Don't thank me. You think that wasn't also for me?" I nod my head down, showing her the evidence. "Move up."

She scoots higher on the bed until her head is on the pillow. The shyness I witnessed earlier has vanished under the satisfaction of release. What a stunning sight to see.

I climb over her, using my knee to spread her legs wider for me. Settling in, I push my dick to where my tongue had the pleasure of being. With my eyes locked on hers, I lower myself to kiss her purely because I want to, then dip to kiss each of her breasts and swirl my tongue around her nipples. Her arms come around my shoulders just as I gently bite, sending her body to jolt like a strike of lightning ripped through her. "Oh God, yes, Griffin."

My name rolling off her tongue has me thrusting inside her. She's said it before, but hearing it when we're so connected is like a hit to my heart, reviving it to life again. I drop my head to the bed beside hers, the feeling of her overwhelming my senses. I've wanted this for so, so long.

Her warmth wraps around me, the heat extending through my bloodstream. I'm realizing now that I don't have the control I thought I did. Not with her. She's the one in charge. I pull out slowly, lifting to hover over her. Planting my weight on my forearms, I lock my gaze on hers and push back in. The parting of her lips, the lust of greens in her eyes, and the rock of her hips against mine, meeting thrust for thrust with as much passion as I have uncoils my desire.

Hold it the fuck together, Greene.

I find a rhythm that matches hers, one that's slower, a pace allowing me to savor instead of devour. Instead of fucking, we make love. Love. Is that the name of this feeling overcoming me?

When her body quickens the tight hold around my erection, she whispers, "Harder, babe. Faster, please."

I oblige for her, but I sure as hell benefit, feeling my release work through me. And when she falls apart, declaring my name as if I'm a hero, I fall with her. The darkness hits, but I push until I see the lights, the fireworks, and feel our tremors mingling until my breath breaks in my throat, and heaven takes over.

And when breathing returns, each one becoming easier again, I drop down on top of her to recover. She may have brought my heart to life, but it's not mine to own. Not anymore. It's all hers, and I give it willingly for her to hold on to. My heart beats even and when I take a longer breath and relax again, she whispers, "Our small town isn't ready for this scandal."

I smile before I even open my eyes. Looking beneath me, I catch her smile, and ask, "What scandal is that?"

"I'm sleeping with the enemy."

"Nah. You're only sleeping with a Greene."

"Same thing around these parts." She laughs, pressing her hands against my chest. "I can't hang on much longer."

I roll to her side with a stupid grin on my face. "We can't have that." I turn to look at her. "Now that we're back together, I don't think I'm going to let you go."

She rolls to her side, rubbing the tips of her fingers over the scruff of my jaw. "That sure sounds a lot like you're planning to stay a while."

"I didn't have a reason before."

"And now you do?"

Leaning forward, I kiss her, then lick my lips just to taste her again when I lie back down. "You're giving me one."

Her smile falters for the briefest of seconds before she retrieves it to put back on her face. "I hope so. You've broken the dam wide open. Now that I've been with the great Twenty-two, I'm going to need a lot more of that action."

"You know how to make a guy feel good, Ms. Dover."

Rolling back again, she raises her hands. "Only telling the truth." She turns to get out of bed but stops and looks back. "Will you stay the night?"

"What about your son?"

"You can leave early before he wakes up."

I sit up and lean toward her. Kissing her shoulder blade, I reply, "How can I refuse an offer like that?"

She smiles as if there's a silent understanding. *There is.* I like that everything doesn't have to be said. Maybe it's being older and supposedly wiser, but I want to believe we don't have to complicate the feelings growing between us. Cricket goes to the bathroom, and when she returns, I take my time cleaning up and taking care of business before coming back to bed.

When I lie down, I open my arm for her to snuggle in. She does, resting her head on my shoulder. "Six thirty. Jacob gets up at seven." Placing a kiss as if it's a promise she's making me, she rests back down and closes her eyes.

I lie awake long enough to hear her breathing even out and feel her heart steady in her chest. Her soft sleeping sounds bring a comfort I didn't expect. My eyelids close, and sleep takes hold of me.

IT's the gasp of death that startles me into sitting straight up. "What is it?"

"It's eight!" she shouts, catching herself by ducking as if

that will lessen the sound of her voice carrying. She pushes against my arm like she can actually move me. "Get up. Get up. Get up."

Shit. I'm barely awake, much less functioning, but I drop my feet to the floor and stand with a fast rub of my eyes. "Okay. I'm up." Looking around for my stuff, I find a piece here and a boot there.

Snapping her fingers doesn't help, but neither does the high-alert mode she's shifted into. She opens a drawer and grabs a long T-shirt that hits her mid-thigh. Recognizing the design, I say, "I was at that rodeo."

"That's great, but you need to hustle out of here. Go through the window."

"The window?" Last night is still hazy from sleep deprivation. "What story are we on?"

"The first."

Thank God.

A lady's voice and then her son's sneaks under the opening to the door, causing both of us to freeze where we are. As soon as it goes quiet again, she moves closer to me. "Oh my God, Griffin." Panic strikes her pretty features, making them sharper. She points at the window again. "You have to go."

"I don't even have my pants on."

"You need to go right now," she demands just above a whisper. "My son could walk in at any moment."

Pulling on my boxer briefs, I say, "Lock the door." It was locked last night, so I'm not seeing the issue. That is until I look over to see the lock unlatched. "Shit."

"*Shh.* Keep your voice down. Please." Her hands are in front of me like she's afraid to touch any part of my body but wants to. "I'm so sorry to end it like this." She paces away from me with the back of her hand to her forehead. "I'll make it up to you. I promise."

"I'm holding you to that." I give her a little smirk when she stops to look at me again. It's not the first time I've jumped out a window, but it's a first to hide from a kid instead of a gun-toting father. Tucking my socks into my boots, I grab the boots and jeans and move closer to the window. She props it open and pushes out the screen.

I'm about to slip on my shirt when her hands press to my back. "Go. Go. Go," she insists, practically shoving me out the window.

"Okay. Okay. Slow your horses. I'm going."

I'm about to climb out when she adds, "I had a good time."

I chuckle with one leg out the window. What a time to be alive, but I'm happy to take the ego boost. I turn back, and say, "Give me a kiss for the road."

She does without hesitation, then bats me playfully away with a gorgeous and devious smirk of her own sitting proudly on her face. "You're the worst."

Waggling my eyebrows, I laugh. "And the best you'll ever have, babe."

"I'll give you that." She laughs but then quietens with a glance at the door. When she turns back, she whispers, "Now get out of here, cowboy. I'll talk to you later."

I climb out the window, landing on soft grass that can't be native to this part of Texas. Only rich people could afford this luxury in the hot hill country. It's nice to land my feet on, though. When I turn around to duck and dash to the front of the house where I left my truck parked last night, a little boy —shirtless, jeans with a buckle too heavy for his waistband, boots on, and riding a hobby horse—rounds the corner.

His horse comes to a halt a few feet ahead. Blue eyes shine from the short distance as he stares in my direction. But it's the familiar hat that's too big for him sitting on his head, and a gasp behind me that pulls my attention back to the window. Leaning out through the opening with her knuckles whitening as she grips the frame, Cricket says, "I can explain."

The kid doesn't react to her, so I turn back to find him still staring at me. *What the fuck do I do?* "So I hear you like baseball?"

"Oh Jesus," Cricket sighs behind me.

CHAPTER 22

Cricket

Griffin sends me a look with "help me" spelled out loud and clear in his eyes.

Fortunately, Judy comes to the rescue. On the heels of Jacob when she rounds the corner, shock widens her eyes as they volley between me and Griffin, who's holding his boots in front of him like they'd be able to hide him from being seen. I just slept with the man and know damn well those boots aren't hiding much on his build. "Um . . ." Judy starts, covering Jacob's eyes with her hands. "Let's go to the park, Jakey." She scoops him into her arms despite his desperate wriggles to free himself as he yells about a "naked man" in the yard, much to my horror and embarrassment, and scurries back the way they came.

"Griffin, come back," I whisper-yell to the back of Griffin's head. When he looks at me again, he does not look happy. *That makes two of us, bud.* "Get in here."

"Back through the window?" He doesn't bother whispering at all.

"You're lucky I don't have neighbors." I wave him over, as panic is getting the best of me. "Come back in through the window."

Standing straight up, he thumbs toward the front of the house, and asks, "I can't use the door?"

"No. They're going to be out there in a minute. I can't have you crossing paths."

"Crossing paths *again*, you mean."

"Semantics." I back away to give him space to climb back into my bedroom. When he doesn't come, I dip back out. "Griffin?"

He sighs with a shake of his head as he returns to where I'm waiting for him. "This is a first," he grumbles, dropping his clothes and boots in through the opening and hitting my floor with a thud.

"Well, if it matters," I say, pacing away from him to the dresser to pull out a pair of shorts to quickly slip on, "this is not how I saw it going either." I turn back to see his progress. "I'm winging this, too."

Securing his hands to the frame, he lifts, showing off those incredible arm muscles of his, and works the rest of his large frame in sideways to land on his feet. As soon as he clears the opening, I shut the window, lock it, and lower the shades as if there are spies outside. "Get dressed."

"Figured that was the next step, but thanks." He grabs his jeans, shoving a leg through while eyeing me. "A bit demanding, don't ya think?"

"Um, maybe this is another day at the beach for you, but my three-year-old just saw a naked man outside my window. So forgive me if I'm in panic mode right now." I take a breath because I need one to calm down. "I'm sorry."

Chuckling enough to rock his shoulders but not make a sound, he grins. "Don't be." With his jeans hanging open at the top, giving me a nice peek of the trail that disappears into his underwear, I grin. God, I'm brazenly wanton around him. This is what he does to me. He makes my mind and body go wild with intention. Taking hold of my upper arms, he bends his eyes so he's level with mine. "Panicking won't help us. We have a minute to think, so we should come up with a plan. Unless you already have one?"

"I don't have one." I put my finger over my mouth so I can hear the scuffle of Judy and Jacob heading down the hall to the front of the house echoing off the wood floors. I hustle toward the door and start to open it.

"I thought you would have all your bases covered," he says in a lowered voice. "Seems to be how you roll."

"Guess I should have." Tiptoeing into the hallway, I dip my head back in. "Don't leave this room. I'll be right back." I shut the door behind me and hurry toward the front door. Yeah, no contingency plan was in place for this type of situation. But if I had, it wouldn't have included Griffin climbing out my window and running into my son, *his son*, while escaping after having sex all night. *Jesus* . . . I'm out of control. *What am I doing?*

I can't play dumb. I know exactly why I've been distracted, and even worse, I'm in full control of what I'm doing. Does that make it better? Nope. But even in this ridiculous and careless web we're all tangled in, it's hard to regret my actions. All this did was put a damper on my great mood.

Jacob isn't hard to convince of a situation. He's three. It's the inevitable conversation I'm going to have with him, when the time is right, lingering ahead of us that puts a pit of dread in my stomach.

When I walk outside, I quick step to the street where Judy's got Jacob seat-belted into the golf cart. "Hey," I call before they take off. Judy's been great. I've never had a complaint, and Jacob adores her. I hope I didn't make her feel as awkward as I do right now, though mortified is technically more accurate. I stroke Jacob's face and lean down to kiss him on the head.

His little hand comes around my wrist. "Mommy, come to the park."

"I can't today. Two people are getting married down by the overlook. Isn't that exciting?" Excitement isn't what I read on his cute face when his mouth twists to the side. "I'm sorry. Tomorrow, we'll have the whole day together. We can go to the park and do all the fun things."

I've been lucky. He's never been a fussy baby or kid. But he does have a stubborn side that's developing. I have no idea where that came from. Stubborn isn't something I've ever considered myself, and I've never been called it either. He's his own little person, though, and every few months that pass, he gets stronger opinions. I'm glad he's so brave to voice them, even if they contradict my own.

I lean down once more to look into those beautiful blue eyes of his. "I promise, okay, buddy?"

"Okay."

Looking over at Judy, I have no idea what to say. She must see me floundering because when Jacob gets distracted by the hobby horse he's still holding in his hand, she smiles gently and says, "It's okay, Cricket. You did nothing wrong."

She's only in her early twenties but genuinely seems to understand the war I'm waging between being myself and having a life outside of my son and being the mother I want to be for him. It never seemed possible to be both. Maybe I was overthinking it, though. I step back from the cart and wave. "Have a good time."

"We will," they reply in unison. Jacob looks back and waves. "Bye, Mommy."

I wave, then cup the side of my mouth, and call out, "Bye, sweetie." Lowering my hand to my side, I stand there until they travel over a hill and are no longer visible to me. When I turn back to the house, I look at it, seeing it from a new perspective. I never considered it a cottage by the size, but Mom named it that on the property map, so it stuck. The blue siding and white trim were also her design. Although I do love it, it doesn't feel all mine like it did even yesterday. *How is that possible?*

Nothing has changed other than Jacob getting closer to learning the truth about his father, and Griffin finding out he has a son. Pretty monumental, but why does it make me feel somewhat displaced?

As I walk inside the house, I know I'm jumping ahead of myself. Even if Griffin is suspicious, he hasn't had it confirmed. I close the door behind me and walk down the hall. Dread causes my feet to drag. It will be good to finally get this secret out into the universe. He should know. He should have all along, if I had only been able to contact him.

I open the door to find him sitting on the couch, dressed, disappointingly, though logically I know I'm in the wrong to hope for that under these circumstances. *Shameless.* "Would you like a cup of coffee?"

He stands but doesn't rush to move. Shoving his hands in his front pockets, he asks, "No pushing me out the door or having me climb out the chimney?"

"Funny," I snark, half-heartedly. I wish I could muster more, but I'm worried about how this will go. Do I lead or let him? More importantly, what will the outcome be?

Crossing the room, he slides his hands under my jaw.

"Listen, the kid saw me. No changing that, but he'll be okay. I doubt he'll think about it twice."

"And what about you?" I ask, slipping my hands onto his sides to hold on to him. If for no other reason than I might not get another opportunity after this conversation.

Raising his hands, he says, "I was already damaged goods. So a kid busting me climbing out of his mom's window isn't going to cause any harm." Walking into the hallway, he says, "I take my coffee black."

"I probably could have guessed that." I follow him into the living room, and we cut into the kitchen.

While he sets up at the island, relaxing on a stool, I move to the other side and turn on the coffee maker. He says, "Am I that predictable?"

"No. Just thinking how much I love a mocha latte and knowing you're probably the exact opposite." I scoop the beans from a sealed glass jar on the counter into the top of the machine. With the flick of a stainless-steel button, the machine starts grinding them. I pull two mugs from the cabinet and set them in place.

"Are we really so opposite, Ms. Dover?"

I think about the question. "Not in all ways, but some." Turning around, I lean against the counter to face him. "You're tougher than I am."

"And you get that from my coffee order?"

"No. I get that from knowing you this past week."

He gets up and comes around to the counter opposite me. Matching my position, he leans against it but then crosses his arms over his chest. "You aren't weak. And you're way fucking stronger than I am. I ran away when life got tough." Swinging an arm out like he's gesturing toward someone not here, he says, "You stayed and raised . . ." He sighs, but there's no weight to it. It's just kind of resolved from the way his expression can't seem to settle on an emotion as it flips through its options. "Listen," he starts again, this time his voice is softer, fitting our proximity. "You've been raising your son on your own. That's not an easy task, even with help from your nanny."

"I'm usually off on the weekend, but there's a wedding on the property this evening, so I'm—"

"You don't have to justify anything to me, Cricket." Sounds more serious when he says my name instead of calling me Little Chirp or even babe like he did last night. He called me babe like he did back in Costa Rica, and it was just as potent last night in making me feel like the only woman caught in his spotlight.

Liquid starts filling the mugs, and I turn to check on it. When I look back at him, I reply, "I love him, Griffin. With all my heart." I don't know why I feel the need to plead my case, but I suppose it's understandable since I'm on the cusp of losing him part of the time to his newfound father.

Don't assume.

Don't jump ahead.

"I know you do." Coming to the counter next to me, he says, "We need to talk about where we go from here."

"I don't think it's up to me." The machine sputters to a stop, so I take one mug and hand it to him. I move to the fridge to grab creamer, keeping my eyes in the cool air versus behind me. "I'm here. We're here. Me and Jacob." Taking a deep breath, I return to stand next to him. "We're not going anywhere." Glancing at him, I ask, "Are you?"

"Tell me something."

I angle toward him, resting the creamer bottle on the counter. "Okay?" I ask cautiously. This is where my world changes forever. Closing my eyes just briefly, I hope it's for the better, wanting desperately to trust in him.

"When you said Jacob's father was *kind of* in the picture, did you mean he sees him sometimes? Or?" *He's so close—* standing next to me and to the truth. I don't dare turn my head to meet his gaze. The intensity of energy flowing between us is already too much, though I know he's only curious, fishing for something solid to hold on to.

"Kind of," I whisper with my eyes trained on my coffee, hating myself for chickening out.

"You can tell me." He whispers so quietly that I'm drawn into the kindness of his gaze. "Or you can let me jump to conclusions. I'll leave it up to you to decide when you're ready."

"Ready for what?" My breath lumps in my throat along with anything else that would be a lie if I spoke.

He rolls back on the counter, staring ahead. "Did I ever tell you about my niece, Daisy?" Taking a sip, he drops that out there like bait. His demeanor is so relaxed that I start to doubt myself. Maybe he is only making casual chitchat. When he looks at me, he says, "Daisy is three. She's got this light blond hair, so light that in the sunshine, it's almost white." My stomach sinks. *He knows.* "And these blue eyes that . . . *Well* . . ." He grins while facing me again, showing off the color of his own eyes in the process. "That run in the family."

I dart my gaze to my mug again, drowning in his words and trying to think of every way this scenario might play out. I can't think clearly with my mind playing tricks on me. Setting the mug down, he reaches between us and takes hold of my hand. He tilts his head to catch my gaze, and when he does, he asks, "Is Jacob's father in his life?"

"Yes," I reply, barely audible to my own ears. "He's your son, Griffin."

CHAPTER 23

Griffin

"Come again?"

Leaning toward the beautiful brunette, I angle my head to place my ear in direct hearing distance. Squeezing my eyes shut to clear the haze that's come over them, I take a deep breath. I heard Cricket perfectly fine, but my body wasn't ready. I wasn't ready. *Now I am.*

As if she's been holding her breath, she exhales. "Jacob is your son." Throwing her hands in front of her, she adds, "So to answer your question, his father is now in his life."

"As the naked man sneaking from his mom's window? Great first impression." I walk into the living room, needing room to think. Her steps sound against the floor before promptly stopping at the threshold. Is she worried about me? I don't know how to comfort her and process this information at the same time.

With my back to her, I stare out the front window, watching a truck with a bed full of white chairs drive by. *The wedding* . . . I really fucking wish this didn't come out when we are being torn for her attention.

Locking my fingers on top of my head, I turn back, and say, "I would have preferred meeting him at birth instead of in the yard at three years old."

"I would have preferred that, too, but it's not how it's happening. We're here now. Tell me what you're thinking."

I can see the way she's lodged behind the far side of the island as if she needs the protection, or maybe she needs some distance of her own. "I don't know what to think." I drop my arms to my sides and glance toward the front door like Jacob might return any minute. "Where is he?"

"The park is an area of the property that only the family has access to, behind a metal gate with a keypad. He's safe."

"I'm not worried about his safety. I'm worried when I'll get to meet my son."

"Well, that's not going to happen right now." She moves around, running her fingers over the stone counter and stopping just before reaching the edge. "No." She shakes her head like I've crossed some invisible line she's drawn. Staring at me, she snaps, "I need to talk to *him* first. He's three. He won't understand some guy just walking in and claiming to be his father." Her irritation grows before my eyes as she finally leaves the border of the kitchen and comes to stand a few feet in front of me. Waving her hand between us, she tries to level me with a glare. "We're not just hard launching you as his father to a three-year-old and all of Dover Creek. You and I need to figure out a few things first."

"Dover Creek isn't a concern of mine. I'm not from around here. Remember?" The question seems to strike, causing her head to jut back. Pointing at where I assume is the park buried somewhere on this property, I say, "Jacob is."

"If Jacob's your concern, then we need to work together to make this a smooth transition for him."

"He's not changing schools his senior year. He's meeting the father that he should have had all along."

Crossing her arms over her chest, she says, "I don't like your tone."

"I don't like this whole fucking situation, but I'm doing the best I can under the circumstances." I close my eyes to gather my scattered thoughts, so I can get better control of my reaction. "I know you better than the thoughts that are trying to seize the opportunity. You wouldn't have told me if you didn't want me to be in his life." Her mouth drops open.

"Is that being used against me?"

There's no way I'm telling a woman to calm down when I wasn't calm myself. "No. Not at all." I take a breath and even my tone. "We both agree that this is not ideal, but this is the hand we've been dealt. I want to meet him. That doesn't mean I'm going to blurt out that I'm his dad. I want what's best for him, Cricket. Considering his age, this might be a slow process—"

"That sounds like you plan to be in his life. Does that mean you're sticking around? Because if you're not—"

"I'll stick around."

"You didn't have an answer for me the other day."

We're standing here like two strangers arguing over the last bagel at the coffee shop. "Now I do." I move closer, take each step with caution, not because I fear her reactions. I don't want her to fear mine. "We're on the same side just like we were an hour ago. I promise that I don't want to hurt Jacob, but I won't hurt you either." When I get close enough to reach out and touch her, I say, "I didn't get a chance to tell you how much I enjoyed last night. How much it meant to me."

Her arms fall to her sides, and the wall that was hiding the electric green of her eyes from me slowly lowers. She shifts, glancing down at the floor and exhales sharply. When she looks at me, I get a semblance of a grin, but I'm not going to argue about it. I'll take anything she's willing to give. "It meant a lot to me, too, Griffin. I'm sorry that this has spiraled out of control."

"Life came at us fast, huh?"

"That's what I get for taking my eye off the ball."

I smirk but keep it restrained out of respect. "Using baseball analogies now?"

"Tennis," she snarks, twisting her lips to try to hide the smile that bounds forth right after.

With a shrug, I reply, "I'll give it to ya."

Her stance relaxes through her shoulders and hips, and the smile doesn't wash away, but it does soften. "All this trouble because I thought a wild and nameless night was a good idea." A laugh follows, but it's filled with the sound of regret more than humor.

"Hey," I say, reaching over to tap her hand before pulling back. "It was a good idea if it meant I got to meet you not only once but twice because of it." I raise my left arm just off my side. "And we have a son." The words hit harder this time, like they're finally sinking in. I exhale slowly, but that doesn't alleviate the emotions wanting to consume the rest of me, just as they have my heart. "A son." I drop my head into my hand, feeling the weight of the words. The responsibility. The connection I have to him by blood. My blood. My mom's grandson. *Fuck . . .*

Cricket wraps her arms around me and kisses my head. "It's okay." She laughs gently. "I felt the same. It's amazing and shocking all at once." When I lift to look at her, she says, "And the best thing that ever happened to me."

My chest is so tight, the hold this kid already has on my heart feels immeasurable. How is that possible when I don't even know if he'll like me. "What if he doesn't want me in his life?"

Her smile is soft at the corners, but there's a confidence in her eyes. "Jacob's going to love you so much. What's not to love about a dad who plays your favorite sport?"

I want to chuckle, but she's probably not that far off. "I can get this kid to the majors."

"We'll focus on kindergarten first." She gives me a wink. It's playful in nature but comforts me in a way she's not even aware. The tightness in my chest loosens under her gaze and the warmth of her proximity.

"Kindergarten? That's a year late to be starting Little League." He had a solid grip on that hobby horse. All he needs to do is turn it sideways, and he'll be hitting homers in no time. Well, in about fifteen years. Twelve if we work on it. "I'm starting him on T-ball as soon as possible. When's his birthday?"

She slow blinks at me, already knowing I'm up to no good. "His birthday is May third."

"Perfect. He'll be four before the Little League deadline at the end of August."

"Oh lordy." She rolls her eyes and plops in a chair in front of me. "I think you should meet him first."

I sit on the edge of the couch closest to her. Reaching forward, I cover her knee with my hand. Her skin is as warm as her gaze when she looks at me. There's no fear and no anger. All I see are her beautiful greens with trust lying inside. "I want to tell you something."

"Okay," she says with a hint of nerves in her voice. "What is it?"

"I think you're amazing." Her smile returns, and even a glimpse of what I would have typically considered charmed, but I know that doesn't fit. I'm just not sure how to read her eyes when they look a lot like they did last night at Whiskey's.

She covers my hand with hers. "Why is that?"

"The gravity of what you've done, raising our son and keeping him safe." I smirk, though I try not to be an asshole about it. "Teaching him baseball. Thank you." Tears swarm in the inside corners of her eyes, and this time, she drops her head down as if she's too shy to cry in front of me. Moving in, I kneel in front of her and take this incredible woman in my arms. "I wish I could have been there, but since I couldn't, I'm glad he has you as a mom."

As a sob racks her body, I take her into my arms to hold her, console her, or whatever she needs from me. Her tears fall against my neck while I rub her back. Kissing the side of her head doesn't stop her emotions from coming, but when she leans against me, I know it was the right thing to do. I lift her into my arms and situate her on my lap. Her long hair flows over my shoulder and down the other side of her face. Tucking the strands behind her ear, I get to see this stunning woman I'm in total awe of.

As if she could be more beautiful, her eyes are as captivating as she is. I lean down and kiss her on the cheek. "I have to tell you something, Griffin."

Those simple words shouldn't cause my heart to stop like they did, but they do. Her lashes are wet from crying, her lips licked as she stares up at me. She slowly pushes up and angles to fully face me, making me think I need to brace for bad news.

"I didn't," she says, her voice low as she looks nervously at me. "I didn't teach him baseball."

"What?"

"He inherited his interest in it." She steals a kiss, then leans back again with the sweetest smile on her face. God, it's good to see. "And he's oddly good for a three-year-old whose mom never played the sport a day in her life."

She didn't have to say anything to make me feel better about the downsides of this situation. And sure, him showing a natural inclination toward baseball doesn't make up for me missing his birth. *But it sure as fuck gets close.*

I burst into a chuckle that feels a lot like a weight has been lifted from my shoulders. "That's okay," I say, running my hand over her shoulder and higher to her neck just to settle on the delicate curve of it. "He's got his mom's vocal range. Did you hear how loud he was when she was carrying him away?"

She whacks my arm, but it's all in good fun. "You're the worst, you know that, Greene?" *Greene.* Hearing her call me that through feist and fun has me realizing we're getting back on track the way we should be. It was a quick detour on a bumpy side road, but we're going to make it through this together.

Cricket tries to get up, but I hold her right where she is. "Come on, Little Chirp, don't be mad. I'm just playing." I lean in to kiss her just below the ear, but then whisper, "Kind of." She punches my arm harder this time, still holding back like she could actually hurt me. I bring her back onto my chest until she's fully trapped in my arms. She wriggles but gives up the fight a little too easily. I think she likes where she's at. I sure do. "He also has your fight. And that's something you should be proud of."

Her smile gives her away. "Those Greene genes are

mighty strong, though." Leaning down to kiss me, she brushes her lips against mine, and says, "What a lucky kid." Our lips press together as if waiting even a second longer was too hard to bear. It was for me. This time when she sits up on my lap, she runs the tips of her fingers along my temple, then lower over my cheek. "Do you want to go to the park to meet him?"

I answer straight from the heart. "Yes."

CHAPTER 24

Griffin

Cricket shifts her BMW into Park and looks over at me. "Are you ready?"

She felt it would be less of a production if Jacob saw her vehicle with the "naked man" in it, versus her arriving in my truck. *Too much new all at once.* Watching her maneuver through this situation has left me in awe of how her mind works. She covers all the bases with him at the forefront of her motives, selflessly putting herself at the back of the list of priorities. Everything said back at the house was with the best for him in mind.

I imagine it's a way of keeping all the balls in the air that she's been juggling while making sure he's taken care of. But what goes up must come down, and I'm thinking that her family won't be the ones to help pick up the pieces once they fall. At least not judging by how they were the other day when I met them.

Maybe that's something I can help with. Those are the things needing to be worked out. I'm not opposed to being the one there to catch them when they fall. She deserves a partner after all she's had to do on her own. Can I be that man for her? I should slow down. A lot is hitting hard and fast with curveballs thrown in. I can't just rush first base. Though I could steal it.

I lean forward in the leather seat to get a better look at Jacob, *my son*, from this distance while we're parked. I narrow my eyes because my damn vision has changed since I last had it checked. Whenever that was.

"Do you mind if I take a second?"

Reaching over, she rubs my arm. "Of course not."

He's little. Maybe big for his age. I have no clue about these things. What I can see is that the cowboy hat he was wearing earlier is bouncing on his head as he cuts through the field toward the playscape. I lower my head because a layer of crap has gotten in my eyes, causing my vision to blur. Rubbing the inside corners of my eyes, I try to clear the water forming there. No idea where that came from . . .

Cricket's hand rubs over my back and then holds my shoulder. "Are you okay?"

"Yeah, fine." I look up again as she pulls her hand away that I wish had stayed. "Not sure what that was about. Probably allergies."

"Probably," she replies with a compassionate grin, which lets me know she's onto my act. She's just kind enough not to call me out on it.

Knowing I'm not fooling anyone, I might as well lay my heart on the line. "That's my hat, isn't it?"

She'd undone her seat belt already and grasped the steering wheel, but she sits back, keeping her eyes forward on him, like me. I see she's beginning to suffer from the same allergies I am. She takes a few breaths and then rolls her head to face me. "He knows it's his dad's and wears it all the time." A laugh gently rocks her chest. "Sometimes even to bed."

I was smiling from the moment she opened her mouth. These are the details that I never thought I'd get. She gives them to me so freely as well. "You made sure he had a piece of me without even knowing if you'd ever see me again."

"It's all I had to give him." She grins. It's so wicked that I have no idea what she's thinking. "If I'm being honest, it was hard to give away. I loved having it, but he deserved to have it more."

"You made that hat look damn good, babe." I chuckle to myself. "But it's also really fucking cute on him."

Her laughter is louder this time. "It really is."

When the laughter begins to fade, I ask, "Where does he think his dad is?"

"He's asked about his dad once or twice, but he's so young that it's easy to respond without saying much. He doesn't question it. *Yet at least.* I know it's coming." Glancing at me, she adds, "What will I tell him?"

"You won't have to. I'll be here for him."

"You will?" The surprise in her question is shocking.

"I hadn't made plans, but I guess the universe made them for me." I slide my hand over to hers and hold it. "I'm going to be a good dad to him. I promise you."

Squeezing my hand, she replies, "He's all that matters, Griffin." She slips away from me and pops her door open. I'm still wrangling through her response because it didn't sound like there was room in that reply for us. It's not one or the other, but this is going to take baby steps. We were headed in one direction, veered off the path entirely, and ended up in uncharted territory.

Her door shuts, and she starts walking, waving when Jacob sees her. I give her time to greet him without my interference. We didn't discuss what we were going to do or say, but I think she'll lead us in the right direction.

This playscape is quite a structure. Looks new. The Dovers probably had it built for Jacob, judging by the amount of money they seem to have out here.

An entire park for himself? I wouldn't be surprised, but this is a way different life than how I was raised. I thought a rusty hoe was good fun when pretending I was a knight in a jousting tournament, bending the blade straight out to take down an opponent that was only pretend. Thinking about how dangerous it was for me to be riding a horse without a saddle or any reins to hold on to at eight seems monumentally irresponsible. Running that horse fast through the back part of the rocky property, all for my make-believe adventures, was not the smartest for me or the horse's safety. All because I was hiding from my dad, so I didn't have to do more chores. "This kid has it made," I say, opening the door to get out.

How would I fit into his life? *This* kind of lifestyle?

I have all the money I could ever want, that he could ever need, but I don't understand living through wealth at this level. I'm a guy who had to earn his way through life using my skills, God's gifts, and a lot of stubbornness to be the best.

I shut the door and start behind Cricket, who has a good lead on me. Jacob comes running, wearing what he had on earlier, but he's added a white tee instead of being shirtless. "Mommy!"

Holding back, I wait for her to guide me on what's best to do. I shove my hands in my pockets and watch as she catches him in her arms. She wraps him in such a tight embrace that I wonder if he can breathe. I chuckle, remembering how my mom used to do that with me. Didn't matter if I was three or twenty-three. My mom always hugged me like it was the last and it meant the world to her. I wish I had told her how much it meant to me.

Watching Jacob and Cricket, it makes me wonder if this is my mom looking over me, her giving me a chance to do what I didn't with her.

Cricket kisses his head, and tells him, "I love you so much." I thought I'd considered her position in all this, but seeing them together, her holding him like she's about to lose him makes my heart clench.

Jacob looks up at her with the sun shining between them, and says, "Love you." His eyes land on me, still standing near enough to hear their conversation until he whispers in her ear.

She laughs and then pretends to whisper, but replies for my benefit, "Ask him." *Cute.*

When she sets him on his feet again, Jacob eyes me up. "Are you a real cowboy, mister?"

I didn't think wearing my clothes from last night was a positive, but it might be what gets me into his good graces. "I left my hat in my truck, but these are my ranch boots on my feet." Waggling my belt buckle, I reply, "It's not the biggest buckle in my collection, but this one is my favorite."

He looks at his mom again. They hold a silent conversation before he reaches up and she takes his hand. My heart thumps in my chest as they walk toward me. I wasn't nervous about hopping on a bull at sixteen even though I had lied about my age so I could ride in the Wimberly County Rodeo. *I came in third.* I feel robbed to this day.

When scouts showed up at one of my games unannounced to watch me play in my sophomore year of high school, I hit a homer like it wasn't a big thing.

I didn't even break a sweat when I stepped up to the

plate with bases loaded to bat in a playoff game leading up to the World Series during my rookie season. I did what I came here to do and hit it out of the park.

Meeting my son for the first time has me sweating bullets.

When they approach, his eyes are on the buckle. It's not showy, but it means the most to me.

Jacob punches the brim of his hat up, and asks, "Why's it your favorite?"

"My dad won it when he rode in the rodeo a million years ago."

"It's shiny." He bends down to look at his own. The plastic has no sheen at all. "Mine doesn't shine."

"That's okay. Buckles represent different events." I bend at the knees in front of him and eye it up. It's nothing more than a toy costume piece from a store, but everyone deserves to feel good about their wins, especially when it comes to buckles and what they represent. "See that bull and the rider?"

"Uh-huh."

"This is a championship buckle, buddy. You must be pretty good to have won this prize."

Glancing up at Cricket, he giggles. "I got the prize, Mommy."

"You sure did." She kneels beside him and says, "Jacob, this is Griffin Greene." Glancing at me, she smiles. "Griffin, this is my giggle-box of a son. Jacob." She hesitates before adding, "Dover."

Before I can react to something I have no control over, I remind myself that I wasn't around. There's no reason he'd carry any other name than hers. They're a team. They always have been. But that doesn't alleviate the sting of hearing it, a stark reminder of my absence in his life, and all because we didn't exchange names, something so basic kept me out of his life. There's still the hat. That means something. Holding out my hand, I say, "It's good to meet you, Jacob, or do you prefer to be called Champ?"

By how hard this kid is cracking up, he almost has me believing I could make a killing as a stand-up comedian. Shaking my hand, he replies, "Champ." When he leans toward his mom, he twists his arms around each other and looks at her. "Can I play?"

Cricket slips her gaze my way as if I have a say in the matter. As much as I want to talk to him some more and get to know him, he's three, and his attention span is limited at best. Hell, mine sucks, so I can't expect more from him on the first meeting. With the quickest of nods, she says, "You can go play, but remember, I'll be working so I won't be home until late. Okay?"

He's already running but turns right back around to come give her a hug again. This time, he looks at me, and says, "Bye, mister."

"Bye, Champ." I stand back up with her.

As soon as he's out of our hearing range, Cricket says, "It was short. Sorry."

"Short and sweet. That's all it needed to be the first time." We head back to the vehicle. "It went well."

"It did." She's smiling so I take it as a win for both of us. We get in the car, and she starts it. "I don't want you to think I'm rushing you off the property. Twice." She laughs. "I have to work this wedding and need to get ready. You can hang out with me if you want or if you have things to do—"

"I do. A long list of them."

"OH GOD, YES!" Her mouth is wide open, eyes closed, and cheek pressed to the stone. Steam fills the air in the shower as water sprays down.

I drop my head just above hers, fucking her from behind. With her body pressed to the wall, she begs for more, "Harder, Griffin." Reaching around behind her, she holds me, digging her nails into my back and inspired to do as she pleads. I slide my hands up the slick of her body and around to her tits, taking hold and squeezing until she starts to lose control. Her hands swing back to the wall, pressing on either side of her head and then pushing back at her hips.

Catching my eyes over her shoulder, she says, "Please."

Fuck. That's all it takes. I grab her hips and fuck her even harder, faster, wilder, so nothing exists but the feel of our connection.

She meets me thrust for thrust, and the feel of her becomes too much, too everywhere all at once. "So good," I groan, but I know I can't last. The heat of her consumes me, the sounds of our wet bodies hitting together have my thoughts spinning. The coil breaks, sending me spiraling into my release, and the erratic movement causes me to lose rhythm. But there's nothing more that I want than to feel her coming.

"I'm so close."

Reaching around her abdomen, I find that sweet cherry bud of hers and make it taut with my fingers. A pinch and circle, a tap, and tease. I need her to catch up before my orgasm ends and for her to fall apart with me.

She's panting as I thrust into her, hoping she finds the inevitable slip from the cliff. One more breath, and she squeezes hard around me, tremors rippling through her body and breath. She pulls me into the depths of our release with her.

I move until I can't, until the last of me is stripped away. I stay inside her even though our bodies have stilled, and our breaths run jagged. Dropping my head to her shoulder, I try to catch my breath again. I kiss the nook of her neck and along her shoulder.

When I'm steady in my body again, I pull back, tossing the condom to the floor. "I just checked off the first to-do of the day."

She laughs, sliding against the wall for support and turning around. Wrapping her arms around my neck, she smiles at me. "How many more to-dos are on your list?"

"Nine."

Resting her head back, fully amused, and from the way her eyelids hang a little lower, she's properly worn out. "What are they?"

"I'd rather show you." I slide my hand over her cheek and kiss her. Leaning my forehead against hers, I smirk. "How much time do you have?"

CHAPTER 25

Cricket

STARING AT MY NOTES, I tick each item that's handled. Bartenders is the only item left glaring at me. "Savvy, can you get someone to walk the bartenders through the rosé versus sparkling wine, which is which, and the protocol for tonight when serving each type? Remember when they didn't know the difference? I had to run the bar for two hours that night. What a mess."

I'm ready to tick the box as soon as she accepts the delegation of duty. But her silence has me lifting my eyes to find her staring at me. "You had sex."

"Good God, Sav. We don't have to say everything that crosses our mind."

She laughs and then comes closer to whisper and singsong in my ear, "Cricket had sex." She steps back with her all-knowing grin and points at my face. "Look at that glow." She goes quiet when a golf cart of servers drives by, but as soon as they pass, she adds, "I have to say, dear cousin, I'm impressed that you got you some after four years of self-inflicted celibacy with the same man who rocked your world the last time."

If she didn't look so impressed, I might be amused. Just a bit, but I would have. Lowering my phone since she's clearly not going to allow me the hit of dopamine I get when I check a box, I watch the last row of seats being set up as the florist hurries down the aisle, tying ribbons to the ends of each side. "You've got your facts wrong. Trust me, it wasn't self-inflicted."

"Have you looked in the mirror, like ever?" She comes to stand next to me. If I know her, and I do very well, her gaze is noting the setup over at the bar, though she still won't give me the reward of marking it off my list. "You could walk into a Brookshire Brothers Grocers and hook up. So, trust me, it was by choice. Almost like you were saving yourself. *Aww*. How romantic for someone who has always claimed she's the opposite."

Our gazes slide to each other at the same time. "Oh wow." The notion settles into my psyche. "That's what happened, isn't it?"

"According to you, not on purpose." A smirk slips out before she says, "I'm off to work with the bartenders."

I pull up my phone and check the box. I don't get the instant gratification hit I thought I would, but for some reason, it doesn't matter. I had sex today with an incredible man who made sure to check all my boxes. I'll be riding this high all night.

THE CEREMONY WAS PERFECT. The reception is going off without a hitch. I even got a quick hug good night from Jacob between the two events. Seeing him, even for a few minutes looking all cute in his jammies made my night. When he asked if he was going to see Griffin again because he was nice made my heart melt on the spot. *What an amazing day.*

I still can't stop thinking about the significance of seeing them together at the park. My worries were totally unfounded. There was not an ounce of jealousy. Not one iota of fear that Griffin was going to flip our lives upside down for custody. It's early days, but I don't think that's going to happen. Not that he won't want time with him, or that he doesn't deserve it, but more like it was okay to allow the idea in for the first time. Griffin isn't a threat to me by stepping into Jacob's life. He's not replacing me. He genuinely seems to want to give Jacob the dad he deserves.

I think back to the pizzeria when I met Griffin's dad. He was the nicest guy who had this playful rapport with Griffin. There was respect flowing both ways between them. He's had a good role model. They're still very close and put family first. What more could I want for my son? Happiness is the most important thing I can give him.

I see my brother standing on the outskirts of the open-sided white tent where the party has another hour before closing. I walk over to stand next to him. "What brings you by? Spying for our parents?"

He laughs, looking down at me. "Why would our parents send a spy to check on you, Buggy?" That name is the worst. *Will I never outgrow it?*

I'll assume that's rhetorical since we both already know the answer. "I heard you did big things in France?"

Turning toward me, he scratches his temple and then looks around like someone is watching him. "A few deals were closed." He looks at me, and says, "I'm thinking about moving there."

Blindsided, I rock back on my heels. "Will? Why? How? What do you mean?" We've not always been on the best of terms. He's inherited some of my parents' bad habits when it comes to me, but he's also my brother, and he's gone to bat for me when I was under fire.

I stare into his eyes in his silence. A message he doesn't seem to be able to verbalize is written in the irises. He finally says, "Being born a Dover doesn't obligate me to a life on this property."

"Have you told our parents?"

He chuckles like I told a joke. "They're going to be upset," I say, telling the truth. I laugh a little just to down play the dramatics, though.

Taking hold of my upper arms, he says, "You have Jacob and . . . Savvy—"

"Oh wow. You're giving me Savvy." I roll my eyes, knowing I'm lucky to have her whether I ever marry or not.

"You know what I mean." He lowers his arms and glances at the reception festivities as they do the Cotton-Eyed Joe.

"You mean since I don't have a man in my life?"

The guests yelling, "Bullshit," while they dance and sing is quite the statement as we muddle through our own conversation.

Will says, "Didn't look that way the other day in your office."

He's not wrong. Griffin has captivated almost every thought I've had this week. Before he returned, he was still a frequent mind visitor. The tides have turned from fantasy to reality in such a short time. He's here. He's real and appears to be staying, at least for the time being. And the anxiety I had leading up to him finding out about Jacob has all but disappeared. I'm okay taking this journey with Griffin. "You're right, and I don't want to hide from you guys."

"Why would you have to?" His smile sinks into something more suspicious. "Is it because he's a Greene?"

My heart shouldn't drop to the bottom of my stomach, but it does. "Greene isn't a dirty word."

"It is around here."

The party is going swimmingly. I flip my full attention to him and cross my arms over my chest. "And why is that exactly?"

"Shit, whatever happened, it was long before we were a thought."

"That's the thing. No one seems to know what happened a generation, two, or even three ago, but people around town reference it like it was some great war with no details." I look at him, wondering if I can trust him. Such a horrible thing to believe about your brother, but sometimes I'm not sure where his loyalties lie. And that's the real issue, right? Our family is divided. We're rarely on the same side. Except apparently, hating the Greene family is supposed to unite us.

Jacob's a Greene as much as he is a Dover. It makes me question if that changes how my family will feel about him. Maybe Will is right, and it's time to leave instead of feeling responsible for fulfilling the obligations of our parents' demands.

How has everything changed so fast? It's a whirlwind of emotions. I think I need to take one thing at a time. My top priority is Jacob and talking to him about his father.

There's only one way to see if trust still exists between us. I won't tell him anything about Jacob until it's solidified, but I do have other information to drop. "Will?" When his eyes greet me, I ask, "Will you keep Griffin's last name a secret?"

"Not wise, Buggy. They're going to find out. Wouldn't you rather be the one who tells them?"

"No, I wouldn't, if I'm being honest. Nothing will change their reaction, so my trying to convince them he's a good person won't put a dent in their aggravation."

I can see the moment his eyes get over shadowed by deviousness. He grins, and then says, "You help soften the blow about me moving to France full-time, and I won't say a word about your boyfriend."

Boyfriend?

I've never thought of him as a boyfriend before. That might fit someone else I just started dating, but it doesn't encapsulate what Griffin and I are together. Everything is bigger and better with him. We're even co-parents, for God's sake. The thought alone has me smiling, though that secret is staying under lock and key for the time being.

So yeah, boyfriend just won't do for what he means to me. Or my son.

But this isn't relevant for the deal being struck. His silence is, though. "When are you breaking the news to them?"

"Not sure. I'm taking suggestions."

"Hmm." I glance over at him but don't stare. My brother was a big hit in high school with my friends. Annoying. He's always been the golden child to my parents. Their first and proudest accomplishment. This news will send them to an early grave. Maybe that's his plan. Will always had a slightly evil side to him, which has me asking, "How did you know Griffin's last name was Greene?"

Shaking his head like it's obvious, he replies, "They used to have a billboard off Ranch Road 23. Peachtree Pass's pride and joy, all-star baseball player. Don't you know, it's the home of the great pro-baller?"

"I didn't know that. I don't even know where Ranch Road 23 is. Why were you in Greene County back then?"

"The girls were hotter over there in high school, and I'm not related to them."

I snort. "It's hard to escape the family in this county."

"Or get away with anything."

"Good point." *Same one Griffin once made.* And a billboard? Can't wait to ask him about that. I bet his ego loved that.

Some of the party goers have started taking off their ties and shoes to get down on the dance floor. This is when I usually take my leave after a long day of making sure everything turns out perfect for the newlyweds and their guests. I stand on my tiptoes to look for Savvy, but don't see her. "Listen, I need to wrap some stuff up. I've been here since ten this morning, and we're just past eleven. I'm exhausted. Let me think about things, and let's talk this week. You're not in a hurry, right?"

"I'm not unhurried either." That changes things and is highly interesting. My brother doesn't act on whims. He's honestly the most uptight guy after my father. For him to be making what must feel like a rash decision, my mind lands on a theory.

"You're seeing someone. In France." Cocking an eyebrow up at him, I challenge, "Tell me I'm wrong." He laughs, but it's faker than fake, and all for show to throw me off the scent. "Oh brother, I can see right through this ruse." Grinning like Sherlock Holmes after solving a case, I say, "She must be something special for you to risk the wrath of the Dovers to make this move." I start to laugh.

"She is."

It's then that I see the brother I used to know so well. Maybe he's been there all along, but villainous was never a good look on him. Though I must admit, he played the role well. I take a step to the side and bump against him before nudging him with my elbow. "You got yourself a deal."

His arm comes around my shoulders, and he jostles me at his side. "I knew I could count on you, Buggy."

"About the Buggy . . . let's end that, okay?"

"You hate it that much, huh?"

"With a passion. It's cutesy, but it was never used that way when I was little. It was used to make fun of me."

This time, his side embrace feels genuine. "Consider it retired."

"Thanks." With him contemplating a move across the world to be with someone, it has me wondering if I'd move across county lines to be with Griffin. It's fun to think about, but not something that's on the table. It's way too soon for that.

Is it too soon to see him again, though? Knowing Judy is at the house for the night, I check the time on my watch. Is it too late to contact him? For all I know, he could already be asleep. Selfishly, I'm willing to take the chance. But first, I pull the phone from my pocket to text Savvy, requesting her location.

My brother says, "You go on. I can cover with the crew. What do they have, an hour left?"

"Just under." A text pops up from my cousin. "Savvy is restocking bottled water, but she's here as well. She can handle it easily if you don't want to."

"I'll stay. It's been a long time since I've been a part of the events at the winery. It's good to know all the ins and outs."

I reply to Savvy and let her know I'm taking off. I also text: *I'm going to see if I can get lucky. Again.*

Her text pops up quickly: *I knew it. Kidding aside, you have fun. You deserve all this good coming your way, cuz.*

That built-in family best friend really worked out for us. I type: *Thank you. Love you.*

She replies: *Love you.*

When I pocket my phone again, I look up at my big brother. "Hey?"

"Yes?" he replies with a chuckle.

"Thank you."

With a casual shrug, he nods. "It's good to know all parts of the business."

"That's not what I was referring to." I put my arm around his back because my immediate family of Dovers aren't really huggers. But my intentions are good.

His arm comes around me as well. "I know," he says, his eyes trained on the party. "Now get out of here, kid. Get some rest."

I walk away, feeling good about our conversation. It's the first time in years I feel we connected as humans, as siblings, even as equals. I smile. As soon as I reach my car, I send a text to Judy to let her know I'll be out later. Then I send one to Griffin: *You awake?*

I don't see an immediate response, but then the three dots rolling across the screen have me grinning. A reply pops up: *Wide awake. You?*

I type, holding my breath, and then hit send. *I was thinking maybe we could knock another one of those to-dos off your list. What do you think?*

I just know he's already smirking. I can see it so clearly in my head, it's like he's here next to me. His message pops onto the screen: *How fast can you get over to the Riggins's house?*

Me: *Twenty minutes.*

Him: *If you're speeding.*

I remember joking with him about this very thing. So I text: *A few speed limits will be broken, but all for a good cause.*

Griffin: *For a good cause indeed. We need to knock out this to-do list.*

You'd think we hadn't seen each other in weeks or even months. But even the hours from this morning have been too long without him in them. I send one more text before starting my SUV. *I can't wait to see you again.*

CHAPTER 26

Cricket

Last week, my nerves were eating me alive, turning me into a person I don't want to be. But Griffin relieved my anxiety when he stepped up for Jacob. Without question. Without hesitation. He didn't even ask me to prove anything. He just believed me.

I could justify it any way I want to slice it, but the bottom line is, Griffin trusted me. He made me happy for my son to have his dad in his life, but maybe there's also room for me in there somewhere. For the first time, I wonder if fairy tales really do exist?

Without another car in sight and no streetlights, I squint into the darkness ahead. I have no idea where this turnoff is, so I slow down to glance at my phone and the directions Griffin sent. According to him, the turnoff should be right about here. I stop, spotting an opening in the dilapidated fence falling on the right side, and pull in.

Maybe I should tell Savvy where I am, just in case I

pulled onto the wrong property and am about to be murdered. My headlights land on the back of Griffin's tailgate, and I breathe easier. Thank God.

I park next to him. Before I can cut the engine, he's coming around to my door with a big smile on his face. T-shirt just the way I like it, clinging to his biceps, jeans that he sure knows how to wear, and that hair that looks like he's been running his fingers through for the past hour.

He opens my door and takes my hand. I'm swept into his arms and spun until my back is pressed to his truck. Our lips lock, and we share every breath. When he sets me on my feet, he holds the sides of my face like I'm precious. "Do you know how beautiful you are?"

"No, tell me." I give him a dose of his own smirky medicine.

He grins, but it's his eyes that have me wholly captivated. My knees weaken under his adoring gaze, and goose bumps erupt under his touch as he slides his hands down my neck and over my shoulders. When he takes my hand, I would literally follow this man anywhere. "I want to show you something."

"Yeah?" I ask, clinging to his arm on a double step like a giddy schoolgirl. "What is it?"

"A surprise. I think you'll like it. I hope you do." I catch a hint of nervous excitement in his voice.

Although I find surprises hit or miss most of the time, I have no idea what I'm getting into, no expectation other than spending time with him. Anything else is the cherry on top. But I do think it's fun to see this side of him, the one that cockiness has clearly never met.

His excitement is contagious, though, so I kiss his arm as we walk toward the back of the house. "The lights are on inside?"

"I spent some time out here today. Brought my dad and brother out to check the structure." We walk onto the huge back porch that spans the length of the house. It could easily fit a porch swing and a whole host of rocking chairs on one side alone.

When I look at the other side, a daybed hangs from the ceiling. It looks too new, the wood freshly stained. Sheets with tiny floral detailing line the bed with a woven blanket and pillows freshly fluffed. "Did you do that?"

"Do you like it?"

I stand in astonishment, quickly taking in the effort again, and then look at him. "Did you make that for me?"

"Yeah." He looks down at his feet when he scuffs the heel of his boot along the wooden porch. "It's not fancy. Just some wood."

"I love it, Griffin." Still holding his arm, I lean my head against it, staring at the bed that he made for us, for me. When I glance down, I say, "You swept the porch."

"It was a dusty mess. I can't have you covered in dirt."

I don't know when I died, but this must be heaven. My heart is in his hands, and my love is budding for him. Who am I kidding? I felt the stages four years ago. Every day since we've reunited, it's only grown stronger.

He says, "I want to show you around inside."

Holding my hand like it's the only hope of keeping me from floating away, which he might be right about if swoons come in the form of helium, he opens the back door for me. I step inside, unable to hold my mouth closed. "Griffin." It's all I can manage as I look around the house.

I expected old-fashioned and dated, dusty, and doilies for some reason. I suppose because Mr. Riggins was older. That's not what this is. A lamp in the corner illuminates the living room in a golden hue, bouncing the light off bright white walls and delicate sheers on the windows. The furnishings are simple in a structured design, beige with blue pillows, and yellows to highlight the contrast. The blanket tossed over the arm of the couch even appears to be modern in design.

He says, "I haven't touched the other rooms, but I really think I can turn this place around. My brother said he'll help." I turn back to look because I'm not sure I've heard this kind of excitement from him before. "He's just finished renovating his home a few miles up the road from here. That one was in terrible disrepair—"

"This home isn't."

"No, this home is structurally sound and has solid bones to work with. Mr. Riggins was a home builder back in his day. He had things that homes of his time didn't have, like the pot filler in the kitchen. His wife was Italian and loves to cook." He crosses the room and pats the side of a wall that divides the space from the kitchen. "This isn't load bearing, so we can open it up like at your place if that's your preferred style."

I sit in a leather chair, keeping myself perched on the edge of the cushion. I watch Griffin disappear into the kitchen. There's a light, but it's not bright enough to be the overhead. He says, "There's a banquette. I've always liked banquettes." Returning to the living room, he sits on the couch. "I can see a family gathered around the table puzzling together."

"Puzzling?" That's different. "Not playing games?"

"Sure, we can play games, but it would be fun to puzzle together, too." When he jumps from using the word "family" and "we" when this all started with designing it in *my* favorite style, I'm inclined to ask, "Who are you remodeling this house for?"

"I . . ." Pausing his words, he sits forward, turning his gaze to the coffee table in front of him. My heart starts to beat out of my chest waiting for him to reply. For such a large man, his frame is bent forward, the excitement he just had lost to stormy clouds in his usually clear blue eyes. When he stands, he scratches the back of his neck, clearly choosing his next words carefully. He finally looks over at me and says, "I thought it would be easier for Jacob to be in a home like his own."

"Oh . . . um." I blink several times in hopes of keeping humiliation from burrowing under my skin. "Sorry. Of course." I wave my hand for no reason other than those nerves I thought I didn't have are now running rampant through my veins. "Jacob will love it."

I pop to my feet and drag my sweating palms down the front of my jeans, hoping he just thinks I'm straightening the wrinkles out. They're denim, so it's highly unlikely he'll fall for that excuse. *Why is my heart a little broken?* The more we say, the worse I feel. I walk toward the door, thinking it's best if I just remove myself from the situation. "I'm going to get some fresh air."

"Are you okay?"

I look back with one foot on the porch. "I'm fine."

Outside, I turn to see the daybed, made pretty for me. That's something I can hold on to, something just for me. For tonight, at least. *Why am I upset?* Is it really embarrassment over a simple mistake?

Warm hands cover my shoulders from behind, and then he rubs. "You have a really nice home."

I nod, choking on my gluttony of wanting more . . . *more with him.* "It is. It's really nice."

His breath coats my neck before he plants a kiss on the side of it. He comes around and sits on the bed in front of me. "Then what's going on?" Taking both my hands in his, he says, "Talk to me, Little Chirp."

"I got caught up, that's all. It's fine. You don't need to worry. I think it's great that you're doing all this for Jacob. He'll need a place to sleep when he's with you." A pang shoots through my chest. I grab at my shirt as if that will relieve it, but it still clenches inside me.

Griffin pulls me closer to lean against the inside of his legs. "You're always welcome here, babe. Not only when Jacob is here. My door is always open to you."

Finding comfort in his words, I arch into him and loop my arms around his neck. "You're quite the charmer when you want to be."

"Shh. Don't let my secret out." His arms fall around my lower back before his hands slide down to grab a good handful of my ass. That doesn't even make him less charming. It just spurs me on to want more with him on this daybed.

"If it matters, I think your secret is already out." I pull my grin to the side to keep it from growing. *And fail miserably.*

Squeezing my backside, he says, "It only matters what *you* think."

"And there you go again, making me fall for your smooth lines and stupidly handsome face." I kiss him because when I'm honest with myself, I know that's why I wanted to meet up. Does that make me weak to him? I don't think I care anymore. Life just feels good with him, and I want to enjoy it.

But he pulls back, looking me in the eyes, and says, "You think I'm stupidly handsome?" His brows waggle once, but it's that roguish grin that's driving me wild.

"Devilishly good-looking."

Sliding his hands higher, he drags the hem of my shirt with them. "Go on."

I roll my eyes and chuckle. My chest feels less constrained, and my feelings are not hurt anymore. "Deliciously doable."

"Deliciously doable?" He chuckles. "That's a new one, but I approve. Give me more."

"Hey," I say, toying with the collar of his tee. "Shouldn't you be charming me?"

Dragging two fingers over my collarbone, he says, "I can do that, but I'm going to need you to lie down first."

I grin. "Oh, really? And why is that?"

"No reason other than I want to see you naked again."

I tug my top over my head. "Fine. You win, ya big charmer." I already know I'll come out ahead on this deal. The way he looks at me like I'm an aphrodisiac has me ready to come the moment he touches me. So yeah, I toss my top to the railing while toeing off my shoes. I strip off my jeans and then stand there in my navy blue set I've never worn before.

You'd think I was naked by how he's studying my body like he might be quizzed on it later. I'm ready for him to touch me, or even better, make love to me now. He unabashedly gives me a once-over and then has the gall to say, "Spin for me."

Planting my hand on my hip, I eye him. "Are you serious?"

"Why wouldn't I be?"

He stares at me like I'm the one who's acting ludicrous. "Why do you want me to spin for you?"

"I want to appreciate your form." Using his finger, he circles it in the air. "Please spin." I give in, slowly at first, but then sway my hips a little more and raise my arms into the air so he gets a good eyeful. I like his eyes on me anyway, so it's a win-win for both of us. "Now dance for me."

"You're out of your cockamamie mind if you think I'm dancing for you." I shove him back on the bed, then climb over this man who rivals Mount Everest. "You got my clothes off. You had me spin for you." Straddling him, I lean down and hover over his face. "Now it's my turn."

CHAPTER 27

Griffin

Tucking my hands behind my head, I watch this ferocious beauty go in for the kill. And by kill, I can tell by how Cricket tugs her bottom lip under her top teeth that she's not quite sure where to start. "The possibilities are endless," I say, giving her a wink. "Aren't they?"

"I have some ideas." She's great at bluffing.

Lying under her, I don't bother pretending I'm too cool to show how fucking lucky I am to have this incredible woman almost naked, straddling me like she wants me as much as I want her. That's called winning.

I drink in the sight of her—the dangerous curve from her waist to the swell of her hip and the rounded bloom of her breasts and the way the straps slink over her shoulder, inspiring me to want to follow the trail to her backside. The matching triangle of fabric covering that pussy I know tastes so sweet has me dipping my finger in the bend of her thigh and teasing. With a pluck of the silk, I say, "I like that blue on you."

She looks down at her body as if she'd forgotten what she was wearing. Her vibrant greens land back on me just as her back straightens. "You do?" She acts innocent, but she knows how to do some teasing herself.

I slide the tip of my tongue over my bottom lip, slipping my finger across her supple lower lip. "It's my new favorite color."

Planting her hands on my chest, she lowers to me, causing my finger to slip into the need slicking between her velvety lips. Her lids flutter as she takes a deep breath. Steadying her expression, she whispers, "I think the issue—"

"We have an issue?" *God, I love toying with her.* And fucking her, but I'm trying to be a good boy and restrain myself so she has full ownership over this situation. She's making it damn hard. *Literally.* I slide my knuckle slowly through her folds and then down again, my thumb leveraging against my erection.

I'm already so turned on that I may be as patient as I'd like.

One small triangle of fabric keeps me from driving into her.

And my fucking jeans.

"We do." She releases a harsh breath as I coax her body into submitting and giving me what I really want—her orgasm as my trophy. Struggling to hide how she's affected, she shifts on top of me and digs her nails into my chest. The cotton covering of my shirt is only a thin barrier. I feel the pressure she's trying to hide as she resists falling apart for me. The little vixen. I don't mind a challenge.

On a jaded breath, she says, "A major issue. Your clothes are still on your body."

"That's exactly what I was thinking." Reaching up to tap

under her chin, I raise an eyebrow. I make sure to find her clit to circle it a few times before withdrawing my hand from her pleasure despite it being all mine as well. "Not sure if I should be worried, but you're starting to sound a lot like me, babe."

"What's good for the goose—"

"Is good for this gander." Grabbing her hips, I pull her hard to exactly where I want to feel her. "Would you like me to take them off?" I ask, willing to lead my lovely to water . . .

She slips to my side, which is highly disappointing when it was just getting good. "Yes. All of them." When she rests back on her hands, her tits are gloriously prominent on her chest, the tops rounded and the cleavage running deep. She's a good tease when she slides the tip of her finger along the gathering and higher across her collarbone.

"You know what I want to do to you?"

"What is that?" With her interest piqued, I reach for her, weaving my fingers into the hair at the back of her head and bringing her in for a kiss. Just when our lips part, I whisper, "I want to drag my tongue between your tits, tease your nipples with my teeth, then fuck them until I come." I'm so fucking crass when it comes to her. She brings out the best and worst in me without even realizing how she causes me to react.

The silence between us sends a quake of worry through me, so I lean back enough to catch her gaze. The shock I expected isn't there. Nothing that indicates I crossed a line exists in any part of her expression. "Too mu—"

"It's like we share the same mind," she says without a flash of a lie in her eyes. *Damn, she's good.* Magnificent, in fact.

Running her hands over the sides of my face, she says, "I can't wait to do all the things with you." Resting back on my lap, she tilts her head, and a sweet smile reappears on her pretty face. "Maybe not all at once, though."

"We have time."

"That's what I like to hear." Tugging the hem of my tee, she plucks it. "This still needs to go, charmer."

I tug it off over my head and toss it somewhere on the bed. I stand to strip off my boots and jeans without making a big deal about it. I'm just anxious to return to her mounting me. As soon as I hang them on the railing, I turn around.

A cat who ate a mouse looks less guilty than she does sitting there like she already knows she owns me body and soul. She twirls her finger in the air, and says, "Spin for me."

My boisterous laughter bellows into the dark night as I eye her with my arms crossed over my chest. "Funny."

She shifts, bending one knee up and resting an arm across it. "What's so funny, Twenty-two?" There's not one bit of humor in her question, and her expression backs that request. "Can't handle a girl bossing you around?"

"I can handle you just fine. You want me to spin?"

Her grin grows well past her mouth. "I do."

"Careful with those words, or you might find yourself married."

"You should be careful yourself, cowboy." I swear she arches her back as if her tits put the exclamation on that remark. "Tossing around the word married while trying to sleep with me might get you in trouble."

"Trust me, sweetheart, there won't be any sleeping tonight."

"Prove it." The woman's got some moxie in her attitude tonight. So fucking sexy. Wrapping her arms around her knees, she states, "*Spin*. For me."

My girl is going to play this card until she wins, so I might as well give her a show. Stripping off my boxer briefs,

I get a good grip of my dick and slide it up the length once, making sure she's watching. "You see how hard you get me, babe?"

"Hard to miss."

"You're stroking my ego, but I'd rather you be stroking my—"

"Then spin and I'll let you steal second base."

Every time I think she can't be hotter, she proves me wrong. I'm starting to think this spinning business is a prerequisite. All's fair in love and sex. I spin, slowly, allowing her to ogle every part of my body to her desired content. I have a few things to be ashamed of in my life. My body isn't one of them.

When I'm facing her again, I ask, "Anything else, your majesty?"

"Yes," she replies, reaching around to her back and unclasping her bra. After she slides the straps down her arms, baring herself to me, she waggles a finger to summon me back to her. With my knees pressed to the wood of the daybed, I watch her smile soften at the corners as she looks at me. "You've ruined me, Griffin." Not what I expected, which is starting to become a running theme with her. "I feel empty without you inside me."

Relief embellishes my smile as I climb back on the mattress. "I can help with that." I take her thong down her legs and drop it near the bra at the corner of the bed. With both of us naked, we slip under the covers next to each other. Instead of leaning over and kissing her, I say, "I want you on top of me."

This time, free from any barriers, she straddles me again. Bending to kiss me, she whispers against the corner of my mouth, "I don't want you to wear a condom. I want to feel all of you." I turn, cupping her face to ask, but she adds, "I'm on birth control."

The trust she's giving me, the way she's opened not only her heart but her body for me, leaves me at a loss for words. "Okay." I find one through the mess of thoughts running through my mind. "I cannot wait to feel all of you, babe."

I run my hands over her shoulders and down her arms, warming the goose bumps populating her skin. She lifts, positioning my dick at her entrance, taking charge and sinking down. Easing over me causes her mouth to part, her eyes to bat closed, and for her head to fall forward. She takes me inch by aching inch until she's seated on my lap. When her hands drop to my chest, she steals a few quick breaths, then raises her head to look at me again. "It's so much."

The words could be referring to anything, but I know what she means. I run my fingers over her cheek, admiring how she's even more stunning when we're bonded like this. "I feel it." My voice is huskier, her warmth consuming. "It's overwhelming and makes me crave this connection even more with you. Like I never want it to end."

"Me too." She laughs lightly, then adds, "But I really need you to start moving."

Quirking a smile, I chuckle. "I can do that." I get a good grasp of the plush of her hips, holding her on top of me as I start to thrust upward. Her head hovers above mine, and her tits are bouncing. It's better than any view I ever had, and I've traveled the world searching. That she's here, with me, and that we found each other again makes this even better.

When her eyes close, I say, "Look at me."

She does. Her eyes open on my command as I fuck her as hard as I can. Sitting up, she starts maneuvering on top of me, taking my thrusts and anteing up with a few of her own.

When she moans and then calls my name, she trails her fingers down her throat. "You feel so amazing. So good. I'm getting close."

"You come for me, and I'll be there with you." I roll to the side without losing the connection and pick up where I left off. But now I get to see her face when I push her hair back to appreciate the emotion filling her eyes as she stares into mine. As I drive deep inside her, her body slides higher on the bed. She grabs me, working against the tide, for another hit of passion.

The wave starts to crash over me, her heat engulfing me. I hear her chant my name like a prayer on her lips, her body dragging me to the edge with her. I'm ready to fall but detour to her breasts, grabbing one and kneading before bending to kiss the other's hard pink tip.

Each punctuation of my hips sends me deeper—the passion, the pleasure, the headiness of being inside is too much. Too much . . .

A crush of tremors electrifies her body, sending her back arching and her chest against mine. When her mouth falls open, I take possession and kiss her thoroughly as my savior. I reach down between those glorious legs and find the bud that I know will have her tasting heaven. She bucks upon my touch and groans in indulgence when I swirl my finger over it. And when I flick, pinch just right, and then soothe it, her orgasm rips through her body. Her body grips me so tightly that she pulls me into the abyss with her.

Thrusts become jolts. I pull out and plunge into her deeper, and then again until I feel my release striking. I fuck wildly, losing control as I drive myself into the fireworks. And then I feel peace as I float in the aftermath of gratification.

"Griffin," she calls me from the darkest recesses, dragging me toward the light. "Griffin," she says on the verge of breathlessness. Too tired to open my eyes, I remain in the bliss of our union. "Griffin, you're killing me."

I'm shoved to the side and roll to my back. Turning my head to the side, I force myself to lift my lids. Cricket's green eyes are so pretty that I'm glad I opened my eyes. Her torso lifts from laughter, and she says, "I was starting to worry you had died and gone to heaven."

I hold her hand between us. "I did."

Sweet sympathy coats her face. "Aw. It was pretty spectacular for me, too."

Propping up onto my elbow, I bend to kiss her head, then look out at the property. "I can't see a damn thing, but if you listen carefully, we might be able to hear the river."

She's quiet, lifting onto her elbows to stare into the dark. "I can't hear it." Her disappointment streams through the words.

"It's okay. It's quieter at this point in the river."

Lying her head back on the pillow, she watches me as I settle in next to her, then rolls to her side to cuddle against me. "If I ask you something, do you promise to tell me the truth?" she whispers as if someone else might overhear her.

There's no point trying to guess what she's about to ask. She surprises me every time anyway. "I promise."

"Are you really only designing the house for you and Jacob?"

It's as if she reached inside my chest to squeeze my heart. How do I answer honestly and still protect myself? I don't think I can. But I made her a promise I'll keep. "No." If she asked me to be more specific, I would, so I offer my heart up on a platter upfront. "I was thinking of the three of us."

And then I hold my breath, waiting for her reaction.

CHAPTER 28

Griffin

"I was hoping you'd say that."

I hold Cricket tighter in some lame attempt to make this night last longer, though I know I can't keep her here forever. I'd eventually be arrested. The subtle movement of her smile growing against my chest allows me to relax, settling me into the moment for just a minute longer. "That doesn't scare you?" I prop my head up by resting it on my arm so I can see her.

She lifts her head and rests her chin on her arm over my ribs. With her eyes already peering up at me under dark lashes, she replies, "No. It doesn't scare me. I know you're not expecting me to jump the Dover Creek ship." Her eyes glance at the house, then return to mine. "But it's crossed my mind before."

This is news. Stroking her head, I could lie like this with her all night and listen to her middle-of-the-night confessions. It's unwarranted to grin from the possibility that we could be here together one day, permanently, but not everything has to be a well-thought-out plan. "Something I learned while traveling was to let go of what everyone else expected of me. I had the privilege of money, time, and enough youth to be careless sometimes."

"I was careless once." A cheeky smile squeezes her lips together, but that sparkle in her eyes is too brilliant to miss.

"Tell me all about it."

"Well," she says, moving beside me. With her head on a pillow next to mine, she faces me. "There was this sultry night in Central America. My cousin and I reunited with a couple of other friends who moved after high school for a few days of sunbathing, spa treatments, and relaxation." The blanket has been discarded to the end of the bed, and I'm mesmerized by how the sheet follows the flow of her body. Sliding my hand under, I rest it on the peak of her hip. Her skin is warm like the night air, and as my gaze travels the hills and valleys, I land on her lips. The seductive pink plush draws me forward to steal a kiss before falling back into place.

She licks her lips right after, as if she wants to taste me before it fades. "What was that for?"

"No reason. So it was a sultry night . . ."

"Relaxing for two days got boring, so we went out for dinner and dancing." She chuckles to herself as if the memory evoked it. "I wanted to see the ocean and the stars and to cool off by getting out of that stuffy bar. So we left. I didn't get twenty feet from the door before I saw a god among men walking down the street."

"I like this story."

"Thought you might," she says, cracking a bigger smile for me.

Dragging my fingers over her arm and higher to her

neck, I study the bluff of her jaw and trace along the edge. "Tell me more about this god among men."

Her laughter is heartier this time, with no air of tension or rush to return to her home. She doesn't even appear tired, not that I want to waste time sleeping. "Golden tan and wild locks of hair on top bleached from the sun as if he spent his days surfing and his nights sleeping under the moon."

"I like him."

Winning another laugh from her has me grinning like a victor on the podium stand. She leans closer, and whispers, "Me, too, but don't tell him."

"Your secret's safe with me," I murmur, and mime locking my lips and tossing the key behind me. "I think you left off after sleeping under the moon."

Her chest rattles with laughter again. "Where would I be if you weren't here to keep me on track when it comes to him?"

"He's a fascinating man. Books should be written about him."

"I heard there was a billboard once."

Chuckling, I roll onto my back and stare up at the ceiling of the porch, which is another project I mentally add to the endless to-do list of this house. "*Ah*. The infamous billboard." Glancing at her, I ask, "How'd you know about that?"

"Word gets around these parts."

I narrow my eyes at her, not sure that would be something she'd hear recently. "It's old news."

"It's new news to me." She reaches over and doodles on my arm. When I shift my gaze to the ceiling again, two of her fingers travel up my arm, then down onto my chest, where she scrapes her nails lightly across a spot before gently rubbing to soothe it. "Will you tell me about it?"

"The god among men was much more interesting." I roll my head to the side and look into her eyes. I discover something new every time I see them. This time is no different, but it's something I probably shouldn't have noticed after what happened earlier between us—a future together. The subtle change in green, caught between the electric and the sage, settles in on softened marine that has me craving to dive into her again. I blink several times to clear this urgent pull I have to her as if we've become latched together and destiny is cranking the winch.

Draping my arm over my closed eyes, I start to realize how much I care what Cricket thinks, how much I love hearing her speak, the sound of her laughter, and how she looks at me. I realize how much I care about her.

Tethered . . .

"The moment I saw him, I knew he'd be the father of my kids—"

"What?" I'm wide fucking awake and have been dropped right back the fuck into reality. "What do you mean you knew I'd be the father of your kids?"

Cackling, she wraps her arms over her stomach. "I thought I was losing you, so I thought I'd hook you back into the story."

I relax on the exhale of a heavy breath. "I was here."

"You sure?" A dose of sympathy echoes through her expression. "You looked like you either drifted off to sleep or your thoughts had wandered off." Lifting onto her elbow, she says, "I can go if you want?"

Reaching over, I graze my hand across her shoulder. "No. I don't want that at all. I'm listening." I manage a smile despite the hurricane of emotions destroying any reasonable thought I might be having. It's been a week, not even. I shouldn't feel this strongly about her. It's too soon. *Too fast.*

But a niggling at the back of my mind is quick to remind me that this is four years in the making. There's nothing wrong with falling in love with the mother of my child.

Love . . .

Holy shit.

I'm thirty-fucking-five. Love isn't something I've ever recklessly fallen into. With Cricket, though, I'm caught in her quicksand with no way to survive from going under. Shit. I swallow, the sound louder than intended. She glances at my throat and then higher, and asks, "Are you okay? You look a little pale."

"I'm fine. Totally fine. Never better." I clamp my mouth shut to stop the bleeding, but it might be too late. She's already onto me.

"Griffin?"

"Yeah?" She doesn't say anything, but she does stare like I've morphed into an alien. "What is it?"

As if she's holding her breath, she doesn't blink. And then her body depletes when she releases the next one. "What's going on? I can tell something's wrong. Talk to me. Please."

What do I say? I'm having a midlife crisis because I might have fallen in love with her. *Fuck.* That's not even true. I'm lying to myself. There was no *might have* involved. I've fallen for her. *Whoa!* That's heavy stuff right there. "Nothing's wrong." I lie again, this time to her. *Fuck.* The dam's been broken, and the lies flood like water from my tongue.

This is ridiculous. Why am I acting like this is a bad thing? It's Cricket. She's incredible. I'd be lucky if she felt the same. I force myself to look her in the eyes, for her benefit and mine, when I say, "Tomorrow's Sunday—"

"Technically, it's already Sunday." Her smile is softer, her lids even starting to fade with the early morning hour.

"Right." I roll to my side to face her, and because I like looking at her in our bed, this bed I made for her. "I wanted to see if you and Jacob wanted to come over and we could spend some time together."

There's that night bloom of a gorgeous, flowering smile. "I'd like that very much." When her gaze drops to the floral sheet between us, she pauses but then looks back up as if she's talked herself into something. "Do you mind if I ask him if that's what he'd like to do? I promised we'd spend the day together. I don't want him to think that I—"

"That's fine. I understand."

"Would it be here or . . .?"

"I was hoping I could show you, show you both, the ranch where I grew up." The rush of nerves through my veins keeps my voice low, fearing rejection. It could happen at any point, so my hopes are held on standby just in case.

"Would we meet your family?"

"Do you want to?" I counter, not even considering how my family fits into the picture at this point in the relationship or with Jacob.

She scoots closer and snuggles against my side. With her eyes hidden from me, I close mine and kiss the top of her head. "I think it would be nice, but . . ."

My eyes flash open again. "But?" I ask, staring off the front of the porch where I can no longer make out the trees from the dark sky.

"It's not the right time to share who Jacob is to them or you."

I breathe easier, knowing we're on the same page. "I agree. Doing things at a pace best for him is my focus."

She kisses my chest, and whispers, "Thank you."

Wrapping my arms around her, I say, "I could get used to falling asleep with you."

"We can't fall asleep this time." She pokes her head up. "I need to get back soon."

"How soon?" I begin to shift from her hold and move lower on the bed. "And what can I do to convince you to stay a while longer?"

Her legs butterfly open for me, causing my cravings to kick in again. My dick is already hard before I dip under the sheet and slide my shoulders between her legs, ready to satisfy my hunger. I start with an appetizer of kisses before my tongue dives in for the main course.

"STAY over at the Riggins's house most of the night?" my dad asks, looking up from a crossword puzzle book next to an empty plate on the table when I finally show my face after sleeping well past lunch.

Running my hands over my hair, I seem to think I have a chance in hell of taming its rough stage of bedhead. "Yeah. Got back around three."

"What were you doing?"

Replying, *Cricket Dover*, isn't the response to go with, but I'm having trouble thinking of another fast enough. He looks over at where I've stopped on the bottom step, and asks, "Working on a project over there?"

I step down and walk to the fridge. "Something like that." Tugging the door open, I bend down to see what the selection is today. Orange juice, milk, prune juice . . . I glance back at my dad, water and beer. I grab the carton of OJ and set it on the counter. "It's mine now."

"What is?" He shifts in his chair, resting his arm across the back as he looks at me.

"The house. Since he left it to me, it's mine." I pour half

a glass before cleaning my mess. "I didn't know he'd do that, but I sort of feel my return makes more sense now."

"How so?"

I take my glass and sit at the table. "I can't live here forever, Dad. This is your home."

Setting down the pencil in his hand on the bent-covered book, he says, "It's yours as well, son."

"I know, but you also know what I mean. The other house is . . . it's an opportunity for me to have something here in the Pass that's solely my own." I drink some juice and watch for his reaction.

He pushes the book away and angles toward me, giving me his full attention. "It's quite the gift, Griffin—"

"It is."

"But your mom would say it's a gift putting you on the road you're meant to be on."

She's not wrong. A lot of things brought me back to my hometown, but there are even more keeping me here. "Might as well get some use out of it."

"And keep you busy. A man needs to be busy either in mind, spirit, or physically. All three are best, but one or two keep you moving forward in life." He stands to set his plate in the sink. "Sounds like you have a reason to stay."

Jacob, Cricket, the house . . . *all good reasons.* "If I didn't before, I do now."

CHAPTER 29

Cricket

I KEEP CHECKING on Jacob in my rearview mirror. He's content staring out the window, counting cows, horses, and even the odd alpaca he spots across the farmlands as I drive us from one county over to the next.

"Pizza," he says, pointing at the pizzeria in downtown Peachtree Pass.

I see the pizza artwork on the window and smile, thinking about how everything changed after the game that night. A few beers, a couple of slices, and Griffin Greene make for a good time. I slow down on Main Street to look at the progress being made. A new Tex-Mex restaurant sign is being hung at the top of the end space. A cowboy hat sign dangles under the awning three spaces down from that one. But it's one of the spaces across the street with nothing more than the steel framework that has me pulling off to the side.

"Mommy."

I look back between the seats to see Jacob raising his arms toward me and kicking his feet. "I'm only stopping for a minute, sweetie." I roll the windows down because he likes to wave his hand out the opening. That might give me a minute or two to entertain the vision I just had.

Peering through the windshield at the structure, it's not large, but it's a nice size, and the clearing next to it could add more space. What am I doing? This will never get approved. I'm lucky my dad agreed to the charity game because raising money for other people initially left a bad taste in his mouth. It only got green-lit after a lengthy argument and a ten-minute PowerPoint presentation on how it would benefit the business.

"Hi there." A man's voice draws me to look through the open driver's side window. He tilts his head as if he's trying to get a good look at me from under the bill of his St. Louis Cardinals cap. Small world, or maybe he's only someone who supports the hometown hero? I'm thinking there are many coincidences this side of Dover County. "How's it going?" He stops just a few feet back, leaving plenty of space between us.

"I'm good. You?"

He chuckles. "I'm great. Stopping by to see the progress?"

"Yeah. It's been a while since I've been out here during the daylight to see all that's going on. Looks great."

"Thanks." He glances at the building in front of me that appears to eventually be two commercial spaces in total. When he turns back, the sun is in his eyes, highlighting shocking blues that remind me so much of Griffin's. I'm not catching exact features, but they share some similarities. This guy's size for one. The color of his hair peeking out under the ball cap. His smile has a charm about it, and his demeanor is easygoing. The former is a dead giveaway, yet the latter is not like Griffin at all. I inwardly laugh. Though he's gotten more laid-back with each passing day, and he relaxes the more time we spend together. Last night reminded me of that guy I met in Jaco Beach.

I think it's safe to assume this guy and Griffin are related. Both are tall, affable when they want to be. Handsome, but in their own ways.

He comes closer with his hand held out. "I'm Baylor Greene. I own these properties. You looking for a space to rent?"

My smile is quicker than the question leaving his mouth when I hear his last name. "Hi, Baylor." Reaching through the window, I shake his hand. "I'm Cricket." Probably best if I leave my last name out of this. "I wasn't, but when I saw it, I started getting ideas."

"Hi," Jacob says, his voice so sweet and happy. It's cute that he's such a people person.

Hearing my son, Baylor peers from beside the car into the back seat. "Hi." He waves. Glancing back at me, he says, "Cute kid. How old is he?"

"Three, but he turns four in two weeks."

"That's a fun age. My niece Daisy is three." Sort of laughing to himself, he reveals more curiosity. "They could be twins."

I sit straighter and glance back at Jacob again and then at Baylor. "Oh?" I want to gobble up all the Greene information I can get, but is it wrong to hear it from someone other than Griffin? I hope not.

His hand makes a motion above his head, looking back at Jacob. "Yeah, same hair—that light blond with some curls. But his eyes really do look like hers, shape and all." When his attention turns to me, he asks, "You from around here?"

"Dover Creek."

He's good at hiding most of the descent of his smile, trying his best to prop it up. I should laugh that where I grew up evokes such a strong reaction from the neighboring town. But I'm not entirely surprised since most people I know react the same when they hear Peachtree Pass. What is it with this rivalry?

"So not too far."

"No, not far."

Gesturing toward the building, he asks, "What are you thinking for the space?"

"I wasn't until I saw it, so it's not a thoroughly thought-out plan, but a tasting room for Dover Creek Wines came to mind."

"Hill Country wines are growing in popularity." He glances at the potential shop. "It's not a bad idea." He digs a card out of his back pocket and hands it to me. "If you're interested, give me a call or send me a text. I can show you the plans. It's early enough to customize at this stage if you're looking for something special."

I look at the card and his details, but it's the last name that stands out most to me. Dropping it into the cup holder, I turn back to see him take a few steps back. He looks at the building again, and then says, "We have a lot of interest." His smirk is a dead giveaway for another one I'm very familiar with. "It's not a sales pitch to pressure you. We've just gotten a better response than expected."

"That's good for business."

"It's great for business. Means we'll be expanding after we finish these." He takes another few steps back and says, "Good to meet you, Cricket."

"You, too, Baylor."

It's really tempting to ask, but I'm unsure if I should. Why? What's the big deal? "Hey, Baylor?" He turns back, adjusting the bill of his hat a little lower on his head to shade his eyes better. "Figure since your last name is Greene that you might know Griffin."

There it is—the cocky grin I knew he was reserving for a special occasion. "I know him. Why are you asking?"

"Don't worry. I'm not the law or anything. I'm actually driving out to see him at Rollingwood Ranch."

He starts back toward me, stopping again with a few feet ahead of him. "You got business out there?"

"Just visiting." I rest my elbow on the car door. "He invited my son and me to spend some time with him today."

Eyeing Jacob again, he comes even closer. His gaze slides back to me, and he says, "Griffin's my brother." He shoves his hands in his front pockets, and his demeanor remains open and friendly, matching his expression. But I can see in his eyes that his interest is most definitely piqued. "How do you know him?"

"We're old friends. We ran into each other again and . . ." Leaving it open-ended might be best. I'll let Griffin fill in the rest.

That seems to satisfy his curiosity, though he does glance back at Jacob again. "I won't keep you any longer. You drive safe, Cricket, and say hi to my brother, will ya?"

"I will."

When he walks away this time, he steals a look over his shoulder before crossing the road and heading into the Peaches' Sundries & More store. I roll up the windows but lean forward once more to look at the potential before me, and then shift into reverse, and get back on my way again.

I pass the Riggins's house, slowing down like I did in the middle of the night to get a better look at it in the daylight. It's set far back from the road, but close enough when I put my glasses on to see tracks of peeling paint across the siding and a crooked shutter on one of the upstairs windows. The landscaping has overgrown the beds, and the driveway isn't but two dirt lines worn into the ground.

Most people would pass this gem by or want to knock it down to build something new, even modern. I like the shape of the house, and the style has such a charm that blends in with the surroundings. After seeing inside last night, Griffin's right. The bones are solid. It will be so pretty when he brings this farmhouse back to life. "Do you see the house, Jacob?"

"House," he repeats with a flap of his arms. Knowing it's a place where he'll have his own room and a dad, room to play baseball and a river where they can fish has my heart aching to be a part of it.

I drive on, pondering how it's possible to maneuver through this new relationship with Griffin while making sure the transition goes smoothly with his son. Jacob must come first. I'll take whatever is left after that.

The large Rollingwood Ranch sign can be seen a mile away with only flat prairielands on either side of an empty two-lane highway leading up to the entrance. I drive over the cattle guard, and the rattle of the tires over the bumpy surface makes Jacob giggle. "That's fun," I say, peeking into the mirror at him again. So different from when we enter the winery.

Griffin told me to park near the first house I see. It's easy to find. A smaller farmhouse with a large front porch and what look to be well-loved rocking chairs and a couple of pairs of old boots dropped near the door. The white house looks like it recently got a fresh coat of paint and holds as much charm as the one Griffin's redoing, which, if I'm not wrong, is less than ten minutes from here. I feel gooey inside from him choosing to stay so close to his family. Soon, Jacob will have the bonus of an entire side of family who are going to fall in love with him. Maybe they'll give him the warmth my family lacks.

As soon as I park the car, the screen door is pushed open, and Griffin walks outside. I pop my door and step out. "Welcome," he says, his grin the biggest I've ever seen it as he trots down the steps to greet us.

"Hi," I reply, closing my door and walking around to the other side to get Jacob out of the vehicle. "That's quite a sign."

"Yeah. It's much bigger these days than it was when I was growing up, but so is the business of the ranch and Greene Farms."

He reaches it the same time I do but pulls me just far enough back to steal a kiss. "That's pure evil, leaving me hanging like that."

"I won't leave you hanging for long. I promise." He opens Jacob's door for me. I unbuckle him, then pick him up to hold him on my hip.

"I'm holding you to that." I look around. "So this is the ranch. The sign fits. It looks like a massive property."

"Thousands of acres." He comes around to Jacob's side of me and says, "Hey there, Champ. Do you like horses and tractors?" He nods with pure enthusiasm. "Your pick. Where do you want to start?"

"Horses." I set him down, and he immediately hits the ground running. Literally. I'm not too worried because I know I can catch him, but seeing the wide-open spaces eliminates any concerns I would normally have when he does that. "Hope you know what you've gotten yourself into."

"I do," he replies with a confidence that can't hide his happiness. There's no cockiness, though there is a time and place for it . . . usually after he's made me come several times in a row.

Chasing him, he scoops him up, sending Jacob into a fit of giggles. When he sets him on his feet again, Griffin points toward the grassy field behind the old wooden railing fence.

I let them have a long lead, giving them moments with me near but not hovering. I think this approach will work best. I have no idea. Neither of us does. We'll just do the best we can. I'm sure we won't scar the kid. I hope not . . .

"Carrots," a man with a raspier voice says, coming toward me from the house. I remember him from the pizzeria as Griffin's dad.

"Pardon?"

"The horses. That little boy of yours might enjoy feeding them."

That's when I notice the carrots poking out of a small basket hanging from his hand at his side. "Yes. He would enjoy that. He doesn't get to see horses up close too often. He's not allowed near the stables where we live."

"The Dover estate?" His eyes are trained ahead on the others when I look at him.

"How'd you know that?"

Turning his gaze on me, he replies, "Horses are a business for the Dovers. Our horses work the ranch with us and are what some would cringe hearing, but they're part of the family."

Holding the handle of the basket in front of me, we start walking together. "I don't cringe hearing that."

"I could tell you were good people when we met."

I stop again, this time facing him. "We haven't officially. I'm Cricket."

"Hmm." It's not rude, but that is not the reaction I expected. Maybe I should. This feud between the families hasn't been a part of my life much, but here, dang, the grudge appears to run deep after meeting Baylor and now Griffin's dad. "Cricket Dover, if I'm not mistaken."

"You're not. That's my son Jacob Dover." *Why hold back now?*

"Bryan's daughter?"

"Yes, sir." This man has not done one thing to hold importance over my head, but the mere mention of my father has me falling in line like his little soldier. Wouldn't want to embarrass Delancy either. "Do you know my father?" The only memory I have of my parents mentioning the Greenes revolves around this man's wife, who passed away. My stomach clenches, remembering how distraught my father was and my mom more determined than ever.

"We played some football against each other in high school. School and county rivalry kind of thing. Never officially met, but I'm glad to meet you. I'm Thomas Greene."

When he offers a hand, I shift the basket to my left to shake it with my right. "Thank you. It's nice to meet you too."

He's the first to take another step, so I start walking with him. "Looks like they've met before." Not a direct question, but easy to read.

"Just recently."

I see him nod in my periphery. *Silent judgment?* When I peek over, he's smiling, though. I exhale a breath, knowing I don't need to walk on eggshells, and I have nothing to be ashamed of. "They get along well."

"Seems so."

Griffin looks back when we approach. "Hey, Dad," he says, turning around. "I see you met Cricket."

"I did. Ms. Dover was telling me about her big guy here."

Griffin's eyes shoot to mine—concern and panic starting

to cloud them over. "She was?" He gulps for the entire universe to hear.

I hand him the basket of carrots. "I was saying how you recently met Jacob, but you two already get along like a house on fire."

"House on fire," Jacob repeats and giggles, hanging like a monkey from the rail.

I add, "Your dad brought carrots."

"Just call out the word, and they'll come running," Thomas says, glancing at me with what appears to be a permanent smile on his face.

Squatting down next to Jacob, he tells him, "If we yell the word carrots really loud, the horses will come visit." Jacob holds his arms up for Griffin to hold him. My heart is clenched from the trust he's given. Griffin hands him the basket, then lifts him on top of his shoulders, securing him by holding his legs. Jacob accidentally bangs the basket against Griffin's head. He winces but grins at me. "Okay, Champ, you ready?"

"Ready?"

Together, they yell, "Carrots," several times. The depth of Griffin's tone drowns out the pitch of Jacob's voice, but they work as a team, and it's adorable to see.

A black horse comes from a distance, galloping from behind a lighter, brown-colored horse. Both head in our direction. Griffin says, "The brown horse is named Sunrise."

Jacob holds a carrot and calls, "Sunrise?"

Giving them space, I stand behind them next to his dad. Griffin says, "The other one is called Nightfall." Sunrise makes it to the fence, where they step up.

I don't have a lot of experience with horses despite the stable of ten at the Dover property, so I gnaw on the side of my cheek, a little anxious.

"He's in good, capable hands," Thomas says. "They won't hurt him."

The timbre of his voice is calming, and I find myself gravitating toward easily trusting him. "He is. Jacob's taken right to him as well."

"Does he like baseball?"

I laugh lightly, glancing at him. "It's his favorite."

"That works out well. How about you?"

"I manage operations for the Armadillos and the stadium." I hate how I switched into business mode. I don't have to sell anything, not even myself for Greene approval. I just need to tone it down and enjoy the day.

"By choice?"

"Not at first, but I wouldn't trade it now. I've come to appreciate the sport more recently."

"Is that how you and Griffin met? From that all-star fundraiser?"

Like his other son, I'm tripped up over how to answer this question. The honest response is not one I'm particularly looking to talk about.

"Hey, Dad?" Griffin nods for him to join them. "I was telling Jacob how you can neigh just like a horse."

"Sure can." As he neighs, messing around with them and causing my kid to lose it laughing, Griffin smiles at me.

He mouths, "You okay?"

"I'm okay," I silently reply. Better than okay, actually. When I look at the large grassy pasture and the land ahead past the barn, it looks so much like our property, which isn't a surprise, but the buildings and the vibe feel less manicured, less picture-perfect, and more lived-in. It makes me feel like I can be myself here. I'm not sure I can be when I'm with my family, only in my own home.

The rumble of an off-road utility vehicle draws my attention before I see it coming from a deeper part of the land. A woman with a wide-brimmed hat and a man with his own on his head sit inside the open-topped vehicle. A bobble of blond curls is barely seen in the back seat, and I don't see the baby strapped to his chest until they park and get out.

I'm thinking this is his sister's family. I remember her from her rodeo days and being awed that she was allowed to barrel race. I didn't dare dream of being allowed to do something like that.

She's tall, again, not surprising after meeting her brothers. The man is near Griffin's height but not quite. A little terror of tousles waves her hands wildly in the air as she runs to Griffin. He kneels, and she asks, "Who's that?"

"This is Jacob. Jacob, this is Daisy. She's three like you."

"I'm," he says, holding up four fingers.

"Not quite, buddy," I say, not letting him get away with even an exaggeration. No one likes liars. "Two weeks."

His sister takes hold of the baby in her arms, and comes closer with a welcoming smile on her face. But suddenly gasps. "They're twins."

Oh no.

Everyone starts glancing between the two kids, and then his sister looks at me. "Are we sure these two aren't related?" She laughs, as does her father and husband.

Griffin and I are in a standstill of panic over what to do, his eyes hitting mine. When we are at a loss for anything that would make sense other than the obvious truth, his dad says, "Best to air these things out before they stink up the house."

The smiles fall from their faces as they look from Griffin to me twice before a young boy I didn't notice joining in the fun, says, "What'd I miss?"

CHAPTER 30

Cricket

GRIFFIN LAUGHS, but there's nothing real in it. I roll my eyes while shaking my head, but then that makes me laugh for some reason.

Turning to me, he starts to laugh for real. We're two fools laughing like that, hoping it will throw them off the scent. Other than staring at us like we've lost our dang minds, his brother-in-law finally throws us a lifeline. "Hi, I'm Tagger Grange. This is my wife, Pri—Christine, Griffin's sister." He comes closer for a quick handshake.

"I'm Cricket . . ." Do I tell them and go through the whole hullabaloo again?

"Dover," Griffin states. "Cricket Dover, and this is her son, Jacob." Turning around to find the boy, he adds, "You didn't miss anything, Beckett. This is my friend Cricket and her son."

"Whoa. I thought that was Daisy on your shoulders."

"Silly, brother." Daisy cracks up, then kicks him in the shin.

"Daisy!" her mom scolds while Beckett hops around on one leg like they might have to amputate. "You don't do that. Now tell Beck you're sorry."

"But I'm not sorry." She takes off running along the fence line. "Come on, Sunrise." The horse gallops along with her, which is so entertaining to see. I've never seen a horse do that before.

Christine watches until they near a curve in the bend, then turns back. "I'm sorry, Beck. Are you okay?"

Annoyance produces a scowl on his face before he grumbles, "I'm fine."

When he takes off running after her, his dad says, "Be nice, son."

As if a little embarrassed, Christine closes her eyes and sighs. When she reopens them, she says, "She's wild like the flower she was named after."

I'm not sure if I should fear her wrath or applaud her spirit, but that Daisy is going to love having a cousin her own age to play with. I'll have to make sure Jacob is up to the task, though. Other than going to play gym twice a week, he's not used to the dynamics of other kids, much less ones who kick.

Tagger says, "Beckett's my oldest. You've met Daisy, and this here is baby Julie Ann."

"She's precious. How old is she?"

"Four months and just the best baby," Christine practically coos. "We named her after my mom. She's so sweet and already sleeps through the night, which is a win."

My gaze darts to Griffin who gives me a reassuring smile. When I turn back, I say, "I remember that period well." My gut twists when I realize what we're saying in front of Griffin though. He didn't get the opportunity to be there for his child like we did. His expression is one of indifference, but I've learned he holds a lot inside that he tries to hide from everyone. "Well, I'm glad you guys get to sleep as well now."

She says, "If Baylor and Lauralee were here, you'd get to meet the whole family."

"Oh." I hold a finger up. "I met him."

Griffin does a double take. "You met my brother?"

"Yes. Downtown. He was really nice. Talked to me about one of the available spaces." They all groan in unison, causing my jaw to slip.

Christine laughs. "Sounds like Baylor. Did he get you to sign on the dotted line?"

"No," I reply under a gentle roll of laughter.

Moving closer to me, Griffin sets Jacob, who's still clinging to the empty basket, back on his feet. "He's really good at closing deals."

"No deals were closed today. At least, not with me." When I see Griffin smirk, the gaffe I made glares like a beacon. This man closed a few deals himself last night on that back porch daybed of his. I wouldn't be opposed to closing a few more after hours, except I can't. No babysitter on duty tonight.

Griffin comes to stand next to me, his hand on Jacob's shoulder like it's natural. I don't even think he realizes what he's doing, and I know Jacob doesn't mind because he's still standing with Griffin like he's his new favorite hero. My son looks up at me, and says, "Potty, Mommy."

I look at Griffin. "Do you mind if I take him inside to use the bathroom?"

"No. Go right ahead. We'll be here."

Taking Jacob's hand, I lead him toward the house. Conversation picks up behind us, but from the words I catch, it's casual and jovial. When we enter the house, I do a quick scan, knowing we're running low on time before he has an accident. I gesture toward the hall. "Come with me."

The bathroom is tucked under the stairs. We slip inside, and I help unlatch his belt buckle. He takes care of the rest. I'm used to stark white and marble bathrooms designed by my mother. This bathroom is decorated in gold-hued towels with matching flowers on the shower curtain. A dark brown rug is situated over laminate flooring. Although the style has probably passed by a decade or more, the colors are warm, and it makes the small space feel cozy.

After a quick handwash, we return to the front of the house, but instead of going straight for the door, Jacob dashes upstairs. The fastest kid. Wonder where he gets it? It's not from my Pilates-loving body. "No, Jacob. Come back. This isn't our home." Completely ignored, I huff. I glance at the front door, then back up to the top of the stairs, where he's already disappeared. "Jacob?" I really don't want to get busted like I'm snooping around the place, but this kid's not listening to me.

I'll be quick, retrieve him, and get out.

I dash up the stairs and stop on the landing to whisper-yell, "Jacob, come here right now."

No response. "You're going to get into trouble if you don't come out here." The sound of a small crash has me dashing to the farthest bedroom from the stairs. I push the door all the way open to find Jacob sitting on the floor with a baseball glove close to fitting on his hand. I whisper, "We can't be in here, buddy. It's not our house."

"Glove."

"Yes, it is." I drop down to my knees to take it from him but then stop. Seeing him look so proud as he holds the leather in his hands has me wishing he could have it. Unfortunately, it's not mine to give. I let him play with it a moment longer when I notice a baseball card sandwiched in acrylic knocked over at his feet. I pick it up and run my finger over the front. Griffin was much younger but still sports a familiar smirk as he's caught in action, throwing a ball.

"It's my rookie card." Griffin's voice carries from the doorway, but there's no anger attached to it. "Might be worth some money one day or, like me, left with no value at all."

I stand and go to him. With the card still in hand, I glance down at it and meet his gaze again. "You have more value than a card ever could."

"Tell that to the collectors."

Poking him in the chest, I reply, "I'm telling that to you."

He slides his hands around my waist before quickly retreating when his eyes land on Jacob again. Shifting around me, he sits on the floor, leaning against the bed, and pulls Jacob onto his lap. With a little tug here and an adjustment to twist the glove so it's on correctly, he says, "Fits like a glove."

"Was that your glove?"

"When I was his age. It's just memorabilia my mom saved that's collecting dust. He can have it if he wants."

I set the framed card on the desk under the window and sit on the edge of the bed, my leg bumping up against his bicep. "We can't take that."

"Why not? It's going to sit here, and the leather will just crack even more if it doesn't get conditioned and used like it's meant to be."

Jacob hasn't made a peep, sitting contentedly on his lap and playing with the glove. I rub Griffin's shoulder, and say, "That's very generous of you." But as much as he wants to shrug it off like it's nothing, I know what he's doing. It's not about being conditioned or used. It's about giving his son a piece of his legacy, a part of him. Tears start to fill the corners of my eyes, so I tilt my head back in a fruitless attempt to force them to return to where they came from.

It doesn't work. One slips down, and another slides down the opposite cheek. I wipe them away with the inside collar of the shirt I'm wearing and then look around the room. Trophies line two shelves hanging on the wall next to the window, ribbons with medals adorning the bottom dangle from hooks underneath. A column of baseball bats lines the wall from ceiling to floor in one area of the small room. And cowboy hats for all occasions appear to float on the light blue painted wall facing the bed.

The bed. I actually laugh from the size of it, which feels so good after having my heart squeezed from the loft of what I've witnessed between them. "You don't even fit on this bed, and you've been sleeping here?"

"I've been sleeping here because it's the only bed I have." He looks up at me behind him, and says, "Anything bigger wouldn't fit in this room, so I make do like I always have."

"You can stay at mine." The words came before I had a chance to think them through, my heart just throwing out an offer like it's the one in control of my head.

Jacob gets up, leaving the glove for Griffin to have. He rummages through a bookshelf and then climbs onto a box to investigate the top of the desk. Griffin gets off the floor and comes to sit next to me. With his hands in his lap and his shoulders slumped forward, he's still taller than I am. "Is that a real offer?"

Logically, I shouldn't have made it without thinking it through, but I can't manage to regret saying it anyway. "It's a real offer, Greene."

With Jacob busying himself with coins he found in a jar, Griffin leans over and kisses my cheek. "I appreciate it, Dover. I'll think about it."

"Ouch."

"No ouch," he says, laughing. "I just don't know if you understand what you're getting yourself into."

"So the rejection is for my benefit?" Now I'm laughing.

"I'm a Greene. The enemy of your people. I probably won't be welcomed with open arms."

I open my arms wide for him. With a grin bigger than the Grand Canyon, he leans over, and I embrace him. "It's just you and me. No enemies involved." I kiss the back of his head as he complains about having to get up. "We should get back to your family."

"Nah." He sits. "They've already gone about their own business. My dad went with my sister, so we have the house to ourselves."

Darting my gaze to the little one who's content to count money that he has no idea how to count, I point. "Almost to ourselves."

Griffin gets up and scoops Jacob into his arms, then tosses him over his shoulder. Now staring at me as he's being carried away, he giggles. "Come on, Mommy."

I get it and cross the small space to the desk. Bending down, I look at his rookie card once more before my gaze spots a framed photo hidden in the back corner by a box of tissues. I slide it aside and smile, seeing him with his mom posing in front of a baseball field. She's very pretty. Her eyes are bright like his, and her hair color is even similar. It's easy to see why my father was once in love with her.

"You coming, Cricket?"

"Yeah." I shift the box back in place and scurry out the door. They're already downstairs when I reach the landing. Coming down, I hold the railing and catch a glimpse of them in the living room.

Sitting on the couch, Griffin shows our son a puzzle

piece and places it in its rightful spot. "This is called puzzling."

Leaning against his leg, Jacob rests his forearm on Griffin like he's known him for years. "I puzzling at home."

"You puzzle? No way," Griffin exclaims like this is the coolest news he's ever heard. "What kind of puzzles do you have?"

It's tempting to jump in and respond for him or whisper in his ear to remind him, but these conversations are important for them to have just the two of them, even if he stumbles on his words. Jacob looks at me for answers. I nod, and say, "You got this, buddy."

He turns back to Griffin. "States and animals."

"Whoaaaa, so neat. Will you show them to me the next time I'm over?" Jacob nods, grinning with pride. When Griffin picks up a piece from the table, he says, "I used to puzzle with my mom." His voice is lower, his tone reflective. I can't get a good look at his eyes, but this giant of a man becomes a little boy again when he shares stories of childhood. He was forced to grow up faster than he should have, yet his parents aren't to blame. We do what we can to survive, but his mom's death haunts him in a way that I'm not sure he'll ever escape.

I have no idea if he'll be open to talking about that, but he makes me want to try.

"My mom doesn't puzzle," Jacob blurts out, then laughs. Well, at least he didn't lie.

Griffin tries to appear in total concentration mode, but I see the grin on his lips when he asks, "What do you think about puzzling being one of *our* things, Champ? It can be something we do together, the two of us."

"I want Mommy to puzzle."

"Your mommy can puzzle with us." He glances at me. "I hope she does."

When Jacob runs around the table to throw himself around my leg, his head drops back to look up at me. "We can puzzle together," he says with exuberance. "Griffin said so."

I bend down, wrapping my arm around his back. When I catch Griffin watching us with a sincere smile on his face as if he feels lucky to witness this, my heart beats faster and my pulse races. This feels real with him. Is it logical to fall this fast? Not one bit. But why deny something that feels so right? I don't want to live like that. I want to puzzle with him and lie in a daybed in his arms outside at night. I want—I take a breath, picking up Jacob and holding him in my arms. Although I've had family around my whole life, staff, and coworkers that I know better than my own father, for the first time, I don't feel alone.

Hugging Jacob to me, candidly, I smile just for Griffin, sharing my heart the only way I can right now—quietly, but fully. "The family puzzle night is making a lot more sense now."

He says, "It's a tradition I'd like to carry on."

I nod and shift more to the edge of the living room. "I think it's a great idea."

As if drawn by some imaginary rope pulling him closer, he gets up and comes to me. He rubs Jacob's back and then my arm. His eyes dip to my lips, and I can only assume he wants to kiss me as much as I want to feel his lips against mine. "Thanks for being so supportive. Of . . ." His gaze shifts to the mop of curls on Jacob's head, which he scrubs his hand over playfully. "This and of me."

Jacob turns to cling to Griffin, who happily takes him without hesitation.

I say, "You make it easy to support you." No decisions have been made about when we'll tell Jacob about Griffin's role in his life. But it doesn't seem as earth-shattering as I once believed. I'm not losing my son. He's gaining a part of who he is—an entire history and an amazing family. I smile, seeing them together, but Griffin has made it clear that it's not only about the two of them. It's the three of us, together. There's power in that, strength to help me maneuver through any confusion, and to stand up for what I want for the first time in my life. I've never felt so confident in the direction I'm heading. With him, we're on firm ground as we begin this journey.

I couldn't ask for more.

Although I'm not naive. *The real battle still lies ahead.*

CHAPTER 31

Griffin

One week later . . .

"My dad knows how to do everything." Beckett's voice carries up the ladder where I'm holding a nail to a board.

I look down. "Your dad learned by just doing what needed to get done. Hands-on experience is the best teacher." He only has a hand holding onto the ladder, and if we're being honest, he's using it to rest against more than to secure my safety against falling. It's a good confidence builder to think you are trusted to save a life. My dad used to do the same for me when I was young. I'm not sure Beck needs a confidence boost, but since he's here, I'm putting him to work. I hammer the new board into place, adding nail gun to my list of things to purchase, and start down the ladder. Landing on my feet, I ask, "Did your friend Macon get picked up?"

"Yeah, his mom got him."

"That was nice of you guys to offer to help." And by help, they went out in the boat, hiked a good fifteen acres up the river, explored a cave they claim had something with glowing eyes living in it, and panned for gold in a ground full of granite. I remember those days from when I was younger. Baylor and I used to have so much fun on random adventures and getting into trouble.

He shrugs. "We got nothing better to do."

I drop my hammer into the tool belt hanging around my hips as we walk out from the house, stop, and look back at the progress made today. Crossing my arms over my chest, I stare at the two new siding boards I put in place. You'd think I built the home from scratch by the pride I feel inside. "What do you think?"

With his arms crossed over his chest, Beck mimics me as he studies the house. "I think you have a long way to go, Uncle Griffin."

Ruffling his hair, I reply, "I agree." We head back to the porch to take a water break. After digging out two bottles from the cooler, I sit on the landing of the porch, settling my feet three steps below.

He comes to sit but scoots to lean against a post.

"Got your eye on any girls at school?"

Beckett laughs, but I see his cheeks redden a little too. "Nah. I'm too young for dating. That's what my dad says."

"Your dad is right. Just have fun with your friends and leave those troubles for after high school."

"Is that what you did?" He rolls the bottle over his forehead. He's a funny kid, out here looking like he's been sweating out at a construction site.

"I made mistakes and dated girls I probably should have steered clear of like my mom warned me. Trust your parents. They have good instincts." I rest my palms on the floorboards, scanning the property all the way to the river's edge.

Weeks ago, I had no direction. Now, I'm rebuilding a house for a life I never imagined I'd be lucky enough to have. Some would call Jacob an accident or a mistake. I call him the anchor I need to ride out the rough seas of my life. The sails that have given me direction on sunny days. Cricket, that's easy. She's the captain steering this ship. I glance over at the daybed, grinning just thinking how sexy she'd look in a captain's cap and nothing else.

The role of a ship's engineer is the one I gravitate most toward. None of us works without the other to get to our destination. We're a team now.

"Hey, Beck, see the Cypress at the water's edge? The biggest trees other than the oaks?"

"Yeah."

"When I was traveling, it didn't matter where I was, I could close my eyes, and I'd be flying off a rope swing into the river or climbing up the trunks and perching up on the branches for hours." I glance at him. "I once fell asleep cradled in the legs of the roots. My parents couldn't find me. Scared the living daylights out of them."

"What happened?"

"The police were at the house when I showed up. I totally missed all the commotion. Those trees are home to me."

"Was that a lesson I'm supposed to learn?"

Chuckling, I shake my head. "Nope. Just sharing a bit of my childhood with you, buddy."

The relief of "not learning" creates a smile on his face. "Baylor always tries to wrap these big life lessons into his stories."

"Ah." I rest my arms on my legs when I lean forward. "I

get it." I didn't take my brother as the purveyor of deep truths, but like the rest of us, he's changed, and good for him for helping our nephew. "Do you like baseball?"

"I'm going back to soccer. Everyone here is too intense about the sports they played. I just want to play for fun."

I start to chuckle again. "Yeah, we take our sports seriously around here." I don't know why I'm about to ask, except that I'll get an unbiased opinion, because if this kid is one thing, it's honest to a fault. "Jacob's a cute kid, huh? I was thinking about asking his mom if we could host his birthday party at the ranch." His silence draws my attention to him. "What's up?"

He looks at me, but then his gaze goes to his shoes. "I overheard Grandpa saying that's a Greene if he ever saw one." Guess letting it drop did us no favors. It only allowed their imaginations to fill in the blanks. "Is Jacob a Greene?"

Beckett is a Grange after his dad, my sister being his stepmom, but he's a Greene in the ways that run deeper than blood. Like the rest of them, though, he's not dumb. How do I answer this without starting a field day of family nonsense I'm not ready to address? "He's . . ."

"Is he your son?"

"Yes." My response isn't rushed, but I don't want to beat around the bush. "Jacob's my son."

"Why doesn't everyone know? Why didn't you tell them?"

The details of the story aren't meant for a kid his age. It's not something I need to put into his head or have him asking more questions than are necessary. "I need a little time to work through a few things before telling the family. Can you keep this conversation between us?" I hold out my hand for a fist bump.

He bumps right back. "Yep." After sipping on his water,

he says, "It's Daisy. She was the giveaway. They do look like twins." He takes another chug and then caps the bottle again. "She'll like having him around."

"Instead of following you everywhere?"

"We have fun sometimes, but I want to do dude stuff, too."

"Dude stuff" makes me want to grin, but I don't because I want to be a trusted sounding board for him. We all need that, and sometimes he won't want to talk to his dad. "Is that why you wanted to get dropped off here after school?"

"Yeah."

I tap the toe of my boots against his sneaker. "You can come over anytime." Standing, I take another long drink of water. I look at the pile of wood I bought a few days ago, which hasn't gotten smaller despite my progress. "Want to help me replace a few more boards, or are you ready to go home?"

"Home. It's too hot out here."

Yep, honest to a fault. "Wait until summer." We start down the steps to the truck. "I'll take you home, kid."

Trailing me, he says, "You didn't ask, but I figure I'd tell you since I got a good sense of the situation."

I lean against the driver's side of the front of my truck to look back at him. "What situation is that?"

"Christine says I have a knack for seeing situations for what they are instead of the front people put on. I called it with her and my dad before they knew they were meant to be together. Lauralee and Baylor were too easy to predict. They were the worst at hiding their feelings. Basically, they couldn't."

My jaw has dropped. "You have a sixth sense for predicting relationships?"

Raising his hands, he says, "I don't question my gifts. But

I will tell ya . . ." He stops to put his weight against the truck as he looks at me just over the top. It's a big truck.

I legit have no clue where this is going. "You casting a prediction for me? I'll take all the help I can get." I laugh, waiting, the suspense killing me.

"I know why you got upset when I killed that bug."

I don't know what his ambitions are in life, but he's going far in whatever he decides to do, which apparently isn't sports. Two thumbs down on the no pro ball in his future, though. "Why'd I get upset?"

"Because she's your secret ingredient."

"Who is?" I know who, but I still play dumb because it's weird to have an eleven-year-old calling out your personal life like that.

"Cricket. Grandma Grange said that when you find it, you'll know it. She's the love that's been missing from your dish."

"And my dish is my life?"

Waving his hand carelessly as he moves to the truck's door, he replies, "Something like that. It's a dash of this and a pinch of that, but I'm not sure how it all works. Cricket's the ingredient you've been missing." He opens the truck and climbs inside.

I might need a few minutes to process what this kid just laid out for me. The success of his prediction continues. Welp, good to know the universe is behind us. After I drive Beckett home, I get back in the truck, still thinking about what he said. My sister is right about his abilities. It aligns the thoughts I was already having but hadn't revealed to anyone. Before I head back to the house, I text my girl: *Want to bring Jacob over for dinner at the house tonight?*

It's early, just after four, so she's probably still working. A message pops up along with my smile: *We'd love to.*

CHAPTER 32

Cricket

"Wait for Mommy, Jacob?"

Famous last words. He's holding his cowboy hat on his head, making a mad dash around the back corner of the house before I've had a chance to lock the vehicle. I rush after him since Griffin has made this house his mission, and the back has become a construction zone.

Before I pass his truck, Griffin steps out with Jacob already in his arms. "Missing something?"

I smile from just everything. "Seems you found it."

"I think he found me. I was up on the ladder. He was three rungs up before I had to jump off and grab him to impede his progress." He picks Jacob up under his arms and holds him out to the side like a stinky shoe just so he can give me a kiss without him catching us.

I giggle and then lick my lips before he brings Jacob around to face me again. Setting him down, he says, "Hey, Champ, I found some old spray paint in the garage." He glances at me. "I was thinking we could do art on this wood I pulled off the wall. What do you think?"

"I think he'd love it."

Turning back to Jacob, he says, "Your mom said yes."

"Yes!" Jacob fist pumps the air and then bumps Griffin's hand. He grabs Griffin's hand and starts tugging him toward the back again.

What a goofball Griffin is, acting like this kid is yanking him. It's so adorable that my heart melts. Following them, I take it wide around the back to get a look at the changes. My feet come to an abrupt halt, almost jerking me forward. New boards are littered throughout the back siding, the shutters are down, paint colors are being sampled at the far end, and the porch is covered in fresh stain. "How did you get so much done in the past few days?"

His casual shrug doesn't cover his tremendous progress. "I have time on my hands."

"Are you going to renovate this whole house by yourself?"

Standing a few feet away, he turns back to look at the house again as if he's not decided. "I'll do what I can. I'm not an electrician or plumber, and I don't plan to acquire those skills. I prefer to leave those things to the professionals. Baylor, Tagger, my dad, and even Beckett have been out here to survey the damage and offered to help with the other stuff."

I walk over to where they are. Griffin has boards laid out flat in the grass, rows stacked on top of each other. Spray cans line one side and are color coordinated from brightest to darkest. I won't mention it, but I do think it's cute that he did that. "I love how your family does so much for each other."

"That's what families d—" The comment was so natural

and off the cuff, but he catches himself, and I know why. My family doesn't do that. Jacob's Dover side doesn't. It makes me grateful to connect with Jacob's other side of the family even more. Not that I needed a reason when I have Griffin right in front of me.

Now if I can only convince him to start staying over at mine at night . . . I get his hesitation. My family. Enough said.

Kneeling away from me, he sits back to rub the back of my leg. "Sorry."

"You don't have to apologize. You're not wrong. That is what families should do. Instead, mine is more divided than ever." Do I drag our business out into the open? It's not something I've ever done before. The Dovers are vaults when it comes to family secrets. It's probably why we know so little about each other. So freaking sad. Another reason to be so thankful I have Savvy in my life. We can tell each other anything. Though I haven't talked to her about my brother and his plans. No particular reason, other than I was waiting to hear from him again. He doesn't seem to be making plans to jump ship yet, so I'm not rocking this boat by bringing it up.

"Orange," Jacob says, getting up from the grass and running to grab the can. He hands it to Griffin. "Show me." He's having a ball. I'm just happy for the distraction.

Griffin clips something to the nozzle and hands it to Jacob. "You squeeze this handle with both hands, and it will spray paint everywhere. Remember what I told you when we came over here?"

"Keep the paint on the canvas. What's the canvas?"

"The wood." Griffin taps it. "This is the canvas. Okay?"

Jacob squeezes, hitting him right on the arm. "Not the

canvas," he says, his mouth flattening as he turns slowly away as if Griffin won't notice.

Looking up at me, Griffin says, "It's just an old undershirt." But he sounds like he's trying to convince himself more than me. He moves next to Jacob again and says, "This time, paint the wood. Not your da... not your friends."

"Not my friends." I don't like the devious look I get from Jacob before he puts both hands on the lever again. "Not your friends. Not your Mommy." *Oh no.* I grab his hat, not wanting it ruined by paint, and rush to the porch to set it down. I don't mind the distance when paint is involved. He squeezes, spraying orange paint exactly where it should go —on the wood.

"Good job, buddy," I say, moving in a little closer again. He doesn't stop, now getting the hang of it and letting his creativity flow.

Griffin joins him with royal blue on his side of the wood, but instead of a design, he writes Jacob's name. The paint sputters on the C and sprays air after he gets a barely readable O. He stands and steps back next to me. "It's old paint. I'll just use another..."

I watch as he walks up to the wood again, standing with his hands planted on his sides. Jacob's having way more fun, especially since no one is monitoring the situation. He's doing just fine, so why ruin the good time?

But Griffin, on the other hand, dips his head down and rubs the bridge of his nose. I move in behind him to rub his back with my hand and quickly place a kiss there. "What's wrong?"

"His name." He turns back to face me.

Jacob drops the can. "I want a new color."

Griffin's eyes are set on mine when he replies, "Pick any color you want, Champ."

"You named him Jacob."

I don't get it. The question is lost in translation between us. "Yes." *Ohhhh*. My eyes dart to the wood where his name remains unfinished. JACO.

When I look back at him, he says, "You named him Jacob for Jaco Beach."

"The details sometimes slip away from me." It's not a reason to be upset, and he's not, but I do feel the need to explain myself. "I was . . . alone. I felt so alone. Even with my cousin by my side at the hospital, I wanted you there. I was running every moment we shared, every word you said through my mind. I had your hat sitting on my belly when they were wheeling me to the birthing room. When they asked me what his name was, I said Jaco but corrected myself. His name is Jacob. Jacob Justin."

Jacob is tugging on Griffin's jeans so he'll put the lever on the can of yellow paint. He bends down and swaps out the contraption, but I see him stop to look at Jacob, to really look into his son's eyes. "There you go."

"Thanks." His voice is sweet, but it was how he looked at Griffin, a bond already formed, that has my heart racing. I love them together.

"You should tell him, Griffin."

He stands, the minutest shake of his head backs the confusion populating his eyes. "Tell him what?"

"Who you really are."

His gaze whips back to our son before it meets mine again. "Are you sure?"

"It's not up to me anymore. If it feels like the right time to you, I support you."

Searching my eyes for any doubt comes up empty for him. Reaching out to take my hand in his, he kisses my palm, and with glossy eyes, he whispers, "Thank you."

The feel of his lips lingering on my skin causes goose bumps to ripple up my arm. "You don't need to thank me for you telling him what he should have known all along."

"I was thanking you for giving me a child. It's not something I envisioned ever having, but now that I do, I can't imagine life without him."

His realization is one I had a long time ago. My life is better because Jacob is in it. Now I get to spend time with his father. Life is good. "It's funny how that works."

Not bothering to hide us anymore, he kisses my cheek, then turns back around. "Hey, Champ, I was wondering if I could talk to you for a few minutes."

"Sure." He's squeezing the lever so hard, but nothing is coming out. "It's broken."

"We have more, but how about we go talk on the porch?" Jacob takes his offered hand, and the two of them walk to the back of the house. Griffin holds the hat so Jacob can sit next to him.

I wait for it because I know it's coming. Like everything else, one thing leads to another, and secrets don't stay buried forever. His gaze slides up from the hat. He says, "Jacob Justin."

Cutting through the grass, I think back to so many moments when that hat kept me company and filled in for the partner I didn't have. I wore it in the middle of the night while feeding my baby. I took photos of him on his first birthday wearing it. "I looked at that label more times than I can remember. Justin. The brand just came to mind when I needed a name that meant something. That hat was the only tangible thing I had from our night together, the only souvenir I got." I laugh. "Other than Jacob."

"I not souvenir," he states defiantly even if not said

perfectly. He doesn't even know what a souvenir is, which makes me laugh a little louder.

"You're my baby."

"I'm big boy. Almost," he says, holding up four fingers again.

Griffin asks, "Almost how old?"

Turning to look up at him, Jacob grins, the little goose. "Four."

"Yeah, four. Exciting stuff." He looks at me and laughs. "They're quality hats." Griffin's smile spreads like wildfire across his face as he sets the hat on his son's head. "I was wondering if you had plans for your birthday next weekend?" He glances at me.

I reply, "We were having cake and ice cream at the house with Savvy and Judy."

Jacob's eyes brighten. "Cake!"

Griffin asks, "What do you think about having a little party at the ranch with my family?"

"I want that." Jacob hops on his butt down the steps and then climbs back up. "Cake with Griffin."

"I can't wait," I say, sitting on the other side of Jacob. My eyes meet Griffin's over his head, and I nod. He doesn't need the go-ahead. He already has it, but I just want him to know I'm here to support him as well.

Griffin wraps his arm around Jacob's shoulders and brings him into his fold. "I have some great news to share with you, Champ."

CHAPTER 33

Griffin

BIG BLUE EYES that match my own, my mom's, my dad's, brother's, sister's, and nieces' stare into mine with all the hope in the world shining in them. The moment I met this kid, my son, my kid, I felt an indescribable bond. I think he feels the same as he rests his hand on my leg. *Trust.*

I look at Cricket, who has her gaze directed toward the river in the distance and tears welling in her eyes. I thanked her for giving me a child, but she did so much more than that.

She gave me my life. *Back.*

She gave me a purpose. *Something to look forward to.*

She gave me her heart. *Without any conditions.*

And this incredible little human. *And made me a dad.*

When the quiet starts to stretch, she looks over at me with a smile that could make any man's heart weaken, but it gives mine strength. No words need to be said. She's given me more than I ever deserved. I won't let her down.

I open my hand. Jacob slaps his down on top of it. So

small, it fits within the confines of my palm. I was his father from the beginning, but I want to remember this, the day I officially became his dad. "You know, Jacob, we have a lot in common."

"Baseball."

Chuckling, I say, "Yep. Baseball. And we both like bull riding." I back up to gesture toward his belt. "You're even a champ."

"You are," he says, twisting his arms together shyly.

"Third counts."

Cricket says, "Third counts when you're riding a bull. Good lord, if you ever have this kid—" She waves her hands like she's washing the windows. "Nope. Don't even want to think about it. Not going to happen."

Reaching around Jacob, I lean to rub her back. "You okay over there?"

"No bull riding, okay?" Her voice is firm despite the kindness in her eyes.

I look at Jacob. "No bull riding. You heard your mom."

"Aw, man." He stomps his boot with fisted hands, but only once. I'm thinking his interests lie more in the buckle and prize than his ambitions for the sport. It's not one I'm going to push. It's fucking dangerous. I was stupid for doing it.

She seems satisfied, and says, "Carry on."

Resting my back against the post, I angle his way. "You know what else we have in common, Jacob?" He's looking at me with such anticipation that I hope I don't disappoint him. "Our eye color is the same. Hold out your hand like this." I hold my hand out palm down next to his. "Our hands. Look at that."

He says, "Whoa. The same."

I hear the soft giggle from Cricket but try hard to

restrain mine. It's tough with this kid being as cute as he is. "Do you know why that is?" He shakes his head, staring right into my eyes as he waits for the answer. "It's because we're related."

"We are?" He shoots his gaze to his mom.

"Hey," I say, tapping his shoulder to bring his attention back to me. "Do you know how you met my dad at the ranch?" He nods vigorously, so much so it's tempting to catch it before he rattles his brain. "I'm his son. He's my dad, my parent. You have your mom, who is your parent. But you also have me, your dad." The ending clogs in my throat and doesn't come out as strong as I hoped, but I clear it to set them free. "I'm your dad, Jacob. Your father."

He looks at Cricket again. She smiles, lifting the hat that's barely hanging onto his head and brushing his hair back from his sweaty hairline before lowering it again. "I'm your mom. Griffin is your dad, buddy. Isn't that great news?"

When his face whips back to me, his eyes study mine. He blinks a few times, and then says, "I want to paint."

Cricket's and my eyes meet under laughter. She doesn't say a thing, though. He's waiting for me to respond, so I nod toward the distance where we were doing the art. "Go paint, Champ."

He hops down the steps, holding his hat, and then dashes off. He doesn't get very far, though, before he turns around and comes running back. "I'm glad to have you as my daddy." This time, he runs straight into my arms, into my life forever, and right into my heart.

CHAPTER 34

Cricket

*O*NE WEEK LATER . . .

I LIFT on my tiptoes to scan the higher shelf, but even with my glasses on, I can't see far enough. The text on the spines is too small, and the gold lettering has faded from age and wear and tear.

I go to the far corner of the library and drag the ladder on the track over to the section I believe is where the Dover family records have always been kept. I used to flip through some of the pages of these old records when I was a teenager and bored out of my mind.

Scanning the other books as I climb, I stop when I reach the fourth set of shelves a few feet below the twenty-foot-high ceiling. I'm not afraid of heights, but I'm not used to being up here in the heels I mistakenly chose to wear to work today.

"Duck. Duck. Duck. Duck. Duck." I drag my finger along

the wood instead of the books to help preserve it. "Goose." *Bingo*. I remove books 1878–1928 and 1929–1979 from the shelf and carefully climb back down the ladder.

"What are you doing in here, Buggy?" My dad's voice is gruff with the irritation he's harbored inside most of his life. It used to startle me. I always thought I was in trouble. I finally realized that's just who he is. He's always been impossible to please, and his demeanor reflects it.

Strange for a man who was given everything from money to an empire that had already been built for him to lead. He has cars, a yacht, four vacation homes, and a wife who will do anything to keep the Dover name in good light and company at the table.

"Research." I set the books on the large wooden table in the center of the room and smile. "Hello, Father. How are you?" Apparently, etiquette is reserved for business dealings and friends, not his grown children. Correction, *not me*. I know he loves catching up with William.

"On?"

He glosses right over the niceties like I hadn't said a dang word. "Our family."

He shuffles his finger in the air between the books and the ladder. "Put those up. You can ask me. I can tell you anything you need to know."

"Actually, no one tells me anything, so I decided to do the research myself." I sit down, setting my clasped hands on the wood in front of me, prim and proper, like what was always expected of me.

His footsteps are heavy against the wood floors as he crosses the room. Coming to the side of the table, he asks, "Don't you have work to do?"

"You're starting to make me think I might discover something you don't want me to know."

"You're not an ingenue, Cricket. You're a mother with no husband." He shoves his finger in the direction of the entrance to the library. "That child has no father. I think you understand very well that every family has a dark past."

The heat of my boiling blood reaches my cheeks. The fire burns in my eyes as I stare at him. I may be used to this treatment, but when he drags my son into it . . . "Jacob is not a part of your dark past. You created that all on your own. He's the only good thing to come of this family." I almost feel bad for not mentioning Savvy, but she'd rather me make the point than water down my argument. "Anyway, you're wrong."

"How so?" His fingers begin a sonata of heavy taps against the wood table. Playing piano used to bring him joy. He stopped playing years ago, but it would benefit him to pick up the hobby again.

I sit back under a shrug, and reply, "The Greenes don't seem to fall under that concept. They're the nicest people I've met in a long time."

His pause is slow; his eyes narrowed on mine. "What are you going on about, Buggy?"

"Please don't call me that. I have never liked it, and you know that. Is that why you still use it? To upset me?"

Resting his hand on the books in front of me, he leans down. "Are you challenging me? You do realize everything in your life is because I gave it or allowed it?"

An undercurrent of that darkness he mentioned shifts his mood. "I'm trying to talk to you like a daughter to her father, but you entered the library with built-in resentment. Is it me that you resent? Is it that I had a child out of wedlock, and you lost your spot at the men's club for two years? Is that what bothers you? You got it back, so there should be no issues."

"I bought it back for a quarter-million-dollar donation." He walks away, stopping in front of the ladder that reaches to the highest shelf. Crossing his arms over his chest stretches the shoulders of his suit. The threads pull as if hanging on for dear life. It's not worth mentioning, as he would view it as a slight instead of helpful.

"Seems like a lot of money to pay people you used to call friends."

He hits me with a glare, but it doesn't last before he turns away from me again, walking to the windows on the far side of the room. "Why is everything with you a confrontation lately?"

"Me? I was just using the library." Playing dumb is not a defense. I need a strategy, but I'm too tired to fight his battles. "Why is there a feud between the Dovers and the Greenes?"

His head jerks as if he had been slapped. There's no other reaction or word spoken. I almost wonder if he didn't hear me. He paces past me and then stops at the side of the table again. He taught me one golden rule in sales: the first one who speaks loses. "Why would that be of any interest to you?" His voice is not one I recognize. Nowhere in there is the stanch, cutthroat businessman. The harsh tone he used with me as a child has softened.

I haven't been nervous until now. My palms are sweaty, and I press my hands to my thighs to stop them from shaking. I don't back down, though. I raise my chin and ask, "Were you in love with Julie Ann Greene?"

His face drains of color, and he walks away from me. Sitting in a leather chair with his back to me, he stares at the stained glass window. "Did you know your mother made this with her own hands?" He glances back at me.

I look at the colorful glass again and see the bluebirds

and cardinals sitting on the tree branches. The sun works through the leaves, and the flowers dot the grass freely as if there were no plan, just like in nature. "I didn't know that. It was always my favorite growing up." I push up despite my unsteady hands and cross the room to sit in the chair next to him. My heart thunders in my chest, and I keep my eyes ahead, but whisper, "Griffin Greene is Jacob's dad."

The weight of his stare blankets me like a shroud. I refuse to be scared of him, and I won't let that control me anymore. Releasing a deep breath, I turn to him, ready to face his wrath.

He drops forward, his forearms to his legs, and hangs his head down. I'm not sure what to make of it. I reach over and touch his back, realizing I don't remember the last time I've been this close to him. "Dad?"

Turning his head, he looks at me. "Is that Julie Ann's son?"

"Her eldest."

When he sits back, a breath is knocked from him. "Destiny, karma, the universe always finds a way."

I sit back, feeling small like I'm supposed to be learning some great lesson as I soak in the knowledge. It's just ramblings that make no sense out of context. "What does that mean?"

"I respect your mother. I haven't made it easy on her, and she still stood by me, holding the family together, keeping our name out of the gossip groups and gutter." He casually angles toward me like we do this all the time. *God, I wish we had.* "Julie Ann Greene." He sighs, messing with a button on his jacket. "You want to know what's in those books? You want to know why the Dovers and Greenes chose a fight instead of being allies?"

"I do. I want to know all that because I can't find anyone

else who does. They don't even know why we supposedly dislike them."

That manages a grin out of him. Not a full one, but one that shows the story entertains him. "Seven generations back, the families settled here at the same time, became friends, and you can imagine," he says, spinning his hand briefly to fill in what I assume might be the naughty parts a.k.a. the good part. "What happened after that? Someone fell in love. Someone got hurt. They stopped speaking and remained on bad terms." He looks younger somehow when he seems happy. Is he happy? *I am.* This is the dad I always wanted him to be—talking, showing interest in me, treating me like I matter.

"That was a long time ago. We're still holding grudges because of a broken heart from seven generations back?"

"We Dovers are good at grudges."

"We sure are." The story has me thinking whose heart got broken? "It had to be the Dovers with the broken heart."

His interest has him sitting straighter and eyes widening. "Why do you say that?"

"Because we're the ones holding the grudge. They're not."

A humorless laugh escapes him as his brows knit together. "They're not? At all?"

"Nope. Not at all. They're very happy, actually."

Seemingly stunned by this information, he replies, "Remarkable." He touches my arm like we're close. An ache in my chest floats to the surface. Maybe one day. This conversation gives me hope. "The story doesn't end there."

"It doesn't?"

"No, it gets better." Did he just waggle his eyebrows? "Five generations ago, a girl from the Greenes and a boy from the Dover clan ran away together. No one knew what became of them. Could've been killed. Texas was a lot wilder back then. Could have gone off to Hawaii and lived their remaining days on the beach." When he shrugs, his shoulders relax instead of stiffening again. "It's a mystery I've investigated many times over the years. Their tracks end just west of San Antonio."

"That's sad. Doesn't sound like they got very far."

"But I think they did." Excitement glimmers in his eyes. "One day, I hope to prove it."

"I could help you with that."

He smiles. *HE* smiles. It's genuine and real. "That might be a fun project to do together." Griffin and Jacob have their puzzling. My dad and I can solve family mysteries together.

Leaning in, he rests his arm on the chair closer to me. "Three generations from mine—"

"There's more? I'm so invested. Who knew our history went back that far with them?"

"I did."

"Oh right." I'll just clamp my mouth shut and let him finish telling the story.

"So three generations back, my great-grandparents had ten kids. One got pregnant by a Greene—"

"Seems it runs in the family," I joke, nudging him with my elbow. The joke doesn't land. Oops. "Sorry, go on." I zip my lips and try to keep myself from thinking we're further along than we are. Baby steps. Or maybe he just doesn't appreciate one-night stand humor. It's probably that when I think about it. Then a random thought occurs that has me sweating on the spot. "Oh my God, please don't tell me I'm related to Griffin."

He sighs, but his expression doesn't harden. I'm kind of waiting for that to happen. Unkind? Possibly, but a few words with dad's personal interest don't negate the disrespect he walked in with. But for now, I'll try to enjoy the moment in case all things change at the stroke of midnight.

"You're not related. The baby didn't make it, which added fuel to the already burning feud."

"So much sadness."

"Times were hard back then. The Greenes had lost their fortune from some wayward members of the family, and as you know, our family thrived."

"Probably on their hard time."

"Probably. Nobody comes by fortune by being kind."

Crossing my legs, I get more comfortable by slumping just a little into the chair since it doesn't seem we're in a hurry. "That's too bad. I'd rather lose a fortune than live a miserable life surrounded by money."

"Poppycock." It's not something I'm going to argue about with him. I have the privilege of not having to worry in life, so far, but that may not last forever, so I'll choose love to carry me through.

I wait for the story to continue, but he doesn't say anything. "What happened next?" The lightness he'd allowed through seizes, and the lines of his face harden again. I knew I was on borrowed time but didn't realize how much. Recalling where the story left off, I think about three generations and following the pattern that means it would jump to—*Oh.* "Julie Ann and—"

"As I said, out of respect for your mother, it's not a story that bears repeating. Nothing came of it anyway. No great legend to be added to the books. No fateful ending . . ." He closes his mouth and sits back, his thoughts wandering somewhere else.

"Dad?"

He looks at me, and says, "No fateful ending for us. Only hers." Trying so desperately to hide an emotion that might tip me in one direction or the other, he fails. Pinching his lips together, he releases and then adds, "You and Griffin Greene finally broke the curse." Relaxing deeper into the leather cushion, he smiles. It's not toothy, but that wouldn't be him. "It's only broken if you're together. Are you seeing him, Cricket?"

"We're together." I don't need to question Griffin's honor or loyalty, if he's staying, or if he loves me. The words haven't been exchanged, but Jacob and I feel them.

This time, he's the one who reaches over and covers my hand with his. "I'm happy for you."

"What's going on?" My mother comes around to stand in front of the stained glass. "What are we celebrating?"

My dad's hand was already back in his lap, his back stiff and his expression miserable again. Such a disappointing end to what was one of the highlights of my life. I stand, swiping at the back of my pants to smooth any wrinkles. She looks at me, though her gaze doesn't reach that deep.

My mom was the It Girl of Central Texas. She could even claim the title all the way up in Dallas. She had the last name, the money, the connections, and the ambition. Her mother made sure to connect her with the most eligible pedigreed bachelor she could find. My father entered stage left and never left her side again.

I think there were plans for me to take over one day, wear the crown, win affection, and whatever else comes along with the title. Unfortunately, she got stuck with me as a daughter. And placating society was not something I was interested in. Add in being a single mom, and that dream of my mom's was destroyed. But I don't care anymore. I'm tired of pretending that our last name matters. I'm happy, and that is more important. "I'm dating Griffin Greene, and he's Jacob's dad from a one-night stand in Costa Rica four-plus years ago." Her ruby-red lips open in shock. "Your grandson's birthday is this Saturday at Rollingwood Ranch. You're both invited. He loves baseball, cowboy stuff, and has recently gotten into graffiti with his dad, if you need present ideas."

I start to leave, walking around a large console toward the door. I stop just on the other side of it and turn back. "I want to open a wine-tasting shop in downtown Peachtree Pass, and I'm going to marry Griffin one day. We're not engaged, and we've not said I love you, but he's my soul mate. It took seven generations for this to happen, and I'm not going to waste time trying to explain to naysayers." I head for the door again and open it.

Before I have a chance to close it, my dad asks, "What time is the party?"

I look back over my shoulder with my heart in my throat and happy tears threatening to fall. With a smile I give him wholeheartedly, I reply, "Two to four. Hope to see you both there."

The smile doesn't leave. I couldn't wipe it away if I wanted, so I just wear it all the way back to my car parked in front of their house, get in, and squeal from joy. I don't know what happens next in the big picture, but for me, I need to see Griffin.

CHAPTER 35

Griffin

"Griffin?"

I hear her before I see her. Standing on the roof of the porch, I look at where we park, and call out, "Cricket?"

"Griffin?"

Climbing down the ladder, I jump the last five rungs and land on the ground, racing toward the side of the house in a panic. "Cricket?"

"Umf!" Catching her as she collides into my chest, her arms thrown around my neck like a lasso, I lift her and then shift to tighten my grip. Our mouths crash together in a flurry of lips and tongues, passion and urgency. I plant my boots on the ground and slide my hand into her hair, kissing her glorious mouth like it should be. Appreciative, enticing, and sensual.

Left breathless and panting for air, she pulls back with a smile, cracking her cheeks wide open. "Griffin," she starts, her breath coming out in heavy waves. "You'll never believe what happened." Tightening her legs around my waist, she shamelessly rubs her center against my abs. I don't mind, but there are growing consequences she'll have to deal with.

"I missed you, babe."

The corners of her eyes soften along with the tails of her smile. "I missed you so much."

"Those twenty-four hours were hell."

She laughs. "It was about sixteen, but who's counting?" A melody of exhilaration rings through her words that has me smiling in response.

It's early May, but it's already feeling hot like summer here in Texas. Her body makes it even hotter, but there's no way I'll put her down. Grabbing hold of my face, she kisses my nose and bursts into laughter. "I did it," she says. "I told my parents about you. About us. About you being Jacob's dad."

Shifting my gaze from one of her eyes to the other, I search for the background story to fill in the details. "And you're here to tell the tale?"

"I am. I survived, but more than that, I told them everything. No more secrets. No more hiding. No more being the perfect daughter." Tilting her head in amusement, she puckers her mouth wickedly. "Not that I ever was, but it's so freeing." She abruptly drops back in a trust fall with her legs still leveraged around me. She's damn lucky I'm so strong and catch her in my arms. I have a feeling she knew I'd never let anything happen to her.

Throwing her arms wide, she closes her eyes and soaks in the feeling. She lifts, pulling herself up by holding my shoulders and coming right back in for another good kiss.

"I know the history of the feud. There are so many stories of broken hearts and tragedies over seven generations of our families. My dad—"

"Your dad?" This news comes out of the blue. She's

happy, so that means I don't have to go kick anyone's ass, but this is quite the turnabout.

"Oh, Griffin, it's been an amazing day. He and I spent time in the library talking." She takes a quick breath, and then says, "I'll fill you in on everything soon, but I need to tell you the most important part now," she says, her words rushing from her mouth.

"What is the most important part, babe?"

"We are." Pure delight lights up her expression. "We're together. We broke the curse. You and I are ending the war between our families."

It's not just excitement; it's love I see so boldly in her eyes as she stares into mine. It's our future and life together. It's grandkids and great-grandkids around us as we grow old. It's a life we build as one. "I want to hear more, but I like this ending."

"We're the fairy tale."

"I promise you happily ever after." I kiss her again, though I'm a sweaty mess from working outside all day. It doesn't seem to bother her because she doesn't move an inch. She's content right where she is. I move to the porch, though, carrying this gorgeous creature to where I really want her. The daybed. I stripped the sheets, covers, and pillows to keep them clean, but the mattress remains, so I lay her down and then take her in a solid once-over. Most guys wouldn't consider work clothes sexy, but damn does she make me want to play office with her. Bent over the desk, fucking her from— "Hey, Twenty-two," she purrs, bringing me back to her. "What's on your mind?"

"You. Always you, babe." Her top is light, the fabric shifting with the slightest of breezes and giving me a good view of the sexy line of her collarbone right now. The sky-high black heels have me thinking she most definitely needs to be wearing those once I get her naked. I kiss her, then pull back to take off my shirt. "No holding back anymore. No keeping secrets from anyone. Gossip be damned. You, me, and our son can now be a family." Her breath hitches, her hand covering her chest like she might need help. "Is everything okay?" I ask, ready to resuscitate her, if necessary.

"Griffin." My name is all she manages to say.

I bend over her. My eyes align with hers, and our mouths are just more than a breath away. "What is it?" I whisper, capturing wild strands of her hair and pushing them back from her face.

"You're staying."

Her words confuse me, and I shake my head. "What do you mean?" I climb onto the bed, situating myself between her legs and anchoring my elbows into the mattress beside her head. I want to be as close as I can to her. "Did you think I could lose you twice and exist without you?" I kiss her with gentle pressure, only pulling back to look into her beautiful eyes. "Impossible. You and I broke the timeline. We did it."

She cups my jaw, dancing her fingers along the edge with a smile that makes me feel alive each time she grants it. "We did it," she whispers. "We broke the curse."

I drop my head. "I traveled the planet, went to the most remote beaches and towns, thinking I was escaping the failures of my life. I wasn't. I was only dragging out the inevitable of facing my troubles."

Her palms settle on the round of my shoulders, and she asks, "What made you leave? What failures sent you searching?"

Sounding weak is not attractive, but I know to her, honesty is. "My mom died." I fall to my back, needing air as my heart starts thumping in my chest. She rolls to her side, dipping her head against me and giving me time to say what I need to say without her staring.

"I'm sorry," she whispers.

I take hold of her hand and kiss it before resting them on my body. "She'd call me before every game. She was the first and only person I called after I played. I could ramble about a missed catch or slow return. I could boast about getting a player out when bases were loaded or hitting a homer. It didn't matter to her. She just wanted to hear my voice. I wish I could hear hers now."

Cricket wraps her arm over my midsection, her breath warming across my skin every time she exhales. She doesn't understand the comfort she brings me. I tighten my arm around her. "She sounds like an amazing mother."

I swallow down the balled-up emotions lumped in my throat, though it's not easy. "She was. The best." I kiss her head, and say, "You two have that in common."

A tremble runs through her, and then the softest sniffle as if she's stifling her tears from releasing. I contort to the side to see her eyes. "Hey, what's wrong?"

"I know ..." A tear slips to my chest, and her gaze finally meets mine. "I know how much she means to you, so to hear that you think I could be that kind of mom to Jacob is just so ... It's so touching. You're an incredible man, Griffin."

"It's true. Our son is fortunate to have you. I am, too. Who knew you'd slum it with a guy like me twice."

That warrants a little laugh out of her. "Feels like two different lifetimes, but then the years have sped by quicker."

It's these moments when time seems to slow down, and we get to process the present. Maybe it's time to release myself from the past so I can be with her and Jacob fully now ... "I got in a fight with my teammates. That's what led to my suspension. And then it went downhill from there. No fucking way was I going to apologize. I was so full of anger and resentment, and taking it out on the guys giving me shit made sense in my jaded brain. They threw the insults. I threw the punches."

She shifts onto her stomach and rests on her elbows. "What led to the fight?"

I pause to think about what to say, not because I don't know, but because the story has never been given my voice before. It didn't matter what the sports channels or the broadcasters said, and it didn't matter that others happily gave their side of the story. I wasn't and didn't. I can now because I trust she'll love me for who I am and not the lost cause I used to be. "I was waiting for my mom to call." My stomach jerks, the memory wanting to cause a revolt. "They didn't tell me until after the game. My family knew, but I played like she was watching." I laugh because I'm such a fucking fool. "It was one of my best games ever, too."

Cricket places a kiss on my arm, then goes higher, dropping one on my chest before reaching my lips. When she settles back, she says, "You didn't play that well because she was watching. You played that well because you'd spent your entire life building up to that moment. That was your payoff for all the hard work you'd put in."

A surge of anger begins to roll through me, but it fizzles out before it makes headway. I want her to be wrong because if she's right, I spent years punishing myself for nothing. I pinch the bridge of my nose to keep the tears away. *Fucking hell.* I'm fighting myself at this point. It wasn't the world against me. It was me versus me, and my ego won out. Holding this magnificent woman in my arms, it's time for a new start. "I know you're right, but I missed the calls and got stuck in my head. My game went to shit."

"You didn't grieve. One day, you should allow yourself to

feel it, to release it, and to heal. Your mom would want that for you."

"She would," I admit, which might be a first for me. When I slide down to see those greens I'm so in love with, I say, "There's no living this life without you in it, though. I want us to be together, Little Chirp."

"A family," she says this time with no fear in her eyes. "No more stories of fated love to be told generations from now." Her smile grows as she coaxes mine to return, too. "We did it. We brought an end to the feud and brought our families together. That's the power of our love."

"It is." I could tell her that being in my life has changed me for the better, but she knows her worth. I find that so fucking sexy. I run my hand over her cheek, then lean over to kiss her temple once, twice, three times before whispering, "I love you."

This time, she pulls back, grabs hold of my wrists, and looks at me. Her mouth opens, but then a crush of emotions temporarily drags her under. When the wave subsides, she says, "I love you, too, so much."

"WHAT IF THEY DON'T COME?" my girl asks as we circle the table with cardboard baseballs and cowboys, placing them down as decorations.

I stop and look at her across from me. "Why wouldn't they? He's their grandson. Are they going to hold a grudge against you, which I don't think they have a right to, based on what you told me, against a four-year-old? If that's the case, they can stay gone from my family."

The word family has so much more meaning for me

these days. I started with the best, but somehow, it got better and bigger.

My sister comes out of her house to see the table we set. "Looks great." She sets down a pile of napkins and small plates with all different floral patterns on them. "I find it so interesting how Jacob is into the same things as . . ." She stares at me. The look alone tells me she knows. She still doesn't say it, even if they're all thinking it. "As my big brother here."

Cricket laughs, and nothing is subtle about it. She doesn't even bother to conceal her expression, which reaffirms my sister's theory. That traitor will be properly handled later. I smirk.

It's a day of family in celebration of him, so it's best to just get it all out on the table so we can enjoy it. "Jacob's my son." I stand at one end of the table, my sister at the far end. Her smile grows along with the reveal. "I know you know. I know all of you know. So there it is. Your suspicion is confirmed, sis. Happy?"

"Very," she says, opening her arms wide and making a beeline for Cricket. "I'm so happy to have you both in our lives. I have a nephew. So exciting!"

Their embrace is sincere and warm. To see the woman I love being welcomed into my family without hesitation reminds me of how lucky I really am. I don't have my mom anymore, but my family is steadfast, and the love is even stronger.

When Cricket turns to look at me, her cheeks are pink. To my sister, she says, "I'm so grateful for your family. Both Jacob and I are so happy to—"

"Be a part of it," I add, making sure she knows she's every bit a Greene even though she doesn't carry the moniker. I come around behind her and wrap her up in my arms. After kissing her head, I look up to see my sister watching us.

"You make a beautiful couple and adorable kids, if I do say so."

As if cued, Daisy runs from the corner of the house with Jacob in tow and Beckett trying to wrangle them. "Come on, guys, I mean it. We have to wash up."

Daisy laughs like the maniacal terror she is and yells, "*Neveerrr*."

"Never," Jacob shouts and giggles right after as they leg it up the steps and run into the house.

I say, "That's trouble if I ever did see it."

Cricket glances at me over her shoulder. "Should we be concerned?"

"Nope." He's led a life that was more on the sheltered side and wasn't exposed to other kids as much. He'll get more than he bargained for on the ranch. It will do him good, and he's going to love it. "We're going to let that kid be a kid. Sometimes he's going to fall and scrape his knees. Sometimes he's going to lead the charge and start some shit. But he's going to have the best childhood. I promise."

Tagger comes out with a platter of fresh fruit, and my dad follows with two bags of chips. Baylor comes from the other side of the house, holding tongs in his hand. "Are we ready to eat?"

Lauralee comes out of the house as if she can sense her husband's presence, takes a sip of lemonade, and sits down. Rubbing her baby's belly, she says, "Two more months."

Cricket sits next to her, and they start chatting like old friends while I go inside to get my gift for Jacob. I got him something I'd like to share with him privately before the birthday festivities kick off.

I duck inside the house and grab Jacob midair just as they were taking off up the stairs. "Gotcha."

"I'm playing, Daddy," he whines with a few kicks, but the sound is music to my ears because he called me Daddy. I'll never take that for granted.

Spinning him sideways, I carry him under my arms to the living room, where I let his present down earlier. "I wanted to give you a gift." Apparently, the magic word was said because he stopped fighting me. I plop him on the couch and sit next to him. Taking the small, wrapped box, I hand it to him, and say, "I want you to have this, Champ."

He tears into it like a gift-opening pro and lifts the lid. His eyes dart to mine. "Your buckle." When he looks back at it, he pulls it from the box. "Your favorite." He's the politest kid I've ever met and handles it with care as he wiggles it in both his hands to catch the light on the shiny surface. "Whoa. Did you see that?"

He caught a ray of sunshine sneaking in through the window, and it hit just right. "I did." For a kid I'm pretty sure is big for his size, he's still so small next to me. It's weird to have this feeling of wanting him to stay this way, with him only seeing the good in the world and rushing for him to get bigger so we can do all the things together. "Do you like that?"

Nodding, he holds it to his heart. "It's my favorite, too." He stands next to me, looks at the buckle with a big grin, and throws his arms around me. "Thank you, Daddy."

I hold him, closing my eyes and feeling the full weight of the blessing this kid is in my life. "You need to take care of it, okay? It was grandpa's and then mine, and now it's yours."

Even when he leans back again, he's still staring at it in awe. "Okay." I help him put it on his belt and send the little cowboy out to the pasture to play.

With everyone back outside, I take a moment in the quiet of the house to soak this in—the good I've been given, the second chance at having a real life, and the gift of family.

"How ya doing there, Greene?"

I look up to see Cricket standing behind a chair, with nothing less than admiration lifting her features. I'm so fucking lucky. But I'm also starting to think it wasn't luck at all. It really was the universe bringing us together. "I'm good. How are you?"

"Happy."

"You deserve that, babe."

"So do you," she says, coming to sit next to me on the couch. "That was really nice of you to give him your buckle."

Sitting back, I stretch my arm over her shoulders. "Figured it would be good to pass something else down other than a feud between families."

"We squashed that, so we get to focus on the good generational stuff like belt buckles." She leans over and kisses my cheek. "The hot dogs and burgers are ready."

"I'm starved."

The front door opens, and Savvy stops when she sees us. "Two things." I've gotten to know her cousin enough to know she's really speaking to Cricket when she has something to get off her chest. She has strong opinions, just like my girl. "What are they feeding them over here in Greene County? Goodness. They're giant and gorgeous. The men working downtown and, well . . ." She gestures toward me with her hand. "Jesus. Then you got this family." Looking straight at me, she asks, "Got any spare brothers or cousins around here? Sign me up or, better yet, hook me up, Griffin."

I start to chuckle along with Cricket when she replies,

"Yeah, I'm not sure why we were hanging around Dover County when all this sexiness was just over the county line."

"What about Blake?" I ask, but am quickly shot down with two level-me-to-the-ground glares. "My bad. I'll just keep my mouth shut." Cricket gives my hand a little squeeze.

Savvy says, "Second, Blake and I broke up."

"What?" Cricket jolts forward.

She waves her off like it's no big deal. "I take it you didn't see the online photos? Yeah, the team is in Nashville, and photos surfaced of him making out with some girl and then walking into his hotel together, which means the team knew." Shaking her head, she half laughs. "If I weren't so mad, I might be upset, but really, it was a long time coming. Even when we tried to put in the effort, all was forgotten the next day, and we were back to being better roommates than lovers." As if she reminded herself, she says, "The man is horrible in bed. He stares at photos of himself in his baseball uniform to get off."

"Yikes," Cricket says, standing up. "Look, you are better off without him. Your guy, someone who will fall madly in love with you, is out there waiting for you. I just know it."

I follow them back outside just as Tagger asks, "Hey, did you guys meet my brother?"

Savvy's the first one off the porch with her hand out, ready to greet him. "No, we did not. I'm Savvy Dover."

"Ace Grange."

Not sure if it's her little double skip forward to shake his hand or the way he just looks like he met his soulmate, but I think she's going to come out of this breakup just fine.

A trail of dust in the distance draws my eyes up to the road by the barn. I immediately glance at Cricket, who's already spotted the car. I take hold of her hand and ask, "Are you ready?"

"As I'll ever be." Taking a deep breath, she says, "Here we go."

CHAPTER 36

Cricket

My mom's feet are the first to land in the grass where the black SUV is parked in front of Christine and Tagger's house. Her spike heels are not the wisest for the ranch, but she doesn't do casual.

Dad slides out after her, offering his arm for her to hold. He closes the door, and they come toward the house with everyone gawking. I should probably make it easier on them to approach by meeting them halfway, but I think this is a good experience for them to feel like guests rather than owning the place, which is their typical modus operandi.

Even Savvy is popping grapes in her mouth on the porch swing, sitting next to Ace and watching like she's about to see a fireworks show. She might if I can't keep my temper in check.

I eased some of the torture by walking down the steps of the porch and waiting there for them. Griffin is by my side without asking. Christine comes to stand next to me and asks, "Your parents?"

"Yes."

"Hello," she says to greet them by cutting across a few feet of grass. Introductions are made quickly with references to everyone who's here. "Hot dogs and burgers are coming off the grill. Make yourself at home," she says before returning to the porch to let them mingle.

I hadn't noticed Thomas standing by his son's side until my parents approached us. My mom air kisses my cheek, and then says, "You look so pretty in that dress, Cricket." The compliment takes me by surprise and causes me to look down at what I'm wearing. It's a sundress I ordered, nothing fancy—white with blue flowers like the prettiest jacquard prints in Paris.

"Thank you. You look pretty, Mom." She always does, but I felt the need to tell her this time as well.

My dad leans in and wraps his forearm around my neck. These grounds we're breaking will come in all forms. He's trying despite always being a family of non-huggers.

Shaking Griffin's hand, he says, "I hear congratulations are in order."

Griffin glances at me like he has no clue what he's talking about. "Thank . . . *you*?"

My dad starts to guffaw, never ceasing to amaze me. I haven't heard him laugh in years. "You're the father of my grandson and won my daughter's heart."

"Ah," Griffin starts, "Well, it's a funny story actually that starts in—" I slam the back of my hand against his chest.

"Save that story for another time. We have a birthday to celebrate, and you're starving, remember?"

He rubs his hand over his stomach. "I remember."

But my mom and dad are moving down the row of us like we're a receiving line, ending face-to-face with Griffin's dad. I hold my breath as they shake hands. "It's been a long time, Bryan," Thomas says with a pat to the upper arm.

"It has been." Okay, this is good. *Light. Conversational. Surface.* I hope they can keep it that way. Just when I think it's over, and I'm ready to redirect them to the table to find a seat on the porch, he says, "I wanted to give you my condolences. As you know, I held a high regard for Julie Ann."

"Yes, I know. I appreciate it. It's been hard, but she'd want us to all move forward and live life to the fullest." He spies Jacob running by, and adds, "She'd love all these grandkids. She'd be amused that we're family in a way." They finally release hands. Thomas pushes his into his pockets, and says, "You know, I never did talk to you at the funeral."

I see Griffin visibly shake, and I reach to slip my hand in his. His eyes look down at me next to him before rubbing the bridge of his nose to hold back his emotions.

My dad replies, "You didn't need to. I wasn't there to draw attention away." He takes my mom's hand in his own act of reassurance. "I was there to pay my respects, and you allowed me to do that." Glancing at my mom, he gives her a knowing smile that evokes one of her own. They're a team, and by how the aura feels different around them, it's not against me. *Anymore.* He adds, "Delancy brought gifts. I should get them out of the Suburban."

Before he does, he moves closer to Griffin again, and says, "I was thinking we could put this feud behind us, once and for all, now that you're with my daughter."

"I think that'd be alright, Mr. Dover."

"Call me Bryan. All my friends do." They shake hands once more before my parents walk back to the vehicle.

As soon as we're alone again, I lean against him and look up. "How are you?"

Taking a sobering breath seems to ease the tension caught in his jaw. "That went better than expected. How are you?"

"Optimistic? Is it wrong to feel this way?"

"It's healthy. I think we take it as it comes. It's possible to get things on the right track. What do you think?"

I start to smile again. "I think the path to healing takes time. You're right. I'd rather take it at present value than keep holding on to the past."

His hand comes around my lower back, and he kisses my forehead.

Another slam of a truck door has us seeing Peaches coming with boxes of goodies in her hands. "Sorry, I'm late. Had to wrap up the lunch crowd at the pizzeria."

Lauralee gets up to greet her mom. "I can't believe I left the cupcakes at the shop. Pregnancy brain. Thank you for bringing them."

"No worries, honey." She rubs her cheek before turning to Thomas and giving him a quick kiss. "What fun did I miss?"

Maybe that shouldn't make us all laugh, but we do, and it feels good to feel like we're in this together as a family. Family. Mine. Griffin's. Us together.

I'm caught in a hug of warm fuzzies from the family and the celebration of the day when Griffin pulls a phone from his pocket and stares at the screen. His light mood turns heavy, and he says, "I have to take this," and walks away from the party.

Everyone goes about filling their plates as they sit around the table, sharing stories and getting to know the guests at the ranch. Although I get Jacob to eat a hot dog, he'd rather be playing. I shrug and promise to call the kids back over when it's time for cupcakes.

The chatter is strong, and my name comes up here and there, but I can't take my eyes off Griffin. Pacing through the far end of the field, closer to the edge of the forest that leads to the river, he occasionally looks back, but he has his head down and pressed to the phone most of the time.

I want to go to him, to be the person who walks alongside him in moral support. I'm also damn nosy and have been anxiously picking at my cuticles for the past half hour. I force myself to stay put, to eat a hot dog, and drink lemonade. It's a party and should be enjoyed after all.

But when he shoves his phone into the back pocket of his jeans and starts back this way, I stand and rush down the steps that will lead me to him. I'm walking and then I'm running, my heart racing as fast as my feet until he catches me in his arms. The side of my head is covered in kisses, and when my feet land back on the ground, he takes hold of my hands, and says, "I just got called up."

"Called up where?"

"To the majors."

THREE MONTHS LATER . . .

THIS BUTTON IS GOING to pop before it holds my boobs in properly. *Damn, Savvy.* She knew what she was doing when she ordered this Cardinals jersey for me. Griffin is going to love it, especially with his name on the back this time.

Waiting outside the gate for the players to come out of the locker room with all the other baseball bunnies isn't my idea of a good time. I heard cleat chasers once. I don't know the official term, but I do know they're looking to score. I'm looking to . . . *okay, fine*. Maybe we're not so different. At least I'm guaranteed a good time with the man I'm madly in love with and with whom I share a kid.

The guards open the gate to let a few players into the parking lot. With bodyguards keeping a path clear for them, some load onto a bus, and others have rides waiting for them. I turn back when I hear a scream, with Griffin shouting in the middle of it. Two players part, and I see him, my sexy and oh, so handsome man. I join in with the others because I'm bursting at the seams and excited to reunite with him. It's been a few weeks since he hit the road to travel with the team, and I was back working and spending my time with Jacob in Dover Creek. We watch the games with his family, and sometimes at his dad's house. I work on the puzzle that he started and never finished, saving the last piece for him to complete when he gets back.

Since everyone else is calling his name, I cup the side of my mouth, and call, "Hey, Twenty-Two."

He looks up, the tension knitted between his eyebrows releasing when he sees me. His cocky grin goes rogue and weakens my knees. As soon as he passes through the gates, he reaches for me. Our fingertips touch, but another bunny shoots her shot and grabs his hand. Griffin frees himself from her clutches, then tells a guard to help me.

It happens fast. They surround me and move me through with their large bodies, covering me. I'm released into his arms, his eyes that are bluer than summer Texas skies, and his lips pressing to mine before he whispers, "Little Chirp."

We're maneuvered in front of the bus, where he takes me to a lineup of cabs waiting for a fare. Before we get in one, he kisses me again. "What are you doing here?"

"I missed you."

This time, his smile is so sincere that it makes my heart ache from its absence lately. He says, "I missed you, too." His eyes dip to my chest, and all sincerity is replaced by hunger. Licking his lips, he tugs me tightly into his arms. "Damn, you look good."

"I wore it for you. Has your name on the back and everything."

He cups my face and kisses me again as if he doesn't want the moment to pass us by. "I've been thinking about that."

"What about?"

"How do you feel about it being your name as well?" Everything stops—my heartbeat, my breath, my thoughts, my body, the world on its axis. "This isn't romantic, babe. It just comes from the heart. I love you and want to marry you. I want to be your husband and you be my wife. Wake up together when I'm home and go to bed together at night." He runs his hand through his hair and sighs. "I could have done this better—"

"I'll marry you."

As if I hadn't said anything at all, he says, "I'll make it up to you and ask for your hand in mar—"

"I'll marry you, Griffin."

"Wait, you will?" Disbelief is overcome by elation. "You'll marry me? For real?"

"For real. I want to marry you." I lift to my toes and kiss him to seal the deal because he said it. He put it out into the universe. I'm no fool. I know a great thing when I see it. Even more when I kiss it like I'm kissing him now.

EPILOGUE 1

Cricket

Two months later . . .

Griffin puts the piece in place, then stands over the puzzle, gazing down with a grin on his face. It wasn't a huge puzzle or anything like that. I think he just remembers putting it together with his mother. Looking over at me sitting at the table in his dad's kitchen, he says, "That is so satisfying."

I laugh. My guy's a puzzler, what can I say? "I ordered some puzzles for the wine shop. They can spend a few hours drinking wine and putting puzzles together, or purchase them to take home. Surely, you can't be the only one so into them."

He crosses the room, stops in front of me, and pats his thigh. I place my shoe against his leg. He starts trying to fasten the tiny buckle on the ankle strap of my shoe since I had no luck. "When does the tasting room open?"

"If you make the playoffs, you won't be there."

He chuckles. "Let's hope I'm not then. I'd like to be there. Is the date flexible?"

"For you, anything. It's the first thing that's all my own. Bought and paid for with my own earned money. I want you there if it's possible."

He kneels to inspect the situation closely. When his eyes peek at me, he says, "I won't miss it, babe. Though these shoes are fucking annoying. If we can't get them on, how am I going to get them off?"

"Good point. I'll just go barefoot."

The door opens just as I slip the shoes off. Jacob says, "Uncle Baylor said we need to move this along before Aunt Lauralee has the baby."

He's so stinking cute. "Tell them we're coming."

Jacob turns to yell, "They're coming." Not exactly what I meant, but it got the job done.

Griffin pulls me into his arms, and we start to slow dance on the linoleum. "This is it. Are you ready to tie the knot, Ms. Dover?"

"So ready, but soon it's going to be Greene. Quite the adjustment."

"I think I'm up for the challenge." His gaze dips to my mouth before reaching my eyes again, and asking, "How do you feel about it?"

"I have no doubt you are, and maybe it doesn't feel so shocking to me. I think I've felt like one with you since you accused me of stalking."

Dropping his head back in laughter, he says, "Oh, we're going to do that, are we?"

"We are. Do you think you can handle me?"

He grazes his fingertips under my jaw. "It will be the honor of my life, Little Chirp."

"I love you, Twenty-Two."

Chuckling, he says, "I love you, too." Taking my hand, he leads me out the front door of our house. We stopped calling it the Riggins's house a long time ago. Now it's just ours, and nowhere close to being done, but the yard cleans up nicely, and the sound of the water makes a beautiful backdrop for our nuptials. "Now let's go hitch this horse to a cart."

I roll my eyes. "Charming."

"How about this?" He stops just before opening the door since Jacob slammed it closed again. "I regret that we lost four years that could have been spent together. I'll not waste another day taking our life for granted."

"If I hadn't already said yes, I would be now." He kisses me just as the door reopens, flooding us in sunshine, but I don't care that our families see us caught up in each other. I love him. My soul always knew he was the one.

GRACIE GREENE MADE her debut just after seven o'clock tonight, and she is absolutely beautiful with her dark hair and cute curls. Lauralee and Baylor couldn't be happier. More family is the best gift any of us could ask for. *Except one.*

After talking to Jacob privately to see how he feels, he confessed that he wants his daddy's last name. I'm not offended. He agreed to keep it tucked in the middle for me. The gift came in a card Griffin opened in the waiting room of the hospital. He had his one chat with Jacob to make sure. When I saw them hugging and the way Griffin's eyes glistened, I knew the right decision had been made. All three of us sharing the same name means just as much to me as it does to him.

The rain kept us inside as it got torrential outside for thirty minutes. It was swept away just as fast as it came, and we've been given the most stunning pink and orange, yellow and blue sunset.

I'm not sure how I got talked into this, but in the parking lot of the hospital with Jacob tucked in his car seat, I rev the engine of Griffin's truck, and ask, "Are you sure?"

"I'm sure," Griffin replies, standing on the other side of a huge puddle. "All's fair."

"It's petty, and I don't want to be petty with you. I believe you when you say splashing me was an accident. Does that help?"

He grins. "I'm giving you the chance to get revenge, babe. No one's getting hurt. I'm only getting wet. It's no biggie. Just do it."

I back the truck up and align the tires. That arrogant smirk deserves to be drenched, but there won't be any satisfaction in revenge. I shift into park, then climb over the console to the other captain's chair in the cab of the truck.

When he's still standing there, ready to take his punishment, I reach over and honk the horn. "Come on. I have other ways to get you wet." I glance back to see if Jacob reacts like he would somehow know what I'm talking about. He's fast asleep. It's been a big day.

Griffin opens the door and climbs in. "You're too good for me."

While he buckles up, I say, "Savvy said she'll watch Jacob tonight."

Reaching over, he grabs my knee and leans in to kiss me. "What do you have in mind?"

"A lot of sex on our wedding night."

"That might be the hottest thing you've ever said to me."

"Words are hollow. Wait until I show you what I have in mind."

We showed each other about four times, but I forgot if oral counts with equal value in the equation. If it does, seven was a great number to celebrate.

EPILOGUE 2

Griffin

Two months later . . .

"You know who I am, Joe. I'm tired. I traveled all night and just want to see my wife and kid."

"Sorry, you're not on the list. So unless you prove—I'm just kidding, Griffin." The gate lifts at the Dover estate, and he says, "Go on."

"Thanks, man."

"Hey, way to make us Hill Country folk proud. Two homers in one game. Big accomplishment. Bet those will help in negotiations for next season."

"We'll see." I wave with two fingers, then drive onto the property to Cricket's cottage. The house is almost done, but not quite. At least we have this place where we can stay until it is.

Contracts . . . Talks will be happening soon. Who knew the team would get footage of me playing in the fundraiser game? I owe my second chance at pro ball to Cricket for making it happen. If she hadn't organized that game, the online footage wouldn't have gone viral. I would never wish an injury on another player, but Pete Scholtz breaking his leg by motocrossing during preseason feels a lot like this was meant to be for me.

I'm playing the best of my career, but at thirty-five, my entire body hurts. Decisions will need to be made and pros and cons weighed. Do I keep playing for my pride, for the payday, and struggle walking when I hit my fifties like my dad? Or stop while I'm ahead, settle down in the Pass, and enjoy my family? Sucks it's an either-or situation.

I sneak into the house just after two o'clock in the morning, lock the door, and get a glass of water before making my way down the hall. First, I peek into Jacob's room because I miss him so much when I'm traveling. I kiss his head and touch his little chubby cheek, then kiss it, too.

I'm careful when closing the door, then I continue down the hall to the last door on the right. When I open it, it's dark. *Really fucking dark.* The place is kept immaculate, so I don't worry about tripping over anything while I make my way into the bathroom to shower before climbing into bed with my wife.

I close the bathroom door when I'm inside, then flip on the light.

"Looks like you hit another homer," she says, propped on the counter with her legs crossed.

"Fuck me." I grab at my heart, hoping I don't end up in the hospital. "If I didn't feel old already . . . fuck, babe."

A strip of cotton clings to her tits. Not much else from what I can tell is below her waist. She knows how to welcome a guy home from a long month of travel. "What are you doing in the dark?"

"Stalking you." I'd laugh, but the delivery was a little too deadpan for my liking. She then laughs, though, the sound airy and soothing to my heart. "That was an amazing homer."

I move in to kiss her, knowing I might not be going to bed anytime soon if I do. "You like that? I did it just for you." I'm willing to make the sacrifice.

She shifts, propping one leg up, and nope, there's nothing down there. I was tired, ready for a shower and two days' worth of sleep. I'm wide awake now and prepared to go to heaven with this beauty. "It wasn't the homer in the game I was referring to."

"No?"

"It was this one." She reaches behind her and slides something on the counter next to her. My gaze shoots to hers and to the stick again. I close the gap and tap the small screen that reads "Pregnant." I'm not sure what I can say. I'm not in shock and it's not negative. It's the opposite. She's giving me another second chance to be there, to be a part of this huge event from the beginning. "Even birth control can't stop you from scoring."

I move my hand over to her thigh and run it up to slide around to her hip. "You're pregnant?" The crack in my voice can't be hidden, so I just own it. "You're having a baby?"

"Your baby." She grins. "Again." When she covers my hand, she brings it up and rests it on her chest. "Feel that? Can you feel how my heart races for you?"

The strong and steady beat is showing off for me. "I can. I feel it, babe."

A tear slips down her cheek, and she says, "I've never been happier in my entire life than when I met you and all the amazing things that have happened since. Thank you, Griffin, for coming back to my hotel room that night."

Laughter slips out. "I mean, imagine if you had been five minutes later or passed by ten minutes sooner."

I grab her ass and slide her, legs spread, against me. "Let's not imagine that." Envisioning my wife meeting some other guy is the last thing I want to think about. "We could have blamed it on the moonlight, but let's just call it what it is."

With her gorgeous smile on full display, she strokes her hands down the sides of my neck, and asks, "What is it?"

"Meant to be."

Ten months later . . .

THE YELLOW HOUSE with white trim, blue shutters, and a matching door stands as a point of pride behind us as our backdrop. With my son seated on my shoulders, my wife at my side holding our new baby, River Greene, named after the water where we fell in love, we say, "Cheese."

It's not until we get the photo back, framed and ready to hang in our new home, that I see Cricket wasn't smiling at the camera. She was smiling at me. Luckiest bastard in the world because she saw something in me when no one else did . . . *My looks helped*. The attraction between us was instant. The love will last a lifetime.

I hang the photo on the nail on the wall that leads up the stairs, then look at the others that help make this house a home. One of my parents, siblings, and me. Another of my dad chasing me at three when I escaped the bathtub and made a run for the pasture. Cricket says Jacob and I are twins at that age. I'd have to agree. Cute kid.

I reach up and touch the one of my mom holding me in my first photo. Dad took it of her in front of their home the day I came home to the ranch from the hospital. Whatever was broken inside me, Cricket healed, as if my mom had a hand in our reunion. I wouldn't be surprised. She always did love a great love story, and my wife and I have one of the best. Breaking curses, we were generations in the making, in fact.

"Hey, Twenty-Two," she calls from the living room. "Game is starting."

"Coming." I step back and take in the photos of her and her family, who have grown closer, and her mom has thawed in time. Her brother taking off to Paris might have helped that relationship along since they're stuck with us now.

Eyeing the photos in the middle of the stairs where Jacob's story begins, I move my attention to him holding his little brother for the first time. But the blank walls just beyond don't bother me. We have years ahead to make more memories. Lucky bastard.

I walk into the living room, where my dad hands me a beer. "What did I miss?"

Delancy says, "The Cardinals are taking the field." That there is a plate with two chicken wings next to her is huge progress. Baseball. Now wings. I can only imagine how things are going to change from here.

When I sit on the couch next to Cricket, she leans her head on my shoulder, and asks, "Do you miss it? Do you miss being a part of the game? Or playing for the Cardinals?"

"No." *God's honest truth.* "It was fun to live the dream again, but I missed being here with you more. My body isn't destroyed—"

"It sure isn't, sexy stuff." If she keeps looking at me like that, we might be making another baby before the sixth inning. *Vixen.*

"I didn't get to do this the first time. I want to be here for you and the kids. This is the dream I didn't know I wanted until I met you." I kiss the top of her forehead, then reach over to hold the baby.

She slides her glasses from the top of her head to the bridge of her nose, tucking her feet under her. Looking up at me with stars in her eyes, she whispers, "I love you, Greene."

My wife doesn't realize her stars are only a reflection of the ones I carry in my eyes for her. "I love you, too, Greene."

THE PEACHTREE PASS **Series is now complete. Read Now:**

Long Time Coming
Lead Me Knot
Small Town Frenzy

YOU MIGHT ALSO ENJOY

Recommendations - These are books you'll enjoy reading after *Small Town Frenzy in addition to other Peachtree Pass series books.* These books will grab your heart and have you falling in love along with the characters.

Read in Kindle Unlimited and Listen in Audio

Long Time Coming (if you haven't read book 1 in the Peachtree Pass series) - You met Tagger and Christine in Small Town Frenzy. Now read the captivating and joyous journey as they find their way in this small town, big ranch, single dad love story. Free in Kindle Unlimited. *Turn the page to start reading*

Read in Kindle Unlimited and Listen in Audio

Lead Me Knot (if you haven't read book 2 in the Peachtree Pass series) - Falling in love with Lauralee and Baylor is easy in this Small Town, Best Friend's Brother, Marriage of Convenience romance. She owns a bakery. He's in finance in New York City. Coming home for him becomes a lot more fun as he falls hard for the girl who bakes the goodies. Free in Kindle Unlimited.

Read in Kindle Unlimited and Listen in Audio

Head Over Feels - Friends to lovers at its finest. The banter, the wit, the teasing, the sneaking around is so fun in this New York City love story where Bachelor of the Year is brought to his knees over the girl next door friend he's crushed on since college. Free in Kindle Unlimited.

ACKNOWLEDGMENTS

Thank you so much to this incredible team:

Kenna Rey, Content Editor
Jenny Sims, Copy Editing, Editing4Indies
Kristen Johnson, Proofreader
Andrea Johnston, Beta Reading
Cover Design: S.L. Scott
Audio Producer: Erin Spencer, One Night Stand Studios.
Narrators: Savannah Peachwood & Tor Thom

Thank you Super Stars and my awesome Facebook group members. And sweet thanks to my amazing friends!

My husband, sons, and little dog, Ollie, are my entire world. I love you more than the universe! Thank you for your beautiful support and love. Love you always. XOXOX

ABOUT THE AUTHOR

Suzie loves a great view of the ocean, spicy margaritas, and spending her free time with her family and sweet dog, Ollie.

New York Times and *USA Today* Bestselling Author, S.L. Scott, writes character driven, heart-racing, and swoony romances that will leave you glued to the page. With stories ranging from witty beach reads to heart wrenching and heart healing, her stories are highly regarded as emotional, relatable, and captivating.

Her books are more than escapes for the voracious readers of today. They are journeys of the heart that always come with a happily ever after reward at the end.

Find her at: www.slscottauthor.com